HERETIC SPELLBLADE

K.D. ROBERTSON

MAPS!

The following page has a map for the immediate area of the story. Check out the link below for a detailed map of the entire archipelago that the series takes place in.

You can find the full versions at:
https://www.kdrobertsonbooks.com/heretic-spellblade-maps/

MAP OF DOUMAHR

Soreaux

The Den

TRAFAUMH

REPUBLIC OF ARCADIA

Pearlescent Canyon

Elysia

Aurelian
Spires

Straub

Castle
Fisselburg

Kravum Rock

Medstejn
Castle

ANFANG
EMPIRE

Tartus

Fort Taubrum

AMICA
FEDERATION

Aleich

Trantia

Gharrick Pass

HOUKEEM DESERT

Fei's Village

Carence

LEGEND

- Capital
- City
- Major Town
- Major Fort/Castle
- Binding Stone Fortress

FACTION NAME

REGION NAME

SUBFACTION

Note: Only locations
important to the plot
will be on the map

KURAI PENINSULA

Ruins of Sorami

CHAPTER 1

The last day of the world arrived with little warning. A scouting report sat unread in an office. The lights were off and moonlight shined through the window. If somebody scanned the report, he'd learn about unusually powerful activity in the nearby demonic portal.

The owner of the office, Nathan Martel, stumbled in and fumbled with the light switch. Two wrought iron lamps flickered to life as magic ran into the lighting elements within them. Nathan scanned the room for a few moments. His dark blue officer's jacket hung off his shoulders, and his shirt buttons were undone. Given his unkempt black hair, it seemed unlikely he was here for work.

His eyes fell on the report. He picked it up, flicked through it, then frowned. He hesitated, going over it once more. Almost a minute passed in silence while he considered what he had read.

Then he snapped the report shut, dropped it on his desk, and turned off the lights.

The report could be dealt with in the morning. He had an alluring subordinate waiting for him in his bedroom.

Light crept into Nathan's bedroom at dawn. He was already awake. He remained under the silk sheets of his bed as the sun's rays crept over his face. His eyes were wide open, and he stared at the black hair of the woman sharing his bed. A bushy black tail lay wrapped around his body as he spooned her, and her tufted black cat ears twitched every few seconds as she dreamed.

Nathan absently rubbed her belly while they spooned. His mind was elsewhere. He glanced at the ticking clock on the wall. The ornate golden hands had moved by at least an hour since he last looked. Licking his lips, Nathan realized he needed to get up. The bed was alluring, but work needed doing.

He rolled out of bed and the woman stirred. She tossed the sheets aside as she blindly groped for him, her eyes still closed.

"Nathan," she moaned. "Come back to bed."

"Go back to sleep, Jafeila," he said.

She opened her eyes and pouted at him. Her arms reached for him, palms out and welcoming. He kept his expression still, but found it difficult. She knew his weaknesses. Every muscle in his body called him back to bed.

"You know you want to," she sang. "Come on, this is the first time I've had you to myself all week."

"Go back to sleep," he repeated. "I'll join you once I finish something I should have dealt with last night. It's probably nothing."

She blinked at him and lowered her arms. Her brow furrowed as Nathan retreated into the adjoining bathroom.

The rhythmic pulsing of hot water on Nathan's back allowed him to focus his thoughts. Something about that scouting report was off. He was no stranger to stopping demonic invasions, but he couldn't put his finger on what was wrong with this report. Little things jumped out in his mind that didn't add up.

Handling this was Nathan's duty. He was the Bastion of the Far Reaches, and the commander of this frontier fortress. As Bastion, he had special magic to suppress demonic portals and destroy their armies. And only Bastions could create Champions, who were magical warriors with the power to destroy entire armies of demons single-handedly.

Nathan turned the shower off with the brass taps and dried himself off. A clean and neatly pressed uniform lay in a basket near the door. He smiled at the sight. For years he had refused to accept any servants, but somehow his subordinates kept sneaking in and doing pointless things like this. This morning it saved him the trouble of putting together his own uniform and appearing ragged.

Given the choice, he would have chosen to appear ragged rather than waste any more time. Every passing minute weighed on him. The voice of experience warned Nathan that he had made a grave mistake last night.

Jafeila stared at him when he stepped out into his bedroom in full uniform. She was curled up around his pillow, her tail pressed against her face and ears flat against her head.

"This isn't 'probably nothing,' is it?" she asked.

Nathan frowned. "'Probably' means that it may also be something."

"Don't be coy," she said.

She sat on the edge of the bed and glared at him. Her tail swished back and forth along the sheets and sometimes brushed her curvy thighs. Her large bust bounced with her movements, drawing his eye to the three glittering amethysts inset directly into her collarbone. Those gems marked her as one of Nathan's most powerful Champions.

Nathan sighed. "I need to follow-up on a scouting report I saw late last night. Something about it doesn't sit right with me."

"A scouting report?" Jafeila repeated. Her eyes narrowed. "This is about the portal, isn't it?"

"Could it be about anything else?"

"It could be a war..." she trailed off, her lips thinning.

"Against who? Falmir is the last nation left on Doumahr." Nathan laughed bitterly. "I'm hoping it's nothing, but..."

"If you're this torn up over a scouting report, then it's not nothing," Jafeila said. She stood. "I've only been with you for a few years, but I know your reputation. Something is very wrong."

Nathan appreciated the ego-stroking.

"Give me a minute to clean up and I'll join you," she said.

He held up a hand. "No. I'll go now."

She blinked and her tail froze. It resumed its movement a moment later.

"I need you to gather Narime and Vala," he said.

A pause.

"You think you'll need all three of us?" she asked, running her hand over the three gems in her collarbone.

"If it's as bad as I suspect, I'd rather be safe than sorry."

Jafeila looked away for a moment, then back. "Right. I'll clean up then get the other trigem Champions. Should I let anyone else know?"

"Not yet. Once we know more, I'll let the three of you take charge," he said.

Before he could take a step toward the door, Jafeila intercepted him. Her arms and bushy tail coiled around him. She pulled his head down and crushed her lips against his. He reciprocated instinctively, his tongue slipping inside her mouth and eliciting a moan from her.

When she pulled away, she had a grin on her face. "I'll see you in a little bit," she said impishly.

Nathan left his bedroom. The halls were dimly lit. Only one out of every three lamps were on, a measure to save magical energy when nobody was around. The moment he stepped into the hall, every lamp lit up as motion-detecting magic sensed his movement.

"Bastion, good morning," a woman greeted Nathan. She stood next to the door in full plate armor, a longsword at her side and a tower shield strapped to her back.

"How long have you been standing guard, Ciana?" Nathan

responded. He glanced around the hall. Had she been standing perfectly still? He couldn't imagine how else she had avoided activating the lights.

Ciana was a curious woman. Only slightly younger than Nathan, she had served as a Champion under several Bastions until he finally recruited her. She had platinum-blonde hair and a fine silken horse's tail. A pair of diamonds shined from within the gorget of her armor. A single iridescent horn protruded from her forehead, parting her platinum bangs and marking her as one of the rarest of the beastkin: a unicorn beastkin.

Neither Ciana nor Jafeila were human, like Nathan was. They were beastkin, a race of humanoids with animal-like features such as ears and tails. Their appearance varied significantly based on the region their race originally came from. Many beastkin races had been lost to history over the centuries. Ciana's race of unicorns were so close to extinction that Nathan had never seen another in his thirty-plus years.

"Sen and I changed shifts four hours ago. Sunstorm was to guard you during the day, but it appears you have work to do early in the morning," Ciana said. "The scouting team—"

"I saw their report last night. I'm heading to the monitoring station now," Nathan interrupted.

Ciana followed behind Nathan as he walked through the empty stone hallways. The fortress was sprawling, but Falmir had long stopped supplying enough soldiers and staff to keep the place full. Nathan's power as Bastion kept the fortress running regardless of how many people were present.

A half-dozen men and women sat at glowing desks in the monitoring station. Holographic charts and figures hovered above the occupied desks. Another twenty or so desks were unoccupied and unlit. The far wall was lit up with more charts and figures, and formed a central monitor for Nathan and everybody in the room to use as an overview. A pair of statues stood in the far corners, depicting the Watcher Omria, the only goddess of the world.

Nathan froze as he entered the room, his eyes running over the central display. Ciana's hand closed around his arm. She looked up at him in concern.

"Bastion, you're here early," an analyst said, noticing Nathan's arrival. "Have you seen—"

"Have you confirmed the scouting report?" Nathan interrupted.

He strode forward into the center of the room. Everybody stopped what they were doing and looked at him. Looking around at their faces, he realized they didn't understand what they had given him last night or what they were looking at.

"Well, all night we've been—" the lead analyst began to say, but stopped when Nathan looked at her. She gulped. "No, sir. None of our readings match what the scouts reported about the portal. Monitoring devices installed next to the portal, scanners in the walls, and even the leyline activity readings built into the fortress are all at normal levels. The sorcerers can't detect anything out of the ordinary either."

Nathan nodded slowly. "You've re-calibrated everything?"

The lead analyst paused and looked to her subordinates. They nodded. "Yes, sir. At least what we can. We don't doubt the scouts, but..."

"Do the calibration again. Tell Captain Murdas to send out a different team of scouts. I'll check the binding stone and see what I can read from the fortress and leylines directly," Nathan ordered.

Nothing happened for several long seconds. Nathan sighed.

"We need to confirm if the scout report is correct. If it is, then I know what is happening and can take the appropriate counter-measures," Nathan explained, looking each of his analysts in the eye one by one. "If it's wrong, then we can all get some sleep and laugh this off as a false alarm. Understood?"

"Yes, sir," the analysts said in unison.

While the analysts got back to work and several left the room to contact others in the fortress, Nathan turned inward.

Lurking beneath the surface of Nathan's mind was a gargantuan presence. It seemed to grow in size as he turned his attention to it, threatening to consume his mind. With long practice, he dove into it—mentally, that is.

What had appeared to be a singular, all-consuming entity revealed itself to be a sprawling mass of mental nodes and magical links. Nathan followed a mental tether to the closest node. This was the binding stone of this fortress.

Nobody knew who created the binding stones. They littered the world of Doumahr like discarded relics of an ancient race, but even the oldest records of the First Peoples stated that they were here before them.

What Nathan knew was that Bastions trained themselves to control binding stones, and through them, they controlled the world around themselves. Through the fortress's binding stone he sensed the world around the binding stone in impossible detail: the temperature of the earth; the heartbeats of every person inside the fortress; the flow of magical energy through the leylines connected to the binding stone.

Time passed at a fraction of a rate it did normally. Nathan watched Ciana blink in slow motion. Her brow was furrowed, her worried expression cute despite the circumstances. She still held onto his arm. He couldn't feel her grip.

That was the price of focusing his senses through the binding stone. He lost access to his body's senses for the duration. Fortunately, he normally only used the binding stone for brief periods and the time dilation effect prevented him from coming to harm or missing anything important.

Nathan pulled away from the fortress's binding stone, and the web of leylines and other binding stones under his control.

Only seconds had passed in the world around him. He looked around.

"Nathan?" Ciana asked quietly.

He ruffled her hair, his hands tickling her pointed horse ears. She gave him a flat look.

While Nathan liked playing with the hair of his Champions, and especially tickling the animal ears of the beastkin, many of them expressed a preference for him not to ruffle their hair. Naturally, he did it anyway.

"I can't sense anything through the binding stone," he said. "But I expected that. There's... something off about it."

"Off?" she asked.

"Do you ever get that feeling of 'too normal?'" he asked.

"Sometimes. Is that what this is?"

"Probably."

Nathan took a seat. The desk lit up with fancy holographic diagrams, but he ignored it. Only the return of another scouting team could confirm or allay his fears. Ciana stood next to him.

Almost an hour later, Jafeila entered with two other Champions. All three women had a trio of gems inset into their collarbone. These were Nathan's trigem Champions. His greatest warriors.

"What the hell? All readings are normal? I thought you said there was a problem, Fei?" one of the new women said. She was Vala, a human Champion. Her body was noticeably thicker than the other women, with thighs capable of crushing a man's skull and plenty of muscle packed in under her uniform.

"Eh? But I..." Jafeila trailed off when she saw Nathan's expression.

The remaining trigem Champion stared at Nathan, her expression darkening. She glanced up at the central monitor, then looked at the busy analysts nearby.

"You think it's a Messenger, don't you?" she said.

Nathan scowled as the room froze. Everybody looked at the Champion who had just spoken, as if in disbelief at the words that had come out of her mouth.

"I am waiting to confirm the scouting report," Nathan said after several moments.

The last trigem Champion was Narime, a mystic fox from the now-uninhabitable Kurai Peninsula, and she was as wise as she was outspoken. Seven voluminous silver fox tails hung behind her slim, buxom frame, and her robe was severely cut to accentuate her figure and reveal her luscious thighs.

Narime pointed a finger at Nathan.

"But if it's correct, then there's little else it can be," she said.

"Yes," he admitted.

"Wait, how can we get a Messenger when our demonic activity readings are this low?" Vala asked. She scratched her head, making a mess of her dense brown hair.

"Messengers can interfere with our detection magic," Narime explained. "We've seen it in the past. It's how they conquered Trafaumh practically overnight."

"A Messenger?" an analyst blurted out. The others exchanged terrified looks, although at least one seemed lost.

"Um, what's a Messenger?" the confused analyst asked. He shrunk in on himself when everybody glared at him.

"Don't look at him like that," Nathan admonished his subordinates. "All of you were like him once."

Jafeila nodded. "I remember being like that a little too vividly, back when I first fought a Messenger during the fall of the Anfang Empire. They're the generals of the demonic armies. The weakest of them are equal to a trigem Champion. The stronger ones have taken out multiple Bastions."

"Multiple weak Bastions," Vala corrected. "I don't remember any Messenger ever defeating a Bastion with three trigem Champions. And Nathan has countless duogem and monogem Champions. We've got this."

The room calmed down at Vala's projection of confidence, but both Jafeila and Narime remained reserved. Unlike Vala, who had fought under Nathan all her life, the two of them came from nations that had fallen to Messengers. They knew the true power of the demonic threat, even if Nathan had eventually been the one to slay those Messengers.

"We can't let our guard down," Nathan said. "Messengers vary in strength too much, and I don't want to lose anyone." He looked at each of his Champions, and they smiled in return. "If the scouting report confirms my suspicions, we'll ready everything we have."

Another hour passed. Captain Murdas reported in person, carrying handwritten notes from the scouts. He saluted upon entering and focused on Nathan. Two of the trigems, Vala and Narime, hovered on top of him, while Jafeila lingered behind him.

"Bastion, I have the second report here," Murdas said. "Do you want the summary, or the details?"

"Does it differ at all from the first report?"

"No."

"Then I don't need the report." Nathan sighed. "Send your scouts back out to place the live monitoring crystals. We'll need them in place as soon as possible."

Murdas nodded, a grimace crossing his face. He saluted again. "I'll get everybody to work now."

His footsteps echoed in the room after he left. Then, silence.

Nathan drummed his fingers on the desk. All eyes turned to him. The analysts, Jafeila, Ciana, Narime, and Vala.

"We have to assume this is a Messenger," Nathan said. "If the portal is showing signs of physical activation, but all the readings are telling us the opposite even after calibration and double-checking, that means somebody is tampering with our readings. In the past, that's always been a Messenger."

He looked at his trigem Champions, who were almost sitting on top of him.

"The three of you know our defensive plans. Vala, you have the outer layer of walls. Narime, you take the inner wall and provide support fire and command the summons. Jafeila, the inner fortress is yours, as well as the siege weapons and reserve force. Should Vala need to retreat—"

"I won't, so don't waste your breath reexplaining things," Vala said, rolling her eyes. She plopped herself into Nathan's lap. Her dark brown hair blocked his vision for a moment as she cuddled against him. "You're always such a worrier. Just let us lovely Champions take care of you."

One of her hands wandered below his chest and down to his crotch. He held back a gasp. This needed to stop before it went too far, he thought.

"Enough, Vala," Narime said with huff at her rival.

She leaned in and pulled Vala away from Nathan. The brunette collapsed unceremoniously on the floor with a laugh. Not that Narime let her own opportunity pass. Her lips closed over Nathan's and her tails closed around him like a fluffy prison.

"Although she's not wrong. You should find some time during the battle to prepare for our celebration," Narime breathed out after the kiss. She winked at Nathan and pressed her breasts up as she pulled away.

"You shouldn't tease him so much," Jafeila whined.

"You don't tease him enough," Vala said. "Anyway, let's get down to brass tacks and sort out our battle plan. Make sure to prep the summons for us, Nathan."

The three of them left the monitoring station. Nathan pulled himself together and sighed. Vala's last request was important. He needed to summon as many defenders as possible using his binding stones. Ciana ruffled Nathan's hair while he was distracted, and he glared up at her.

There was an army on his doorstep, and only hours to prepare for its arrival.

Once he won this battle, he could go back to his normal day-to-day life as the ruler of this fortress, with countless dedicated Champions and soldiers. A life spent fighting off the unending waves of demons.

CHAPTER 2

A clear image of the demonic portal shimmered on the wall of the command center. Three demonic portals, actually. Nathan had never seen a portal split apart like this.

A visual feed of the portals was projected onto the stone wall at the far end of the room. A couple dozen administrative staff monitored terminals powered by the binding stone's magic. Uniformed soldiers stood guard nearby.

In the center of the room glowed a three-dimensional projection of the fortress. Innumerable blips of light dotted the hologram and marked life signs. Many gold chevrons moved about within the projection, and these indicated Champions.

Nathan looked back at the portals. They looked like tears in the fabric of the world itself. Black and white scars that stood dozens of meters high and flickered strangely. Staring at them brought stars to Nathan's eyes and a sharp pain in the back of his head.

The pain was muted because Nathan was staring at an image of the portals, rather than the real thing. Nathan imagined how painful it must be to be outside. Normally, a projected image only caused mild discomfort. Nathan's growing migraine proved this portal was different. This might even be the worst portal he had encountered in over a decade of fighting demons.

Not that he needed any reminding of that fact.

Beneath the portal was a heaving, seething mass of demons. Thousands. Tens of thousands. Nathan didn't know how many demons there were. The monitoring devices still didn't work, so he couldn't get an accurate estimate. His scouts estimate had been so enormous that Nathan had refused to share it with anybody else.

The wasteland surrounding the portal was vast and ringed by steep cliffs. Demons covered every inch of the bare volcanic rock. And every single one of them pushed their way forward, toward the valley that led to the fortress.

Explosions rippled through the mass of monsters occasionally. They were the work of long-range siege weapons that took out entire formations in conventional battles. Here they appeared completely ineffectual. By the time the dust cleared, the demons had already filled the gap created by the dead. An endless tide of animalistic demons poured forth from the portals. Fortunately, the monitoring crystals didn't capture sound.

Nathan knew from experience how awful the sounds were. How terrifying it would be to be a Champion on the front line.

Vala…

The visual feed cut out. The fortress shook and dust fell from the ceiling. Screams rung out. Hands grabbed at Nathan's arms.

"Nathan!" Ciana shouted.

"We're fine," Nathan said, shaking her off. The other hand didn't let go.

"Ifrit… Ifrit says we should retreat," a young woman said. She didn't have any gems inset into her collarbone, but she emanated magical power. One hand clasped Nathan's arm, and the other wrapped itself tight around her stomach.

Nathan frowned, feeling troubled by the words. "We'll be fine, Sen. I have you here."

He ruffled her white hair. Despite looking just shy of twenty, she was the same age, if not older, than Nathan. In exchange for her immense magical power, she had stopped aging.

"But... Okay, Nathan," Sen said. She tried to look brave, but the inner voice of Ifrit was clearly troubling her.

"She's right," another woman said. A single onyx was buried in her upper chest. "This reminds me of when I saw the demons invade Aleich and bring down the Anfang Empire. The demons appeared to be endless. Just like now."

Ciana looked away, her face pained. The Empire was her homeland, and she had fought during the fall of Aleich, when the Empire had been destroyed over a decade ago.

The fortress shook again, but nobody screamed.

"Vala, status report," Nathan asked aloud. He spoke into a device embedded in the command terminal. "And Choe, this isn't the fall of the Anfang Empire. None of you need to worry about that."

"Don't call me Choe in front of everybody. I'm Sunstorm," Sunstorm muttered, twisting in place.

"Vala?" Nathan repeated, speaking into the communication device again.

"Little busy! We're holding the outer wall and—"

Every light flickered at once. A bolt of lightning ran through Nathan's veins, and he slumped to his knees. His breath came up short. For a long moment, he couldn't feel his body. His limbs felt like they were made of lead.

The fortress rumbled. Echoes of some massive noise blasted through the halls and into the command center. The floor vibrated.

Nathan looked up. Ciana, Sunstorm, and Sen surrounded him, saying things he couldn't hear. His hearing was shot. Their arms reached for him, but he couldn't feel their touch.

A gargantuan magical attack had hit the fortress hard. Harder than he had imagined possible. He had gone toe-to-toe with

Messengers before. He knew the depths of their strength, and how hard they could strike his defenses.

Nothing had ever hit him like this. It felt as if his opponent had somehow struck his mind and body directly, ignoring the countless layers of stone and magical barriers between him and any attacker.

Nathan dove into the mental world of his binding stone. He saw cracks spreading from within it, and many of the tethers he had to other binding stones had been severed. Hurriedly, he repaired what connections he could and slapped together some hasty mental fortifications.

For several long moments, he stared at a part of his mental world he had built but never thought he would use. Years ago, he had devised a secret weapon. It had only one purpose and was to be used in only one scenario. The worst possible scenario.

He activated the weapon but kept it separate from the rest of his mental world. That weakened it, but he was concerned about another possibility. This Messenger might be able to attack him through the binding stones.

He came back to reality to find his Champions pulling him to his feet.

"Nathan!" Ciana shouted in his ear. "We need to get you to a healer."

"Stop," Nathan growled. "I'm fine. Just a little shaken."

They gave him an odd look. Before one of them could say anything, somebody shouted.

"I just got my connection back. We've lost the outer wall! And... and the inner wall? This can't be right," the man said.

Nathan stared at the chaos surrounding him. Most of the terminals in the command center had gone down. They were slowly lighting back up, but the results were bad. Communications were still down. The command terminal wasn't working, and Nathan couldn't rely on the holographic projection to monitor the battle.

There was another way. Nathan reached out for his Champions through the binding stone. A wave of relief washed over him as he sensed those who were alive. Then guilt.

Vala and Narime were alive. But most of his Champions weren't. He should value all of them equally, he felt. How many had already fallen?

"Vala and Narime are still up," he said. "Jafeila will lead her reinforcements to pull them back. The fortress itself is the most heavily warded defensive line. I always intended the walls as an extra layer of defense."

As if to punctuate his point in the worst possible way, the fortress shook again, and the terminals winked out.

Silence fell. Nathan closed his eyes.

He should go out there and fight. Years ago, he would have done exactly that. But things were different now.

A Bastion held all the power of the binding stones and granted power to his Champions. At his best, Nathan's skills as a spell-blade allowed him to match a duogem Champion, albeit with significant help from his binding stone. But he had three trigem Champions, and each of them was worth ten Nathans. The power differential between the grades of Champion was massive.

And this Messenger was so obscenely powerful that he struggled to imagine her raw strength. If Nathan died, all of his Champions lost their power and the fortress's defenses failed instantly.

So Nathan could only watch, give orders, and strengthen the defenses of the fortress using the binding stone.

"Sen, Sunstorm, I need you to go help Jafeila," Nathan ordered.

"But—" Sunstorm tried to object.

"No buts. She is going to need every Champion I can spare to help her. I don't need three of my most capable Champions protecting me," he said.

The two looked at Nathan, then at Ciana. The unicorn beastkin stared at Nathan, as if daring him to order her away too. He didn't.

He knew well enough that she'd refuse to leave him.

With several glances backward, Sen and Sunstorm left the command center. Soldiers, sorcerers, and administrative staff shouted over each other and ran around in their wake. The two Champions gave Nathan a last wave from the doorway. He smiled at them and gave them a salute. They smiled back and vanished from his sight. His heart felt empty.

How many Champions had he failed to say goodbye to today?

The fortress rumbled. The terminals hadn't come back to life since the last tremor. Nathan felt his defenses fail one after another. His Champions were fighting as hard as they could. Vala, Narime, and Jafeila were all still alive.

What did he have left to throw at the demons? What was his next step?

He was about to dive back into his binding stone to buy time to think when the room rumbled violently. The stonework visibly shook. An explosion rumbled in the distance. Fire and lightning ran through his veins as that attack from earlier struck once more. He realized that the Messenger was attacking the fortress this time.

"Get down!" Ciana shouted.

She pulled Nathan beneath her. Dust billowed from the ceiling. Stone plummeted down in whole blocks. Screams and shouts. Nathan grabbed every ounce of magical energy he had and tried to project a defensive barrier.

All vanished into blackness.

Nathan awoke seconds later. Or maybe it was hours. Everything was dark, but there was something warm on his body. Pain consumed his left arm. He felt like he hadn't slept in a week, after doing ten rounds with Vala.

The castle hadn't crushed him to death. He created a wisp of

light and saw that the rubble was being held above him by a
glowing barrier, but only by a fraction of a meter.

Something glittered and caught his eyes. He turned. Then he
looked away, his breath caught in his throat.

Ciana hadn't made it.

Channeling his binding stone, Nathan vaporized the rubble
above him. It took several blasts to create a tunnel large enough,
and he used yet more magic to keep it stable as he crawled out.
The entire fortress must have fallen on him. Had the Messenger
brought the whole thing down? How was his binding stone still
active?

He dove into the binding stone and his mind turned to
horror.

His mental world was a ruin. Almost every tether was
destroyed. He remained connected to this binding stone, but the
tethers to the others had been severed. Nathan was now reliant
entirely on this individual binding stone and the leylines directly
connected to it.

But he still had his secret weapon. It had fully activated itself
now and was burning with magical energy.

Pulling away from the ruins of his mental world, Nathan
instead faced the ruins of the real world. The fortress had been
flattened. Dark stone rubble was strewn as far as the eye could
see. A few stray walls remained standing. Dusk had arrived, and
the purple rays of twilight peeked over the horizon.

Nathan wanted to believe this wasn't real. He reached out
magically to check on his Champions.

He found only emptiness.

They were all gone. Ciana, Sen, Choe, Jafeila, Vala, Narime,
and countless others.

A gargantuan double door gate stood in the middle of the
ruins, seemingly untouched. It was barred shut and covered in
runes. The locking bars shimmered with crystals, and the entire
structure exuded an awe-inspiring power. This gate separated the

demonic portal from the actual world, and so long as it remained closed, the demons couldn't get in.

In front of the gate was a young woman.

No, not a woman. A Messenger. The four curly horns protruding from her skull gave her away, as did the demonic power roiling off her. She was petite, barely five feet, and scantily clad. Nathan could generously describe her as showing a lot of skin, but it was more like she was wearing underwear with some translucent silk cloth attached to it. Platinum hoops and bangles hung on her thighs, hips, and arms, and each gleamed with an otherworldly magic. Her trim black hair was cut to her jawline and her skin was bronzed.

Despite the situation, Nathan found his eyes drawn to her curves. He blamed her lack of clothing. She lacked much in the upper body department, but her flared hips and plump thighs more than made up for it.

The Messenger turned to face Nathan, and he saw that she had violet eyes with red pupils. She raised an eyebrow at him.

"So you are still alive," she said. "That explains why this gate won't open. You're a tougher nut than I expected. When your outer wall went down to my first attack, I thought this was another wasted world, but you somehow survived. And now you've survived an entire fortress falling on your head. Well done. Clap, clap, clap." She clapped her hands at the end for an extra-patronizing effect.

"I still control the binding stone, despite your best efforts," Nathan growled out. "And I know a trick or two."

"Like regeneration, I suppose." She stared at his left arm. "I always find watching flesh regrow itself fascinating. Sadly, I don't really have the time. You've been more entertaining than expected, but I need you to open this gate so that my demonic armies can spill forth from the portal. You've made me think there may be something worthwhile in this world, and I'm rather impatient."

He stared at the Messenger. Was she serious? Did she think he was going to open the gate for her? He had devised this last ditch security measure explicitly to cut off the portal if the fortress ever fell. It would buy time for Falmir to raise an army and defend itself.

Then he met her eyes and realized the truth. She was patronizing him.

He smirked. "You think killing me will open the gate and undo my defenses? You're wrong. The spell operates independently. The battle was over the moment you triggered it. It'll buy enough time for the other Bastions to raise their armies and gather Champions to suppress you and your portal. Assuming you can even keep a portal this large open for that long."

"You set this up to operate even after death?" she asked. She sounded impressed. Her eyes ran over the gate again. "Huh. Quite the dead man's switch. Well, no matter. I can wait."

"What?"

"I said, 'I can wait.' Did you not hear me? Did the fortress falling on your head perhaps damage your hearing?" She smirked at him. "You think a combined army will be enough to stop me, but that's not how this works. The other Bastions will come to me, saving me time and effort, and I'll get what I want so much sooner. It's rather funny how you've done my work for me. All I have to do is sit back and wait."

Nathan stared at her as she stretched her arms out and yawned theatrically. This Messenger was so confident in her power that she thought she could defeat the combined might of the remaining Bastions of Falmir?

Then again, she had effortlessly crushed him. Could she pull it off?

He swallowed. Then dove into his binding stone and did something he had never thought he would ever do. Something he had sworn to never do.

The Messenger froze. Her eyes met Nathan's the moment his mind returned to reality.

"Did you seriously just..." she trailed off and licked her lips nervously. Her dismissive manner from earlier disappeared. She took a step forward, her eyes focused entirely on his. "You did, didn't you?"

How did she know what he did? It's impossible for somebody to sense what another Bastion is doing in their mental world. She should be clueless as to what he had done.

But she wasn't.

"What are you?" he asked.

"Ahaha, finally, somebody asks the right question." The Messenger grinned. "I am known as Sister Kadria. But just call me Kadria. You know me as a Messenger, but I am much more."

"But you're not going to answer my question, are you?"

"You wouldn't believe me if I did. I learned long ago to place little faith in humans. Your minds are rather fragile, and you're good at denying reality when it doesn't fit your preconceived notions. But you can tell that I am no mere Messenger, can't you? That's why you're so troubled, hmm?"

She took another step forward.

"It doesn't matter. None of this does. If you know what I've done, then you know what comes next," Nathan said.

"I know what comes next. Do you, little human?"

"The binding stone detonates. A chain reaction ripples through the leylines. The explosion will turn everything in a hundred-mile radius into an uninhabitable wasteland. No plants will grow here. No sorcery or magic will ever be usable here. Everything and everyone will die."

Nathan swallowed and closed his eyes for a moment. None of that mattered, given the people he cared about were already gone. He reopened his eyes.

"More importantly, the portal will collapse. Without magic, and without the binding stone or leylines, no demonic portals can be sustained here. Your army will vanish. Everything you've done will be invalidated. This is the end," Nathan said.

He made to dive into the binding stone again.

"Wait!" Kadria shouted. "Do you really think that's it?"

"Is this where you try to convince me not to do it?" Nathan sneered. "Don't bother."

"Oh no, feel free to blow yourself up after I speak. But understand, you cannot stop me with this. No magic or technique born from a binding stone can kill me. You will buy time. Losing my army and this portal will hurt. I am impatient, so I can't say I'll be happy with the result. But the end?" She laughed. "Hardly."

He stared. "You're bluffing."

"Maybe. But I can tell you that the next part isn't a bluff. You have two choices: die, or accept my offer."

For a moment, Nathan wanted to ignore her and finish detonating the binding stone. Her arrogant attitude grated on his nerves. He forced himself to listen to her. He had nothing to lose. Even if she killed him here and now, the binding stone would detonate by itself within minutes.

"What offer?"

"You want to save this world, don't you? Well, maybe not this world," she said, waving a hand at the ruins surrounding them. "But the world you grew up in. Filled with so much hope, greenery, friends, and lovers. I imagine that's why you're a Bastion. You're trying to stop the demons and Messengers from ending everything, yes? But here we are, in the ruins of your life. The ruins of this world, even."

"Are you done?"

"Listen for a minute, will you? I'm selling you on this," Kadria said, glaring at him.

"Your sales pitch is kind of shit."

She ignored him. "What if you could save that world? Go back to before everything had fallen apart and stop the world from falling apart? A second chance at life, but with all of your current knowledge and ability. Would you take it?"

Silence reigned.

Nathan didn't breathe. Couldn't. He stared into space as he tried to comprehend her words. Everything faded into nothingness around him as he fell into fantasy.

"Are you saying you can send me back in time? Messengers are capable of that?" he asked.

"If we make a deal, then I can send you back to the world you so desire to save, instead of this ruin."

"Why me? And why offer such a deal if you can destroy the world so easily?"

"Because I don't want to destroy the world. Our objectives aren't too dissimilar. Neither of us wants this world. You want to save and live in a world that hasn't been despoiled by horrible demonic armies. Would you believe that I want the same?" Kadria raised an eyebrow at him.

He looked around at the ruined fortress. "No."

"I said you wouldn't believe me."

Nathan frowned. Her statement irritated him because it was true. If what she was offering was possible, did he have a choice? A chance to save everybody who had already been killed by the demonic hordes was something he had only dreamed of.

And if she was lying, then he could detonate the binding stone regardless. There was nothing to lose.

"Fine. But why me?" he asked again.

"Because you're the first Bastion I've met who's been able to bypass the protections of the binding stone like this. They're not supposed to explode, you know. If they could, then the world would be in too much danger to let any random human manipulate them. So that makes you my best candidate for what I want to do. Anything else?" she asked.

"Anfang," he said. "I want to go to Anfang. Not Falmir. If you can actually send me back."

She tilted her head to one side and held a finger against her bottom lip. Slowly, a grin crept across her face.

"Ah, I see your game. The Anfang Empire. The first great nation to fall, and the beginning of the end. You think you can stop it from collapsing, and thereby stop the demonic hordes from ever taking hold? Amusing. I know exactly the time and place to send you, then."

Kadria rushed forward. Ignoring his instincts, Nathan remained still. Every part of his body told him that he was about to die. The power oozing off her terrified him. His very essence screamed that she was vile, and he was making a mistake.

Her hand grasped his, and he felt something reach into his mind. He gasped. That feeling vanished in an instant.

"I just needed the connection," she muttered. "But you are cuter than I thought. All that dust and blood does you no favors."

Nathan looked away. His eyes fell on a half-broken statue of the Watcher Omria. He averted his gaze.

Did he have any right to gaze upon the figure of the goddess when he had now become a heretic? He was consorting with a Messenger.

He could still detonate the binding stone. It would only take a moment.

"And done," Kadria said. "See you on the other side."

Nathan opened his mouth to say something. No sound come out, and he realized he couldn't hear anything. White light crept over the edges of his vision. Kadria vanished a moment later, leaving him to stare into an endless white void.

Then all thought stopped. Nathan Martel ceased to exist.

CHAPTER 3

Dappled sunlight filtered through the dense canopy of leaves high above. Birds chirped and tweeted as they flitted from branch to branch. The bubbling of a brook could be heard in the distance, although it couldn't be seen.

It was a calm day in the middle of spring. A carriage trundled down a bare dirt road through the forest. No horses drew the carriage, and it seemed to propel itself through some form of invisible power. The carriage was fully enclosed, and the windows couldn't be seen through from the outside. The exterior was painted black, with faded and cracked silver trims and regalia.

Nathan opened his eyes and found himself staring out from within this carriage. He spent several seconds staring out the one-way windows. Taking in the sight of an undisturbed and peaceful forest. Only the trundling of the carriage broke the peace.

He started, leaping high enough to hit his head on the roof of the carriage. Cursing, he sat back down. His hands ran across his body. He no longer felt any pain, and his wounds were gone. Not from healing, but as if they had never happened. He was no longer covered in dust and grime from the collapsed fortress. Blood no longer caked his face, arms, and hands.

He froze. His uniform was black.

Had it worked?

Had that Kadria woman been telling the truth?

Nathan examined his uniform thoroughly. He was wearing a black and silver officer's uniform, with the regalia fitting of a Bastion.

This was the uniform of a Bastion of the Anfang Empire. Officially, their colors were black and gold, but the Empire considered the color gold a symbol of the royal family. As such, the military wore silver as a sign of subservience to the Emperor and the Archdukes.

The carriage showed signs of belonging to the Empire as well. And Nathan had a duffel bag of belongings that did little to dispel the illusion that he had gone back in time. If this was fake, then Kadria was a master illusionist.

Nathan swallowed and leaned back against the worn seats. Almost a minute passed as he let his thoughts wander. He had failed. His fortress had fallen. Everybody he had loved had died. Everything he had accomplished had been for nothing.

Had he truly been given a second chance? A chance to prevent everything from going wrong?

He sat bolt upright. Would he have the chance to find them all again? Jafeila, Vala, Narime, and the others? More than anything else, they were the driving force in his life these days.

If he had gone back to the time of the Anfang Empire, they'd be much younger. So would he, in fact. He'd been a teenager when the Empire had been invaded by its neighbors and all out war had broken out across Doumahr. A teenager apprenticing as a Bastion, thrust into a war that nobody really understood.

Something shined from within the bag. His bag, he remembered. Things didn't feel right, but he needed to remember that this was now his life. He must have a past in the Anfang Empire, and a family here. How else could he be a Bastion in the Empire?

Reaching down into the bag, Nathan found a small hand

mirror. Was he so vain in this life? Small jewels decorated the outside of the mirror. On the back was an inscription. A family motto, signed with what he somehow knew was his mother's name.

The mirror was a gift from his mother, he realized. No, a way to remember her. He wasn't vain. It was simply a way to remember lost family. Nathan grimaced at the thoughtless way he'd insulted the person whose body he'd inherited.

Somebody moved in the mirror. Nathan looked closer and realized it was himself. But that was impossible.

After all, that somebody looked far too much like Nathan did before he had come back. Shouldn't he be much younger?

Nathan blinked. He carefully analyzed his features and checked his hands. Despite his assumption, he looked almost identical to his old self. When Kadria had sent him back, he had somehow thought that meant he would become young again.

Stupid. She said nothing about that. He was still in his thirties, but sent back in time.

After putting the mirror back in the bag, Nathan took the time to think. Actually think. Since arriving in this time, he had been making assumptions and jumping at everything. He needed to stop for a few minutes and assess everything he knew. And everything he didn't know.

He had a rough idea of where he was, but not when he was. Exactly how many years in the past had Kadria sent him back? If the Anfang Empire was still intact, that meant that all out war hadn't broken out.

In Nathan's youth, the world had been relatively peaceful. Nations still bickered. Wars were still fought. But the network of Bastions kept the demons in check, and there were no massive invasions by demonic hordes. No Messengers capable of defeating several trigem Champions effortlessly. In fact, trigem Champions were so rare that they were considered legends, known by name across the entire world.

All of that changed when the Empire started a war with its northern neighbor, the religious Order of Trafaumh, known by most as Trafaumh. While the Empire's armies were busy in the north, another nation had invaded from the east. The Empire began to collapse, its Bastions falling, and the resulting loss of protection allowed hordes of demons to escape into the world.

The Empire's capital of Aleich fell, and a Messenger tore apart most of its lands. It took years to vanquish the Messenger, by which point more Bastions had fallen, and more demonic hordes had taken root. War had become normalized, and the collapse of the world began.

Falmir had been the last nation standing by the time Kadria attacked Nathan's fortress in the Far Reaches. Every other country had fallen to the Messengers, and their lands left to rot in the hands of the demons. Kadria had been right to say that Nathan didn't truly want to save that future.

But back in the past, before the Empire had fallen? There was so much opportunity here. All of Nathan's friends and lovers were still alive. And he had a chance to avoid some of his past mistakes.

Nathan's biggest problem was that he didn't know exactly when or where he had been sent back to. He was a Bastion, so he could claim a binding stone and use that to gain more power and Champions. But if he was in the wrong place, then he couldn't stop everything from going wrong.

He didn't know where this carriage was taking him, either. Was there even a binding stone nearby? Although he had remembered his mother in this timeline, he found it difficult to remember other things.

There was no sign of Kadria. She had said she would see him on this side, so where was she? Somehow, he knew that he had unleashed a true monster into the past.

Perhaps he should have let himself die and trapped her in the future. If she needed a talented Bastion in order to travel back in time, then did he do the wrong thing to allow her to travel back with him?

He shook the thoughts off. This was his chance to fix things. He would deal with Kadria when he found her.

Absently, he reached into his mind to see if he could feel a binding stone. As expected, the connection wasn't present. There was no overwhelming presence of something ancient and over-whelming threatening to consume his very essence.

But there was an odd feeling he hadn't felt before. Like he was tethered to something he couldn't see or feel. Whatever it was, it never became more than a strange feeling in the back of his mind.

Nathan knew something or somebody was tied to him in his mental world, but he couldn't see who or how. Was this Kadria's work? Or a lingering aftereffect of losing access to his binding stones?

The carriage slowed, pulling Nathan from his thoughts. He put everything back in the duffel bag and closed it.

When the carriage stopped, he opened the door and stepped out into the ancient ruins of a fortress. Lichen and moss grew over mountains of limestone. The ruins were thick with grass and trees. The remains of a keep, maybe three stories tall, stuck out like a sore thumb in the rubble. Nathan saw the worn-out interior of the keep in places, where the walls had fallen away.

He knew this place. Almost any student of history did.

"Oh! Are you Nathan Straub? Sorry, I mean Bastion Nathan Straub. Sir," a youthful voice chirped. It sounded familiar to Nathan, but he initially wasn't sure why.

He turned to face the speaker. A young beastkin girl wearing black-painted armor, with a scimitar at her side. Her black cat ears twitched constantly as Nathan watched, and she scratched her cheek. She had a massive bushy tail, which swished back and forth faster with each passing second, kicking up dust from the ground. Her legs twisted back and forth. She placed her arms over her chest nervously, hiding her hefty bust from view. But she couldn't hide the rest of her generous curves, particularly in her tailored uniform.

"Um, am I right? You're wearing the uniform of a Bastion," a much younger Jafeila asked slowly, looking at Nathan through upturned eyes.

He continued staring at her.

When had Jafeila been this cute?

Nathan blinked. Wait, Straub?

Something clicked in his memory, without Nathan even thinking about it. His surname wasn't Martel in this timeline. It was Straub. He had inherited the surname of an Imperial noble, as well as the body of one.

"I am," Nathan said. He paused despite himself. He'd naturally spoken in Imperial, the native tongue of the Empire, rather than his birth language. Was this another effect of whatever Kadria had done to send him back, just like these memories of his new life that were rising within his mind?

He shook the discomfort off. "You're Jafeila?"

"Eh? You know who I am?" The beastkin's tail and ears shot bolt upright before flattening. "Sorry, I mean—yes, I am. Champion-in-training Jafeila reporting for duty, Bastion."

It took considerable effort for Nathan not to stare at Jafeila in shock. She had never been so cute and nervous before. He felt that he was seeing an exotic animal that must be cherished and protected. A side of his lover that she had never spoken to him about and that he had never seen.

Jafeila had been the fourth trigem Champion to join Nathan's service, although he had known her from earlier in his career. By the time he met her, she was a hardened veteran from years of fighting demonic hordes. She had survived the fall of the Empire, the roving bands of demons in the aftermath, the invading armies of greedy neighbors, and much, much more.

He remembered his first meeting with her vividly. She had been a monogem Champion serving a Bastion from Trafaumh.

Nathan had been a relatively new Bastion. He was popular in Falmir due to a heroic victory against a demonic horde, despite the odds being stacked against him. They had met in a field of demonic corpses, and Jafeila had dismissed him with a glance.

The nervous looks she gave him right now were a far cry from dismissive. She pressed her fingers together and licked her lips as her tail beat up a storm behind her.

"Champion Jafeila," Nathan corrected. "You're no longer in training as of now. Walk with me."

Jafeila half-squeaked, half-screamed in delight at the news that she had finally been promoted to a full Champion and bounced behind Nathan. He ignored her for a moment, letting her burn off her nervous energy.

Hopefully, she'd be a little calmer once she settled down and got to know him. But a niggling thought ate at the back of his mind.

Would any of his women be the same as they were in his time-line? Could they be the same given he planned to change the course of history?

He suppressed the thought and looked at the ruins around him. Striding toward the remains of the keep, he recalled what this place was.

Gharrick Pass. One of only two major land routes connecting the Anfang Empire with its eastern neighbors through the Gharrick Mountains. It was through this fortress that the Empire had been attacked from behind.

This ruined fortress indirectly caused the end of world.

No wonder Kadria had said she knew exactly the place to send him. She had held up her end of the bargain so far. If Nathan could protect this pass, he could stop the collapse of the Empire.

Nathan felt the slight pull of a binding stone from beneath the keep. With a wave of his hand, he told Jafeila to follow him and entered the ruins.

Gharrick Pass had been abandoned centuries old. But with

the binding stone's power, Nathan could rebuild the fortress practically overnight. That made finding it his highest priority.

There might be a slight complication, however.

"Lady von Clair wanted you to visit her once you arrived," Jafeila said. "She said she would organize everything you needed. Do you know her?"

Consulting his implanted memories, Nathan decided he didn't. He'd never even heard the name in his life.

"I don't, but it's normal for Bastions to work with the ruling nobles," he replied, taking a stab in the dark regarding Lady von Clair's status. "Although we serve as soldiers of the Emperor, and are part of the Imperial Army, Bastions spend most of their time keeping the peace. It's a lot easier for us to do our jobs if we work with the nobles."

"Ohhhh."

Jafeila fell silent for a little while. The pair stepped over rubble and stagnant pools of water. One of the staircases down was flooded, presumably blocked, so Nathan looked for another way down.

"So what sort of things will she do for us?" she asked suddenly.

Nathan smiled wryly. "It's more accurate to say what she'll ask us to do for her."

"Eh?"

The next staircase was too dark to see down, as there were no cracks in the roof for sunlight to stream through. Nathan summoned a ball of light with a snap of his fingers. The beastkin stared at the hazy glowing ball in wonder.

"Like I said, we keep the peace. The ruling noble of the region does the same, so she'll try to offload her duties onto us. She'll grease some wheels and help us run the fortress and feed ourselves. But we don't need most of what she can provide. Once the binding stone is operational, I can use its magic to build the fortress myself, and summons make better soldiers than humans for the most part."

Nathan gave Jafeila a nod. "And I have you, my Champion. With a boost from the binding stone, you can probably defeat Lady von Clair's army single-handedly."

Wide green eyes stared back at him. He looked away before her adorableness mesmerized him.

"So why is that message so important?" Jafeila said. "She seemed to think it would be the first thing you'd do."

Ignoring her for a moment, Nathan stared down the dark, damp tunnels. Centuries of rain had caused water to seep through from above, but there had been no signs of recent rain. The flooded tunnel from earlier must be above them, and the water slowly seeped through the earth and stone. Once he activated the binding stone, his next steps would be to clear out the underground and make this place safe.

He worried that it might fall in on him at any moment.

A dim light emanated from a room at the end of the current corridor. He made his way toward it, and Jafeila followed.

"We're about to find out," Nathan said.

"Find out what?"

Nathan stood at the doorway and stared at the glowing monochrome orb in the next room. Although it looked like it sat on a pedestal, he knew better. The orb was fixed in place. If he smashed the moss-covered limestone pedestal beneath it, the orb would hover there, perfectly still.

This was a binding stone. Nobody knew what they were made of, where they came from, or what powered them.

But the Bastions knew how to control them.

The binding stone was roughly half of Nathan's height, and perfectly round. It glowed a very dull white, almost gray, color. Two bands of black ran across its surface.

Those bands were a good sign. Binding stones could be sealed away, made inert. Legend had it that the Watcher Omria sealed away binding stones that were not in use, preventing miscreants from abusing them. Once sealed, only another binding stone's power could break the seal.

Nathan didn't control a binding stone so he couldn't awaken a binding stone. If this one had been sealed, he would have needed assistance.

"Find out if the binding stone was still inert," he explained, answering her question from earlier.

He walked up to the stone. It didn't react to his approach. Jafeila remained standing at the doorway, staring wide-eyed at the glowing orb. Her ears flattened against her head.

"Is that safe?" she asked.

"For me? Yes. For your average person? Also, yes. I suspect it's still not active," Nathan mused. He placed his hand against the binding stone. It still didn't react to him, even when he probed it with magic. "As I thought."

"Oh. So is that why Lady von Clair wants to see you?"

"Probably. This binding stone has been warded against intrusion. An untrained Bastion or casual intruder cannot easily activate it. Most likely the Bastion who unsealed the binding stone placed the wards on it to prevent anybody from using the stone, unless they were from the Empire."

Fortunately, Nathan knew how to unravel most of the protections the Empire used. Falmir and the other nations had uncovered them over the course of the war, as they claimed the Bastions and binding stones that had once belonged to the Empire. Later, Falmir did the same to other nations, as the demons destroyed country after country.

A few minutes passed as he used a few spells and tricks to connect himself to the binding stone. Jafeila watched from the doorway at first, before creeping up next to him. Her tail batted against his legs with every swish, but he couldn't slip out of his focus to tell her to stop.

Luckily, he had years of experience with beastkin physically distracting him with their fluffy tails and ears. A single tail brushing against his legs was nothing.

Then, success. He dove into the new binding stone and tethered it to himself. Time slowed down around him. A rush of sensations blasted into his body. Cold, freezing cold. Everything was so damp. He felt like he was frostbitten and decaying away. Like he had been left to rot in a tundra.

Nathan pushed away the sensations from the binding stone before they overwhelmed him. Old binding stones were dangerous, as the world around them was often in such disrepair compared to a normal binding stone that they physically hurt the Bastion. Normally there would be an older Bastion coaching Nathan through this, but he didn't need one.

Chances are that was what Lady von Clair's role was. Wait for Nathan to arrive, then let another Bastion know that he's ready to have his binding stone activated. She could spend a few days helping the new Bastion familiarize himself with his surroundings, and the more experienced Bastion wastes less of his time with a newbie. Win-win.

But Nathan wasn't a newbie and didn't need help. Plus, he didn't want to waste a day without access to a binding stone.

Nathan scanned his surroundings. Then he scanned the power now available to him. Nobody had used this binding stone for centuries, so its reserves were overflowing. He immediately put them to work.

The underground area needed to be cleaned up and reinforced. Then the keep repaired, given he and Jafeila would live here. Afterward, he'd clean up the rubble and vegetation outside. Only after all of that was done could he rebuild the fortress proper and fortify the pass against external assault.

The tasks assigned, Nathan withdrew from the binding stone. Moments later, the keep groaned. Water vanished from the ground, stone shifted, and lamps sprung out from the walls.

Jafeila jumped. She grabbed Nathan's arm.

"We need to run! It's collapsing," she screamed.

He held her in place and tried not to laugh. "It's fine. Calm down," he said.

"Eh?"

He briefly explained what he had done while the binding stone did its thing. The stonework appeared to repair itself as magic poured into the keep. His brief explanation turned into a long one about how binding stones used their internal magic stores to control and manipulate reality in their vicinity. He didn't know how much of it sunk into Jafeila.

"Now, I believe we have somewhere important to be," Nathan said. He stood up and brushed off the dust from his uniform.

"Oh, so we're still visiting Lady von Clair?" Jafeila asked.

"Not yet." He frowned. "We need to check on the fortress's demonic portal."

CHAPTER 4

A double door gate stood in the center of the keep. It was nowhere near the size of the gate from Nathan's fortress in the Far Reaches, standing only three to four meters tall. No runes or jewels decorated it. Only a single steel bar held it shut.

Nathan placed his hand against the gate and felt magic sealing it shut. The seal felt old. Faded. That meant somebody had sealed the portal away long ago, perhaps even before the fortress fell and the binding stone was abandoned. Whatever the case, no demons from the portal had broken into the real world.

"Um, do we need to go through there? We only just activated the binding stone. Don't we have ages before any demons invade?" Jafeila asked.

"The portal may already be active. The first step any Bastion should take upon claiming a binding stone is to confirm the state of the attached portal, and whether they need to suppress it," Nathan explained.

"Already active? But how?"

Nathan stepped away from the gate, realizing he had to explain a few things first.

Around him, the keep was being rebuilt by magic. Cracks in the limestone filled themselves in. Staircases folded out from the walls. Sand appeared from thin air and melted into glass. Statues and suits of armor poured themselves into existence from molten metal and liquefied rock.

"You've been taught that demonic portals activate whenever a binding stone is used by a Bastion?" Nathan asked.

Jafeila nodded. Her ears pricked up in anticipation of his next words. Her tail curled behind her back.

"That's wrong. Well, not entirely wrong." Nathan chewed on his lip as he thought on his next words. "If we could keep the demons out by sealing away all the binding stones, don't you think that somebody would have sealed them all away decades or centuries ago? Or that the Watcher Omria would have done so, given the goddess's prime directive is to protect Doumahr from the invaders?"

Jafeila nodded slowly, but said nothing.

Nathan continued, "Each binding stone has a portal attached to it, but the portals can activate of their own will. This gate is sealed to keep the demons out in case the portal does activate. Think of it like insurance, and it keeps demons from invading through unprotected portals. If the portal is active then a demonic horde may be ready to invade any day now."

"Shouldn't we wait until we have an army before we enter, then? What if we're ambushed upon entering?" Jafeila's tail shot bolt upright.

"Relax. If there really was a demonic army large enough to be a threat, they'd have already broken down this gate and invaded," Nathan said, giving Jafeila a cheery grin.

She glared at him. He ruffled her hair, squashing her cat ears. She darted away, cursing him.

"You're so blase about all of this," she muttered. "I don't remember learning half this stuff."

"A lot of what you get taught in the academy is watered down so you don't get scared," Nathan admitted.

Or the trainers didn't know it, he thought darkly.

"You're so much more experienced than I expected. I was told you were a new Bastion, so I expected somebody closer to my age and experience," Jafeila said. She froze, including her tail, then looked at Nathan with wide eyes. "N-Not that I'm not extremely happy that you're my Bastion, Nathan. Lord Straub. Bastion. Uhhhh…"

"Call me Nathan," he said, a broad grin crossing his face.

"Really? Thank you." Jafeila paused. "So, how do you know so much more than me? We both came from the academy. Everything is so complicated and obscure, but you seem like a master."

Nathan's memory agreed with Jafeila that he was a brand-new Bastion, so he needed a convincing lie. The Jafeila from his timeline was a great liar and could keep a secret. He wasn't convinced that the Jafeila in front of him was the same. At least, not yet.

Fortunately, his memories provided a grain of truth he could rely upon.

"I am a new Bastion, but my father was also a Bastion," he said. This was true in this timeline and the last. Although neither ever told Nathan anything about the truth of being a Bastion.

One swore an oath to the Watcher Omria to not needlessly spill many of the secrets of Bastions, in order to limit the damage if the wrong people abused the binding stones. A twinge of regret ran down Nathan as he remembered that oath and the method he had used to travel back in time.

"Ohhhh, so you became one to follow in his footsteps?" Jafeila asked. She frowned. "At over thirty?"

Chuckling, Nathan shook his head. "Not quite. I'll tell you the full story later." His memories were still jumbled, and he got the sense that he hadn't become a Bastion for the happiest of reasons.

People rarely did.

For now, they had a portal to investigate. He placed his hand on the steel bar blocking the gate. The magical seal pushed back against him, preventing him from removing it. Nathan applied a gentle push from the binding stone. The seal snapped, and the bar slid free, grinding along a century of rust and crashing onto the stone below.

Nathan pushed the gate open.

Beyond lay a volcanic wasteland.

Fantastically huge cliffs ran along the valley the gate opened into, but they cast no shadow. The ground was rocky, uneven, and lined with finger-wide cracks. An eerie purple light emanated from deep within those cracks, with no obvious source. The rock itself was volcanic in nature, with the telltale glassy appearance and texture, and was a deep, dull gray.

There was no sun or moon in the sky, nor any other source of light. But the entire world was perfectly lit. Soft, diffuse shadows were cast directly beneath everything. The sky itself was a hazy red, as if in perpetual sunrise.

"Only a few demons," Nathan muttered, taking in his surroundings.

He wandered into the hellscape and scanned the valley further. Jafeila followed behind him, her scimitar out and ready for action.

"How can you be so calm walking into Hell?" she asked, voice low.

"This isn't Hell. Or wherever the demons come from," he said. "If it were, they wouldn't need portals to get here, they'd live here. This is a place between worlds. A transitory world of some form. I wish we knew why it connected to our world, or how it sprung up next to the binding stones."

In the distance was a much larger clearing with a small mound of dirt and rocks in its center. A trio of goat-headed demons sat next to it, doing nothing in particular. Nathan had never known what demons do when milling about in this world, and he didn't care to learn now.

There were two more demons closer to him, standing in the narrow part of the valley. The demons hadn't noticed the new arrivals yet.

"So, where's the portal? This place is so small," Jafeila said.

"The portal isn't active, so you can't see it."

"I know that much at least." She pouted at him. "But I can't even see where it's supposed to appear. Isn't there supposed to be some massive pile of rocks, or a spire, or something where reality tears itself open?"

Nathan wordlessly pointed at the tiny mound in the middle of the clearing. Jafeila stared at it for several moments, tilting her head.

"Oh. That's it?"

"That's it. Which is very strange."

"Isn't a small portal good?"

He shook his head. "That's not how this works. The demons are always going to invade. It's in their nature. Given this fortress has been abandoned for centuries, there should be some buildup here. Or the protective seal on the gate should have been restored much more recently, after an invasion. Instead, nothing's happened and the portal is practically nonexistent."

There were a few possible causes that came to mind in Nathan's head, none of them pleasant. Most of them made little sense given the time period. He had yet to confirm the precise date that he had been transported to, but the fact that this was Jafeila's first assignment as Champion told him that the invasion of Gharrick Pass was imminent. So that meant many of his theories were out by default.

He resorted to voicing his thoughts aloud to Jafeila. "Demonic energy builds up in portals the same way that magical energy builds up in the binding stones. Demons then use it to expand the portal or invade. They clearly haven't done either, as this portal is one of the smallest I've seen, and they haven't invaded, because the seal was intact."

"That means…"

"I don't know."

"Oh. I thought you knew everything." Jafeila bit her lip. She didn't mean it as a jab, but it sounded like one anyway.

He sighed. "I can speculate, but knowing something is different to guessing. Something or someone has likely bled the demonic energy off. Maybe a major invasion took place nearby and used this portal's energy." He shrugged. Too many possibilities. Too little evidence.

The portal was inactive and tiny. Nathan turned and made to re-enter the fortress. A squeak of surprise caused him to stop.

Jafeila blushed as he looked at her.

"Um, shouldn't we get rid of these demons?" she asked, fiddling with her sword hilt.

"A few demons won't cause any problems."

"But... but..." she mumbled. Her ears flattened against her head, and her tail ran against the ground, picking up dust.

Somebody was going to need to give her tail a proper clean after today. It was filthy, and her black fur had lost its sheen.

"Fine. You can have your fun," he said. She perked up and spun around. Before she leaped away, he grabbed her by the shoulder. "But we have something important to do first, Champion."

"Eh?"

"Did you forget the most important part of being a Champion?" Nathan pointed at himself, then at her. "There's one last step, then you'll be a true Champion."

A moment passed. Then two. Jafeila stared at Nathan in visible confusion. Then her eyes widened.

"Wait, you mean—" she cut herself off and gulped. "You're going to grant me a gem?"

Nathan blinked. "No. Not yet."

"Aww."

"In time," he said. Her tail perked back up. "There are four stages to being a Champion. You should remember this."

"Enhancement, monogem, duogem, trigem. I know. But I hoped you would skip straight to monogem," she muttered.

"Impossible. A gem won't take unless a Champion has enough experience with the power of a binding stone. To get that experience, I must enhance you first. Trust me, this is a significant step." He smiled at her.

"I know, I know. We get enhanced during training." She scowled at him.

Nathan's eyes gleamed. Jafeila had gone from nervous and adorable to pouty and adorable, all because he had disappointed her. She was so openly emotional now, compared to the Jafeila he knew. Maybe he enjoyed this too much, but this felt like being able to pig out on a buffet after a lifetime of only ever eating food a single plate at a time.

"Like I said, trust me. Now, what type of enhancement do you prefer?"

"Type?"

"The typical ones are strength, speed, or endurance. They're self-explanatory. Or you can mix and match. More advanced stuff includes focusing enhancements on particular facets of your body, like your legs, or enhanced senses." Nathan paused, noticing that Jafeila was staring at him with very wide eyes. "You can also increase the magical side of things, but I don't think you know any sorcery, so best to stick to physically enhancing your body with the binding stone."

"This is permanent?" she asked.

"More or less. Your training enhancements are to prevent you from dying when you fight demons, not to help you slay them. If they gave you a full enhancement straight away, you'd probably get a little overconfident and not train properly. But you're a full-fledged Champion now. I need you to be a one-woman army, Jafeila."

She mouthed her name after he said it. He realized that was

the first time he had spoken her name aloud after the initial greetings.

"So? Strength, speed, or endurance?" he asked.

"Wait, now I can only pick those three?" she squeaked. Her ears flattened. "I was thinking about what I'd mix and match, too."

"You can change your enhancement at any time until you get your first gem. I recommend you change it up regularly until you know what suits you best," Nathan explained. "So stick with the basics at first."

"Oh. Then speed. I wanna chop up those demons into ten pieces before they can even blink. Like in the stories of the trigem Champion Tarako, and her Nine-Tail Slash." Jafeila grinned at Nathan and bounced up and down on the spot.

He grimaced at the mention of the fictional trigem Champion. Or at least, every mystic fox he had ever met insisted that she was fictional, despite the statues and countless stories talking about the nine-tailed fox Tarako and her centuries of exploits.

Speed was a predictable choice by Jafeila. It had been her enhancement in his timeline. He was hardly surprised that she chose it this time. Somehow, her predictability comforted him.

"Stand still and don't move. This will only take a moment," he said. "It might feel a little funny, but you can't move from that spot. Also, don't try to resist in any way."

"I trained for this. I'm ready, Nathan," Jafeila breathed out, her voice husky.

The pair fell silent. Not even a wind blew past them, as there was no wind in this world. The faint sound of the keep rebuilding itself could be heard from the other side of the gate. As could the distant grunting of the demons farther down the valley.

Nathan gave Jafeila one last look. She stood still, her muscles tensed and eyes closed. Both her ears and tail stood bolt upright. Her fingers tapped against her leggings.

She seemed ready, so Nathan decided to proceed. He dove into his newly activated binding stone, exploring his mental world. There wasn't much to see. In his old timeline, he had connected himself to countless binding stones over his life. Here, he only had the one.

His mental world only contained the one binding stone, the tether to his own mind, and the leylines directly connected to that stone.

Plus that strange tether that Nathan still couldn't detect, but that he knew was there.

Shrugging off that odd feeling, he concentrated on his existing binding stone. He plucked a spare bit of magic from it and left his mental world. Time resumed. Jafeila continued to tap her leg.

Her magical presence hovered in front of him, faint but still there. Ordinary people barely existed with regard to magical detection. Nathan suspected the only reason he could detect Jafeila so quickly was because she had trained as a Champion. That process had increased the magic within her body.

Most ordinary humans and beastkin were practically invisible to Nathan when it came to magical detection, unless he cast a dedicated ritual to detect them with his magic or used the binding stone to detect them.

Now that he had found her magical presence, Nathan connected his own essence to hers. The moment he made the connection, he felt her mind push back against him. He mentally grasped the magic of binding stone, just in case he needed it to force the connection.

Then she stopped resisting him. Her body relaxed, and a sigh escaped her lips. Over the next few seconds, a sweet scent drifted through Nathan's nose. Jafeila hummed lightly.

He pushed onward into her essence. Her power surrounded him. It seemed to caress him, welcome him in.

In reality, it was a threat. If he misstepped, her power would try to crush him in defense. The binding stone could protect him, but he was still in danger.

Eventually, he reached her core. Slowly, he drew on the piece of magic that he had brought with him from the binding stone. Then he cast the enhancement ritual on Jafeila.

How many times had he done this? Never to Jafeila. But dozens to other Champions.

But in this timeline, this enhancement ritual was his first. That made it special.

After a minute, the ritual was done, and Nathan withdrew from Jafeila's essence.

She stood in the same place as before, but her body was noticeably looser. A cheerful grin spread across her face, her palms were open, and she swayed from side to side. A light moan leaked from her lips.

"How are you doing, Jafeila?" Nathan asked, trying to bring her back to reality.

"Fei," she mumbled, staring at him with glazed eyes. "Call me Fei. I don't like being called Jafeila."

She didn't? That was news to him. In his timeline, it had been the opposite. Everybody else called her Fei, and he called her Jafeila at her request.

He hid a frown at the deviation from his memories and nodded. That sweet scent lingered in his mind, slowly fading away.

"So, how are you doing, Fei?" he repeated.

"Umm, getting there?" Fei said. She shook herself out, her tail waving back and forth out of sync from the rest of her body. "Wow. I can't imagine what that must be like if you enhanced a guy. I thought my books exaggerated things." A blush crossed her face, but she grinned at him regardless.

"There's a reason Champions are almost always the opposite gender to the Bastion, or at least a matching gender preference," Nathan said drily.

"Gender preference?"

"I'll tell you when you're older."

She scowled at him. "I'm an adult."

That he knew, in more ways than one. And he was very thankful for it, given the way his body was reacting to the sweet scent she had let off during the ritual.

"Of course you are," he said with a grin. He reached out to ruffle her hair.

She darted back in a blur, taking several steps faster than he could blink. Then she froze and looked down at the ground.

"Oh. Oh my goddess," she said. She ran forward and nearly bowled Nathan over with her speed. "I'm so faaaaaaaast!" With those last words, Fei became a black blur charging across the valley toward the demons.

Nathan pumped some magic into his eyes so he could keep up with her movements.

The demons looked up, their massive eyes narrowing and focusing in on the strange blur charging right at them. One of them bellowed, leaping up and hefting an axe the size of a man.

Too late. Fei whirled behind him. The hand gripping the axe began to fall, almost in slow motion. The demon's eyes widened. He shouted.

Fei's scimitar ripped right into his groin, then tore upward. The demon screeched. Nathan looked away for a second, not wanting to watch what came next.

Except the demons kept bellowing, and Fei let out a shriek. Looking back, Nathan saw that Fei's sword was stuck. She rolled back, leaving her scimitar buried halfway up the torso of one demon, who had keeled over in the dirt.

The other demon slammed a two-handed hammer into the ground. Each strike left small craters in the rock. A single hit from that would cave in Fei's skull. As a Champion, she would survive it, and Nathan had access to basic healing from the binding stone, but he didn't want her to take that much damage in her first fight.

He reached for the longsword at his hip. Before he could draw it, Fei pulled a dagger from her belt. She darted in, dodged the demon's blow, and slashed open its neck twice. Blood fountained out, but the demon only staggered.

Too shallow.

Fei noticed. She spun around. The demon turned, hefting its hammer into the air.

A human warrior, and even a Champion, would have been slowed by a major wound like that. Not a demon. They felt pain, but wounds didn't slow them. Nobody understood why they even had internal organs, given they didn't use them. Puncture a demon's heart and it fought on, as if it had been tickled.

The only way to kill a demon was through sheer bodily damage. Cut them open, slash off their limbs, smash them, blow them up, pelt them with magic. Anything worked, so long as she physically damaged their body enough that they eventually died.

Fei hurled her dagger at the demon. It slammed right into its eye and the demon froze. Then it shouted and charged forward. She scowled, grabbed another dagger, and met its charge.

Three charges. That's what it took. Each time, she slashed its chest open and darted aside before it crushed her with its hammer. Eventually, the demon collapsed to the ground, unmoving.

After retrieving her scimitar from the gory mess she had made of the first demon, Fei waited for Nathan to walk up to her.

"I know. I messed up," she mumbled.

Nathan ruffled her hair. She let out a squeak, her ears pricking up around his hand, before flattening under his attention.

"This is normal for your first battle. Demons are the primary threat to the world for a reason. If they were easy to defeat, we wouldn't need so many Bastions and Champions, would we?"

"I guess not."

"Take out the three in the clearing, and you'll feel better," he suggested.

This fight went more smoothly. Fei didn't lose her scimitar and kept her attacks more reserved. She struck at their limbs, slipping in and out of the demons' reach with her superior speed before they could react. By the end of the fight, she had collected a hand from each one, and was sawing off the head of another.

"Do you need the head?" Nathan asked as he approached.

"I figure a huge demonic goat head makes for a better trophy than some hands. And this guy is the biggest of the lot." Fei grinned up at Nathan. Her face, fur, and hair were liberally covered in blood from the battle.

Not that it bothered him. Blood-covered Champions were a common sight. If anything, this was a nostalgic sight. He had first met Fei in the aftermath of her slaughtering countless demons.

She hadn't been so cheerful about killing demons back then, however.

"We'll find somewhere for you to put it. For now, let's head back and clean up," he said.

Fei looked at him in confusion. Then at herself. "Oh. Right. Clean would be good."

Then she followed his gaze and her eyes landed on her tail.

Her scream echoed throughout the empty valley.

CHAPTER 5

"Ah, right there! Mmm! I want to feel your hands," Fei moaned. Her voice was sweet and breathy. She let out a low moan during the next stroke from Nathan. "Where did you learn to brush tails like this?"

"I've had some practice," Nathan muttered.

Years on this tail in particular, in fact. Fei might be over a decade younger, but her tail was unchanged.

Fei arched her back and let out another moan as he moved his hands down her tail to the next segment he needed to brush. Her eyes glistened as she stared back at him, her tongue sticking out, and strings of saliva still connecting her lips.

Her reactions were far more exaggerated now, however. Nathan swallowed and looked away from her in a vain attempt to quell his hardening erection. How many times had he seen her like this when she was older, back in his old fortress? How many times had he lain with her, then enjoyed her playfulness afterward?

Never again, an icy voice in the back of his head said. He remembered that night. The feeling of reaching out for Jafeila and the rest of his Champions and finding nothing but emptiness.

"Nathan, are you alright?" Fei asked.

Snapping out of his thoughts, Nathan gave her a soft smile. "It's fine. Just lost in thought."

"They didn't seem to be nice thoughts," she said. Her hand drifted over his, but didn't touch it.

True enough. He didn't have to worry about his erection anymore. At least for the next five seconds, before Fei let out another sweet moan.

"Just relax, Fei. This will be over soon," he said, changing the subject.

She pouted. "I don't want it to be over soon."

The plan had never been to brush her tail, but she had been so pathetic that he had foolishly offered to help. She likely thought he would simply help her comb out the worst knots, or maybe she wanted some companionship.

Instead, she got the treatment of a tail-grooming master, if Nathan didn't say so himself. He pushed her into the shower, given she wouldn't stop marveling at the sight of her newly constructed and furnished bedroom suite.

Now she was sitting on a thick velvet cushion in her underwear while he brushed out her hair and tail. He had never expected to get so close to her so quickly, let alone like this, but beastkin desired physical intimacy more than other races.

Once he finished, Fei threw herself on her bed. She sank into the soft mattress with a groan of pleasure.

"I've never had a bed this soft," she said, eyes closed. "Nobody said Bastions could create such amazing furnishings. Everywhere else I go is so plain by comparison."

Nathan raised an eyebrow. This was one of the few things his master had taught him in Falmir. He had little positive to say about his training as an apprentice Bastion, but he had learned to craft some very impressive furniture. Being able to conjure up whatever expensive materials and objects he wanted was freeing for Nathan.

Perhaps that meant he had wasted a little bit—or perhaps a lot

—of energy from the binding stone on luxuries and aesthetics in the keep. But he planned to live here and use Gharrick Pass as a base of operations for some time. Why not make it a pleasurable experience?

Therefore, he filled the hallways and open spaces with ostentatious statues, gilded decorations, and decorative suits of armor. Nathan had set aside a small chapel for the Watcher Omria, even if he couldn't bring himself to enter it. He'd even used his power to help Fei mount her demon's head on the wall. The bedroom suites contained massive beds, bathrooms using plumbing technology that Nathan wasn't certain had been invented yet, and ornate rosewood furniture.

"Enjoy it as much as you like," he said. "Use today to explore or settle in. I need to spend some time with the binding stone."

"Oh. Bastion stuff. See you later." Fei waved to Nathan as he left the room.

He spent the rest of the day and most of the morning in a reconstructed office. Unlike most rooms in the keep, this one had survived the centuries relatively intact. Signs of temporary habitation were also present, namely an up-to-date map of the region which allowed Nathan to get a more accurate grip on the world.

His memory was good, but he had been a newbie Bastion when the Empire fell. Most of his knowledge came second hand.

The books and maps in the room had been preserved with magic, and a touch from the binding stone allowed Nathan to restore them enough that he could read them. Not that he could restore faded ink. The binding stone could repair dried paper, cracked spines, and prevent a scroll from falling apart when he picked it up, but it couldn't fill in a word where one had been written centuries ago.

Nathan's next step was to assess the current state of the leylines. The binding stone allowed Nathan to monitor the flow of magic in the surroundings, which an experienced Bastion could use to detect the movements of sorcerers, Champions, or demons.

Right now, there were potential signs of all three, which made little sense to Nathan. Perhaps his detection skills had gotten rusty. He couldn't remember the last time he had used them on something that wasn't a demon. Maybe he had misinterpreted something.

But what he knew was that there was a large draw on the leylines to the east, beyond Gharrick Pass. That felt like a powerful sorcerer actively using a leyline to power their magic. But there were also signs of Champions around there, if very faint. Too faint for a Champion to be actively present.

Closer to home, something felt wrong with the leylines. The flow of magic was disturbed, and that almost always meant demons. This disruption further affected Nathan's ability to monitor this side of Gharrick Pass. For all he knew, Champions had been active here as well, but the leyline disruption covered their tracks.

Which, again, made no sense to Nathan. The portal was inactive and tiny. Demons might overflow to the neighboring region if the portal was actively overflowing with demonic energy, but that wasn't the case.

"Oh, is this your office?" Fei interrupted. She poked her head through the open doorway. "Um, am I interrupting? You look deep in thought."

"No, it's fine. I have an open door policy." Nathan waved his hand at the doorway, which didn't have a door.

Fei tiptoed in, her brow furrowed. She stared at the doorway. Then it clicked.

"Oh. Oh! It's a pun. You literally have an open door," she said. "Huh. I thought you were the serious type, but..." she trailed off into inaudible mumbling.

Nathan waited patiently, leaning back in his chair. A large table sat between the two of them. On top of the table was the map he had found in here, which was dated 407 OA. The OA stood for Omnia's Ascent and referred to her disappearance from the Anfang Empire. Nobody knew where the goddess went, but it marked the beginning of the decline for the Empire.

The Empire had fallen in mid-408 OA. This map was almost up-to-date and reinforced Nathan's assumption that he was reliving the days that led up to the fall of the Empire.

"Anything interesting on the map?" Fei asked. She stared down at it.

The map depicted only the eastern border region of the Empire. It went as far north as Forselle Valley and ended just south of Gharrick Pass. The capital, Aleich, was visible at the western-most edge of the map.

"Apparently, the Empire thinks it controls land on the other side of the pass," Nathan said, pointing at a small region of land on the far side of the Gharrick Mountains from their current location. "I'm worried we'll be responsible for defending that. Perhaps our Lady von Clair will know more."

"You want to visit her?" Fei asked.

"Shortly, yes. I'd feel more secure in a few days, once the walls are repaired."

The binding stone had finished clearing out most of the courtyard, but its reserves had finally run dry. Nathan had turned his attention this morning to drawing in magical energy from the leylines, and would set the binding stone back to work in a day or two.

Until then, Gharrick Pass was unprotected. The keep was fully repaired and fortified, but it was far less defensible without an exterior wall. Nathan would have liked to block off the pass itself, but he lacked the Champions to defend such a long line of wall. Assuming he even had the time to build it in the first place.

Suddenly, a trumpet cut through his thoughts. The note was short, but piercing.

"Champion! Bastion! Are you here?" a voice shouted from afar.

The trumpet blew again.

"I think somebody wants us," Nathan muttered. He rose from his chair and investigated the disturbance.

By the time they reached the entrance of the keep, the trumpet had blown three more times. Each time was further apart, but the shouting became incessant.

Nathan wanted to leave the nuisance be, but there was only one reason somebody rides up to a Bastion's keep and requests their presence like this.

Well, two reasons. But the person blowing the trumpet would have been less panicked if he was here to summon Nathan on behalf of Lady von Clair or some other noble.

"I'm here, soldier," Nathan called out as he pushed the keep's gates open. A man wearing an Empire uniform sat on horseback in the courtyard, riding around in circles. Most likely a private soldier, given he lacked the emblem of the Emperor. Maybe one of Lady von Clair's men?

"Are you the Bastion?" the soldier called out.

"I am. Nathan Straub. You're one of von Clair's men?" Nathan asked.

"Yes. I'm so glad you're here." The soldier closed his eyes for a moment and his horse whinnied nervously, picking up on the mood of its rider. He stroked the horse's neck. "Calm down, girl. It's fine."

"You're in a hurry. I take it you need help," Nathan said.

"Lady von Clair formally requests your aid, Bastion. She understands you only just began your posting..." The soldier's eyes lingered on the gleaming keep behind Nathan. He surely knew it had been a ruin not long ago.

"Leave the formalities for your lady. Where do I need to go?"

The soldier stared at Nathan. He opened his mouth to say something, then closed it. His horse tried to move forward, but he pulled her back.

"Trantia. Lady von Clair is under siege at Trantia. Please help her," the soldier said. "I need to keep going, Bastion. Lady Nair must also be told of this attack."

Nair?

"You mean Vera Nair, the sorceress?" Nathan probed.

"That's right, Bastion. I'm sorry, but I must be off," the soldier shouted, already riding down the pass.

The soldier's figure vanished from sight while Nathan and Fei watched. His horse was fast, and possibly enhanced with magic.

"Trantia? That's too far on foot," Fei said. "He must have left hours ago to get here so fast. And the carriage left last night."

The horseless carriage ran automatically on magic. The spell commanded it to return to the capital after dropping Nathan off, so it had. That left Nathan and Fei with no immediately obvious transportation methods.

"Maybe not hours. That horse is fast, and Trantia didn't look that far away on the map," Nathan said. "I'm more curious why Lady von Clair is sending a message to a famous sorceress by horseback. Surely she has some means to contact the region's protector using magic or some faster means."

"Protector? I thought you said that's our job?" Fei protested.

"It is, but Nair's a fairly well-known sorceress. We can work with her," he said.

When the Amica Federation had attacked the Empire from behind, Nair had been the only line of defense the Empire had at Gharrick Pass. She had gone down in history as a sorceress who fought until the end for her country. Naturally, she lost, and the Empire was destroyed. But her name had lived on through almost every retelling of the fall of the Anfang Empire.

In Nathan's mind, she was a comrade fighting to stop the end of the world.

"In any case, let's worry about that later. For now, there's a town under siege. Hopefully things haven't gotten too bad," Nathan said. He reached for the magic of the binding stone.

"Should we really go by ourselves? If they need this sorceress, and Lady von Clair's soldiers can't handle it, then can we?" Fei asked, eyes wide.

Nathan ruffled her hair. "You're new to being a Champion, but consider this to be your first actual mission. Chances are the attackers are only bandits, and anything less than an enemy Champion, sorcerers, or demons are too weak to threaten us anymore."

"Really?"

"Really. You'll understand that once you crush your first bandit army single-handedly." He chuckled.

Ignoring her pout at his dismissal of her worries, Nathan drew on the binding stone. It was low on power, but he only needed a tiny amount.

He cast his hand out and white sparkles drifted out. Where they landed, a pair of metallic horses sprung into existence, seeming to unfold into this world from thin air.

The horses were made entirely from steel. Empty space filled voids between overlapping plates of metal, and they had no actual heads. These were metallic automaton horses, rather than real ones.

The binding stone lacked the power to summon living creatures, as it couldn't create or destroy life directly. So almost everything Nathan summoned was some form of metallic or earthen creation.

Fei stared at the summons with wide eyes. The horses stood perfectly still, even as Nathan mounted one.

"Are you coming?" he asked.

"I don't know how to ride," she whispered.

With a flick of his wrist, Nathan unsummoned the other horse. Fei flinched and looked down at the ground.

"Fei," he said. "Fei, look at me."

She looked at him. Saw his outstretched hand.

"Are you coming?" he asked again, holding his hand out. "We

have a town to protect."

   She took his hand, and he pulled her up onto the horse in front of him. A moment later, the horse took off toward Trantia.

CHAPTER 6

Dense thickets of pine trees lined the road to Trantia. The forest floor was a thick bed of fallen pine needles, shrubberies, fallen trees, and rocks. Only the road was clear of debris, and tree trunks lined the forest path to keep forest debris and water clear.

Nathan scanned his surroundings while his automaton horse barreled forward at a full gallop. The horse took care of itself, so his mind was free to focus on other things.

A small part of his mind focused itself on the squirming beastkin girl holding on to him for dear life. Her warmth bled into him, and he felt the constant pressure of her body pressing against him. She was a pleasant distraction.

The rest of his mind concerned itself with disparities between what he thought he knew about the Empire and what he observed.

This area hadn't been heavily populated or worked for centuries. Somebody kept the dirt road clear, but the forest showed no signs of human activity. If Nathan tried to run through the forest, he'd trip over within seconds and crack his head open.

Nathan was no expert on trees, so he had no clue how old these pines or the forest itself might be, but he knew that most forests weren't this dense. Any nearby villages and towns would need wood to fuel their homes and industries.

There couldn't be many people living nearby, then. No wonder Gharrick Pass had been left abandoned for so long. There was nobody to protect. This was the wilderness. He'd been sent to the boonies.

The ride took less than an hour. The fact the horse didn't slow down or rest at all made the trip extremely fast.

A small town loomed in the distance.

"No smoke plumes," Nathan said. "They haven't done anything to the town yet. Let's find a vantage point."

With a mental nudge, Nathan directed the horse to a nearby hill. The forest thinned out and vanished well short of the town, and the pair had passed a couple of tiny villages on the way. Now the terrain was flat and open. Any besiegers could see Nathan and Fei coming without even trying.

Trantia looked to be intact. A wall surrounded the entire town, and Nathan could see undeveloped space within the town. Whoever had designed the wall had planned ahead.

Or perhaps they had overestimated the growth of the town.

There wasn't much to see. A large manor house. A town hall far too large for the size of the town. A mishmash of houses built in wildly different eras. Nathan reckoned some buildings were as old as the Empire, and others younger than Fei.

A shimmering blue dome hung over the town.

"Does every town have that?" Fei asked, pointing at the magical barrier.

"Border forts and towns, usually," Nathan replied. "Cities use a more limited variation in their walls."

"Why only at the borders?"

Memories of refugees fleeing burning towns and armies wiped out overnight in "state-of-the-art" fortresses came to Nathan's mind. The demonic hordes had shown little respect for the wondrous power of sorcery.

"Barriers are a fairly new technology. They haven't been tested or made economical yet," Nathan said, telling a half-truth. This was the reason a normal Bastion would give. Someone who hadn't seen the barriers fail in the future.

"Econo—" Fei blinked. "What?"

"They cost too much to be worth it for now. The Empire would go bankrupt building them everywhere."

Fei nodded. Nathan didn't remember her being so... uneducated. She was cute, but he couldn't help but want to teach her all the things she had known by the time he had met her in his timeline.

"I guess that's why those bandits haven't broken in," Fei said, pointing at the mob of the people camped outside the walls. "There's so many of them."

"Really? That's your reaction to that tiny group?"

"Eh?"

Nathan hid his smirk. If he smirked too much, he'd come across as condescending and arrogant to Fei, and he wanted her to like him. Hopefully love him, eventually.

"What was the last thing you told me before we left?" he asked.

Fei paused. She held a finger to her lips for several seconds. Then she nodded.

"'I don't know how to ride,'" she said.

Nathan glared at her. "Before that."

"Um... Something about how dangerous it was because Lady von Clair's soldiers couldn't handle the bandits?"

"Exactly. Now, how many bandits are there, and how many soldiers do you think Lady von Clair has?" Nathan asked.

He waited while she counted the bandits one by one, then stared blankly at the town. Almost a minute passed. They were lucky that the bandits weren't on the lookout for reinforcements. Or maybe the bandits assumed that a single horse with two riders was too insignificant to worry about, given how far away Nathan was sitting.

Both he and Fei had enhanced vision. He used the binding stone to see farther, and Fei's beastkin senses were vastly superior to a human. Where the bandits could barely make them out, he and Fei could see the fine details of the bandits and their camp.

"Fifty-four bandits. Maybe a few more I can't see in the tents," Fei said. "I know Lady von Clair has at least that many soldiers. Don't soldiers come in companies of a hundred?"

"It's her private army, so she can have as many as she likes in a company. But normally, yes," Nathan said. "What does that tell you?"

"She should have sent her troops out to crush the bandits? I don't see any signs of battle."

"Which means a few possibilities." Nathan began ticking off fingers. "This is a trap intended to lure us or Nair in. The soldiers either aren't here or are terrified of the bandits, which I feel is unlikely if we're being called to help."

Nathan held his last finger up. "Or, most likely, the bandits have a sorcerer of their own. It only takes one to upset the balance of a battle, and it explains why Lady von Clair's soldiers are hiding inside the town."

"They're that powerful?"

"Compared to us? No. Compared to ordinary soldiers? Absolutely. A sorcerer's spells punch through steel plate, melt flesh, and harm dozens at a time. Even if her soldiers win, Lady von Clair may lose half of them, and the bandits may simply retreat. Then they attack another day, and she has no soldiers left." Nathan shrugged. "So, what is she to do?"

"Ask us for help?"

"Exactly. Even if this is a trap, there's still likely to be a sorcerer present."

"So this is a real battle then? Because there's a sorcerer?" Fei asked.

"More so than I thought," Nathan said.

He dismounted the horse. Fei watched him, remaining precisely where she was, her hands gripping the reins tightly.

With a thought, Nathan commanded the horse to lower itself to the ground. Fei screamed as the horse dropped, pressing herself against its neck. When nothing happened, she poked her head up and looked around.

"Oh." She giggled and jumped off the horse.

The bandits continued to mill about outside the town. A handful of tents sat roughly a hundred meters from the walls, and a construction site was directly opposite the gatehouse. Open wagons loaded with logs sat next to the construction site. A half-dozen laborers were nailing the logs together into a frame. At the front of the site was a large hunk of misshapen steel.

A battering ram. Normally, it wouldn't be able to break through the magical barrier. But with the help of a sorcerer, it could.

"We'll take out the ram first," Nathan explained, pointing out the construction site. "I can't spot the sorcerer from here, so we'll need to look for one once we've drawn their attention. Once you spot him, dash in and take him out. I'll cover for you."

"Against fifty bandits?" Fei squealed.

"I told you before, it's not the bandits that we need to worry about. Don't worry about them." Nathan gave her grin and ruffled her hair.

She ignored his attempts to boost her morale. "There's over fifty of them!"

This conversation wasn't going anywhere. Fei needed to experience her power firsthand.

Nathan raised his hand and pointed his fingers at the battering ram's construction site in the distance. In his mind, he found the nearby leyline. He could use the binding stone's power, but the farther away from it he was, the more expensive it became to use.

Meanwhile, there was a leyline immediately beneath him. As

Bastion, he had a direct connection to this leyline through the binding stone. Plucking a thread of magical energy from the leyline was trivial, and Nathan turned his attention back to reality after a few moments.

A pair of glowing orange squares snapped into existence around his outstretched wrist. Burning runes scrawled themselves into the surrounding air, embers of light drifting off into the rays of the afternoon sun. Nathan pulled power from the leyline and pushed it into the spell in his hand.

The air shimmered with the intensity of the magic being cast. The runes became blindingly bright. Too bright to read. Fei shielded her eyes, but still tried to watch, her mouth wide open in shock. Shouts rose up from the bandit camp.

Nathan closed an eye and tilted his head to one side. With his spare hand, he placed it over his open eye. He adjusted his hand, lined up his spell, and unleashed the power contained within it.

The battering ram vanished. Vaporized. Plumes of dirt, dust, wood, and ash rose dozens of meters into the air. Flames roared out from within the explosion. The shock wave flattened the closest tents and knocked bandits off their feet. Rocks and massive hunks of earth crashed down, taking out other tents. A bandit went down when a chunk of wood punched a hole through his chest. Dismembered limbs began to fall among the debris.

"That should get their attention," Nathan said. He lowered his hand. "Head down there and see if you can't find the sorcerer. I'll back you up."

Fei turned her head back from the screaming chaos of the bandit camp to look at Nathan. Then she looked back at the bandit camp. She closed her mouth and swallowed.

"Yes, sir," she murmured.

Was that a little too much for his first spell, Nathan wondered. He'd kept the explosion fairly restrained compared to the amount of power he had drawn upon. Most of it had gone up or down, to provide a theatrical effect. He was fighting bandits, not an enemy Champion or demons.

Fei charged down the hill. Her pace sped up after the first few steps, and she soon kicked up a cloud of dust as she sprinted toward the bandits.

A few dozen bandits gathered themselves in groups. The closest to Fei stared at the approaching dust cloud, transfixed. Her scimitar tore through them before they reacted. Their bodies hadn't hit the ground before she flipped over their heads toward the next group. Blood mixed with the dust she left in her wake, and her scimitar gleamed red.

A collapsed tent went flying, and a giant stepped out from beneath it. His armor was battle-scarred, but Nathan made out old markings of the Imperial Army on it. The breastplate fit too well on the man's gargantuan figure, so he had to be a deserter. Bandits couldn't afford tailored steel plate, especially when they're that huge.

"It's just one girl, ya buffoons," the giant yelled. Nathan relied on his enhanced hearing to overhear the shouting. "Surround her so we can get her properly."

Properly? That sounded bad to Nathan's ears. He guessed the giant to be the bandit leader, or close enough.

Sliding down the hill, Nathan checked for any active magic. A wise sorcerer didn't scan for magic in the middle of a battle, given the focus it required, but Nathan wasn't in danger for the moment. If he found the enemy sorcerer first, he could end this battle before it truly started.

Before he found anything, a series of yells brought him back to his senses. A crossbow bolt slammed into the ground next to him. Another hit him dead in the chest.

The bolt snapped on impact and fell to the ground. Pain fountained out within Nathan for a few seconds, as if somebody had punched him very hard in the chest.

Given a crossbow capable of penetrating steel plate had hit

him, he wasn't complaining about a little pain. The magical protection the binding stone gifted him made him nearly immune to non-magical attacks, but they still hurt. And enough physical harm could kill, like having a fortress fall on top of his head.

The yelling stopped. Nathan looked over and saw five bandits. Three of them had stopped mid-charge, axes raised. They wore leather armor and chain mail. Behind them were two more bandits with crossbows. All of them stared at him, eyes wide and jaws dropping.

Nathan raised an arm. A glowing triangle appeared at the end of each fingertip of his hand. The bandits tried to turn and run.

With a snap of power, Nathan blew a fist-sized hole in the torso of each of the five bandits. He didn't wait to see if they were dead. Ordinary humans couldn't survive a hole where their heart should be.

The ground rumbled. Nathan cursed, realizing he had forgotten his primary objective.

An inferno of flames rose up in a straight line from the middle of the bandit camp. Fei was nowhere to be seen. Bandits scattered from the blazing fire, unsure if they were under attack by a third enemy. Their tents burned, and soon the inferno engulfed the entire clearing.

Nathan ran toward the flames. As the original blast faded into ash and smoke, Fei came back into view. She had her arms crossed in front of her, eyes closed and tail tightly wrapped around her torso.

Opposite Fei was another woman. Her figure wasn't entirely clear through the smoke and haze, but she wielded a greatsword almost as big as she was.

"Fei! Counterattack her," Nathan shouted.

Fei's eyes snapped open. She looked down at herself. Pieces of her clothes fell off her body in ashen tatters, and her armor was blackened by something other than paint. But she appeared physically unharmed. She looked at the woman opposite her and grinned toothily.

The two swordswomen traded blows. Fei struck at every weak point she could reach. She dove behind her opponent and cut at her ankles. Despite the unwieldy size of her sword, the bandit swordswoman kept up with Fei's magically enhanced speed.

As the smoke cleared, Nathan saw why. A glowing red hexagon hovered over the crossguard of the bandit's greatsword. While looking at it, Nathan felt the power slowly filling it up. This bandit was a powerful sorceress.

The inferno from earlier hadn't been caused by a sixth rank spell, which the hexagon denoted. Maybe a fourth rank spell at most. If this girl unleashed a sixth rank spell, the power would level the entire clearing. Shattering the barrier wasn't even a consideration. Half the town would vanish in an instant, and the rest would be turned to ash in the ensuing blaze.

And Nathan knew she was casting a fire spell.

After all, he recognized the woman holding the sword. A young woman with short brown hair, who looked just shy of twenty. Her cloak covered up most of her figure, but he knew what she looked like. Petite, short, lithe, toned muscle, tanned skin, and blazing red eyes.

No, not red eyes. Not yet. He didn't know her natural eye color.

"Sen," Nathan murmured to himself, stopped in his tracks for a moment. He was fighting against one of his Champions from his old timeline, and a former lover.

Sen's eyes locked with Nathan's for a moment. Green. Her eyes were green. He memorized that fact.

Suddenly, Sen dropped her sixth rank spell and darted back. She raised her sword. A red triangle appeared at its tip. Fei raised her guard, recognizing an incoming spell.

Nathan raised his hand and cast a protective barrier in front of Fei. An instant later, Sen crashed into the glowing silver wall. An explosion burst from her sword. Nathan lost his view of Sen in the smoke.

"Pull back," Nathan shouted. He reached for the binding stone and pulled a chunk of magic from it. He didn't plan to use it, but Sen was a much more talented sorceress than he had expected to fight.

And he refused to kill her.

Fei glanced back at Nathan in confusion for a moment. His message got through a moment later and she leaped backward.

Drawing on the magical power he had just gathered, Nathan began to cast a fourth rank spell, and a square appeared around his hand. He raised his hand, palm upright, toward where Sen had been moments later. The moment the dust from the explosion cleared, he looked for Sen.

Found her, he thought. He clenched his fist.

Sen's eyes widened. She immediately stabbed her sword into the ground. Magical power poured off her, but no magical shapes appeared around her.

She was trying to brute force her way out of his spell.

The earth exploded upward around her. Like a fist of hardened earth closing over her, Nathan captured her in his prison.

Dust filled the clearing. All Nathan smelled was dirt. The bandits cursed and shouted, trying to run away. The bandit leader was close, shouting Sen's name. That confirmed that Nathan was right, as if he needed the confirmation.

"Derek, get everybody out," Sen shouted. "Please!"

Nathan blinked. She'd escaped?

An enormous hole had been blown in the enclosed fist of hardened earth. Nathan saw no signs of fire or charring. The only answer was a raw blast of wind.

But Sen could only use fire magic in his timeline.

No. Again—like with his memory of her eyes—that was wrong. Nathan shook his head. Sen wasn't restricted to fire magic yet. He cursed his faulty memory and assumptions.

"There's just the two of 'em, girl," the bandit leader, Derek, shouted back.

"Do you want to die?" Sen screamed. "He's a Bastion! And a better sorcerer than me. Run!"

Those words had the bandits running for the hills. Sen had instantly realized what Nathan was, and probably what Fei was as well. But the bandits hadn't.

Many people reckoned they could take a sorcerer down if they had the numbers. There were plenty of stories of brave knights and soldiers overcoming evil sorcerers and the like. The army even recruited less capable sorcerers, and there were plenty of people who thought they were a sorcerer because they could heal a scratch or help crops grow.

But everybody knew the legends of the Bastions. There weren't any stories of a brave group of bandits defeating a man with the power to hold off legions of demons.

Sen never turned her back on Nathan as she retreated. She kept her sword raised. Her eyes were wild. Terrified.

Nathan grimaced as he watched her withdraw. He could stop her, he knew.

He didn't know if he could stop her without hurting her. Or killing her.

"Is it alright to let them run?" Fei asked. "They seemed a lot stronger than you said they were. Or she was, at least."

"She's a spellblade, so that's to be expected," Nathan said.

The barrier over the town winked out. He heard noises from behind the gate. Presumably, the guards were checking that the bandits were gone and that it was safe to come out. Nathan walked toward the gate.

"Spellblade? What's that?" Fei asked.

"A sorcerer talented with both sorcery and weapons. Many Champions can take out a normal sorcerer by getting up close, because sorcerers don't fight in melee. Instead, they bombard you from afar. But a spellblade is dangerous at all distances, and often more dangerous up close." Nathan waved a hand at the burning ruin of the bandit camp. "Think of them like the sorcerer equivalent to a Champion. I'm a spellblade, for reference."

"Oh. I was going to ask. I knew you could use magic, but didn't realize you were a proper sorcerer," Fei said, grinning stupidly. "You were so cool. Nobody told me that Bastions used sorcery like that."

"Most can't. All Bastions need to understand sorcery, or else they won't be able to use the binding stones, but most don't have the talent to be sorcerers." Nathan shrugged. "I'm not an especially good sorcerer, but I know a lot about the theory, and I have more raw power than most sorcerers thanks to the binding stones."

"Not good at it?" Fei said. She looked at the nearby crater and the house-sized fist of hardened earth. She raised an eyebrow but changed the subject. "Um. And when do you use your sword? You said you're a spellblade, like that woman from earlier."

The gate creaked open. Close to a hundred soldiers trooped out through the doors. Each wore the same uniform as the rider who had come to Gharrick Pass.

"I'll use my sword when we fight an enemy who needs me to," Nathan said.

Fei blinked and tilted her head. He sensed she had more to ask, but the arrival of the town guards kept her inquisitiveness as bay.

A single officer stepped out in front of the assembled soldiers. He licked his lips and looked around the destroyed clearing. Sweat formed on his brow, visible beneath his helmet.

After several attempts to speak, he finally said, "On behalf of Lady von Clair, I thank you, Lord..."

"Bastion," Nathan corrected. The officer's eyes widened. "Bastion Nathan Straub. I believe Lady von Clair left a message with my Champion before I arrived." Nathan gestured to Fei, who blushed and bowed. "If she's in, I'd be happy to meet Lady von Clair now."

The officer stared at Nathan. Once again, he looked around the clearing that had been full of bandits only minutes ago.

"Of course, Bastion," the officer said after several seconds of silence. "Allow me to guide you to milady's manor."

CHAPTER 7

The von Clair manor towered over the town but was less impressive up close. Its stonework showed its age and was built with the same limestone as the keep at Gharrick Pass. The fence was wrought iron and held a pearlescent luster from its finish, and the windows were a beautiful green stained glass, with images of the Watcher Omria imprinted in the larger panes.

But the newer elements of the manor only drew more attention to how old and rundown the rest of the building was. The roof needed retiling. A previous owner had added gargoyles, and they clashed horribly with the current theme of the manor. The garden seemed unimpressive and overgrown, even to Nathan's amateur eyes.

The interior wasn't much better. The servants wore what Nathan assumed to be the latest fashion in the Empire: vests, collared shirts, and pleated pants in black and white for both men and women. Given the years between his original timeline and now, Nathan couldn't quite recall what was in fashion or outdated.

But while the servants dressed up, the furnishings were antiques. Valuable antiques, but antiques nonetheless. Over-wrought mahogany furniture cluttered up each room, and any upholstery had lost its original color. Nathan felt like he was walking through a museum.

"Our keep is so much nicer than this," Fei muttered.

"Maybe keep that to yourself," Nathan said. "We should be polite."

A male beastkin with a wolf tail bowed and ushered Nathan into a sitting room. Unlike the rest of the rooms, this room had been redecorated. The coffee table was glass, unlike the back-breaking hunks of wood he had spied in the other rooms. Most of the furniture was made from steel, with natural ebony wood included for decorative purposes. The room was painted in neutral tones, instead of the warmer colors present elsewhere.

On the far side of the coffee table sat a young woman in a flowing black and blue dress that fell just short of her knees. She stood and curtsied to Nathan and Fei, a polite smile on her face. A glimpse of flesh drew Nathan's eyes when she raised her dress above her thigh-high black stockings. She had dirty blonde hair, almost rust-colored, that fell just below her shoulders, and a figure that drew the eye to her broad hips rather than her less impressive chest.

"Good afternoon, Bastion," she said. "I am Lady Anna von Clair. It's a pleasure to meet you. I do hope we'll have a long and beneficial relationship."

A tea set sat on the table, laid out for three, so Nathan made his way to the table. Fei followed.

"I hope so, too. I assume you have a lot of bandits that need dealing with?" he asked before plopping into a seat opposite Anna.

Her smile turned brittle. She glanced at Fei, who pointedly looked away.

"It's not about the bandits," Anna said.

She sat down and poured the tea. It gave off the delightful smell of chamomile. Given where he was, Nathan suspected this would be sweeter than the blend he had usually been served in his timeline.

"What is it about then?" he asked.

"As I said, forming a beneficial relationship." She stressed the last word of the sentence. "It goes both ways. You keep the peace of the region as Bastion, and I ensure the economic health of the region as its ruler. That's what the Emperor expects of us, no?"

"You got to the point fast. Quid pro quo." Nathan sipped at his tea.

Anna stared at Nathan, her smiling slipping for a second. "You have familiarized yourself rather quickly, it seems. I had been informed that I would need to help you settle in, build your keep, and provide military support until another Bastion arrived to give you a hand. At the very least, I can still help with you rebuild your fortress at Gharrick Pass."

"Nathan's already rebuilt the keep," Fei chirped.

All eyes in the room turned to Fei, who preened under the attention. Nathan noticed the beastkin from earlier lurking at the entrance.

"How long have you been here?" Anna asked Nathan quietly.

"I arrived yesterday," Nathan said.

Anna slowly placed her teacup back on the tray. She topped it up. Her face was expressionless. As slowly as she had lowered her cup, she raised it again and drank her cup in almost a single go.

"I had been told that you may be a little odd," she said. "This isn't the odd I expected."

Nathan wracked his brain for the reason for her reaction. Was it the keep being rebuilt so quickly? That was pretty normal for a Bastion to be capable of. The power of a binding stone was enormous and constructing a castle was rather straightforward.

Although perhaps doing it in a single day was going overboard. Nathan hadn't built a keep from scratch until he'd been a Bastion for years, and he couldn't remember building it so quickly even then. Oops.

"Given the situation, I'd suggest you want odd. Or at least, out of the ordinary," he suggested.

"And what do you think the situation is? You've barely let me attempt to explain anything." Anna glared at him over her cup, slouching back in her chair. "You're a noble. There's something to be said for politeness, even if you prefer to be more straightforward. We've only just met!"

"Your facade melted fast," Nathan commented.

She smirked at him, showing some teeth. "I'm happy to smile emptily, simper, and pander to you all day long if that's what you like. But I'm absolutely certain that's not what you want."

"What do you think I want?" Nathan asked.

"Answer my question first."

Nathan paused. She had asked him what he felt the current situation was. A fair question to ask of a new Bastion, especially when he hadn't let the meeting play out the way Anna wanted it to.

"I think you're the countess of an old, failing noble family in a region plagued with issues. You lack recognition and are under-resourced," he explained, leaning forward and cupping his hands together. "The land is undeveloped. You rule from a township as if you're a mere baroness, but you have your own military, so you must be a countess at least. The nearby bandits are brave enough to openly lay siege to towns, which suggests you've lost control of the region."

Nathan took Anna's widening eyes as a sign that he was on the mark, and continued, "To make matters worse, tensions are rising in the Empire. Last year's campaign against Trafaumh failed, and there are worries that another will start any day now. Some are even worried about the Amica Federation and what they'll do, but they won't say it aloud. You should be receiving recognition and military support equal to the countess of a border region, but you're only now being sent a brand-new Bastion with no additional support."

Leaning back, Nathan spread his hands as if to ask if anything he said was wrong.

Anna frowned at him. "There's one thing I'm confused about."

"Name it."

"I heard that your father passed over you in your line of inheritance. That's why you became a Bastion."

Really? Nathan hid his surprise at the revelation and checked his implanted memories from this timeline. They had grown less fuzzy over the last day.

She was right.

He had been raised to take over his family's county in the north of the Empire. For years he had effectively run the land in his father's stead, commanded its military, and learned sorcery on the side, while his father was busy being a Bastion.

Then war broke out with Trafaumh last year and his father abruptly returned, named his younger brother the new family heir, and left again. Nathan had effectively been disinherited. Any possibility of rebellion was quashed by the fact that his father was a Bastion. A single Champion could crush any uprising without even trying.

"And?" Nathan said after he finished processing his false past. Or perhaps his real past. He wasn't sure which was which. Or whether this timeline's past even mattered.

"I can't understand why," Anna said. She sipped her tea. "Unless your brother is one of the brightest people to walk Doumahr, I cannot see him being more worthy of the county than you."

"We only just met," he said, echoing her earlier words. "You're making quite the assumption about me."

"Cute," she said, shooting him a smirk. "But you understand the situation better than most. Better than some of my own advisers, even. I don't need a Bastion to quell some bandits. I need a Bastion to keep the Federation from invading, to make the region desirable, to make the Empire remember that my county even exists." She nearly slammed her teacup onto the table, but stopped just short.

"Somebody could have told me all of that," Nathan responded.

"There's exactly one man in Aleich who understands what's happening here, and he never tells anybody anything that they don't already know," Anna said. "I requested a Bastion over a year ago. Vera's been complaining ever since I took over the county from my father that the Empire doesn't do enough. She's right, but her frustrations have made her less reliable in her agreement to protect the region. She used to clean up the bandits twice a year. Now she only deals with them when they attack, and I can't contact her using sorcery anymore."

That was news to Nathan. He finished his tea and placed his cup back on the table. Fei poured him another cup.

"Is she distracted? Or is something else going on?" Nathan asked.

"Both? Neither?" Anna huffed. "I wish I knew. Vera and I are old friends. I never planned to ask for a Bastion, but when my brother got called away to fight Trafaumh last year, I needed more support than Vera was willing to offer me."

"Your brother went up north?"

"He's still there. We're a noble family, and we ostensibly rule a county. My archduke would strip me of my lands and title if I didn't support him militarily." She shrugged. "The bandits were a problem before, but they've gotten worse over the past year."

Nathan leaned back and let her words wash over him. A grandfather clock ticked away in the corner of the room. Seconds passed, and Anna finished off the last of the two pots of tea initially laid out.

"Kuda, more tea, please," Anna asked the beastkin servant in the room.

"Yes, mistress," Kuda said with a bow. He removed the tray

containing the tea set and passed it to a servant outside of the room, before immediately returning.

"A question," Nathan said. "Let's say I deal with the bandits—"

"A brave proposition," Anna remarked.

"I know. I'm amazing, aren't I?" Nathan said blandly. "I deal with the bandits. What do you do next as countess to make it worthwhile?"

"Well, I could give you a curtsy, a cute smile, and serve you some nice cakes, but you seem to want me to do something of substance," Anna said. As if to punctuate her point, her servant placed a tray of cakes and tea on the table. "And it seems you get the cakes as an advance payment, so I'll need to offer something more attractive, won't I?"

"I'd imagine so," Nathan said, trying to hide a smile.

"I'll lower taxes," she said simply. "I've always wanted to do it, in order to attract the peasantry from neighboring counties and develop Gharrick County. But Kuda thinks that so long as the bandits are here, nobody will come. So I need the right opportunity."

"Can't say I know much about that, but if you're confident it will work." Nathan shrugged.

Anna gave him an odd look. "You ran your father's county longer than I've run this place. Don't you have an opinion on it?"

"Aren't you the one relying on Kuda's advice?" Nathan replied, nodding at the male beastkin standing by the door.

"The plan is my own. Kuda is merely an adviser, and I disagree with him."

"Then why not go through with the plan, if you're so convinced that you're right?"

"Because that's what it means to have a trusted adviser. If I ignored him, he'd be pointless." Anna sighed and bit into her cake. She spoke again after a few seconds, "I think I'm right, but I trust Kuda. And if I'm wrong, I risk bankrupting the county. Now that you're here, I don't need to wait."

"What if I don't get rid of the bandits? You lowering taxes isn't much of an incentive for me," Nathan said, keeping his face expressionless. Unfortunately, Fei looked at him in shock.

Anna smirked, and pointed at Fei. "Your poker face is good, but hers needs work. Besides, you drove away the army outside the gates without any offer of reward. I imagine you became a Bastion for a good reason. Trying to retake your lost county, hmm?"

Anna's eyes bore into Nathan's, her smirk widening.

Perhaps that had been the drive for the original Nathan of this world. Revenge. Without the power of a Bastion, it was impossible for Nathan to take back his inheritance. His father was too powerful.

But for the Nathan sitting in this room right now?

"I'm a Bastion. I use a binding stone to rewrite reality. I have an adorable Champion by my side. Why would I care about some old territory?" Nathan said, before stuffing a hunk of cake into his mouth.

Anna burst into a fit of laughter, genuine mirth spilling out into the room. "I never thought of it that way." She wiped tears from her eyes and met Nathan's gaze. "It sounds like something my father would say. You remind me of him."

"I remind you of your father?" Nathan asked incredulously.

"It's in your manner. Arrogant, overconfident, certain that you're making the right decisions. You're the type to ask me a question when you already know the answer you expect to hear, and you'll educate me on why I'm wrong if I don't give you that answer." Anna's smile turned wolfish. "Am I wrong?"

She wasn't. The description was everything Nathan worried he was becoming.

"I'm not sure I like being compared to your father," Nathan said. "We must be close to the same age."

"True." Anna gave him a critical look. "You should lay off the condescension a little until you have the gray hair to pull it off without pissing people off. You're a little too cute to pass as a wise but embittered mentor."

"Cute?" Fei repeated, her voice low and eyes narrowed. The tip of her tail circled in the air.

"Do you describe your father that way as well?" Nathan drawled.

Anna paused and tilted her head. Her cheeks turned red, and she looked over Nathan's shoulder for several moments in silence.

"That's not what I meant when I compared you to my father," she said. "I was talking about how you behaved."

"Uh-huh."

"Can we pretend this didn't happen?"

"Can you never call me cute again?"

"Deal."

Nathan raised his empty cup. Seconds passed. Eventually, Anna realized the purpose of his gesture and raised her cup in return. He clinked his cup against hers and nodded.

"To a long and beneficial relationship," Nathan said.

CHAPTER 8

"You should see Vera once you settle in," Anna said as they left.

She saw them out through the rear courtyard of the manor. Monstrously tall hedges hid them from sight as she led them down a marble path. A solid wrought iron gate blocked the exit, and Anna stopped short of it. Her servants, including Kuda, stopped just outside of hearing distance farther down the path.

"You mentioned she's been hard to contact," Nathan said.

"She responds to messengers, but I can't get through using magic at all. I'm not a very proficient magic user, so I don't know why. But neither the two-way communication mirror I share with her works, nor the wireless." Anna grimaced and looked up at the odd metallic box protruding from the top of her manor house.

Wireless communication was a burgeoning field of magic. Sorcerers had always communicated long-distance between each other, or enchanted objects to do the same. But making it available more widely had only become a reality during Nathan's childhood.

Nathan knew that only nobles and the military used the wireless at present. The boxes were expensive, used rare magical catalysts, and needed to be located close to leylines to be effective.

They also weren't portable. But they enabled transmission of audio and images to anybody else along the same unbroken leyline connection of the wireless. Sorcerers had been battling over what to name the technology, but most people called it the wireless.

In the future, it would become reliable enough to use over short distances and dominated all forms of communication. Nathan had used it to transmit the visuals of the demonic portal in his last stand, and the technology had become vital to the monitoring of demonic portals across the world. But it would be years before sorcerers would make the advancements necessary.

"That's likely because the leylines are disrupted," Nathan mused aloud, responding to Anna's worries.

"Disrupted? How can the leylines be disrupted?" Anna asked. She folded her arms and gave him a quizzical look.

"Usually because of demons."

Anna gasped, but he gestured for her to calm down.

"But I don't know. I've been here a day. The first thing any Bastion does is check on the leylines and the portal. The portal is fine, but the leylines aren't. I can probably kill two birds with one stone and deal with the bandits while checking on the leylines. Nair might know more," Nathan explained.

Most likely, Sen had convinced her group of bandits to locate themselves on top of a leyline. Her magic would be greatly enhanced, and she could recover her stamina much faster. Nathan hoped she hadn't, but Sen wasn't stupid. She would take every advantage she could get.

"Hmm," Anna let out a low noise as she eyed Nathan. "In any case, you should be off. I'll send Kuda along to Gharrick Pass with some soldiers and staff in a week or two."

Nathan blinked. "What?"

"I said—"

"I heard you. Why?"

"I'm the countess of Gharrick County. I need to help my

Bastion run his fortress, don't I? And keep an eye on my invest-ment." Anna smiled. "Who better to send than my most trusted adviser."

With those last words, Nathan and Fei left the countess and the town of Trantia.

The remains of the bandit camp smoldered outside the walls. A handful of carts sat near teams of laborers piling up wood, rocks, and messier things. The people helping were exclusively male, and the soldiers pitched in to help with grim faces. Nobody tried to break apart the fist of earth that Nathan had created.

Before he returned, Nathan took the opportunity to break down the remains of his spell and burn the bodies of the fallen bandits. Fei wanted to stay for longer to help clean up the rest, but the red rays of sunset peeked over the horizon.

The automaton horse trotted up in response to a mental command from Nathan, and the two mounted it. Waving good-bye, Nathan returned to Gharrick Pass.

Outside, he found the messenger from the morning. He was drinking from the well in the courtyard. The soldier saluted Nathan with a slap of his chest, but his expression showed his confusion.

"Bastion, you've returned?" he asked, looking past Nathan for something that wasn't there.

"We have." Nathan lowered the horse to the ground and dismounted after Fei did. "I went, I saw, I chased away the bandits. Once I find out where they're hiding, I'll finish them off."

The messenger gawked at Nathan. "That... That fast?"

"I am a Bastion. Haven't you read the legends?" Nathan walked past the messenger, then turned back. "Did you want to come in? You've been riding all day, I think."

"I... No. I need to pass on Lady Nair's message to Lady von Clair as soon as possible." The messenger looked troubled. After a pause, he saluted again and said, "Thank you for helping us, Bastion."

Clearly Nair wasn't in the mood to send help. Nathan hadn't passed anybody on the way over, and nobody accompanied the messenger.

Something was awry with the relationship between Anna and Nair. History spoke of Vera Nair as a brave defender of the Empire, who fought to the bitter end to protect her country. He'd been here for a day and learned that she might be an embittered defender at best.

Or perhaps something else was at work. Nathan recalled the activity from Champions he had sensed on the far side of Gharrick Pass. The signs had been faint, but was it possible that Nair was being threatened by the Federation? If she was preoccupied with a rival nation, or in danger, then leaving her tower was dangerous. The Federation could seize her tower while she was away.

The messenger left after refilling his canteen at the well and saluted Nathan again.

The keep hadn't changed while Nathan and Fei had been away. If it had, he would have been worried.

"I'm going to finish what I was doing this morning," Nathan told Fei. "You should get some rest."

"Rest? Why? I've spent so long sitting around." Fei pouted. Apparently, a brief tea party allowed her to forget the battle she had fought earlier.

"Just be sure not to push yourself."

Fei rolled her eyes. "Lady von Clair's right. You are like a father."

Nathan froze. "Goddess, don't call me that."

Fei stared at him with wide eyes. A broad grin stretched across her face, giving her a genuinely catlike appearance. "Oh? Why not?"

"I'm not that old," he muttered.

"Really?" Fei purred. Her eyes ran up and down Nathan's

body. For the first time in a long time, Nathan felt self-conscious. He felt that she was sizing him up like a piece of meat.

It was a nostalgic feeling. Most of his lovers had long since stopped sizing him up in his timeline.

Fei remained silent, but her eyes lingered on Nathan's crotch for longer than he felt was necessary.

"Maybe you should say that you're experienced?" Fei said after close to thirty seconds of silence. "I'm beginning to appreciate experience." She licked her lips, her cheeks turning red, and cat ears flattening against her head.

Something told Nathan that Fei wasn't thinking of a family-friendly sort of appreciation right now.

"Yes. Let's say that I'm experienced. And that I'm definitely not your father," Nathan said, looking Fei squarely in the eye.

"Yup," Fei said.

Then she spun on her heel and walked away. "I'll see you in the morning, Nathan."

He watched her, his eyes tracking lower on her body. Her bushy black tail swished back and forth with each step. But his focus was on the toned ass that tail was attached to, and he wondered how different her body felt compared to his memories.

"She's teasing me," he muttered, and headed up to his office.

He froze the moment he stepped inside it.

A matte black door stood at the back of the office. Impossibly, a shield hung in mid-air over the doorway, hovering in front of the door itself. Nathan had restored the shield yesterday, turning it from a faded, rusted mess into a decoration bearing the emblem of the Imperial Army. He figured he needed to put on a show of loyalty in case somebody visited.

Now a monochrome doorway had popped into existence behind that shield. It had appeared while Nathan had been away.

He pulled the shield off the wall. The mounting bracket hovered in mid-air. He needed to use magic to pull it out, and flakes of stone puffed out when he did so. Where was the stone coming from, he wondered.

The doorway felt solid, and Nathan couldn't feel where the old wall had been. But when he dove into his binding stone, he couldn't sense the new door, only the wall that he couldn't see.

What the hell was he seeing? Had reality broken down?

A lump formed in Nathan's throat. Given the color of the door, and the impossible nature of its existence, he had a bad feeling about it.

He gripped the knob of the door.

Nathan pulled on the door. It didn't move.

Nathan pushed the door. It didn't move.

Frustrated, he banged on the door and tried to force it. Nothing worked. He stepped back, growling.

The door swung inward. He saw only solid white light in the gap it created. He pushed the door all the way open, but only a white void appeared.

The binding stone still told Nathan that there was no door here. Only a wall that he had stuck his hand through.

Nathan closed his eyes and stepped through the strange doorway. For an instant, he felt his entire body warp. Or shift. Or something. The sensation was unlike anything he had ever experienced. The closest thing he could compare it to was the feeling that his entire body was being transformed from the ground up.

When he opened his eyes, it felt like nothing had changed. He wore the same clothes, his hands looked the same, and he thought the same thoughts.

"Finished appreciating the ship of Theseus paradox?" an all-too-familiar voice asked.

CHAPTER 9

Nathan looked up and blinked.

Kadria lounged on... something in front of him. She looked exactly as she had on the night he first met her, when she destroyed his fortress and his timeline, and gave him a second chance in life. She had bronzed skin, wore nothing but underwear, and had terrifying eyes of red and violet that bore into his soul. She raised an eyebrow at him.

More concerning was what was around her, and under her.

The entire room, if Nathan could call it that, was an outline. He couldn't see any objects, only outlines. The white void had become a black void, and everything inside this space was outlined with white lines. Nathan felt that he had stepped into a world where everything wasn't merely monochrome, but lacked depth.

Had he been blinded?

And what was a ship of Theseus?

"What the hell is this?" Nathan asked, horror creeping into his voice.

Kadria blinked, eyes narrowing. "You can see them?"

"Them?"

"The furniture. The room. The cushion I'm sitting on."

"I can see outlines. Have you blinded me? What the hell have you done?" Nathan nearly yelled. His breath quickened.

"Calm down. You're not blind. This room isn't like your world. Think of it like the world that the portals appear in. A 'place between worlds,' I think you described it as to your would-be squeeze?" Kadria explained, leaning into her cushion.

"I can see just fine in the portals." Nathan tried to calm down, however. He had to believe his vision defect was temporary.

"The portals are closer to your world than not." Kadria shrugged, and it did interesting things to the thin strips of cloth covering her admittedly small chest. "This place isn't. Not yet. I'm able to connect it to your world thanks to you, but the fact you're able to see anything other than me is a miracle." She paused and eyed Nathan cautiously. "Honestly, most of this has been a miracle. You're a more talented Bastion than I thought."

"Why thank you," he muttered. He had calmed down now and was regaining his bearings.

The room—assuming it even was a room—wasn't especially large. Perhaps the size of a minor noble's bedroom. The walls were rounded, lacking corners. The outline of a bed occupied most of the room.

Nathan blinked. The bed appeared to be massive, larger even than those Nathan had created, but the objects alongside it didn't quite line up. Nathan took a step forward, in case the problem was because of his poor depth perception was staring at the outlines of shapes.

The room seemed to shift, and nothing felt right. Nathan took a deep breath and instead focused on Kadria. The Messenger lounged on her cushion, watching him intently.

"Don't stare too closely. Like I said, this room isn't very close to your world," she said gently. He didn't know her voice could be so soft.

"What the hell does that mean?" he mumbled, rubbing his eyes in an attempt to quell the migraine he felt coming on.

"It's complicated. Suffice it to say that I'm not from around here," Kadria said, shrugging off the question. "Tell me, does your talent usually cause you so much pain?"

"I say again, what the hell does that mean?" Nathan growled, more annoyed than confused now.

With a wave of her hand, Kadria summoned an image on the floor between the two of them. Nathan saw the space between him and Kadria become farther apart, saw her face become smaller, but the room somehow didn't seem larger. Kadria was distorting space itself on a level he had trouble comprehending.

Closing his eyes, Nathan realized he was in well over his head. He reopened them and stared at Kadria, who pointed at the image between them.

Sen's face appeared there, from the battle earlier today. Every pore on her face was visible, the sheen of her lips, flecks of dirt, the slight whiteness of a scar that must have recently healed.

And terror. Raw terror was evident in her eyes and her expression.

Nathan looked away with a scowl. He couldn't stand to look at Sen's face like that any longer. The memory was too fresh.

"Let me ask again. Does being such a talented Bastion usually hurt you so much?" Kadria asked. She wasn't taunting him, he thought. "This 'Sen' girl of yours is terrified of you. Terrified of your power. Wasn't she one of your precious Champions from your world?"

"I'm a Bastion. She's a bandit. Of course she's scared," Nathan said.

"She knew you were a Bastion the moment she saw your adorable little catgirl run up and try to cut her arms off. It wasn't until you started throwing around complicated sorcery like it was child's play that she became genuinely frightened." Kadria crossed her arms.

"All I need is the chance to talk to her, and make her realize that I can help her," Nathan said, looking over the image at

Kadria. He did his best not to let his eyes drift down to the only other colorful thing in the room.

"Oh, yes. I'm sure she'll be keen to listen to the man who killed all her friends." Kadria sighed. "I am trying to help you here, if you'd stop being so defensive."

"Help me?" Nathan resisted the urge to scoff, if only because he realized he had no reason to doubt Kadria. She had been true to her word so far. "Why? Haven't you already gotten what you wanted from me?"

She raised an eyebrow and changed position on her cushion. Her lithe legs shifted about until they crossed at the ankles, which only drew Nathan's eyes further in, to the tiny strip of cloth covering Kadria's nether regions. Her panties were far too thin, he felt. His imagination didn't need to try very hard to create an image of what she looked like without her underwear.

"Neither of us have gotten what we wanted yet," Kadria said, a broad grin crossing her face. "The fact you can't bear to tear your eyes away from my crotch is proof of that."

"You're tempting me," Nathan said, raising his eyes.

"I am a Messenger." Kadria wagged a finger at him. "But that's not even my point here, as much as I adore your attention." She took a deep breath and schooled her expression. "I sent you to this world to prevent it from turning into a wasteland. We both agreed that's what we wanted. And while it's not a wasteland right now, it still has a shockingly high likelihood of becoming exactly the ruin that I collected you from. So, no, I don't have what I want. And neither do you."

Kadria's violet eyes bore into his, and he felt her red pupils were ablaze. "We're still partners. You need to claim binding stones, empower Champions, and prevent the world from falling apart. I'll help you overcome any seals, enjoy the women you want to turn into Champions, and find what's going to be the next problem. Sound like a good deal?"

Something about her end of the deal didn't sound right to Nathan's ears.

"You'll what?" he said.

"Too crass? I figured you'd like that given how badly you're lusting after your catgirl and me," Kadria said. "Champions don't just stick to their Bastions, they become sticky." She gave him a lewd smile. "So yes, my part of the deal is to help you with problems such as this 'Sen' girl."

"And to stop other Messengers? Or is that too much work," Nathan asked, trying to avoid the topic of Sen.

"You need to stop the Messengers, but I'm more than happy to point out when they're coming and give helpful tips." Kadria ran a finger along her belly idly. "I don't want them horning in on my territory."

Nathan let that slide, as much as he disliked the way it sounded.

"How exactly do you plan to help with Sen?" he asked.

"Your problem with her—with all of your former Champions from your world—is that she doesn't have a reason to trust you. Those years where they built up trust in you, and were filled with trust by you, are gone. But not to me." Kadria waved her hand and the image between the two of them changed to that of the older Sen, with red eyes and white hair. "I can make the Sen in this world remember you in the same way that your Sen did."

Nathan's eyes widened. She could bring Sen back? His Sen?

"Wait," he muttered. "You're going to implant memories from the Sen in my timeline into the Sen in this timeline?"

"Is there a problem?"

"You did that to me. And it completely changed me," Nathan said, enunciating every syllable clearly as he thought through something that had been bothering him since he arrived. The disquiet he had felt when exploring his implanted past in Anna's manor grew. "I'm Nathan Straub in name and remember that past, but I only feel and care about the memories and things that Nathan Martel does. When I look at my memories from this timeline, it's like I'm reading a book. It's fascinating, but it's not my life. Nathan Straub has been overwritten with the existence of Nathan Martel."

Kadria stared at Nathan, her eyebrows almost vanishing into her black bangs. "Oh my. And here I thought you were completely lost on the ship of Theseus. I really have underestimated you. No wonder you're terrifying those around you."

"Who even is Theseus, and why do you keep bringing him up?"

"A myth from a much, much different world." Kadria tilted her head, and the bangles in her ears chimed. "Don't think too much about it. Mostly because I'm not saying I'll restore Sen's memories."

"Then how will she remember me?" Nathan asked.

"Her emotions. Her feelings of trust toward you. Her love. She'll remember the parts of you that will make the Sen here feel the same way about you as the Sen from your world. But she'll still be the Sen from this world." Kadria smirked. "I can do that to any of your former Champions. If you'd like, I can give your catgirl a push. She's very into you, but add on the emotions of her other self and she'll be slobbering all over your cock tonight. That's what you want, right?"

Nathan glared at her.

In response, Kadria sat forward and shifted her legs slightly to make her crotch more visible. The tiny black cloth stuck so tightly to her body that she might as well have worn nothing. Her hardened nipples poked through underneath her bra. She ran her hands along her naked belly before cupping her small breasts. Her tongue slithered out of her lips for a moment. Nathan could smell her arousal, but he couldn't describe the scent as anything other than distilled lust.

"That's what you want, you mean," Nathan responded coldly. "Only one of us is talking incessantly about sex, and it's not me."

Kadria's smirk widened. "Your pants are straining to contain you and you're chastising me about being lewd?"

Nathan took a step forward. The room shifted, the projected image of Sen vanishing, and he found himself face-to-face with Kadria. Or crotch-to-face, as he towered over her while she sat on her cushion.

Hot air blew over his crotch. Kadria's breathing quickened. She glanced up at him, but her focus quickly returned to the bulge in front of her face. Her hands wandered up his legs and pulled his cock free. He finished hardening in response to the fresh air.

Something wet touched his balls. Kadria ran her tongue along his shaft and gobbled up what was leaking out of the tip. Her eyes lidded in pleasure and he felt the pressure of her swallowing with her lips pressed against him.

"I was right. You want this," Nathan said. He tried to step away but couldn't. His legs wouldn't move. They were frozen. Not merely glued to the ground, but frozen. His entire lower body was stuck in place.

Kadria giggled. "Let me feast for a minute or five. You taste amazing. So much magic has been distilled into you that I can only imagine this is going to be like sucking down a long, thick, gooey milkshake."

A what? And those words didn't sound right together to Nathan.

Realizing he couldn't escape, Nathan was damned if he'd let the demon have her way. He grabbed two of her curly horns. She gasped, freezing in place.

"Let me go," he growled.

She stared up at him but didn't answer. Her tongue flicked out and suckled on his tip, and he groaned. Her eyes curved, and she continued to ignore him and instead focused on pleasing him.

He wanted to pull her off. Ruin her fun and take control. But she knew what she was doing, and her ministrations felt amazing.

As lust overtook him, Nathan realized he could control a different way. He pulled his arms in.

Kadria's eyes rolled into the back of her head as her lips kissed the base of Nathan's groin and he filled her throat. He felt her pressing down against him, felt pleasure rising within his balls.

He pumped her back and forth along his length. A wet sound joined the bubbling and gurgling Kadria made with each movement. Looking down, Nathan saw her fingers buried in herself, splashes of liquid flying out onto her bronzed thighs or vanishing on the black void floor.

A climax rose up within Nathan, and he rammed himself as deep in her throat as possible, pulling her horns hard. Seconds passed as he emptied himself more than he thought possible. Kadria tried to moan around the thing in her mouth.

Nathan freed himself from her with a pop and leaned back with a groan. Kadria's eyes watched a little bit of white leak out afterward, and she quickly lapped it up.

"You should use the binding stone to get yourself ready for more," Kadria said. "I feel like I've filled myself up with the greatest milkshake humanity has ever produced."

"The binding stone doesn't work on living things," Nathan said, all his fire gone for a moment. He watched Kadria clean him up and wondered how much she would moan when he got hard again.

"Uh-huh. And that's why we're still in your world, surrounded by a ruined fortress, right?" Kadria said.

She pulled back and licked her lips. Feeling returned to Nathan's legs, and he tried to move forward, but an invisible force stopped him.

"Let's stop here for now. I've had my taste, and it was as unexpectedly good as everything about you has been. But I like my relationships slow, and this is already going a little faster than I'd like," Kadria said. She gulped as she stared at Nathan's throbbing length. "Plus, it's important for you to remember who is in control."

Nathan knew who was in control. He knew all too well.

And it wasn't the Messenger staring at his cock with her fingers buried in her crotch.

CHAPTER 10

The next two weeks passed in a blur. Before Nathan knew it, a convoy of soldiers arrived on his doorstep.

"You work fast, Bastion," Kuda said. Nathan recognized him as Anna's beastkin adviser, and possibly also a servant. His red wolf's tail remained surprisingly still behind his body.

If Nathan were to describe Kuda in a word, it would be "disciplined." It was common for beastkin to be servants, but they were often unruly. Their animal features weren't for show. They often displayed animalistic behaviors, and those behaviors couldn't be trained or educated out of them. It was part of their nature, the same way that fairies needed to fly, and humans breathed.

Wolf beastkin were social animals, desiring constant contact with those they accepted or desired. At the same time, they were wary of anybody outside of their social circle. Nathan sometimes spent days convincing a wolf beastkin to speak with him at all when they first started working for him.

So for Kuda to have no issues at all being Anna's liaison with Nathan surprised him. Trusted adviser or not, Kuda's faith in Anna must be absurdly high.

Or somebody had somehow trained the shyness out of Kuda.

The man's poker face was too good for Nathan to tell if the beastkin was anxious.

"Construction is something I'm good at," Nathan said. He looked past the beastkin at the half-dozen wagons. "I expected more soldiers and fewer clerks."

"As you proved at Trantia, ordinary soldiers are no match for the power of a Bastion, Champion, or sorcerer. Lady von Clair is happy to provide you one half-company of her private guards to help with patrolling the keep. The rest are to assist me in my duties," Kuda explained.

The two men watched the hundred soldiers unload their wagons. Armor, weapons, food, barrels of booze, spare uniforms. Typical stuff.

The other wagons were of more interest to Nathan.

"I understand that. But the clerks?" he asked.

Kuda smiled and said nothing.

Two of the wagons had carried people, rather than goods. Unlike soldiers, civilians aren't used to marching all day long. While Nathan had expected some administrative staff to help Kuda, there were far too many clerks here.

A couple dozen paper pushers bumbled around the wagons, doing a terrible job of unloading their supplies. One wandered over to the outer gatehouse, looking thoughtful. The rest seemed awed by the fortress they found themselves in.

Nathan had been busy these past two weeks. One item he had knocked off his to-do list was finishing the fortress. The keep stood tall, casting a shadow over everybody in the courtyard. But it now stood on top of a hill, giving it a height advantage, and a thick wall ringed the entire courtyard. Nathan hadn't wasted much effort making the wall too high. Ten meters was plenty. Champions could still hop over the wall, but it was enough to deter a normal army.

Especially as two layers of defenses sat outside the wall. One was a simple ditch. It was empty, but any attackers had to first run uphill, then traverse a three-meter-deep ditch. When the attacker got past the first ditch, he'd find himself facing another ditch.

Except this one was filled with barbed stakes.

It wasn't the strongest fortification that Nathan had built, but he felt it would cause a lot more trouble to a conventional army than they likely bargained for. The limestone in the wall was reinforced by the binding stone, so siege weapons would be less effective than normal. With another week or two, Nathan would have the power to add a magical barrier to the fortress, preventing a sorcerer or Champion from easily destroying the wall or ditches.

Given the fortress had been a pile of rubble two weeks ago, he forgave the clerks for being a little shocked.

"The clerks?" Nathan asked again.

"This is the border with the Amica Federation. It is also the fortress of the Bastion responsible for keeping the peace of the county," Kuda explained. "Lady von Clair plans to re-institute the tariffs she is lawfully allowed to collect on goods entering and leaving the Empire. Furthermore, I suspect you will need some clerks to help you. You seem to be by yourself here. When merchants and others come to take advantage of the security of your fort, you'll need a hand."

Nathan grimaced. Kuda was right.

Almost every fortress a Bastion set up attracted its own populace. Bastions were popular, which meant a certain type of people wanted to live near them. A Bastion's fort was also one of the safest places to live, as they had Champions and soldiers present in large numbers at all times.

And Gharrick Pass was a thoroughfare for trade. Nathan had noted that traders passed through almost every day, sometimes in large convoys. He had chatted with a few when they stopped to rest or request water. One had even stayed the night, trading some intelligence about the Federation's growing military near the border in exchange for a night's accommodation.

"Why haven't you collected tariffs in the past? Surely that

would have solved a lot of financial issues and allowed Anna to lower taxes to attract more peasants," Nathan asked.

"In case you haven't noticed, we have something of a bandit problem," Kuda said drily.

"They're attacking the traders?"

"Enough that if we charged a tariff or toll, they'd almost all go the long way, through Forselle Valley to the north."

"That's a long trip. Easily another week or more for your average merchant," Nathan mused.

"Compared to the cost of paying for guards, paying an eighth of your best product in tariffs, and then risking bandit attack anyway? Only the larger convoys dared to come through when we did have a tariff. For the most part, that's what we see. The bandit attacks ceased when we stopped trying to collect tariffs a couple of years ago."

Nathan stared at Kuda. "And that's not suspicious to you?"

Kuda laughed. "Goddess, no. Even Bastion Leopold felt that the Federation was funding the bandits. A lot of the wealthier families in the Federation use this route to trade with the Empire, and it's big money for them."

"And he still did nothing?" Nathan pressed. Bastion Leopold was Nathan's direct superior, and the Bastion who had appointed him, according to his implanted memories. Although Nathan knew of the man from his own timeline.

"The Empire's focus is to the north, on Trafaumh. Bastion Leopold's hands were tied, I understand. We tried taking other steps, but they never went anywhere. Politics, you see." Kuda sighed. "Eventually, we applied for and got you. Despite my concerns, you seem a cut above the average Bastion."

"You don't think much of Bastions, do you?" Nathan asked.

"Experienced ones? I think very highly of them. Bastions deserve their legends. But newer ones are like conscript soldiers. Until they've been blooded, they're useless." The beastkin gave Nathan a measured look. "Typically."

Nathan wasn't sure what to make of Kuda. He looked young, younger than Nathan, and had an oddly handsome appearance to him. At the same time, he was deceptively knowledgeable, and seemed aware that Nathan knew too much for a new Bastion.

The new arrivals to the keep added a much-needed atmosphere. Meals became more than Nathan eating in his office, with Fei in an empty dining hall, or a quick snack while patrolling and investigating the leylines and bandit activity. Nathan made the time to join at least one meal a day in the dining hall. Kuda had brought a few cooks, and at least one of them knew what he was doing.

Technically, Nathan could make food using the binding stone. But it was awful stuff. Filling, but unsatisfying. Like eating raw dough in the shape of actual food. It had the nutrition of actual food, but nobody would call it food.

It was during breakfast that Nathan found himself being asked about the fortress. Fei sat next to Nathan, her tail rubbing against him every couple of seconds as it beat back and forth. Kuda sat opposite him, cutting into an omelet.

"What you've done is impressive, but how do you plan to expand?" Kuda asked. "You could build a separate partition for the fortress, closer to the pass, but you'll lose the height advantage and have to dig up the ditches. Binding stone or not, that's a lot of wasted energy."

Nathan waved off his concerns. "I can shift the wall and ditches out as I expand the hill. No wasted energy involved."

"Shift?" Kuda froze, a piece of omelet hanging in front of his mouth.

"Displace? Move without changing? I'm saying that I don't need to dig up the ditches or rebuild the wall," Nathan said. He dug into his own omelet while waiting. It was beautifully golden and brimming with chunks of ham.

Kuda slowly lowered his knife and fork. They clinked against his plate. Then he steepled his hands and eyed Nathan closely.

"You're saying that you can make the hill larger. And move the wall and ditches along the hill. After building this place in a couple of weeks," Kuda said, his voice low.

Nathan shrugged. Internally, he realized he might have made a mistake.

Spatial displacement of physical objects wasn't something he learned from his homeland. Narime had taught him the principles, when he had recruited her while trying to save the Amica Federation from destruction at the hand of Messengers. He didn't know if other Bastions knew much about the method.

Surely if Nathan had picked the technique up from a mystic fox sorceress, then other Bastions knew the technique. Kuda likely hadn't encountered it, because most Bastions didn't explain to others about their methods of using the binding stone.

"I believe there's someone you are overdue in meeting," Kuda suddenly said. "Lady Nair."

"I'd hoped to have more information on the leylines before I wasted her time," Nathan admitted. "But I'm not having much luck tracing the source of the disruption."

"All the more reason to see her now. I feel she would be very interested in you," Kuda said. He resumed his meal.

"Guess I'll make a day trip of it," Nathan said. "Fei, get your things ready once you're done. We're heading out."

"Eh?" Fei blurted out, spraying bits of food onto the table.

Nathan looked at the mass of food on Fei's plate. White sausages, huge slices of smoked ham, whole hard-boiled eggs. Protein, protein, and more protein, stacked as tall as Nathan's fist. Fei easily had enough food on her plate to feed ten men.

Half of her plate was a scene of destruction, as it was almost every morning. Fei ate enough to require her own personal cook, and she had to show up at specific times to get her food. She was never late, naturally.

"I said, we're heading out after breakfast." Nathan took a bite of his omelet, which he felt was plenty for a normal person to eat in the morning. "So finish demolishing your buffet and get ready."

Fei pouted. "It's not a buffet. All of you just eat too little. Especially you, Kuda. How do you even function with so little food?"

"Very efficiently," Kuda said.

CHAPTER 11

"Why do sorcerers always live in tall towers?" Fei asked as she and Nathan rode up to Nair's tower. "Is there some reason behind it?"

Nathan gave her a sideways look. Fei's smile looked innocent, and her ears and tail remained still. Although that might have been because she was riding an automaton horse. A few weeks of lessons during patrols helped, but she was still uncomfortable on horseback by herself.

"What sort of reason are you thinking of?" Nathan asked.

Fei's smile twitched. That was all Nathan needed to see to know she was faking innocence.

He sighed.

"You realize Nair is a woman, don't you?" Nathan said.

"Maybe she wants what she can't have?" Fei broke out into a fit of giggles. "I mean, why else live in a gigantic penis." Her giggles strengthened.

Her joke was an old one. So old that Nathan remembered reading it when he was little. Everybody made the joke. Sorcerers lived in towers that resembled phalluses. Were they compensating for something? Lusting for something? Were the towers symbolic of the true nature of sorcerers?

No doubt somewhere there existed a group of people who believed that the phallic nature of sorcerer towers was some sort of plot or conspiracy.

"Towers are easy to defend, given their height and the ease of protecting one with magical wards and barriers," Nathan explained. "A handful of defenders can hold the entrance, and you can hurl all the spells you like from up on high. It even applies when the tower is breached."

"So they climb the—" Whatever Fei was going to say dissolved into a mess of giggling.

Nathan decided not to bother trying to explain any further. Fei's mind was lost to her lewd jokes.

Nair's tower was uninspired by sorcerer standards, if taller than Nathan expected. Perhaps because it was old. The dark granite exterior was overgrown with vines and moss, and the stone looked aged.

A low wall of limestone surrounded the tower in a perfect circle, with a gatehouse located at each of the cardinal directions. Fairly normal stuff for a sorcerer. Their type loved this sort of symmetry. The plain outside the wall was empty save for paved roads leading to the gatehouses from the nearby highway. Not a shred of vegetation could be seen within half a mile of the wall.

Two suits of armor stood guard at the gate that Nathan and Fei rode up to. He eyed them warily. The magic within them was simple to detect.

They were summons. Good ones, too.

Although Bastions were renowned for their summoning talents, nothing stopped an ordinary sorcerer from creating their own summons. Nothing except the vast amount of power necessary to create and run the things. A binding stone was an all-in-one magical generator and battery that eclipsed anything created by humans or any other race. For a sorcerer to try to match one was folly.

But that didn't mean a sorcerer couldn't create a handful of good summons. What made Nair strange was that she had summons outside of her tower. Most sorcerers that Nathan met only used a handful of summons—sometimes as few as one—and kept them close. A summon was an indefatigable defender. They didn't sleep, didn't eat, were unaffected by darkness or deception, and were far more powerful than any non-magical warrior. Assassins didn't have a chance against one.

But a summon couldn't defend you if it was a hundred meters away.

Nathan tried to open the gate. It didn't move. Looking around, he couldn't see any obvious method to contact Nair or any occupants.

With no other options, Nathan banged on the wooden gate. The loud thuds echoed across the empty clearing.

After close to thirty seconds—long enough for Nathan to want to leave and Fei to become bored—a voice spoke from the air.

"I'm assuming from your uniform that you're the new Bastion?" the voice asked. It was too distorted for Nathan to know who or what the speaker might be.

"I am. Bastion Nathan—"

"Nathan Straub," the voice interrupted. "Yes, I know. Anna sent a message letting me know that you were here, among other things. Let us talk in person."

The voice vanished. A moment later, the gate creaked open. Somebody needed to oil the hinges.

Nathan and Fei approached the tower. He was all but certain the speaker had been Nair herself, given she spoke of receiving a message from Anna. Regardless, he needed to keep his guard up.

For all he knew, the Federation had already replaced Nair with an imposter and this was a trap.

By the time Nathan and his Champion reached the base of the tower, the double doors at the front of it were open. A beautiful young woman stood outside, waiting to greet them. Vera Nair herself, Nathan assumed.

She wasn't wearing a uniform, which meant she wasn't part of the military. Instead, Nair wore a blue robe cut to reveal plenty of thigh and cleavage. Definitely not military issue. Atop her robe was a combined jacket and cloak that almost glowed white in the morning sun. Her flowing red locks contrasted against her cloak, as did the golden adornments on her jacket and her many pieces of jewelry, such as her rings.

Nathan noted the two badges on her cloak, connected to one another by brass chains. One badge identified her as a member of the Imperial Sorcerer's Lodge, which was the only recognized authority for sorcerers in the Anfang Empire. The other was a badge of knighthood from the archduke of the region.

So, Nair was an actual lady—a noble serving the Empire. Nathan had assumed others referred to her as Lady Nair out of respect for her position as a sorceress, but she was the real deal.

He didn't know what to make of this revelation. If anything, it was further proof of her allegiance to the Empire. A knighthood was hereditary in the Empire, unlike in many other nations, and granted many noble rights to the holder.

"Lady Nair," Nathan greeted, dismounting from his automaton horse. "It's a pleasure to meet you."

"I imagine the pleasure is all yours," Nair said. "And call me Vera. We're equals, are we not? You're a Bastion, I hold a knighthood and am a sorceress."

Fei didn't even try to hold in her displeasure and shot Vera a scowl. But Nathan patted the beastkin on the shoulder and gave her a look before she said anything.

While the sorceress was clearly being disrespectful, Nathan had nothing to gain by biting back. And she was technically correct.

In terms of nobility, a Bastion was one of the lowest ranks. Equal to a knight, but above an untitled and unlanded noble. All nobles who had been granted land as part of their titles—known as landed nobles—were superior to a Bastion in rank. Baronets, barons, counts—it didn't matter. Holding land made a noble superior to a Bastion.

"She's so rude," Fei muttered as Vera led the two of them into the tower.

"The purpose of a Bastion is to serve and defend," Nathan explained. "She won't be the first noble to try to remind us of that."

"But we're the ones doing the fighting," Fei protested, her voice raising slightly. Vera didn't respond, but Nathan knew she heard Fei.

"So is the army. The nobles rule the land, and we help them keep the peace." Nathan raised his voice to make sure Vera could hear him. "Bastions hold the same rank as knights for a reason. We're all protectors of the Empire."

Vera paused in her step. Would she turn around?

She didn't.

The three of them ascended through several levels of Vera's tower. The tower was a simple construction, with a single open atrium rising all the way to the top. Each level had a staircase at the opposite end and required them to walk around the circumference of the tower to get to the other side. The rooms of the tower were locked off behind windowless rooms and closed doors on each floor.

Nathan glanced down and saw that it was a long drop.

He could probably survive the fall. The natural enhancement from the binding stone made him physically sturdy. Crossbow bolts snapped on his chest, and even long falls weren't as lethal as they otherwise should be. This tower hadn't been built to be defended against a Bastion or his Champions.

"Is that what I think it is?" Nathan asked when he spotted an archway placed against a solid wall. They were close to the top of the tower.

"And what do you think it is?" Vera replied.

"A gateway to another mage tower."

"It is. Well, almost. I can turn it into a gateway." Vera grimaced. "My predecessors have used it, so it is active on this end. But the sheer expense in organizing a connection to somewhere else prevents me from using it."

Nathan nodded. A gateway was convenient, but somebody needed to constantly feed it with magical energy and catalysts to keep it active. Even as a powerful Bastion, Nathan had been sparing in his use of gateways.

To say nothing of the downsides to gateways that he knew about from his knowledge of the future.

Eventually, Vera led them into a separate room in the second-highest level in the tower. This room was still windowless. Wisps bumbled about near the ceiling, filling the room with soft light. A single table dominated the room, and a map of the nearby region was spread out in plain view. The leylines were drawn over it, as were the region's borders.

"I see you know why we're here," Nathan said. He walked up to the map.

"I know why Anna says you're here. Whether you're worth my time is something I'll decide," Vera replied.

"Let me cut to the chase then," Nathan said. "Why aren't you dealing with the bandits? Anna says you had an agreement. It sounds like it goes back quite a while, possibly to whoever held this tower before you. The two of you even seem to be friends. So I'm surprised that you're so keen to blow me off when I'm helping Anna with your job."

The temperature in the room dropped several degrees. Vera's face darkened, and she only barely avoided glaring at Nathan or baring her fangs at him. The wisps sensed the anger building, and scattered to the corners of the room, casting shadows over the map.

Nathan threw up a ball of light in the center of the room. Vera blinked at his casual use of sorcery.

"It's rather impolite to use sorcery in another's domain," Vera said.

"I'm a Bastion. I can't say I care," Nathan responded.

Vera stared at the ball of light. She looked down at the map and kept her gaze fixed there. Her fingers crept out and ran over the leylines on the other side of the pass, close to Trantia and the Empire.

"I haven't been able to talk with Anna as much as I'd like," Vera said. "The leylines have been disrupted and—"

"Bullshit. Anna is sending messengers on fast horses to you. It's not even a day's ride." Nathan sighed. "Look, I'm not stupid. I'm a Bastion. Part of what I can do is sense major movements of magic. And I know that the Federation's Champions have been slinking around nearby. Have you seen them? Do they have a base of operations here?"

Vera seemed taken aback by the change of topic. She looked up at Nathan with a blank face, her mouth opening and closing several times.

"What?" Vera eventually said. "The Federation has a fort just to the north, but it only has a Champion there. I don't know if there's even a binding stone there."

"There is, but it's inactive," Nathan interrupted. "There isn't enough activity coming down the leylines."

"You can sense that?" Vera asked, surprised. She leaned back, placing a hand over her chest. She was breathing deeply, and each breath drew Nathan's eyes to her substantial cleavage.

Vera was beautiful. Genuinely, strikingly beautiful. Nathan wondered why she was out here, living in a tower in the middle of nowhere, instead of working for a powerful noble deeper in the Empire. Pride? Politics? Some sort of secret? Was the tower and this land part of her family line?

Because Vera could easily have found success elsewhere. Sorcerers were in high demand everywhere in the world right now. Her summons outside were proof that she was a highly competent sorceress, and her looks could easily win over some doddering fool of a noble.

"I don't understand why you're focused on the Federation," Vera said. "Their Champion is likely poking around, but isn't that normal for you Bastions? You're investigating the leylines as well."

"I wouldn't dream of crossing the border of another nation without their permission," Nathan said. "I could start a war. But the Federation doesn't seem concerned about that."

Vera stared at him. "You think they're up to something?"

"I'm wondering why you don't think so." Nathan crossed his arms and placed a finger on the map, pointing at Gharrick Pass. "Kuda explained the situation regarding the tariffs. You know Kuda, don't you?"

"Anna's adviser. He's older than he looks and helped raise her when she was a teen," Vera said.

Nathan filed that piece of information away. Given Kuda's handsome appearance and angular features, Nathan had guessed that the beastkin was a few years younger than himself, but for him to be hired to raise Anna well over a decade over, and be as educated as he was, made that impossible.

"The Federation appears to be supporting the bandits. I'm told Bastion Leopold agrees."

"Bastion Leopold says a lot of things," Vera said, her face splitting into a scowl.

"You don't like him?"

"He's the Emperor's right-hand man, responsible for keeping the peace at home while the Empire focuses on Trafaumh. Leopold is a political animal. How can I trust anything he says, especially when he does nothing to help?" Vera huffed and waved a hand in the air.

A curious interpretation. She wasn't wrong, however.

Leopold Tyrim was the oldest Bastion in the Empire, and a close friend and ally of Emperor Gorthal. In Nathan's timeline,

Leopold had fought to the end and died defending Aleich. He was sung as a hero by almost every Bastion who knew him, and every Champion who had anything to do with the Empire. At the same time, those not from the Empire had more negative opinions of the man.

Nathan had never met him. Leopold was now Nathan's direct superior, which made everything far more complicated.

"I'm inclined to agree with Kuda and Bastion Leopold on this," Nathan continued. "Especially with a Champion sniffing around near your tower. Bandits attacked Trantia. The leylines are being disrupted. The Empire is distracted up north. War is coming."

"War? Are you insane? The Federation is a gathering of merchants and minor nobles. What would they have to gain from a war?" Vera sneered at Nathan.

This was the argument Nathan had worried about the most. Anna had seemed to understand that the Federation was interested in the Empire's territory, but that was because she had been fighting them for years. But to most people, the idea that a smaller nation would attack the Empire was insane. The Empire might be weakening, but it was still easily one of the greatest nations on Doumahr.

But Nathan knew that the Federation would attack, and that the Empire would collapse.

How to get this across to Vera? Nathan wasn't a politician. And he definitely wasn't the brilliant noble that his false past painted him to be. He had spent almost his entire life as a Bastion, fighting in wars and stopping demonic invasions.

"I don't know," Nathan said. "But I know what I can see."

"You've been here a few weeks, what can you possibly—"

"I know that the leylines are being deliberately disrupted and have been for months. If this continues, there's a risk of a demonic invasion outside of the portal at Gharrick Pass," Nathan snapped.

He'd had enough. Who cared if Vera Nair was supposedly a

valiant defender of the Empire? Right now, she was actively sabotaging his attempt to save her life and the world.

"You've holed yourself up in your tower for some inane reason, probably to work on your summons in some silly attempt to crush the bandits as if you're a Bastion, while the county you're supposed to protect is tearing itself apart," Nathan raged. "If the leylines aren't restored, then it doesn't matter if you think the Federation wants a war or not, because a horde of demons will bring it anyway."

Vera stared at him.

"You didn't know that, did you?" Nathan asked coldly.

"How could I?" she said, voice barely audible. "You Bastions never tell anybody your secrets."

"Well, I'm telling you now, aren't I?" Nathan sighed.

A hand ran through Nathan's hair. He looked over to see Fei standing on her tiptoes, reaching up to pat his head. Her ears sat flat against her head and her tail almost brushed the floor.

"I'm fine," he said, removing Fei's hand. "Look, Vera—"

"There is a cairn not far from Trantia," Vera interrupted. "It's huge. Much larger than the small ones you may have seen elsewhere in the county. If the bandits are hiding anywhere, it's here."

Vera pointed a shaking finger at a precise point to the northeast of Trantia. It was deep in the forest, if Nathan remembered correctly.

"What's a cairn?" Fei asked, tilting her head.

"They mark locations where the leylines are easier to reach for sorcerers," Nathan explained. "The bigger ones often have runes in them that also pull magic. It's common to build towers or camps on them, if you're a sorcerer. Given our bandits have a powerful sorcerer with them, and they're disrupting the leylines, they're likely using the cairns to assist them."

Vera nodded. "I've been preparing my summons so that I can take them out in a single fell swoop, but I didn't know... I'm sorry." Her voice nearly dwindled away completely.

"Like you said, nobody told you. I never told Anna the danger of the leyline disruption either," Nathan said. He crossed his arms. "But if I know where at least one bandit camp is located, I can slow things down. Can you mark down the other cairns? That will save me a lot of time when patrolling?"

"Can't you sense them?" the sorceress asked.

"Not while the leylines are disrupted. I know that your tower is built on top of a large cairn, but my side of the pass is unreadable."

"I see. I'll prepare a map then." Vera turned toward a desk in the corner.

"Then I'll be off."

Vera spun. "Already?"

Already halfway to the door, Nathan and Fei didn't stop. Instead, Nathan raised a hand and waved goodbye.

"I'll visit you another day to collect the map," he called back. "I have bandits to get rid of."

And a Champion to recover. Nathan was going to recruit Sen to his side, whatever it took.

CHAPTER 12

"Wait!" Vera shouted.

Nathan turned and saw her run out the front of her tower. He and Fei stood outside. Their horses sat in front of them, waiting to be mounted.

Vera carried a staff tipped with a chunk of obsidian. It looked expensive.

"Wait," she repeated, then doubled over to catch her breath.

"We're waiting," Nathan drawled.

Vera shot him a glare, then winced and tried to look less angry. After a few moments, she calmed herself enough to speak.

"I'll come with you," she said.

"I gathered," he replied, nodding at her staff. "Do you have a mount?"

Vera opened her mouth, but then saw the automaton horses. She gulped and looked away, a grimace crossing her face.

"Not one that will keep up with yours," she muttered. "My summons are more like golems. Slow, sturdy bulwarks that can punch a hole through steel plate. Not tireless steel draft horses."

"You can borrow one then," Nathan said. "I'd create another, but the expense this far from the binding stone is too great, and we're going to battle today."

He waved Fei over to him. The beastkin's bushy tail wagged back and forth once, before freezing as she understood what she was being asked to do.

"Eh? But that's my horse," Fei protested. She whined for a few seconds while creeping over to Nathan's side. He scratched behind her ears and enjoyed the sight of her face melting in pleasure.

The sight of Fei being petted bothered Vera, but she suppressed her annoyance and mounted a horse. Nathan lifted Fei up and got up behind her, her tail tickling his chin as she unconsciously begged for more attention.

"It'll be a rough ride, so hold on to the reins," Nathan warned.

Then they were off. The gates opened when they started moving, and they bolted through them without pausing. The ground became a blur as the horses galloped without rest or making noise.

Clouds, dark and brooding, had formed while they had been inside. Nathan doubted they could escape the rain much longer. He called the group to a halt before entering the pass. They found a rest stop that somebody had constructed years ago. The stonework was overgrown with ivy, and the wood decayed to a severity that he doubted it could keep out the rain.

"Let's eat now," Nathan said. "If it rains on the way through the pass, I'd rather try for the cairn."

"Eh? Shouldn't we go into the keep?" Fei tilted her head in confusion. She pulled out the pack full of food from the saddlebags.

"The bandit spellblade used fire heavily. That's likely her primary affinity," Nathan said. "We shouldn't waste the opportunity to catch her with her pants down."

A strange smile crossed Fei's face at Nathan's comment, even though she still looked confused.

Vera huffed. "You haven't explained anything about sorcery to her, have you?"

"She's a Champion who uses a sword, not a sorcerer," Nathan said with a shrug.

"All the more reason she should know. How can she defend you if she doesn't know her opponent's weaknesses or how to defend you properly?" Vera pressed. "Also, that's far too much food."

Fei gave Vera an odd look and kept pulling food from the saddlebags. Dried fruit, jerky, slices of salted meat, and cured cheese covered almost an entire table. In normal circumstances, Nathan would have agreed with Vera, but almost all this food was for Fei. As it was, Fei would probably complain about the portion Vera ate of her lunch.

"Why don't you explain it then?" Nathan suggested. "And maybe mention the reason behind your change of heart while you're at it."

Vera scowled. "It's not a change of heart. I said that I didn't know how severe the consequences of the leyline disruption was. If I'd known, I would have intervened earlier. I can't believe you've wasted the past two weeks."

"Wasted?" Fei growled.

"It's fine, Fei," Nathan said.

The beastkin grumbled and gobbled down a hunk of cheese. Vera's eyes widened as she saw Fei's absurd appetite firsthand.

"And I'll happily explain sorcery," Vera said. "Put simply, all sorcerers have affinities with the natural elements of the world. The primary elements are water, wind, earth, and fire. The secondary elements are derivatives of these, such as sand and metal from earth. There are other elements, but don't worry about those."

"Why not?" Fei asked.

Vera frowned, and Nathan saw in her eyes what would come next. A long-winded explanation that Fei wouldn't understand.

"Because extremely few sorcerers can use anything other than the natural elements," Nathan explained instead. "They're mostly discussed with regard to Bastions and Messengers."

Vera and Fei blinked.

"Messengers?" they both asked.

"Demonic generals. Don't worry about them for now," Nathan said, waving them off. He should not have said that.

Vera gave him an odd look, although Fei seemed satisfied.

Sighing, Vera picked up some dried fruit and nibbled away. Fei demolished most of the food while listening.

"Sorcerers usually have one or two primary affinities. They can also have none, but that's rare," Vera explained. "However, the natural elements have their weaknesses, and those weaknesses suppress a sorcerer's magic. If the spellblade we're going to fight only has a fire affinity, then rain will weaken her fire magic immensely. The opposite can also happen. I have a fire affinity, and my flames become stronger during a heatwave."

Nathan grimaced at the news. "Do you have another affinity?"

Vera chuckled. "I have a wind affinity. And a secondary light affinity."

The three of them finished their lunch. They'd only packed two canteens, so Nathan shared one with Fei. He could refill it with magic in any case. The clouds continued to darken and swept in from the west. Light flashed within them. A storm was coming.

"Um, are you sure we can't stop at the keep?" Fei asked as they relaxed for a minute longer.

"Did you forget something?" Nathan asked.

She appeared to have everything. Her armor and scimitar were present. Unless she wasn't wearing something underneath them. Given the way she squirmed, that was possible.

"No, no, no. I just..." Fei looked down. "I wanted to change my enhancement. That's all."

Nathan stared.

"I didn't do very well against that spellblade last time. I was faster, but she was so much stronger. And her flames went fwooosh and nearly ate me up. The enhancement protected me, but if I was stronger, then I could beat her. Maybe speed isn't everything," Fei mumbled, her voice trailing off as Nathan continued to stare at her.

Nathan felt lost. Fei had always used a speed enhancement in his timeline. Why did she want to change it?

"Can... Can I not?" Fei asked, eyes wide as she looked up at him.

Beside them, Vera remained silent but looked between the pair with a questioning gaze.

Nathan took a deep breath. "You can. You're supposed to try out different enhancements to see which works best. But you've only fought one actual battle with your speed enhancement, so maybe you should try it out for longer."

"No, I know that something else could be better," Fei protested. "Like when my sword got stuck in that demon and I couldn't get it out. I don't want to rely on the enhancement's protection. I want to be stronger. Physically stronger. What use is being able to slash somebody nine times at once if all my attacks bounce off?"

She had a point. But that was why Fei had supplemented her speed with strength-enhancing gems in his timeline.

"You'll get gem enhancements to help round you out later," Nathan said. "Speed from your enhancement, the ability to punch through armor from your first gem. Something like that."

"But we're going into battle now, right?" Fei bit her lip and looked down. Her ears flattened against her head and her tail beat against the ground.

Vera spoke up, "I'm far from an expert on Bastions and Champions, but I thought you could change the original enhancement? Maybe we could stop by the keep? Make some additional preparations before gallivanting off?"

Now it was two on one? Nathan frowned. Was he on the wrong end of this?

He blinked. Of course he was. What reason did he have to refuse Fei's request to change her enhancement? She didn't have a gem yet. Until she did, Nathan could change her enhancement at will. She should try out different enhancements until she found the one that suited her best.

Somehow, Nathan still felt off. Fei should have a speed enhancement.

"No, it's fine," he forced himself to say. "Did you want a strength enhancement? Or something between both, Fei?"

"The second one," Fei said. She brightened up, her tail beating up a storm behind her. "So we're going back to the keep?"

Shaking his head, Nathan reached out for the mental tether he had with Fei. "No need. Changing an enhancement is child's play. I can't do it mid-battle, but we don't need to use the binding stone once you've become a Champion. So, talk me through what you want."

Several minutes passed as Fei rambled about upper and lower body strength and how she wanted to be fast but strong. As was typical for more detailed enhancements, she didn't know what she wanted, but knew how she wanted it to feel. Vera rubbed the bridge of her nose as she listened, appearing to grow more frustrated with each passing minute.

"So you want to run fast and be able to dodge swiftly, but be able to hit hard and cut through armor and demons easily," Nathan summarized.

"Um, more than that—" Fei tried to correct.

"Some of what you said isn't possible with an enhancement," he said, stopping her. "But I can let you keep your speed, increased reaction time, and leg strength, while increasing your ability to land heavy blows."

Fei paused. Then she nodded slowly.

Having gotten her agreement, Nathan slipped into her mind

using the tether. She didn't even attempt to resist him. If anything, she welcomed him and he heard her sigh in pleasure beside him. After a few minutes, he had made the adjustments to the enhancement and returned to reality.

Fei twitched in front of him, drool falling from the corner of her mouth. She moaned, her eyes curved in pleasure. That same sweet scent from when he first enhanced her wafted through Nathan's nostrils. Vera held a hand over her face.

"Maybe do that in private next time?" Vera suggested.

After Fei cleaned herself up, the trio rode through the pass. Droplets fell toward the far side of the pass, and a light shower fell as they reached the checkpoint.

Nathan pulled his horse to a halt in front of the guards and clerks, who sheltered within the guard posts. A guard wandered out, saw who it was, and waved them through after saluting.

As planned, they didn't stop at the keep now that it was raining. The storm deepened as they galloped north along the road. Their horses kicked up mud and splashed water everywhere as they rode, but their magical nature allowed them to keep going without regard for the slickness of the road. As the rain fell harder and denser, the forest became hazy and vision dropped. Eventually, the road fell away, and the horses had to slow to a trot.

Magic guided the horses to their destination, which was good as Nathan had no damn clue where they were. He could find his way back to the fortress using the leylines, but getting to the cairn relied entirely on the original orders he gave to the horses.

Trees fell nearby, brought down by the winds. A crack of lightning in the distance started a fire that the rain soon doused.

The good news was that Sen wouldn't be using fire magic.

The bad news was that this was not good weather to fight in. He'd underestimated how bad the storm would get. At the same time, he didn't want to retreat. If he could capture Sen, then he could recruit another Champion.

More than that, he would have one of his old lovers and friends back. Nathan wanted that more than anything.

Shouts drifted across the storm. Nathan felt the thrum of magic, deep within the soil.

"They're nearby," he called out to the horse next to him.

Vera nodded beneath the hood of her cloak. He couldn't see her face. Fei burrowed against his chest and pulled his cloak farther around herself.

After what felt like a century lost in the storm, they spotted the bandit camp in a small valley. Huts built from logs, and tents reinforced with stones and tree trunks. Some of the tents had collapsed. A tree had been uprooted in the storm and taken part of the embankment with it, pouring rocks and soil into a section of the camp. Dozens of filthy men and women were out in the rain, pulling belongings from ruined huts and tents.

In the center of the camp was a huge pile of stones stacked five or six meters high. It glowed in the storm. Countless lines of red light snaked all the way to the apex of the cairn and met at a single point.

Two women stood in front of the cairn, shielded in a weatherproof bubble. Nathan recognized both of them.

One was Sen, bundled up in her cloak but with her hood off. Her short brown hair was a dead giveaway.

The other wore the uniform of a Champion of the Amica Federation. She had short, spiky black hair, and angular facial features completely unlike almost anybody from the Empire or most nations on Doumahr. A pair of curved short swords hung from her hips.

Most importantly, a single onyx glimmered on her collarbone.

She was Sunstorm. A monogem Champion who had fought for Nathan and become close to him in the last couple of years of his timeline.

Now he had two former Champions to capture in this bandit camp.

CHAPTER 13

A monogem Champion, a spellblade, and a camp full of bandits.

Nathan's decision to charge out and capture Sen as swiftly as possible looked more and more foolish with each passing second. The storm hadn't passed, and visibility was terrible. Even the magic in Nathan's eyes barely let him see the center of the camp. He didn't know how good Fei's or Vera's vision was in the mist.

He waved Vera back from the lip of the hill from where they had been overlooking the camp. It took several seconds before she spotted his gesture, but she followed him back.

"What's wrong?" she asked after they dismounted, leaning in close to him.

"There's a Champion down there," he said.

Vera froze, her eyes widening.

"Onyx gem, black hair," Nathan continued. "Only a monogem. I can handle her, but I'll need the two of you to handle the rest of the camp."

Vera unfroze, but looked uncertain. Huddled in his cloak and pressed against his chest, Fei looked up at Nathan.

"I'm your Champion," Fei protested. "I should be protecting you."

His hand clumped up in her wet hair when he tried to pat her head and she shook him off, sending water flying everywhere and demonstrating how sodden her tail was. She scowled at him.

"I can use the binding stone to support my sorcery," Nathan said, drawing his sword. "A monogem Champion will tear you apart. Either of you. But the spellblade will be weakened. I'll provide some summons to support you, but the plan of attack is simple: we blast apart the camp, scatter the bandits, then focus on the Champion and spellblade. I want to capture them alive."

"Alive? How?" Vera said.

"Earth prisons, shackles, dogpile them with summons. I don't care. I need to know what the Federation is up to," Nathan said, lying about his reason for capturing them. "You can't deny that they're behind the destabilization of the leylines anymore, and if there is a Champion here, then that means a Bastion is involved."

And if a Bastion was involved, that likely meant that the Federation was intentionally trying to start a demonic invasion in the Empire.

Had Nathan uncovered the truth behind the fall of the Anfang Empire, and, consequently, the rest of the world? That the Federation had been willing to unleash demons on the Empire for the sake of their own expansion plans?

He pushed the dark thoughts aside. Whether they were true or not, he didn't have time to deal with the consequences and what they meant for his long-term plans.

"Fei, I need you to support Vera," Nathan told his beastkin Champion. Her ears pricked up when he said her name. Droplets of water scattered from her fur and splattered onto his chest. She nodded at him in acknowledgement.

With directions given, the three of them split up. Fei slunk over the hill and into the valley, Vera right on her heels. The rain bucketed down harder than earlier. Nathan could only see the shadows of the bandit camp now, and their shouting was barely audible.

The bubble in the center of camp stood out like a sore thumb, however. It crackled and glowed in the distance, marking the center of the camp.

Nathan reached out toward the binding stone. It felt distant, as it should. The leyline was directly beneath him, and the cairn brought even more magic to the surface. He didn't dare approach the cairn, however. If Sen had claimed the cairn for herself, then she could sense another sorcerer trying to use it.

The binding stone didn't have as much power as Nathan would have liked, but it would suffice. If they wanted to defeat a monogem Champion, Nathan would need a constant flow of power from the binding stone. Hopefully, its meager reserve would be enough.

The storm had caused him to lose sight of Fei and Vera, so Nathan checked on Fei's relative location with magic. She was close to the bandit camp. That meant the duo would attack shortly.

Go time.

Using a big bundle of power from the binding stone, Nathan summoned a half-dozen armored soldiers at once. They were slimmer than the armored knights Vera used. Their armor comprised a bronze breastplate, gauntlets, greaves, armored skirt, and helmet. Each soldier wielded a round shield the size of their body and a long spear. No flesh resided within the armored husks.

Nathan hadn't developed these summons himself. They were a popular summon used in the western nations, such as Falmir and the Empire. Supposedly, soldiers had once worn armor like this millennia ago, back when the Watcher Omria walked among humanity. They had been known as hoplites.

The bubble in the center of the camp vanished. Nathan heard Sen screaming at the bandits, but he wondered if the bandits heard her. The storm was ferocious. The roar of the wind might have buried her orders to the bandits.

Sen had sensed the summoning. That was why Nathan had waited. Powerful magic stuck out, and Nathan had done the equivalent to slapping his dick on the table while screaming nationalist slogans.

With a mental order, Nathan sent the hoplites into the camp, with orders to kill any bandit they ran into, dogpile Sen if they found her, and avoid Sunstorm.

Then Nathan pointed toward the far side of the valley and vaporized a sizeable chunk of the hillside.

The roar of the storm was drowned out by the rumbling of falling trees and rocks. Countless tons of rock and soil poured down into the valley, and whole pine trees tumbled down with it. Although Nathan couldn't see them, he heard the panicked screams of bandits as the other side of their camp was taken out by the landslide. The ground itself seemed to groan and begin falling in on itself to fill the gap that Nathan had made. More trees toppled over and made the situation worse.

Something began flying across the bandit camp. A tornado full of logs, tents, and bandits hurtled across the camp for several seconds before vanishing as quickly as it appeared, sending everything hurtling toward the ground. Nathan didn't watch the aftermath. It was bound to be gruesome.

He ran down into the valley. The bandits weren't putting up any real fight. Between the landslides, the storm, and the bombardment of sorcery, they were terrified. Dozens of them fled their own camp, carrying whatever they had on them.

Blasts of light punched holes through the remaining buildings, and through any bandits foolish enough to be in the way. Vera calmly strode down the hill, her arms outstretched and white triangles spinning in front of her palms. She blew blast after blast of magic into the camp.

Farther down the valley, Fei scythed through the few bandits foolish enough to fight back. Her footwork was as swift as earlier, but her blade was slower. She no longer targeted limbs and instead went straight for the torso. Her scimitar gleamed crimson. Sparks showered and blood flowed as she cut through steel, flesh, and bone alike. A single slash was enough to bisect a man now, no matter what armor he wore.

Nathan couldn't see Sen or Sunstorm. Then he felt Sen. Or her power, more accurately. The light of the cairn glowed ominously, and magic built up in the area.

Cursing, Nathan realized that Sunstorm might have ran away. Or perhaps she was waiting for a better opportunity. Her gem was perfect for stealth, after all.

As such, Nathan focused his efforts on Sen. He pointed his sword where the surge of power was coming from and unleashed a triangle blast of force. The hut blocking his view transformed into sawdust, and a massive puff of shadow exploded into the air. Nathan saw Sen and Sunstorm standing next to each other for a moment, a glowing red hexagon around Sen's greatsword.

Then that mass of shadow consumed the cairn, Sen, Sunstorm, and the entire center of the camp. The darkness was too dense to see through, and even Vera's blasts of light had no effect.

Sunstorm hadn't run away. This shadow was part of her gem's ability. She controlled it.

Her name was deeply misleading. Sunstorm had always complained about her gem's ability.

Nathan scattered half of his hoplites to take care of the fleeing bandits, then called the rest toward the shadow. The bronze automatons hovered at the edge of the dark mass, shields raised and spears at the ready. A lull fell over the battlefield. The roar of the wind picked up. Rain pelted Nathan's face and chilled his body to the bone.

The shadow lingered.

Somebody had to break the stalemate. Nathan sheathed his sword and drew on magic from his binding stone. The shadow summoned by Sunstorm didn't belong to any natural element.

That was why Vera couldn't dispel it, even though light normally overpowered darkness element sorcery.

But the power building up in the golden square around Nathan's open palm didn't belong to a natural element either. The magic of the binding stone pumped through Nathan's mind and into his spell. He focused it. Aimed it. Released it.

The mass of shadow shuddered as if it were a great ball of jelly. Its edges shimmered with an odd translucency.

Nathan clenched his fist, which glowed gold.

The shadow condensed into a ball roughly the size of a man's head, all within a single instant. A great rush of air followed, along with an audible crack. The rain seemed to halt for a moment, then exploded outward across the clearing. Fractures appeared along the ground. The few remaining huts burst apart into splinters.

And in the middle of all of this stood Sen and Sunstorm, who bore the brunt of the blast. Sunstorm shook like a leaf swaying in the wind, blinking rapidly beneath her black cloak and leather armor. Her Champion enhancement protected her, and she likely felt little more than a tickle.

Whereas Sen collapsed to her knees, holding a hand to her chest for a moment. When the explosive force blew out, she slammed backward into the ground and appeared to scream. Nathan couldn't hear her, so he wasn't certain.

Sunstorm stared up at the ball of shadow hovering above her. Then she looked at Nathan, who held a glowing golden fist aloft. Her eyes narrowed.

She was a sharp one, he remembered. Nathan hurled the ball of shadow high into the air, where it burst into a mass of shadow once more. A moment later, the shadow vanished. Sunstorm must have unsummoned it.

The hoplites closed in on the downed Sen. Looking around her, Sunstorm realized she was surrounded. Her pair of single-sided short swords appeared in her hands. A moment later, she vanished, and a hoplite fell to pieces. Nathan barely caught a shimmer of a shadow dart past the collapsing bronze automaton.

True to her orders, Fei charged toward Sen. The bandit spell-blade was already rising to her feet, using her greatsword as a crutch. Her eyes were wide, and she looked around wildly. Vera should have blown her off her feet. Nathan couldn't see the sorceress amid the storm.

A shadow shimmered in his peripheral vision. Nathan spun to his left, raising his guard. Sunstorm ran at him, torso parallel to the ground and arms straight out to her sides. Dark mist roiled off her body.

Nathan sighed. He held his hands together and a pair of golden triangles appeared on the back of each palm. A moment later, a shimmering barrier appeared around him. Something slammed into it from behind, and an explosion of shadow ensued. Immediately, Nathan spun, dropped the barrier, and unleashed a blast of wind in that direction.

Her blades spinning, Sunstorm darted backward. The wind blast met her blades in a blast of shadow and vanished. A beam of light slammed into Sunstorm's side, and the Champion dropped to one knee with a curse.

Vera strode up and fired off another beam, but Sunstorm blocked this one. The Champion crouched on the ground, glancing between Nathan and Vera. Her eyes made it clear she knew was surrounded. She charged at Nathan. Two beams of light shot at her.

In a puff of shadow, Sunstorm vanished. Nathan whirled, sensing her appear behind him. She was a Champion, and like all Champions she stuck out like a sore thumb magically, shadow abilities or no.

Sunstorm glared at Nathan. She kept her distance, swords up, and glared at him.

In the distance, Fei dueled with Sen. The red hexagon spell had flickered out of existence when Sen had been knocked to the ground. Sen kept trying to hit Fei with third rank spells. The cairn flared with power, and Sen swung her greatsword each time.

Except Fei kept hitting Sen with the strength of a hundred men and sent the other woman sprawling in the mud. Their speed was equal. Sen's magic could disintegrate the Champion and her sopping wet tail in an instant if she got off a single good spell. The bandit spellblade knew from their previous encounter that the beastkin didn't have the raw strength to match her, either.

But this time things were different. Fei didn't slip around Sen's massive swings, or try to slash at her from behind five times each second. Instead, Fei went for the jugular with every swing. Blow after blow rained down against the spellblade. She held on for as long as she could. Rolled with every blow she took and avoided letting Fei cut her open. Her greatsword slowly chipped away.

Then Sen slipped in the mud. Her guard went down. Fei was there. An instant later, Sen's arm twisted and snapped. Her sword fell into the mud. Sen fell down, holding in a scream. Red light burst from the cairn as Sen prepared one final spell in a last ditch effort.

A moment later, Fei ended Sen's resistance with a knee to the jaw. Sen flopped over into the mud. Before Fei could blink, the hoplites were on the bandit spellblade, dogpiling her and grappling her. The fight was over.

Fei had won her first true battle as a Champion. She looked up to where she knew Nathan was and tried to shield her eyes against the rain.

Both Sunstorm and Nathan had seen the cairn sputter out as Fei put Sen out of the fight. Only one opponent remained for Nathan. One person to capture.

His eyes focused on Sunstorm. "Care to come quietly?" he asked.

She took a step toward him and shook her swords menacingly at him.

"I take it that's a no." He sighed.

A pair of hoplites closed in on her. She exploded in a burst of shadow and turned one into a pile of armor, before returning to her previous position.

Nathan didn't have a clue how he'd capture her. He didn't have the power to take her quietly. If he tried to force her, most likely he'd hurt her a lot. Or kill her.

Another blast of light flew toward Sunstorm, and she deflected it. Her attention turned toward Vera, who was slowly moving closer.

Nathan's hand closed on his sheathed sword and his eyes narrowed.

Sunstorm froze. Her eyes turned to him. "You haven't even been taking me seriously, have you?"

"I'm taking you seriously as a threat," Nathan responded.

Sunstorm cursed. "Your nights are limited, Bastion. Arrogance is a curse."

Shadow exploded around Sunstorm. Nathan whirled and fired off a wind blast where she knew she would appear, this time empowering it with the binding stone.

As before, Sunstorm blocked it with a sword. She screamed as the blast knocked away her sword and cut her hand open. Blood flew, mixing with the rain for a moment. Her hand was still there, but long gashes ran along it. She glanced between her fallen sword and Nathan, her eyes wide.

Then she vanished in another puff of shadow.

"Like hell she's getting away," Vera shouted.

With a gust of wind, Vera took off into the mist.

"Stop!" Nathan yelled after her. He cursed when she ignored him.

If Sunstorm stopped to fight, then Vera would get herself killed. Nathan glanced down the valley. Fei was standing guard over Sen and waved at Nathan.

"Keep watch over Sen," Nathan shouted. "I'm going after Vera."

Fei tilted her head for a moment, as if confused by something, then saluted as an acknowledgement.

The mist was too dense to see either Sunstorm or Vera, so Nathan had to follow them using their magical presence. Fortunately, both were using their magic so were easy to track. He stumbled through the forest, trying not to trip over fallen branches or slip over in the mud.

By the time he found Vera, Sunstorm was gone. Her presence had vanished almost a minute earlier.

Vera kneeled in a small clearing, her staff held before her in both hands. A half-dome of solid white light stood in front of her, projected from her staff. She was shaking, staring at the ground. Her arm and face had slashes on them, but otherwise she appeared uninjured.

"You're alright," Nathan said. It wasn't a question. Given who she had chased, these were very light wounds.

"Physically," Vera said quietly, with only a hint of fire in her voice. "My pride? Not so much."

"Your pride can recover from a loss. Your body can't recover from being decapitated," Nathan said.

Sunstorm was an assassin by trade. She enjoyed chopping off heads. Vera was very lucky.

"Speaking from experience?" Vera asked, a hint of a smirk on her face.

Nathan stared at her. Vera's smirk vanished, and she looked away.

"Let's head back," he said. "Fei's captured the spellblade. We can rest up, wait for the storm to pass, then ride back to my keep."

CHAPTER 14

"So that's what gem abilities are like," Fei said on the ride back. "I thought a monogem Champion would be stronger."

Vera gave Fei a look of disbelief. The three of them were riding back on the horse automatons, with Sen tied up on a third one accompanied by the hoplites. The storm had taken a few hours to pass, and it was late afternoon. By the time they returned, Nathan expected that dusk would have fallen.

"Stronger?" Vera rolled the word over her tongue as if trying to understand Fei's mental state. Evidently, the sorceress came up empty. "She deflected third rank spells like they were pebbles. And what was that explosion you caused, Nathan? It took out half the valley, but she barely felt it."

"Third rank?" Fei repeated.

"The triangle spells," Nathan said offhandedly. "You really haven't learned anything about sorcery before, have you?"

"I grew up in a fishing village to the south." Fei bit her lip and looked away.

"It's fine. I just need to teach you more," Nathan said. He knew about her upbringing, but somehow it hadn't occurred to him that the reason she knew so much in his timeline about sorcery was because of her experience, not because she was taught it as a Champion.

Vera looked between the pair of them, an annoyed expression on her face. When Nathan looked at her, she glared back at him as if to say "So what?"

The sun rolled over the horizon while they rode. The keep wasn't in sight yet.

"Fei, you've felt the power that your enhancement gives you, right?" Nathan asked.

"Um, among other things." She blushed.

"I mean in battle."

Fei nodded, her blush fading.

"The binding stone provides a certain level of power to Champions on top of the enhancement itself. That applies to me as well. Magic now runs through your veins. Strictly speaking, Champions and Bastions are no longer human. Or beastkin, in your case." Nathan eyed Vera, who was listening intently. Much of what Nathan was explaining wasn't common knowledge.

Everybody knew Bastions were inhumanly powerful. But Bastions kept a lid on the exact reasons why.

"Oh. Does this relate to how I was always warned that once you become a Champion you can't turn back?" Fei said. "I never really had a choice, but lots of people got cold feet when they found out. The meisters spoke to everybody in private several times before we left the academy."

Vera's eyebrows shot up. Nathan gave her a warning glance, and she raised a finger to her lips with a nod.

At least she understood that he was being kind by letting her hear this. Perhaps he could chase her away, but the conversation had otherwise been fine up to this point.

"More or less," Nathan answered. Fei shifted in front of him. She tried to look up at his face from her seat on the horse. "Gems cannot be removed. And each gem increases your bond with the binding stone, and with your Bastion."

"My bond," Fei whispered.

"That's why a monogem Champion is powerful, even if her gem abilities don't seem as dangerous as they appear. The Federation Champion not only had a base enhancement as strong as yours, but she had more power from the binding stone and her shadow ability from her gem." Nathan bopped Fei on the head to make her pay attention. "So a straight fight between you and her would have been extremely dangerous."

Fei scowled up at him. "You came out fine."

"I can draw directly on the power of the binding stone. I used a lot of it to enhance my sorcery so that I could overpower her gem." Nathan sighed. "That's going to cost me if the Federation attacks soon. I planned to use that power to slap a barrier over the keep."

Dusk arrived. The keep came into sight, and a patrol of guards wandered out to greet them. At the sight of Sen, bound and tied to an automaton horse, the guards signaled the keep using a lantern. Lights flashed from the walls in response. The gate rolled open, and more guards spilled forth, saluting Nathan as he entered.

"I saw it from afar, but you really have been busy," Vera muttered. "This place has been a ruin for as long as I remember."

"Feel free to stay the night. I can send you back with a horse if you'd prefer," Nathan offered as they dismounted in the courtyard.

He waved off the guards when they attempted to carry Sen off. Nathan wanted to deal with her personally. Despite his gesture, they milled about nearby, still wary of the bandit spellblade.

For how long had Sen tormented this county that the guards recognized her so readily and glared at her with such ferocity?

"No, I'll stay. A hot bath would be nice." Vera ran a finger through her matted locks of hair. While she was still beautiful, the storm had dulled her glossy appearance somewhat.

Fei was in a similar state, moaning at the state of her tail. She shot puppy dog eyes at Nathan in an attempt to convince him to brush it later.

Nathan gave Vera a nod while waving off Fei. "We can talk in the morning then. I need to interrogate this one." He gestured to Sen. "And then contact Bastion Leopold. Now that I have confirmation that a Federation Bastion is involved, he may be more interested in acting. If not, I'll continue as planned."

"What about the leylines?" Vera asked, biting her lip.

"It will be a few days before I can tell if this lot were the only ones behind it. Unless I find out more." He locked eyes with Sen, who glared at him. "If the leylines remain disrupted, I'll need to patrol around the other cairns and look for other sorcerers and bandits. If they begin to restore themselves, then..." Nathan trailed off.

There was a risk of something much worse happening, he thought. Now that he knew the cause behind the leyline disruption, and that a Bastion was behind it, everything had changed.

And he really meant everything. He had always thought the demonic invasion had been an accident. That the demons had slipped through while the Empire had been weakened from a two-front war, and the Federation had been too weak to quell multiple portals opening at once.

But if the Federation was weaponizing demons, it meant that Nathan needed to change his thought processes.

The war that consumed his timeline had already begun. He had arrived too late to stop it. All he could do was prevent it from taking the world with it.

Leading Sen to his office, Nathan tried to push down the thoughts. The black door stood at the far end. Somehow, Nathan had gotten used to its foreign presence. He blocked it out most days and kept his back to it when doing any paperwork, reading, or going over the map.

Sen's eyes scanned right over the door. Despite its foreboding appearance, she didn't react.

Nathan knew this was because she couldn't see it. The binding stone couldn't sense Kadria's little pocket dimension, and nobody other than him could see it. It was as though Kadria was living in his mind.

The door scratched at Nathan's thoughts when he looked at it, so he led Sen to the far corner and dumped her in a chair. He then took a seat himself and faced away from the black portal.

Sen glared at him. He removed the wooden block gagging her mouth.

"Not going to spit at me?" Nathan asked as he cleaned off the wood with a nearby cloth.

She threw a sullen look at him. "You killed Derek."

A picture of a hulking giant wearing scratched and faded Empire armor appeared in Nathan's mind. "The deserter? Was he your leader?"

"My friend. And you killed him." Sen's glare grew fiercer. "And he didn't desert. The Empire betrayed him. Left him for dead."

Nathan didn't care about some random bandits. He dropped the wooden block on the table and leaned back in his chair.

How could he go about this? The Sen glaring at him felt so different to the timid, clingy girl he had known.

"I'm Nathan. Nathan Straub," he said.

"I know. Sunstorm told me," Sen said. "Why should I care anyway? Why do you care?"

So much fire in her. So unlike the Sen he knew.

By the time Nathan met Sen in his timeline, she had become timid. She never spoke about her past, and all Nathan knew was that the Amica Federation had forcibly recruited her when they invaded the Empire. He hadn't even known she was close to Gharrick Pass at the time of the invasion.

"Because I don't want to be your enemy," Nathan said. "I'm a Bastion. You're a highly capable spellblade. I can help you."

Sen stared at him. The fire in her eyes didn't vanish, but a look of disbelief appeared.

"If you wanted to help me, you'd have left me alone," she muttered.

Looking into her green eyes, Nathan's heart fell. This Sen was too different from the one he knew. What had the Federation done to her in the few years between now and when he met her in his timeline? How had her spirit been broken so badly?

Could he ever meet his Sen again? He wondered if the quiet, clingy girl with white hair—the one who came to Nathan for comfort after a nightmare, a battle, or whenever she smelled ash in the wind—was gone forever.

"Why were you working with Sunstorm?" he asked, leaning back and rubbing the bridge of his nose.

"Not going to ask my name?" Sen said.

"It's Sen."

She stared at him in shock.

"Again, why are you working with Sunstorm? I'm going to be kind and assume you don't know what destabilizing a leyline does, but you must have had a reason to work with the Federation. The moment the Empire cottoned on to the fact you were working with another nation was the moment your time was up." Nathan clicked his fingers for effect. Sen flinched at the noise.

"Nobody tells us anything," Sen mumbled.

"So, you played along for no reason?"

"The Federation promised me a future. All of us a future. They've been good to us in the past, back when we helped them stop the tolls. Derek trusted them." Sen bit her lip. "This time felt different. I'd never dealt with a Champion before."

Nathan sighed. A typical reason for bandits. They didn't trust the Empire, but the Federation was a different story as it was ruled by merchants. Where the nobles of the Empire constantly suppressed bandits and their ilk, the Federation knew how to play their game.

Bandits could become mercenaries, guards, or even establish their own trading company in the Federation. They weren't restricted in what they could do because of what family they were born into.

"I can promise you that future, Sen," Nathan tried, feeling his offer was futile.

"I already told you—"

"I heard you." Nathan sighed.

He stood up. Sen flinched and looked down. Her eyes were wide open. Magic began to build up within her body, but she couldn't focus it because of the enchanted rope around her body. She tried again and again until she collapsed in her chair. Her glare tore into the back of Nathan's head.

The black door beckoned him.

CHAPTER 15

Kadria had said she could restore Sen's feelings toward him. Would that bring his Sen back, rather than this furious bandit girl that wanted to turn him into ash and hated everything he stood for?

Nathan grabbed Sen and dragged her to the door that led to Kadria's domain. She struggled, but he ignored her.

The door opened this time without requiring Nathan to knock. Despite his fears that it would be impossible, he pulled Sen into the void with him. The moment she passed through the door, her struggling ceased.

Her eyes widened, and she stared around her. Her pupils expanded as large as they could, almost completely blotting out the green of her irises. She slumped against Nathan's side. Moments later, she shivered.

"Where..." she mumbled. "Where are you taking me?"

Kadria's room looked identical to Nathan's last visit. Outlines of furniture and a black void occupied his vision. Kadria was nowhere to be seen, however.

"What can you see?" Nathan asked. He clicked his tongue as he realized this trip had been pointless.

"Nothing. Is this how Bastions get rid of people they don't

need? Leave them in a void while we waste away, so nobody ever finds the body?" Sen shivered and stared up at Nathan.

"No," he said.

So, she couldn't see anything in here. Probably for the same reason she couldn't see the door when she was outside.

Several seconds passed as Nathan considered what to do. The room was warm, but without Kadria there was no reason to do anything here. He turned to leave, still holding Sen's arm.

"Wow. And here I thought you were looking for somewhere private to ravage her and awaken her memories of you the old-fashioned way," Kadria's voice said, echoing around the room.

"Who is that?" Sen shouted, trying to pull away from Nathan. He held her close to him.

Turning around, Nathan concentrated on the bed. He couldn't sense her, but there was the fuzziest imprint of something there. The outline of the back of the bed looked wrong, he realized.

"Show yourself. You're on the bed," he said.

Kadria appeared where Nathan was staring, her body taking shape as if it were an oil painting. Color oozed from the ceiling onto her and ran down the length of her nearly naked body. She took shape over the course of several seconds, as scantily dressed as always, and running a finger along one of her curly goat horns.

"How sharp of you," Kadria said. "Did you like my trick?"

"An impressive illusion."

"It wasn't an illusion."

Nathan sighed. The room hurt his mind if he thought too much about how it worked, so he wasn't about to consider the magic behind what Kadria had done. He knew the basics of distorting space and manipulating force, but her magic was on another level.

No, not merely another level. Another dimension.

"You made an offer last time," Nathan said. He pushed Sen forward, and she fell onto her knees.

Sen stared up at him, her eyes widening in horror. She looked between him and Kadria.

"You... You're working with a demon?" Sen gasped out.

So she could see Kadria, but not the room?

Also, if Sen remembered this afterward, then he might be in some trouble. He hadn't thought too deeply about what might happen if somebody found out about Kadria, but the results would be bad. A Bastion working with a Messenger wasn't merely treason.

It was heresy. A violation of everything a Bastion stood for.

Nathan might know that what he was doing was right, given the future he had come from, but every other Bastion would see him as a threat to the world. He couldn't blame them. As such, he needed to keep Kadria's existence a secret.

"Oh? I thought you didn't want to lose the current Sen?" Kadria smirked.

Nathan glared at her. "Enough of your games. I'm here. You said you would bring her back."

"Allow me to clarify. I said I would help you by bringing back her emotions, her trust in you, her love, etcetera, etcetera. But I made no guarantees as to the behavior, inherent quality, or—" Kadria began to reel off some sort of bizarre script.

"I remember what you said. No memories, but everything else that makes Sen, Sen. You can cut the crap," Nathan interrupted. He wasn't in the mood for her bullshit.

Kadria blinked at him, then pouted. "You're taking the fun out of this."

"I can leave if you'd prefer."

"Fine, fine," Kadria said. "But I do demand payment for this. The gooey kind. I've been thirsty since the last time, and you haven't visited."

Did she ever stop being horny, Nathan wondered.

"That's not a problem. So long as you're not lying," Nathan said.

"Have I ever lied?" Kadria paused. "Not that you'd know."

"I'm sorry?" Nathan asked.

"Hahaha, just a joke." Kadria grinned.

The Messenger crawled off the bed and toppled onto the floor. Sen's attempt to escape proved useless, and Kadria pulled the other woman into her lap. The two sat on the edge of the bed and faced Nathan. Sen mumbled under her breath while Kadria ran a finger along Sen's tanned jawline and up to her temple.

"This will only be a moment," Kadria said.

Sen fell silent. Her eyes lost their fire and her jaw slackened. Even her muscles loosened.

Nathan felt a pit in the bottom of his stomach as he watched. Had he made a horrible mistake? What was he even doing, trusting a demonic Messenger?

A few seconds later, Kadria took her hand away. Sen moved again, life returning to her body. She blinked once. Twice. The emptiness faded from her eyes, replaced by something very familiar to Nathan.

Nathan's gaze met Sen's. He knew in a moment.

She was back. His Sen.

She still had green eyes, rather than red eyes. And her hair was still brown, rather than white.

But the look in Sen's eyes, the way she stared back at Nathan, and the emotions she expressed on her face told Nathan everything he needed to know.

"Hi, Sen," Nathan said.

"Nathan," Sen whispered. "Nathan!"

Sen hurled herself across the room at Nathan. He caught her and spun around from the force of her leap. Her giggles echoed around the room, quickly turning to sobs. She buried her face into the crook of his neck.

"It's you," Sen mumbled between sobs. "I don't know what happened, but I felt that I would never see you again. It feels like it's been so long. Like I've been in darkness for years, waiting for you. But you're here. You're real. I can feel you. Smell you. See you. Touch you."

Something slammed into Nathan's stomach, but he held on tight to Sen. His eyes stared into the black void around him. Her feelings about returning washed over him, but her words hit hard.

"You remember me?" he asked.

Sen froze. She pulled back and made a face. "I... Huh." She looked at him oddly. "I know who you are. I know that I can trust you. That you comfort me when I'm down, when I'm scared, and whenever I just want to feel you near me." A blush rose to her cheeks. She darted in for a kiss, then pulled her lips away quickly.

But she didn't remember him, or anything from their timeline. Her eyes locked onto his and she smiled. She pursed her lips and leaned in close. Nathan felt conflicted.

A hand wandered over his crotch. Sen's eyes seemed to sparkle. Nathan swallowed, leaned in, and kissed her.

She felt like Sen. Tasted like Sen. Kissed like Sen.

When he pulled away, Nathan's doubts had vanished. He felt uncertain because of her lack of memories, but she felt the same way about him that Sen always had. She cuddled against him. Her hair tickled his chin, and his stubble rubbed against her scalp. Her hand crept into his pants, and she giggled against his throat as he hardened in her grip.

"Always so big," she murmured.

Nathan saw Kadria sitting on the bed. The Messenger sat cross-legged, staring at him and Sen with an expressionless face. She stuck her tongue out a few seconds after Nathan locked eyes with her.

Suddenly, Sen flew across the room. She squealed. Her landing was soft, broken by the bed. But she panicked anyway, kicking her arms and legs out because she couldn't see the bed that she had landed on. After a few moments, an invisible force snapped into place, holding her limbs in place, and preventing her from flailing about.

"Nathan, what's going on?" she asked.

"You're fine," Kadria said. "Now just lay here for a bit while I collect my prize. You can fill yourself up later."

Sen looked at Kadria, who sat next to her. Then she looked at Nathan, before continuing to squirm. Sen appeared to be able to see and hear Kadria, but she hadn't panicked like earlier. Although she didn't like being held down by whatever magic Kadria was using.

"Come here," Kadria said. She curled a finger inward while pointing at Nathan.

Nathan's vision blurred, and he found himself standing over Kadria again. Deja vu, he felt. Hot breath blew over his exposed cock, and he stared down at the excited Messenger. Her tongue lolled out of her mouth as she stared excitedly at his length.

"Mmm, before I forget," Kadria muttered.

She held a finger out, which glowed white. Power thrummed in it. Nathan could feel a tiny thread of energy pour into Kadria through him and stared in confusion.

Had Kadria drawn on energy from his binding stone? Through him? How had she done that?

"Pay attention," Kadria said, slowly lowering her glowing finger. "You said last time this was impossible. You're a smart cookie, so maybe you'll pick up a thing or two from a demonstration. Even if you don't, I know the way I like my men." She grinned. "Insatiable."

Nathan didn't know what she meant by that.

Her finger made contact with his tip and the power poured into him. He gasped as he felt his entire crotch throb in response. Something built up within his length and tried to push its way out. After a moment, Nathan felt like that something had succeeded.

Gasping for air, Nathan looked down. Nothing seemed different at a glance.

"Hopefully that worked," Kadria said, holding her hands either side of his length.

"What did you do?" he asked. His voice was raspy. His cock throbbed like it had never throbbed before.

Before Kadria could answer, Sen let out a squeal. She glared at the two of them.

"Oh, hush," Kadria said. She waved her hand and suddenly Sen appeared underneath Kadria. "Make yourself useful."

Without hesitating, Kadria reached down and pulled her panties open. She then lowered herself onto Sen's face. A strange expression crossed Kadria's face after a few moments, before she sighed in pleasure.

"I'm glad I brought over this part of her," Kadria mumbled. "She really knows what she's doing. Even if bringing over the lovey-dovey part is playing with fire."

Kadria's face was brilliantly red, and her breath hot enough to boil water as it blew over Nathan's shaft. Somehow, he had an idea of what she meant by "playing with fire." By playing with Sen's memories and emotions, Kadria had affected herself.

Or perhaps she was hornier than he thought. No matter.

Nathan gripped her horns. Kadria gasped and obediently opened her mouth wide. Her eyes widened and locked with his, her red pupils noticeably dilated. She was spread flat over Sen, giving him a straight line down her throat. Wet noises filled the room as Sen licked Kadria. Kadria's hands wandered beneath Sen's skirt and pulled her white cloth panties down.

Clear liquid bubbled up and dribbled down Nathan's length. Kadria lapped up every drop even as her fingers explored and exposed Sen. The Messenger began to moan and beg.

"Please," Kadria mumbled. "You promised."

Nathan placed a hand on his shaft, lowered it, and slid it down Kadria's waiting throat. Her eyes curved as her lips pressed against his groin. Using her horns, he used her the way she expected to be used. Her body shuddered as she climaxed from the attention. Sen hadn't let up.

Heat surged within Nathan and he finished. Kadria moaned around the mess in her throat, eyes closed.

Nathan noticed a funny feeling in his crotch. He looked down and noticed he wasn't softening. At all. Kadria began to move, entirely focused on his length.

"What did you do?" he asked again.

Kadria giggled around him. He pulled her off.

"You complained you couldn't get yourself ready fast enough," she said. "I made sure that wouldn't be a problem ever again."

Oh no.

To punish her for messing with his body, he went for as long as he felt possible. Sen tried to tag in, but Nathan focused on punishing one particular Messenger.

Eventually, he gave up. Kadria was insatiable. Nathan felt the same way. He didn't feel exhaustion even after an hour of doing this. Physically, at least. His mind was spent but his body felt fresh.

"Hey, stop that," Kadria protested.

Sen lapped at Kadria's cheeks and lips, sucking up stray bits of white that Kadria had missed. The Messenger pushed Sen away, before using her magic to keep herself protected.

"Mine," Kadria said, collecting everything from her bronzed skin with her fingers.

"Uh-huh." Sen rolled her eyes. "Next time save a turn for me, Nathan. Maybe tonight?"

Nathan met Sen's eyes and nodded. For a moment he felt wrong for agreeing, but the look in her eyes made it clear that Sen wanted this. He'd been with her for years in his timeline and he had her back.

This timeline nonsense drove him crazy. But at least he could get his women back.

He snuck Sen out and back to his room without anybody noticing. If this was to become a habit, he needed to add a bathroom to his office. Or maybe rearrange the keep so that his office and bedroom were closer together.

Once cleaned up and sufficiently filled, Sen stretched and gave Nathan a hug. "I missed you."

Nathan's breath caught in his throat. "I missed you, too." He paused. "Um, about Kadria?"

"Who?" Sen stared at him in confusion.

"The woman from earlier."

She continued to stare.

"Bronzed skin..." No recognition at all.

Had Kadria used some sort of magic to prevent Sen from remembering her? Or was something more insidious at work.

A knock at the door drew Nathan from his thoughts. Sen opened the door before Nathan could stop her.

Fei stared at Sen, then at Nathan. The beastkin wore her nightgown and underwear and was holding her comb and brush. Her tail and ears stood on end, and she bore her fangs.

"Fei, wait, wait!" Nathan shouted. Fei froze, fangs still bared, as Sen stared at Fei in confusion.

Did Sen remember Fei? She seemed to hold her head as if she was trying to, but the look of confusion on her face suggested something was wrong.

"Shouldn't she be bound up?" Fei hissed.

"We've come to an agreement," Nathan said. "She's going to fight for us as a Champion."

Fei blinked. Several moments passed, and an undecipherable expression crossed her face. Eventually, her tail and ears returned to normal, and she held out a hand.

"Jafeila," she said. "Call me Fei."

Sen licked her lips and hesitantly took the hand. Then winced as Fei nearly shattered every bone in it. "Um. Sen. I feel like we've met before."

Another strange expression crossed Fei's face, and she stared at Nathan for several seconds. Then Fei turned back to Sen with a big smile.

"Silly, we have."

Wait, what?

"We just fought," Fei chirped. "I knocked you out. You fought really well."

Sen blinked. Her head tilted to one side. Giggles crept out of her mouth, and soon both she and Fei were uncontrollably laughing.

Nathan scratched his stubble. He felt lost. All's well that ends well, he supposed.

"Nathan, brush my tail," Fei said, bounding up to him.

Sen appeared next to Fei. "Oh, I can do that for you, Fei. Why don't we let Nathan rest?"

Fei smiled back. "Oh, I'm sure he'll get plenty of rest while he brushes out my tail. It's not like he needs to move while I lay on his lap."

The two women smiled at each other for several seconds before turning to Nathan.

Ah, now this was a nostalgic feeling for him.

CHAPTER 16

On the other side of the Gharrick Mountains, a mild rain shower passed over a fortress in the Amica Federation. It was known as Fort Taubrum. Pools of water built up on the arid land outside the walls. A moat around the wall captured some of the runoff, and drainage ditches pulled much of it farther away from the fort.

Soldiers in tan and gray uniforms took shelter. A patrol outside the fort paused, and its lead officer held a hand out to the rain. He shrugged and ordered his men to continue as normal.

Within the walls of the keep, protected from the weather in a palatial office, a woman worked through a small stack of paperwork. A young boy stood at attention at the door. He watched every movement she made, but kept himself perfectly still.

The reason was obvious to even a casual observer.

A pair of jade gemstones glittered from the woman's collarbone. She wore a figure-hugging black dress with a pattern woven it into that evoked the Watcher Omria, and slits were cut into the thighs. In her homeland, this style of dress was relatively commonplace.

The woman was known as Seraph. Nobody knew her true name. Perhaps not even her Bastion knew. That was commonplace for the people from the Kurai Peninsula. They took on a false name when they came of age and only gave their true name to those they trusted.

Seraph finished some of her paperwork and added it to a nearby pile of finished papers. After brushing back her long black hair, she took a sip of wine. The only noises in the office were those she made and the gentle beating of rain on the glass windows behind her.

Her wine glass was empty, so Seraph poured another. She clicked her tongue as only a fingertip of red nectar poured into her glass. It vanished as quickly as it had appeared.

One of her gems flashed and the wine bottle disintegrated into a pile of glittering dust. Seraph didn't utter a word. Instead, she retrieved the next item of paperwork. The office filled with the scrawling of her pen.

The boy stepped forward and placed another bottle of wine on the table. It was the same year and vintage, and he had uncorked it in advance. Seraph gave him a dismissive glance, and he scurried away to retrieve a dustpan and brush to sweep up the remains of the earlier wine bottle.

A shadow appeared in the corner of the room within seconds of the door slamming. It grew into the shape of a young woman, and Sunstorm emerged from the darkness.

Seraph paused. She placed her pen down and turned to Sunstorm, wine glass in hand.

"I didn't expect to see you for another week," Seraph said. She crossed her legs and gave Sunstorm her full attention. "I'm assuming this isn't good news. You're not prancing about the office, for one thing."

"I don't prance."

Sunstorm strode into the center of the room. A set of plush chairs and sofas surrounded a stained glass coffee table, on top of which sat a set of statues of the Watcher Omria. Ignoring the table,

Sunstorm dragged a chair over to the same side of the desk that Seraph sat on.

"You do realize there are chairs there," Seraph said, inclining her head at the pair of simple chairs on the far side of the massive oak desk.

Sunstorm ignored her. She plopped herself down on the plush couch she had dragged over and glared at Seraph. Seraph sipped at her wine and waited.

"We've lost our best bandits," Sunstorm said after several long seconds.

"The ones under the young spellblade?" Seraph asked.

"Sen, yes." Sunstorm scowled. "They were too busy licking their wounds after the new Bastion scared them at Trantia. And they paid the price."

"You wouldn't be so frustrated if that was it," Seraph said.

Sunstorm's eyes lingered on the wine. With a sigh, Seraph snapped her fingers at a cabinet in the corner. Its doors opened, and a wine glass flew across the room. Sunstorm deftly caught it, then held out her glass for a drink.

"Did we lose our other contact?" Seraph pressed. If they had, she would have a tough conversation coming.

"No. I confirmed that there are no issues on that front, despite your concerns." Sunstorm guzzled down half of her wine in one go, much to Seraph's dismay. "The Bastion showed up while I was convincing Sen to continue with our deal. The storm came in, and a moment later, he was there." Her scowl deepened. "His Champion didn't even have a gem. How reckless could he be?"

"Not reckless enough to lose his head," Seraph noted. "Or else you would have strode in here with the heads of both him and his Champion. You lost, I take it?"

"I didn't lose," Sunstorm shouted, rising to her feet. She paused, taking in Seraph's calm gaze. "I retreated, noting the storm and the loss of our resources. He'd blown apart most of the

camp already, the bandits had fled, and his Champion had inca-
pacitated Sen. Further battle was unwise."

"If I thought you capable of learning to be less reckless, I'd
believe you." Seraph gave her subordinate a mocking smile and
drained her glass. She rose and walked over to the glass windows.
"He scared you, didn't he?"

Silence. The rain pattered against the windows. Seraph stared
down into the courtyard, watching as ripples formed in the
puddles below. The land was so arid this close to the mountains,
at least on this side. Useless land for the Federation, she knew.

"His sorcery affected my shadows," Sunstorm eventually
admitted. "I don't know how. Normal sorcery had no effect. But
he blew away my shroud with a single spell and leveled half of
the valley at the same time."

Seraph froze. A single spell? That sounded impossible to her.

"Did you see him cast it?" she asked.

"No. I was trying to get an angle on that stupid beastkin
Champion of his and—" Sunstorm tried to say.

"Did he cast anything like it later? Did you see that? What sort
of spells did he use?" Seraph asked rapid-fire.

Sunstorm blinked. She swirled her glass, the wine forming a
pattern around the outside. "He only used third rank spells. The
earlier spell had to be fifth or sixth rank, though. How else could
he have affected my shadows? Gem abilities are far above the
natural elements."

Seraph sighed. So the girl hadn't paid attention to anything
important in the battle.

This new Bastion was a sorcerer. She knew this, but not where
his talents lay.

"If he affected your shadows, most likely he used the binding
stone to enhance his sorcery," Seraph explained. She couldn't
imagine anything else. How he had done it was beyond her,
however.

Seraph knew of two likely methods the Bastion used to overwhelm Sunstorm's shadows. One of them seemed improbably, given how magic resistant the shadows were. Although binding stones had immense power behind them, they didn't turn their owners into gods. That meant he had likely used the other method, which she had been taught was impossible for humans to use.

After all, human sorcerers were supposed to be restricted to the natural elements.

"Does it matter?" Sunstorm muttered. "He wasn't that strong. Like I said, he didn't have a gemmed Champion. I'll track him down and claim his head."

"Then why don't you have his head already?" Seraph retorted.

"Like I said—"

"Enough," Seraph said. Sunstorm shut up.

After returning to her seat, Seraph poured two more glasses of wine. The boy still hadn't returned with a dustpan and brush. She hoped that Sunstorm hadn't killed him.

"You're being too defensive," Seraph said. "There's no shame in losing to a superior opponent." Sunstorm opened her mouth to protest, but Seraph cut her off with a glare. "And he is superior. You've killed Bastions before. You have nothing to prove to me or Master Theus. If he was the weakling you claim he is, then you'd be requesting to meet with our master and show off your prizes. Not complaining about your missed opportunities."

Sunstorm remained silent.

Continuing, Seraph said, "We've lost the bandits, but we planned around that. Master Theus won't be concerned. You say that our contact is still working with us, which means our plans can proceed. At worst, this accelerates our timetable. At best, the Bastion blunders at his next test."

"Test?" Sunstorm asked.

"Don't worry," Seraph said. "All I need you to do is return to his keep and survey it for me."

"Done," Sunstorm said. She didn't move. "I investigated it on the return trip. It's not that big."

Seraph stared at her. "Not that big sounds bigger than I expected. Explain."

Minutes passed as the younger Champion briefed Seraph on the exterior of the keep. Seraph kept her surprise in check.

"And the interior?" No answer. "You did go inside, didn't you? You weren't so scared of him that you refused to infiltrate his keep?"

When Sunstorm didn't rise to the taunt, Seraph knew something was wrong.

"What aren't you telling me?" Seraph pressed, her brow furrowing.

"He… He sensed me," Sunstorm said, her eyes boring into the tiled floor. "When I teleported, he knew where I'd appear. It's how I lost a sword. He even knew when I used a shadow double. How could he do that so easily?"

"Talented sorcerers can detect Champions," Seraph said. "If you're using your abilities, then it's even easier for him to find you without even trying."

"But it takes time to scan for magic," Sunstorm protested.

"Hence why I say talented," Seraph said. "I did say he is a superior opponent. You've done well today, Sunstorm. Remember that you haven't done anything to upset me or Master Theus. Rest up, recharge your gem, and prepare for your next mission. I'll brief you in the morning."

Sunstorm left. The servant boy slipped through the door a minute later and swept up the remains of both empty wine bottles. When he brought another to the table, Seraph waved him off and retreated to her bedroom.

What a mess she was in, she thought. She threw herself onto the pile of cushions on top of her bed. The mattress swallowed her groan.

The Empire had stopped the leyline disruption far earlier than expected. The new Bastion was orders of magnitude more capable than Theus had claimed. Seraph cursed Theus's arrogance.

Years of experience had taught Seraph that taking a Bastion lightly was the highway to the grave. For every incompetent Bastion that Sunstorm could behead without even blinking, another could blow her away just as quickly. The raw power of a binding stone was not to be trifled with.

But Theus didn't care. All he had told Seraph was that the new Bastion was too weak to be of any concern, and that the Empire had sent him to Gharrick Pass to get him out of the way.

Seraph didn't understand why the Empire would ever promote somebody to Bastion only to put them in a corner and forget about them. But Theus had dismissed her concerns, then pissed off up north with his other Champions. They smirked and giggled behind her back, questioning why she worried about a Bastion that everybody knew was incompetent.

And now that Bastion had built a fortress from nothing in three weeks, defeated Sunstorm and her pet spellblade, and appeared capable of sorcery that Seraph had been told was fundamentally impossible for humans.

She could salvage this. Theus was too arrogant to believe she knew how the leylines worked, but she had been a Champion longer than he had been sticking it in those giggling idiots that worshipped him.

If the leylines stopped being disrupted, then all of that magical energy had to go somewhere. Bastion Nathan Straub would need to prove himself to be a capable commander even swifter than he had built his fortress.

In the meantime, Seraph had the time to prepare her next move. First, though, she needed to tell Theus. Beautiful, stupid Theus.

She opened the connection over the wireless after she confirmed it was magically secured. Almost five minutes passed before he answered.

"Why are you wasting my time this late, Seraph?" Theus grumbled over the wireless, his voice crackling.

"I need your authority to accelerate my plans down south," Seraph said, closing her eyes and imagining something less irritating than his voice. "The Empire is making its move."

CHAPTER 17

Nathan watched the carriages roll up along the road toward his fortress. There were three of them, all decorated in von Clair regalia. A company of Anna's soldiers accompanied the convoy.

This wasn't a social visit. Anna wouldn't have brought so many horseless carriages if she only wanted to see Nathan. In fact, she probably would have requested that he visit her.

Several weeks had passed since they defeated the bandits and recruited Sen. Summer had arrived. Wildlife overran the nearby forests, and pollen filled the air. Nathan's nose was constantly irritated whenever he was outside.

And the leylines had stabilized.

Nathan descended from the wall. It now extended farther than it had a few weeks ago and separated the fortress into two halves.

A massive wall protected the upper section of the fortress and ringed the keep. The soldiers and clerks stayed here and practiced in the main courtyard. An inner wall separated the upper section from the lower section, and it contained a single gatehouse for now.

As Kuda had predicted, merchants and peasants flocked to Gharrick Pass once news spread. A Bastion was in the county, and his fortress promised protection. Caravans began to stop here, and that meant there was money to be made. Trade grew as people serviced the caravans, then shops opened up for the people living in the fortress, and soon families moved in because other people were here.

More people arrived each day. Nathan had constructed the lower section to protect them, given they had begun to build their own town outside the walls. How many years had it been since he had commanded a fortress that needed to worry about and protect the general populace?

Too many. The Far Reaches were practically uninhabitable, even if it had been an important chokepoint. His last fortress had been an isolated one.

Nathan sped up the arrival of people through his bandit purges. Sen's group had been the main one. She had told him as such, and the leylines had begun to stabilize within days. But smaller groups continued to operate with much weaker magic users.

Running around burning out bandit camps had spread the word of a new Bastion faster than normal. Within a month, they'd be spilling outside of the walls again if he didn't do something.

"Do you ever stop worrying about things?" Sen asked him, dragging him from his thoughts.

He looked over and saw her hovering by his side. When had she gotten here?

He waved for her to follow him, then headed to the main courtyard in front of the keep.

"I'm a Bastion. If I don't worry about what happens next, who will?" Nathan replied.

"Somehow that feels too natural coming from you," Sen said. "I'm still not used to this."

"Remembering one past, but feeling completely differently?"

"Yes. That." Sen nodded, her eyes distant. "I get strange feelings of nostalgia sometimes, but I don't know what I'm nostalgic about. Other times I feel like there's a hole in my heart, as if I should remember or associate something with what I'm seeing or remembering, but that thing is missing." Sen suddenly smiled. "You're something of a constant, at least."

Good to know, he thought. Kadria had carried out her end of the deal once again.

The carriages rolled through the gate. Anna's soldiers formed up in ranks along either side of the courtyard to greet her. The officers wore their dress uniforms, their breastplates gleaming for the first time since they had arrived at the fortress. The captain of the guard patrolled the line, chewing out some of his subordinates and reshuffling the formation. He wanted the best-dressed guards at the front for his countess to see first.

Nathan meditated while he waited. He checked on the leylines, did rhythmic exercises to focus his sorcery, and monitored every presence in the fortress. Beside him, Sen leaned on her sheathed greatsword and tried not to make eye contact with any of the guards.

Her profuse apologies had mended things enough that the guards didn't glare at her when she passed. At the same time, the fact she had to apologize so much meant there were things that couldn't be so easily forgiven. She was under his protection now, and supporting him. That kept the guards happy.

Even if they weren't happy, they had to live with it. Nathan could run his fortress without them.

"Sorry I'm late," Fei gasped out, running up to his side. Her tail wagged behind her, batting against Nathan's legs once she took up her position to his right.

Sen smirked. "Are you ever not late?" She paused. "Huh. I get the feeling you're supposed to be punctual."

Fei gave Sen an odd look, but shrugged the statement off. Her eyes scanned the courtyard. A sigh of relief escaped her lips when she saw the convoy only beginning to enter the inner section of the fortress.

"Where's Kuda?" Fei asked. "I saw him at breakfast, so I know he's around."

"You have time to pay attention to other people while shoveling down all that food?" Sen asked.

Fei glared at Sen.

"Be nice," Nathan murmured.

The two women glared at him instead.

With a sigh, Nathan said, "Kuda is preparing the meeting room."

"Eh? Is this important?" Fei asked. "It's only Anna's carriage."

Sen laughed, then tried to cover her mouth and pretend she was coughing. Fei still glared at her. Nathan pushed both their heads down, causing both to wince and stop playing around.

"Anna wouldn't bring three carriages if this was a social visit," Nathan explained.

"I also doubt the soldiers would line up like this," Sen remarked.

"No, that's pretty normal," Nathan said. "How often do you think the officers get a chance to show off how well-trained their companies are? Even a minor visit by the ruling noble is a big deal. You weren't on the wall, so you likely missed the crowds in the streets in the lower section."

Sen grimaced. "No, I saw them. I thought there was a market on today."

"That's at midday."

Sen and Fei continued to chatter while they waited for the carriages to pull up. The soldiers accompanying Anna pulled away from the convoy. They took up positions at the far end of the courtyard.

With so many in one place, Nathan noticed that the guards in the fortress had adjusted their uniforms slightly. While the guards that had arrived with Anna only wore her family symbol, as befitting a private army, those in the fortress were different. They had added a small silver patch from the Imperial Army.

Nathan's historical knowledge of the Empire wasn't complete enough to help him recognize what it was. But he at least knew that the guards in the fortress now identified themselves as soldiers of the Empire, rather than mere hired swords under a noble. For many of them, it was a large step up in status.

The carriages came to a stop. Anna stepped out from the closest one, her dirty blonde hair almost brown in the summer sun. She wore an elegant ruffled black dress covered with silver ribbons and bore a red sash. Her heels were larger than her bust, and Nathan doubted she had any plans to run about much today. She was dressed to impress.

Vera joined her a moment later in the same sorceress robes from the other day. Her white robe gleamed. Clearly, she had cleaned them after the storm.

The lead carriage disgorged a handful of clerks, all dressed up in their puffery and carrying books and pens. They clustered a short distance away from Anna and Vera, talking furtively to one another.

The officers called their soldiers to attention. A clatter of boots and armor resounded across the courtyard. Hundreds of mailed gloves slapped against breastplates. Fei clapped her hands over her ears. Gently, Nathan pulled them down, ignoring her watery eyes.

A lean-muscled giant jumped down from the last carriage. His gray hair was neatly cropped, and his sideburns ran low on his jawline. He didn't wear any armor, favoring a simple officer's uniform that matched Nathan's. A golden badge gleamed from his collar, however.

The badge of the royal family.

Bastion Leopold Tyrim, the oldest Bastion in the Anfang Empire, surveyed the courtyard with a gentle smile. Slowly, he raised his hand to his chest in a salute. He lowered it, then gestured for the assembled soldiers to be at ease.

"Is that him?" Sen mumbled.

Fei shot Sen a look of disbelief. The beastkin's eyes were wide as dinner plates, her ears and tail standing on end.

"How can you not recognize Bastion Leopold?" Fei hissed.

Sen stared at Fei, then looked up at Nathan and shrugged. "That's a yes, then."

Another person descended from the carriage behind Leopold. Nathan stared at her.

He had expected to see her at some point, but not this soon.

Ciana. She had served Leopold briefly before the fall of the Empire. Her opinions of him had colored Nathan's view of him, causing him to take many of the negative views of Leopold with a grain of salt.

She looked so young. Her single horn stuck out from her forehead. Her platinum hair glowed in the sunlight. She had tied it back in a ponytail, pulling back her bangs that Nathan had always encouraged her to keep. Her horse's tail swayed behind her as she followed Leopold.

Anna and her entourage approached Nathan. He greeted Leopold with a salute, and the other Bastion returned it. Ciana stared up at Nathan with cautious eyes, then hid behind Leopold when Nathan looked back at her.

"Forgive her," Leopold said with a chuckle. "Unicorn beastkin are naturally skittish around men. Especially those who are more..." His eyes lingered on Fei and Sen, who hovered close to Nathan's side. "Active? Yes, let's leave it at that." Leopold laughed.

"It's fine." Nathan shrugged, despite feeling the opposite. "But why bring a unicorn here given they are rightfully wary of people?"

Leopold raised an eyebrow. "She needs to learn how to handle others. Men, women, 'active' men, enemies, and eventually demons."

"You're training her to be a Champion?" Nathan asked.

"Blunt, aren't we?" Leopold chuckled. "Let's head inside and continue this."

Anna coughed and gave Leopold a look. He sighed, scratched a hairy cheek, and decided to stay put.

"Ah, yes, the formalities," he said. "Well met, Bastion Nathan. On behalf of His Majesty, I congratulate you on your early victories as Bastion, and for uncovering a plot against the Empire. Suffice it to say that rewards are being prepared and will be doled out once the Federation is sufficiently cowed."

Leopold gave Anna a look. "Good enough?"

"You sound like I'm torturing you," Anna whined. "It can't be that bad, can it? You live in the capital and deal with royal politics all day long."

"And here I am on a delightful holiday, but you're making me carry out my duties as if I'm still in the stuffy halls of Aleich." Leopold winked at Nathan. "Now, shall we go inside?"

CHAPTER 18

O nce inside, Anna forced them to attend to the immediate issue first. Nathan allowed the Ciana conversation to drop, for now.

The meeting room was a recent addition to the keep. Nathan always preferred more casual or military-esque rooms when he was with others. Sitting rooms with a few sofas, or a war room where everybody could stand around a map or other point of interest.

But Anna had visited two weeks ago and complained about the lack of a proper meeting room. Apparently, a large table and chairs are necessary. Nathan hated the trappings of nobility and the boring halls of power that he had dealt with in his homeland of Falmir, but he let Anna get her way this time.

Everybody sat around a single long table. Nobody sat at either end, not even Leopold. Anna showed open annoyance at that fact, gesturing to Leopold with her eyes, but he ignored her.

Ciana tried to remain standing. Leopold then forced her to sit next to him. Sitting opposite Leopold was Fei, whose tail moved at a thousand miles per hour. It moved so fast that Nathan could hear it.

Nathan finished summarizing the situation. The only person

who appeared interested in what had happened was Ciana, whose concern visibly grew the longer that Nathan talked. He ignored her.

"How come you never mentioned what the leyline disruption would cause?" Anna asked, her face marred by a scowl.

"If I say 'you never asked,' will you be angry?" Nathan tried.

Anna's glare answered his question.

"You know now, don't you?" Leopold suggested.

"That explanation is somehow worse," Anna said, turning her ire on Leopold. His smile didn't move an inch.

"I didn't want to induce unnecessary panic," Nathan explained. "While leyline disruption can cause a demonic invasion, it often doesn't. It wasn't until I had confirmed other matters, such as the involvement of the Federation with the bandits, that I suspected what was happening."

"Quite a fast conclusion, I must admit," Leopold said. His eyes bore into Nathan. "Especially as Vera said something different. That you believed a demonic invasion would occur before you confirmed that a Federation Champion was involved."

Had she? Nathan didn't look at Vera, but he imagined she might be avoiding his gaze right now.

In truth, Nathan had been grasping at straws during his conversation with Vera. She had doubted his belief that the Federation would go to war with the Empire. He needed something that would prod her into action, and he had found it. But the idea that the Federation had genuinely been trying to disrupt the leylines in an attempt to cause a demonic invasion?

That thought had never seriously occurred to him before he saw Sunstorm meeting with Sen. He had thought the idea to be too heretical for any Bastion to attempt.

"The demonic portal here was too passive," Nathan explained, trying to talk his way out of any suspicion. "All the energy had to be going somewhere. The Federation were behaving suspiciously, but I'll admit I never seriously thought they were trying to cause a demonic invasion."

"But you think they are now?" Leopold pressed. His smile remained firmly in place.

Ciana looked between Leopold and Nathan, her eyes overflowing with panic. She rocked back and forth in her chair, but refused to say anything. Everybody else in the room stared at her, but Leopold and Nathan ignored her.

"Sen has admitted that the Federation taught her how to disrupt the leylines with the cairn," Nathan said, gesturing to the spellblade sitting next to him. "We battled with a Federation Champion by the name of Sunstorm in our territory. The leyline disruption has ceased now that I'm disabling the bandits. Systematic leyline disruption over the course of several months would have resulted in a new demonic portal opening at the cairn, if we hadn't stopped it."

Ciana froze. Her gaze slowly shifted from Nathan to Leopold.

The room remained silent, although Anna continued to look annoyed. Kuda took the opportunity to slip in and provide coffee and tea cakes for everybody.

"I took a risk when I allowed you into the academy," Leopold said abruptly, lowering his mug. "Your father spoke ill of you. And most suspected you of seeking vengeance, given you had just been disinherited. There were other rumors as well. But those who dealt with you—at least without knowing your background —spoke well of you."

Nathan remained silent. In his timeline, he had never found out why he was allowed to become a Bastion or what made him "better" than his counterparts. He had outlived his entire class. His master had never thought much of him, at least publicly, but Nathan had been given dangerous postings. By proving himself, Nathan rose in status and power. He gained Champions faster than others and eventually became a legend. A Bastion with a trigem Champion, and later, several trigem Champions.

So Leopold's words keenly interested Nathan. Even if they applied to his false past.

"Your father has a reputation," Leopold said. "Your falling out with him piqued my interest. Surely a man who has lost everything will see the world differently? It seems I was right. You're sharp. The meisters noted that you devoured information in the academy. And now you're forging a reputation within mere weeks of arriving."

Nathan blinked. Somehow Leopold's opinion applied to both the false him and the real him.

A man who had lost everything. As sure a description of Nathan as any, he felt.

"You agree with his assessment of the Federation?" Anna asked. She bit her lip, her eyes moving nervously between the two Bastions.

"What do you think of his assessment, Anna?" Leopold asked.

"Are you kidding me?" Anna shouted. "You already know this."

"And now I am asking you to repeat it in his presence."

Anna rolled her eyes and crossed her arms with a huff. "He's right. I've been telling you ever since my father passed away that the Federation has been moving on Gharrick County. This isn't about tolls anymore. The bandits attacked my town." She glared at Sen, who grimaced and looked away.

"I see. And you, Vera?" Leopold asked, turning his attention to the redheaded sorceress.

"I don't see any flaws in his theory. A monogem Federation lurking near our borders is one thing, but actively helping to disrupt the leylines? Even if they weren't trying to cause a demonic invasion, it's still an act of war," Vera said.

Leopold nodded. He stroked his bare chin.

"Leopold!" Ciana cried. She stood up. "Why are you doing this? He's clearly right."

Finally, Leopold and Nathan looked at Ciana. Both of them hid their smiles, although Sen prodded Nathan in the side and glared at him. Clearly Sen had noticed his odd behavior.

"It seems my ward believes in you, Nathan," Leopold said after a brief pause.

"I appreciate your backing, Ciana," Nathan said. Then he froze.

She hadn't been introduced yet. Leopold had skipped introductions earlier, presumably because everybody recognized him.

Ciana's face lit up as if it were on fire. She dropped into her chair and mumbled something inaudible. If anyone noticed Nathan's mistake, they didn't comment on it or raise an eyebrow. Leopold patted Ciana on the shoulder and winked at Nathan.

"Indeed, your assessment is correct," Leopold said. "Sorry for the runaround. I was curious to see if opinion may sour when confronted."

Despite his front as a genial old man, Leopold was a savvy political player. He couldn't be the Emperor's right-hand man if he weren't. Anna scowled at Leopold before straightening up in her chair.

"I believe you asked about Ciana earlier?" Leopold continued. "Her path is not yet set. Unicorn beastkin are exceedingly rare. The Empire may not practice slavery, but the same cannot be said of other nations, and many nobles would stop at nothing to have her in their household." Leopold's face darkened, and Nathan felt his pulse quicken.

Nathan made a mental note not to get on Leopold's bad side. The man genuinely terrified him in a primal way.

"As such, I am training her as my ward. I don't know whether she's a better fit as a Champion or a Bastion yet, but I don't want to predispose her to either choice." Leopold paused.

Nathan nodded. "Becoming a Champion is a one-way path."

"I thought that was only if she received a gem?" Vera said.

Leopold glanced at Nathan, who shrugged. Vera was making an assumption there. Fei had told her about the one-way path bit, but many people already knew about it. If Vera believed that it was because of a gem, then that was her choice.

"Champion gems are permanent, yes," Leopold said. "But all Champion and Bastion enhancements are permanent. One can never stop being a Champion or Bastion."

The frown on Vera's face suggested she didn't understand. Neither Nathan nor Leopold helped her.

They had an oath to uphold. Many secrets of Bastions needed protecting. That the Federation had tried to cause a demonic invasion using the leylines was proof of that. Not even other Bastions could be completely trusted.

Nathan felt like he suddenly understood why his old master never told him much. Had this sort of thing happened in the past? Had older Bastions questioned each other and found that the only way to protect the world was to withhold knowledge? Nathan didn't know. He didn't even know if that was the right choice.

"Um, Leopold," Ciana spoke up.

"In a minute, Ciana," Leopold said. He patted her on the shoulder again. "Speaking of gems, I have a gift for you."

One of the functionaries from earlier brought in a small velvet bag. Within it was a small wooden box embossed with the golden emblem of the Emperor. Leopold held his hand over it for a second, and Nathan felt a pulse of power enter the box. Then Leopold slid it across the table.

Three gems sat within the plush confines of the box. An amethyst, a diamond, and a sapphire. Nathan's fingers shot to the amethyst first. He lifted it out of the box, held it up, and silently probed it with magic.

"I wasn't sure which would be most suitable for young Jafeila," Leopold continued. "Her meisters spoke highly of her abilities, but none were entirely certain of what path to suggest. I heard about her speed, and chose suitable gems to supplement such a Champion, although the abilities from each gem are flexible."

"Um," Fei tried to say. Her ears flattened as Leopold turned his attention to her and she quietened. Her tail stuck bolt upright.

Nathan ruffled her hair, and she slowly calmed down.

"I've changed my enhancement to both speed and strength," Fei said, quiet enough that a pin drop would overpower her voice. "Will these gems suit me still?"

Leopold smiled, and it was a genuine smile, unlike his poker face. "Of course. The amethyst is perhaps more single-minded as far as gems go, favoring strength and offensive abilities. But diamonds are easily the most flexible of physical enhancement gems, and the sapphire offers great variety if you wish to utilize gem abilities more."

"They're fairly standard gems for physical fighters," Nathan added. "And especially for a young Champion. More daring gems can be dangerous to rely on."

Nathan returned the amethyst to the box, noting the way Fei's eyes followed his every move. The box remained on the table for the rest of the meeting, but he kept it firmly shut and within arm's reach.

"Thank you, Bastion Leopold," Nathan said.

Leopold waved him off. "I can spare a few gems. The question is: can Jafeila support one? The academy trained you, so you should know how to gem Champions. But given the coming storm, you will need a monogem Champion now more than ever."

Even a dullard could read Leopold's hidden message: Nathan needed to handle this by himself. At least for now.

There was a war on, after all. Or close enough. Leopold's Champions were needed elsewhere within the Empire.

"Leopold," Ciana mumbled. "There's something else."

"Is there something else, Nathan?" Leopold asked him.

Test after test with this old man.

Nathan squared his gaze at Ciana, who blushed and looked at

the table. He waited patiently for her to look back at him. Almost a minute passed.

Eventually, she raised her head and looked him in the eyes. Her breathing quickened.

"I'm not going to bite," Nathan said gently. "You've been nervous ever since I gave my original report."

"I know," Ciana mumbled. Leopold's hand rubbed her shoulder, and she took a deep breath, her fluffy ears twitching.

"I assume you want to see the portal then?" Nathan said. "I can't imagine why else you've been so antsy since I mentioned the leyline disruption ceased."

CHAPTER 19

The gate leading to the portal was as nondescript as before. Nothing appeared to have changed on the outside, save for a pair of soldiers standing guard outside of it. They saluted as the party approached.

"You're not patrolling the interior?" Leopold asked. He seemed surprised that the gate was closed.

"That's my job," Fei chirped. She froze when Leopold's gaze turned to her and hid behind Nathan.

"I don't recall her meisters saying she's so shy," Leopold mused, his lips quirking upward.

"She's a fan," Nathan said flatly.

Leopold suppressed a grin and elbowed the air between them. For a geezer, he was a sharp one, and far more willing to play around than Nathan had expected.

Stepping up to the gate, Nathan reached for power from the binding stone. Fei jumped in front of him before he could push the doors open.

"I can open them," she chirped. "I have my key."

Nathan smiled at her, then reached over top of her and gave the doors a shove. A tiny pulse of magical resistance pushed back at Nathan, but it melted when the binding stone's power struck it. The doors opened a crack.

"How come you don't have to use a key?" Fei pouted.

"I imagine because he's the Bastion, and he sealed the doors," Leopold said. His smile had slipped, and his eyes focused on Nathan. "A curious method to keep the portal secure. I presume the keys are enchanted?"

"They are. It's the same method used for vaults and treasuries. A small set of keys with an enchantment that can unlock the door, except the seal is coded to a specific magical signature." Nathan shrugged. "I read about the technique in the academy. It's used in Falmir."

"Is it?" Leopold's smile returned. "Perhaps I'll see if it works for any of my portals when I return. My Champions would appreciate being able to keep the demons on the other side without needing to watch the gate all day long. Although I imagine that some may use the closed doors as an excuse to ignore the portal longer than they should."

Nathan winced. More than one fortress had fallen because of Champions who didn't investigate the portal regularly, and Bastions who weren't paying attention. Out of sight, out of mind, was a dangerous mindset, but a popular one.

"Can we go in?" Anna asked. "You've had me on edge since Nathan refused to properly answer Ciana."

Ciana ducked her head when at the sound of her name. Hiding a smile at Ciana's shyness, Nathan opened the gate all the way.

Gasps rung out. Fei shot through the open doors, her scimitar out, and gave the all clear signal. Sen drew her greatsword and took up a watch position beside Fei.

The rest of them trooped inside afterward. Ciana looked around with a mix of apprehension and triumph, as if she wasn't sure if she should be happy or terrified that she was right.

"I thought you said the portal was passive?" Anna said. She

pointed at the bottom of the valley they stood in. "I'm no expert, but that looks pretty ominous. And there are demons here!"

She was right. The tiny valley from earlier was no more. Worryingly, the portal now met expectations for what a demonic portal should look like, at least to a casual observer.

The valley leading down to the clearing had broadened. An army could comfortably march toward the keep without breaking formation. Farther below, the clearing had expanded as well. The central mound had transformed into a massive set of craggy rocks reaching for the sky. Dozens of campfires had been built in the clearing, although only a few were lit.

"Care to take care of the demons, Fei?" Nathan suggested. She was the reason so few campfires were being used.

The demons barely had time to react before she careened into them.

"Putting that speed enhancement to good work, I see," Leopold said. Then he winced as Fei bisected a demon. "Or something else. A bespoke enhancement?"

"She found the speed enhancement too restrictive," Nathan said. "So I've combined the strength and speed enhancements to her liking. I've tweaked it a few times over the last few weeks, although at this point I think she just likes the process."

"Yes, young Champions get like that," Leopold said drily. "This may be wrong of me to say, but I wonder what the goddess was thinking to make the process generate such emotions."

The nearby women stared at Leopold and Nathan in confusion. Sen hadn't gone through the Champion enhancement process. Although Nathan had thought Vera had picked up on the gist of it, perhaps she didn't realize it happened to every Champion.

"Why aren't you surprised by this?" Anna asked, gesturing to their surroundings. "Or worried? Or something?"

"Because he's been trained for situations exactly like this. Isn't that right, Nathan?" Leopold turned to face Nathan, his poker face firmly in place and eyes twinkling.

Behind him, Ciana nodded enthusiastically. She had understood what was happening the moment she found out what happened to the leylines, after all.

But this was a trick question. Nathan didn't understand why, but Leopold was testing him. Again.

The trick was that Nathan could never have learned what was happening right now, at least not the normal way. No book had ever been published or would ever be published describing this. Most Bastions never encountered this set of circumstances either, because it required somebody to commit heresy in the first place.

The portal had been passive when Nathan had arrived. He had known that the energy must be going somewhere else, and any Bastion could determine that fact. The leylines were being disrupted and causing the demonic energy from the portal to flow out into the world. Eventually, that would create a new portal and a new demonic invasion.

The natural reaction was to stop the disruption. Everything should go back to normal. But it wasn't, and it was for the same reason that the leyline disruption had weakened the portal to begin with.

"It's similar, but different," Nathan answered, trying to hedge around his actual knowledge. "This looks and feels like a cascade. But it's not."

"A cascade?" Vera probed.

Leopold gave her a considering look, then shrugged and gestured for Nathan to continue.

"All binding stones and demonic portals are linked through the leylines. When excess energy pours out of one portal, it must go somewhere. Normally this isn't an issue, but when too much energy pours out at once, we call it a cascade," Nathan explained. "This is how demonic invasions can occur at multiple portals at

once or in close sequence. Not all of the energy from the first invasion was let out, so it spills over to nearby portals."

"But that's not what's happening here?" Vera asked.

"It is, but it can't be," Nathan said. "There are no demonic
invasions nearby. The binding stone at Forselle Valley hasn't
reported any, neither have any other fortresses deeper within the
Empire. And the binding stone on the other side of the mountains,
within the Federation's Fort Taubrum, is still inactive."

Leopold nodded, his smile broadening. "So?"

"Like I said, it's a cascade, but it isn't. The effects are the same:
rapid expansion of the portal; constant arrival of demons; an
accelerating rise in demonic energy. Every time I take out a bandit
group, the situation worsens, so I've slowed down." That was a
lie. Nathan had been taking it slow since dealing with Sen,
because he had expected this.

"In other words, you think this cascade is related to the
leylines?" Leopold asked.

Ciana was practically jumping up and down.

"I believe your ward agrees," Nathan said, inclining his head
toward the unicorn beastkin. She blushed but stood her ground
this time.

"He's right, Leopold," Ciana said. "And you know he is. You
taught me about leyline cascades."

"That I did," Leopold said. He patted Ciana on the shoulder
again. "Yes, this is a cascade. It is, in fact, the primary reason I
came out here. I wanted to confirm that Gharrick Pass still existed,
and that I wouldn't need to hold this fortress myself."

"What a vote of confidence," Nathan drawled.

Anna's jaw dropped. After several seconds, she picked it back
up and gathered her wits.

"You thought my county was in danger but did nothing?" she
hissed. "What kind of protection is this?"

"The sort that is focused on the future of the Empire," Leopold
said. His smile dropped. "A Bastion who can't deal with a

demonic invasion isn't useful to His Majesty. That is the cold, hard truth. The fact you appear to be managing the situation is a testament to your ability, Nathan. Most would have suppressed all the bandits within a few days, then been overwhelmed by the ensuing demonic horde immediately. A valiant end, but a pointless one."

Nathan shrugged. Somehow, this colder side of Leopold felt easier to deal with. Perhaps because he felt similar to many other senior Bastions from Nathan's timeline.

"I estimate I have another week or two," he said. "My real worry is the Federation. I can deal with demons, but both at once?"

"Fortunately, you will now have a monogem Champion of your own," Leopold said. "Although I recommend that you make some more preparations." His gaze fell on Sen. Did he realize that she wasn't a Champion yet?

Probably. Nathan hadn't requested permission to grant her the status. Sen lacked the training to accept an enhancement, and there was something else she was much more suited for.

"I have a few more tricks up my sleeve," Nathan admitted. "If we're done here, why don't we have some lunch? The cooks have prepared something special."

The rest of Leopold's visit went smoothly. Seeing Ciana during her cuter phase was heartwarming for Nathan, as his memories of Ciana so young were very distant. But when Leopold left with Anna and Vera, Nathan found his thoughts drifting to the coming war.

War. The very thing that Nathan had come back in time to avoid. He knew what he needed to do to stop his timeline from happening, and the demons from destroying everything. But was that enough to stop the Messengers in this timeline?

He needed to make more preparations.

CHAPTER 20

"Are you sure about this?" Nathan asked Sen.

"I may not remember him, but every bone in my body calls out for him," Sen answered. "I feel like I'm missing a limb."

Nathan finished pouring salt for the summoning circle. Standing up, he sighed. Sen copied him, then shot him a grin when he glared at her.

"You remember the price you'll pay, don't you?" Nathan reminded her.

"I won't age. He'll take up a seat in my mind. I'll lose access to all sorcery that isn't fire element or closely related, but lose my weakness to water." Sen began ticking off fingers. "My hair will slowly lose its color. My eyes will turn red. I'll grow horns—"

"You won't," Nathan corrected. "Grow horns, that is."

"You make it sound like I will."

The pair of them stood in an underground chamber within the keep. Fei knew they were down here, but nobody else did. The door was locked and sealed with magic from the binding stone.

The floor of the room was covered with symbols. Two summoning circles, to be precise. The inner circle was drawn in chalk, was very simple, and nine candles burned around the circumference. The outer circle was drawn with salt and was far more complicated. Spaces had been left for runes to be drawn with magic, and a larger one for Sen to stand connected the two circles.

"Allowing a spirit to possess you is a life-altering decision," Nathan explained, for what he felt was the hundredth time. "And an ifrit is easily one of the most powerful spirits you can summon. If I hadn't already seen you spend a lifetime supporting him in your mind, I would never let you do this."

"But somebody already did in your timeline," Sen said. She smiled. "And I'm choosing to be possessed this time."

Nathan looked away. He hated this.

"I want to help you, Nathan. But I haven't trained in the academy. I haven't acclimated to Champion enhancement. You even admitted you don't know how many gems I might be able to support even if I become a Champion. But you know my potential with Ifrit." Sen took his hands. "Rather than spend years waiting to become a Champion and fight by your side, I'm making the choice to fight with you now."

"I still disagree with your choice," Nathan said. "But it's your choice."

He didn't know how to handle this Sen. One look into her eyes and his doubts vanished. She was his Sen. He knew that. But she didn't act like her.

The Sen he knew was timid. She was terrified of her own power, and sought his comfort because she needed it, not because she wanted to cuddle.

The root cause of the change was the very ritual she was about to undergo. Although Nathan knew very little about Sen's past, he knew that the Federation had forced her to be possessed by an ifrit. Her affinity with fire and natural talent with sorcery made her an immensely dangerous weapon, and he eventually got her away from the Federation. But the damage had been done.

Was he about to put her through the same trauma?

"You're looking at me like that again," Sen said, her voice low. "You need to think less, Nathan."

"Thinking is a large part of my job," Nathan said.

"Think about the right things, then." Sen huffed. "Look, we spoke about this. I'm fine the way I am."

Nathan was torn.

Kadria had held up her end of the bargain. Sen trusted him, loved him, and talked about feelings and emotions that reminded Nathan of his old Sen.

But she didn't have the memories of his old Sen. What she had were emotions about events and people she didn't remember.

Phantom limb syndrome was a problem that caused people who had lost an arm or a leg to still feel sensations from it. Sen suffered from phantom memory syndrome, where she trusted Nathan because of memories she no longer had. For all of Nathan's worries about overwriting the Sen from this timeline, he wondered if it would have been a better choice.

"Nathan," Sen warned.

"You say that you're happy, but you don't know what you're missing," Nathan said.

"Maybe. But I can feel the emotions related to what I'm missing." Sen's eyes became distant, and she flexed her fingers. "Other than you, there's not much positive. Ifrit feels more like a missing limb or a security blanket. But Fei? Anything else I think about? I don't feel that I need my missing memories to be happy."

Nathan scratched his head. Could he disagree with her? He wanted to. Everything about this situation troubled him.

"I want to move forward, Nathan," Sen said. "Can we leave it at that?"

He sighed. "Okay. Like I said, it's your choice."

"Good." Sen smirked. "You know, I get the feeling you need this sort of push often. A reminder to go with the flow, or to get back on track. Did I badger you like this before?"

"Not really. You were more timid," Nathan said, then frowned. "You used Ifrit as an excuse to voice your opinions earlier."

"Ah. Well then, this should be fun for both of us." Her eyes glimmered, and she bounced away to her designated spot in the magic circles. "If you overthink things, I'll bop you on the head. Fair?"

"I don't know if I agree to that," Nathan replied slowly.

"Too bad." Her hand glowed, and she did a slapping motion in the air.

A small force struck Nathan upside the head, just strong enough to irritate him. He glared at Sen. She giggled and said nothing.

"Let's get this show on the road," Nathan mumbled, and made the final preparations for the summoning.

Minutes passed as Nathan slowly poured magic into the summoning circle. The salt glowed, then smoldered. A thin barrier of smoke rose from the salt. Nathan smelled nothing, but the air felt charged with magic. An overbearing presence appeared to enter the room. As if the air itself was expanding and pushing against his body.

The salt burst into flames, and the haze from the smoke and heat became thick enough to be a shield between Nathan and whatever was in the circle.

That was the sign Nathan had been waiting for. He stopped pushing power into the outer circle and instead activated the inner circle. The candles flickered for a moment, then burst into meter high torches. Smoke as black as soot pumped into the inner circle. An invisible barrier kept the smoke within the chalk summoning circle. The smoke spiraled together and congealed as it rose to the ceiling. A form slowly emerged from within the dark haze.

Nathan licked his lips. All summoning rituals came with some risk, but an ifrit was a tremendously powerful being.

Summoning rituals tended to be similar in process. The

summoner opens a bridge to the spirit world, using himself as an anchor and magical power as construction materials. That was it. Everything else was about controlling the bridge: where does it go; who can use it; how big is it?

Most importantly, the ritual circles also prevented the summoned spirit from escaping the circle once summoned. While a djinni—a race of spirits that ifrits were part of—couldn't exist in Doumahr long without a host, there was nothing to stop the ifrit from forcibly seizing a host. A mistake in this ritual could be more devastating than the coming demonic assault.

Hence why Nathan used two circles. The inner circle was the bridge. The outer circle attempted to constrain the ifrit once summoned.

Two burly arms emerged from the smoke, each covered in ruby red scales the size of Nathan's head. The ifrit's skin was craggy, like the side of a mountain, and thin glowing cracks ran across it like magma veins. A demonic head emerged, its maw dripping with liquid fire that spread embers across the room. Two horns as long as Sen jutted upward, and glowing red veins could be seen within them.

The smoke sank to the ground and swirled around the base of the ifrit. The spirit hovered in the air of the room, its horns nearly scraping the room's ceiling. Size-wise, the ifrit stood easily twice Nathan's height. But this wasn't its full height. The ifrit had legs that were hidden within the smoke.

Presumably the ifrit had determined that it couldn't fit inside the room at full height, and had compromised by only showing its upper half. Not that it needed the bottom half to be intimidating.

"Foolish mortals, you dare to summon the great Ifrit?" the ifrit boomed. "I have no time for the petty trials and tribulations you waste your fleeting lives on. Tell me your purpose here, and I will deign to consider your proposals."

Sen stared up at Ifrit. Her body shook as she tried to meet his fiery gaze. Ifrit's eyes were like pits into Hell, and his presence overtook the room.

Moments passed. Ifrit hovered, still silent, and flexed his claws. Sen gulped and looked at Nathan for help.

"Can we skip past the melodrama?" Nathan asked, desperately trying to keep his tone light despite his inner worries. "We all know why you're here, and what we want. It's not like you have anywhere better to be."

Sen's eyes transformed into dinner plates. Ifrit turned his head and glared at Nathan, his eyes narrowing.

"Must you ruin one of my few guilty pleasures?" Ifrit said, crossing his arms. They were thick enough to imitate tree trunks. "The summoning is an important moment for me to impress upon people my power."

"Sure, but we kind of already know about your power. I wouldn't have summoned you if I didn't," Nathan said.

"You're not one for parties, are you?" Ifrit asked. The booming timbre of his voice had settled and now made him sound like a grumbling old man. "I've half a mind to leave and make you respect the next djinni you summon."

"Really? Leave, go back, and do what? Play cards for the next several decades in the spirit world?" Nathan taunted.

"I have some wonderful friends. It's not so bad."

"Excuse me, but what the hell?" Sen burst out.

Nathan and Ifrit looked back at Sen. Sensing a chance to regain his earlier momentum, Ifrit let out a deep cough.

"Well, little mortal, have you dwelt upon your innermost desires and come to your conclusion? For what purpose have you summoned me?" Ifrit said.

Sen stared at him. Her eyes narrowed. "This is just theater, isn't it? You talked like a normal person to Nathan, but now you sound like somebody from a folk tale. Do you think this is funny?"

"No, I feel that it's fun," Ifrit replied. He sighed and stared at the ceiling for several seconds. "Very well, if you prefer it, I shall get to the point. Why do you want my power, human?"

"Well, I want to fight for Nathan and—"

"Your Bastion may want you to fight for him, but is that what you truly want?" Ifrit's gaze bore down on Sen. She shrunk in on herself and looked to Nathan for support.

In response, Ifrit flung a claw out toward Nathan. "Do not intervene, Bastion. I will hear her answer. You Bastions are predictable. I don't need to hear your reasons. Only hers."

Sen swallowed, closed her eyes, and fell silent for nearly a minute. When she opened her eyes, they were filled with the determination that Nathan expected to see from her, even if she had always been too scared in his timeline to show it so openly.

"What I told you is exactly what I want," Sen repeated.

"Why?" Ifrit asked.

"Because I want to support him. He supports me right now, even though my power as a spellblade is too weak to compare to his Champions. And I can't become a Champion easily. I'm already talented at fire element sorcery. With you, I can become a worthy partner of Nathan's," Sen said.

Ifrit considered Sen silently. After several seconds, he turned to face Nathan.

"You are the summoner here. Have you explained the risks?" Ifrit asked.

"I have," he said. "In detail."

"And you still allow her to do this?" Ifrit's voice hadn't changed, but Nathan knew he was being judged.

Before Nathan could answer, Sen cut in.

"It's my decision," Sen said. "The effects on my body, the restraints on my sorcery, the unaging, the need to live with you in my mind at all times. It's my choice. Not yours. Not Nathan's."

Ifrit chuckled. "Not my choice? You realize I'm going to be bound to you until your demise, yes?"

"And what else will you do?" Sen smirked. "Go back to the

spirit world and play cards for the next several decades? This is my choice. Deal with it."

Letting out a sigh, Ifrit turned fully toward Nathan. "She's a willful one. It's rare for me to possess somebody with such mental fortitude."

Nathan wasn't sure how to feel about that statement.

"So you accept?" Sen asked, her voice raising in pitch.

"I thought you said it was your choice?" Ifrit replied, amused. "But I have one final question before I agree to the possession. You may feel that I will agree no matter your answer, but this ritual is an odd one."

The spirit leaned toward Nathan, until his demonic visage hung only an arm's breadth away. The heat let off by Ifrit spilled across the summoning circle. Nathan broke out in a sweat. The barrier was supposed to keep Ifrit in. If his natural heat broke through, what else could?

"Tell me, how and why did you summon me, specifically?" Ifrit asked. "I can recall all circumstances relative to which I have given out my true name, and I do not believe you could know it."

Nathan gulped. Ifrit had asked the one question he'd hoped to avoid until after the possession, but he'd known it was highly likely to come up.

Ifrit's name was not "Ifrit." All spirits possess a true name, which they do not give out lightly. A sorcerer can use a true name to directly call upon a spirit, and the spirit must respond to their true name. The spirit can refuse any requests made, but they must always respond to a summons, and often the mere knowledge of their true name implies a level of trust.

Knowing Ifrit's true name had allowed Nathan to summon the specific ifrit that Sen had been possessed by in Nathan's timeline. Nathan trusted Ifrit. But he shouldn't know his true name. Ifrit had given it to him as a gesture of faith, to be used should the worst occur and Nathan need to summon another ifrit again.

Without those memories, it was natural for Ifrit to be curious, and perhaps even upset.

Taking a deep breath, Nathan decided upon the only answer he felt he could give. Ifrit would possess Sen shortly regardless, and have his own answer.

"You may not recall the circumstances, and you may not think I can know your true name, but I remember," Nathan said, matching Ifrit's terrifying gaze. "We've met before."

Nothing more needed to be said. Even if Nathan tried to explain, the simple fact he knew Ifrit's name was proof that Ifrit had trusted him. Spirits were immortal. Not even a binding stone could slay them. No spirit could have their true name forced from them.

Ifrit stood still for close to a minute. Nathan continued to sweat.

Eventually, Ifrit said, "I see."

Nathan blinked. "You do?"

Straightening up, Ifrit gave Nathan a sidelong glance. "I have existed since time immemorial. While I may not recall the birth of this world, I have knowledge of mysteries and wonders that nobody else has. You are a Bastion. I know your magic well, and the things it can do."

He did? Nathan never recalled Ifrit sharing this kind of information.

"I don't remember any spirits ever speaking of binding stones," Nathan said.

"Because it would be dangerous to do so. You have sworn an oath to protect such knowledge, have you not?" Ifrit held a claw to his mouth, as if to symbolize silence. "I may not believe in the divinity of your goddess, but I know her power."

With that, Ifrit fell silent. Nathan took that as a sign that he had said enough.

"Then you are satisfied?" Nathan asked.

"I am. This will prove entertaining," Ifrit said.

That was the go-ahead to complete the ritual. Unlike the summoning itself, finalizing the possession was simple.

Sen brushed aside some of the salt separating her from Ifrit. The wall of smoke that protected her from Ifrit vanished into nothingness, and she stood face-to-face with the spirit.

Ifrit placed the tip of one of his claws against Sen's head. At that moment, Nathan activated the summoning circle again. The room flashed. Smoke churned about the room, thick, black, and acrid. The protective barrier of the summoning circle shattered, and Nathan instinctively reached for the power of the binding stone.

No need, he realized as the smoke cleared within moments. Sen stood alone, unharmed.

But she was possessed.

Her green eyes had turned red. A single, thick lock of her hair had turned white. No other visible changes had taken place, but Nathan could feel her presence in a way he couldn't earlier. She felt like Ifrit to his senses, an explosively powerful presence that drowned out almost everything else near it. Over the next minute, Ifrit's presence faded, as his power wasn't being actively used.

Sen met his eyes and smiled. Nathan smiled back. She was still herself.

Then Sen tilted her head and wandered over to the chalk summoning circle. She inspected the circle, mouthing things he couldn't make out.

"Huh. You really did write his name down here," Sen said. "That's a little rude. Although I don't have the slightest clue what it means. And Ifrit won't tell me. I get the feeling he was always like this." She scowled. "Goddess, no wonder the two of you get along fine. He's as secretive an old bastard as you are."

"Hey!" Nathan said.

"You're my secretive old bastard, if that helps." Sen winked and caught Nathan in a hug. She froze. "Oh. That's super awkward."

"What?"

"Ifrit reading my emotions. I kind of underestimated what it meant to let another being take up residence in my mind." She shrugged. "At least he pays rent. And I know why I felt like I've been missing a limb. If he's this pervasive, then no wonder I feel like I need him."

Nathan ruffled her hair, finding her annoyance cute. He pulled his hand back when he felt his palm begin to heat up.

"Why don't we take you somewhere else to exercise your new power?" Nathan proposed. "Like outside. Before you try to light me on fire."

"Why would I ever do that?" Sen asked, her smile too wide to be genuine.

After quickly cleaning up the summoning circles, and making sure to obliterate Ifrit's name from the floor, the two of them ventured out to the outer wall of the fortress.

A large clearing lay to the south, away from the road and free of the forest surrounding it. Nathan suspected this area had been populated by the Empire at some point relatively recently. Or else the trees would have grown over the land by now.

"What spells do you know?" Nathan asked.

"Um. Not many?" Sen shrugged. "Fourth rank spells only. I know the one sixth rank spell, but only because it's super famous."

"It's the inferno tornado, isn't it?" Nathan asked.

Sen nodded sheepishly. The inferno tornado was renowned as the spell of choice by the Bastion who founded the Kingdom of Falmir, back when they had split from the collapsing Anfang Empire. Many sorcerers learned the spell merely because of its historical significance.

Also because creating a tornado made of fire was awesome. The nature of the spell meant you didn't even need the wind element, although very talented sorcerers combined the two elements anyway.

"Well, don't use that one," Nathan said. "I don't want to waste power from the binding stone to put out the forest fire you'll start."

Sen clicked her tongue and leaned against the crenellations of the wall. "So, what? I use fourth rank spells against Champions?"

"Don't dismiss fourth rank spells," Nathan warned. "Despite the name, lower rank spells will be your bread and butter for a while."

"What about second rank? Nobody seems to use them."

Nathan held up a hand, and a blue line appeared between his fingers. "First and second rank spells are largely indistinguishable, save for the magic power in them. Common magic users rely on them, but actual sorcerers never go lower than third rank. Unless you're in a pinch and need to brute force something."

"Okay, but Sunstorm seemed immune to third rank spells. What about fourth rank?" Sen pressed.

"That's where things get complicated." Nathan summoned a triangle over his palm. "Third rank spells are usually powerful enough, and far more flexible than higher rank spells. You can cast several at once"—a triangle appeared over each finger in his hand—"or supercharge the spell so that it's effectively one rank higher." The triangles vanished, and one appeared on either side of Nathan's hand.

"And that works against Champions?" Sen asked skeptically.

"Yes. You'll also have Ifrit's power to increase your spell effectiveness." Nathan lowered his hand and the triangles vanished. "The rule of thumb is to use fourth rank on Champions; fifth rank on duogems; and sixth rank on trigems. Some trigems will need higher ranks, though. The innate magic resistance of a Champion is one thing, but some gems can make a Champion immune to spells that aren't strong enough."

Sen grimaced. "Trigems? You really think we're going to fight one soon?"

"No. But a duogem? Maybe. And planning around gem abilities is always smart. Any Champion with a sapphire is likely to have increased magic resistance."

Nathan pointed at the clearing. "Now, test out Ifrit's power."

"Are you sure I can't use the inferno tornado?" Sen asked.

"Don't even think about it," Nathan said.

Sen winced and rubbed at one of her ears. "You and Ifrit said the same thing at the same time." She smirked at Nathan and left her remaining thoughts unvoiced. He knew what she was going to say anyway.

Pointing at the clearing, Nathan waited for Sen to obey. She straightened up, held both hands out, and summoned a pair of red squares into her hands.

Moments later, the clearing exploded. A spiral of flames gushed into the air. When the smoke and dust cleared, a blackened crater had replaced the clearing.

"Oh," Sen said. "Okay, that's way more powerful than what I could do before. I can only imagine how powerful my tornado is."

"Don't get cocky," Nathan warned. "Casting higher rank spells and supercharging takes longer. In battle—"

"Seconds kill," Sen said. "Ifrit's lecturing me about my focus and how long I take to cast spells. Urgh. Getting used to this will take a while." She blinked, then gave Nathan a sidelong look. "Nathan, can I ask you a question? Ifrit's refusing to answer."

That didn't bode well.

Despite his misgivings, Nathan said, "Sure."

"How does this work when we have sex?" Sen asked. "Does Ifrit feel you inside me as well? Does that mean you're technically having sex with Ifrit as well?"

Nathan stared at Sen. Then he placed his palm over his face and groaned.

All of his worries had been for nothing. The possession hadn't changed Sen one bit.

CHAPTER 21

A few days later, Nathan found himself helping Fei to prepare for her gemming ceremony.

At least, that's what he told himself.

Fei moaned and mewled in his lap. He moved the comb slowly, gently, and deliberately so as to not hurt her. Her body quivered against him. Her tail continued to move despite his persistent reminders to Fei that she had to stay still.

The scent in the air was the least arousing thing about the situation, and it was pure arousal. Fei wore only her underwear, as she always did when getting her tail and ears groomed. Her nearly naked body rubbed up against Nathan's. She definitely felt his erection.

In his old timeline, the next step when Fei got this aroused would involve no clothing. This Fei didn't seem to pay much attention to Nathan's arousal.

If she did, he wouldn't be able to control himself. Not that he wanted to. Fei had been his lover in his timeline, and he planned to take her when she was ready.

"How are you so good at this?" she gasped out after he finished. During the grooming session, forming actual words was impossible for her.

She continued to lie across his lap, curled up tightly against him. Her newly fluffed tail tickled Nathan's nose as it swished back and forth.

Holding back was hard for Nathan. Fei pressed her bare stomach against his crotch. But she didn't react or comment on it. Until she showed open interest in him sexually, he'd hold back. Let her go at her own pace, he told himself.

He really hoped that her pace moved as fast as the rest of her.

"I've had some practice," Nathan said, blowing off her question again.

Fei looked up at him, her eyes glazed over and fluffy ears twitching curiously. "Did you have another beastkin that you groomed before me?"

Ruffling her hair, Nathan initially didn't answer. But Fei continued to stare at him, her gaze growing clearer and more penetrating. The movements of her tail slowed until only the tip swayed back and forth beneath his chin.

"You don't have any competition, Fei," Nathan said eventually. "You're the only beastkin in my life right now."

Her ears perked up, and her tail resumed its usual movements. But her expression darkened, and she laid her head on the bed.

"I'm not so sure that means I don't have competition, Nathan," Fei complained.

"What do you mean by that?" Nathan asked, although he had a strong suspicion as to who she was referring to.

Fei sat up. She gave Nathan a sidelong glance, as if to ask him "are you serious?" Then she straightened up in his lap and faced him. Her face sat only inches away from his chest, and he was reminded of her petite stature.

If he leaned forward, he could easily sweep her up in a kiss. Her legs rubbed against his hips as she curled them around his back. Her crotch rubbed against his, and he really questioned if she was acting innocently. He held in a groan as she pressed herself against him and tucked her head beneath his neck. Her cat ears flicked at his chin.

That was it, he decided.

A knock sounded at the door.

"Nathan, are you ready? Fei's not in her room, so I'm guessing she went ahead," Vera said.

Fei sprung to her feet, eyes wide. "Oh no! I forgot that I need to get all dressed up."

The beastkin shot around the room and gathered up her uniform and armor. Nathan had gone ahead and brought her things here while she showered earlier.

"You're taking this too seriously," Nathan said.

Fei stuck her tongue out at him. Or maybe she stuck it out because she was struggling to slip into her breastplate. He walked up behind her and helped her do up the clasps and tighten it around her hefty bust.

Vera knocked again, then opened the door. She blinked at the sight of Nathan helping Fei into her uniform.

"We're almost ready," Fei said, face red.

Vera sniffed the air, then turned her head to the side. "I'll wait outside."

The door closed. Fei turned her head, then sniffed the air. After several attempts, she appeared to find the smell she was looking for. Her face lit up.

Then she glared at Nathan and let out a pout.

"You can smell me, can't you?" Fei demanded to know.

"It's hard not to. You do this every grooming session," Nathan said.

She blinked. "Wow. So I should shower after grooming?"

"What would be the point of grooming you if you immediately mess up your tail again?" Nathan sighed. "Let's get you changed, then we'll head out and begin the gemming ceremony."

Fei remained in a sour mood until they left Nathan's bedroom and scowled at Vera when she stepped outside.

"Interrupted something, did I?" Vera asked, a smirk on her lips.

Fei didn't answer. She strode ahead of Nathan and Vera.

After a couple of corridors, the beastkin fell back into step with Nathan. Vera exchanged glances with him. The three of them walked together for some time in silence.

"Um, are you sure this will work?" Fei asked, her eyes flicking between the floor and Nathan.

"No gemming ceremony is ever guaranteed to succeed," Nathan said. Fei's ears flattened against her head.

He continued, "But I think you are ready. You've acclimated to the power of the binding stone extremely fast. Plus, the first gem is always the easiest one. A well-trained Champion can often be gemmed within their first few months."

"You talk as if you've done it," Vera said.

"If we're going to be sent off on our own, we need to know what we're going to do," Nathan responded.

Truthfully, he really shouldn't know this. At least, not in the Empire.

In his homeland of Falmir, Bastions went through an apprenticeship for a few years before being posted independently. The Empire eschewed this system and preferred to use its vaunted academies to train both Bastions and Champions.

The upside of the academies was that they could quickly assess and train a large number of candidates in a relatively standardized way. The Empire had the largest proportion of beastkin Champions for this reason, as most nations didn't have the infrastructure to train them from nothing.

The downside was that Bastions gained little hands-on experience during their training. In Nathan's implanted memories, he recalled a few brief postings with Bastions and some excursions, but little else. By contrast, he gained a wealth of experience during his apprenticeship in his original timeline in the Kingdom of Falmir.

Because of this, this posting would normally be death for a new Bastion. An enemy nation actively attempting to start a war and unleash a demonic invasion? It was a difficult situation for somebody with experience, let alone for a greenhorn. Fortunately, Nathan had a lot up his sleeve.

The keep's rear courtyard welcomed the trio. Nathan led them to an enclosed spot. Herbs cascaded down from planters and vines twisted along trellises. The cooks used this little patch to help feed the keep.

"Any reason we're getting in touch with nature?" Vera asked.

"This isn't what I'd call nature," Nathan said. "And no. Having more room for Fei to move is good, however."

He pulled a pouch from his pocket and pulled the gemstones from it. Fei licked her lips when she saw the three glittering rocks.

"I get to choose?" she asked hesitantly.

"Along with your final enhancement," Nathan confirmed. "Whatever you decide on now, you will be stuck with for the rest of your life. There is no going back after this point. As part of this ceremony, I will implant the gem into your collarbone and its magic will run through your body forever."

Fei nodded. "I'm ready. Um, which should I pick? I know you went for the amethyst first." She gave him an odd look.

"That would have been my first choice if you had your original speed enhancement," Nathan explained. "Amethysts provide their Champions with greatly enhanced strength, martial ability, and raw power. You would be able to move like the wind and cut through a mountain."

Fei's eyes widened. Her fingers twitched. Was she thinking about Tarako again, the nine-tailed fox who could slash nine times at once?

"And the others?" Fei asked quietly.

"Diamonds are flexible. However you want to boost your physical abilities, a diamond can do it. That's why they're the most common gem for physical fighters."

"Common," Fei repeated. She sounded disappointed.

"Because a diamond can do anything. You can make yourself strong enough to slice through an inch of enchanted steel with your first gem; immune to pain with your second gem; and gain the ability to sweep aside entire companies of soldiers with your third," Nathan explained.

He left out that the diamond was the "jack of all trades, master of none" gem. It did anything almost any physically focused gem did, but slightly worse. An amethyst hit harder; a sapphire provided more powerful abilities; a topaz broke the sound barrier. But a diamond could do all of those things.

The exception was durability. The defensive abilities of diamonds were second-to-none. Immunity to pain. Resilience to powerful blows. Barrier projection for the Champion and their allies. Removal of the need to eat or sleep.

Nathan doubted that Fei was interested in durability, however.

"But lots of Champions have diamonds, don't they?" Fei asked.

Vera interrupted, "I don't think you should pick your gem based on what others are using. Shouldn't it be about what you want and what suits you best?"

Fei nodded slowly, but her tail stopped moving and she twisted her hands together.

Had she always been so sensitive about this sort of thing, Nathan wondered.

"There's also the sapphire," Nathan said. Fei's ears pricked up. "Although it's typically used for spellblade Champions and a certain type of sorcerer, there's nothing to say that you can't use it."

"Um, but I can't use sorcery? Or any magic at all," Fei said.

"The gem will take care of that." Nathan waved off her concern. "Sapphires are entirely concerned about gem abilities. That is, granting you magical abilities on top of what you can already do. Common examples for physical fighters are to wreath their sword in flames; to become immune to or even counter weaker magic; or even short-range instant teleportation."

Fei's eyes widened. "Eh? I could do that sort of thing?"

"The cost is that sapphires don't increase your physical abilities directly. Amethysts and diamonds strengthen your body, on top of your enhancement. But gem abilities have to be activated and used. And they also drain your gem's power reserves faster. That Federation Champion was probably running low when she ran away."

"Oh. Is that why she appeared weaker than I thought?" Fei bit her lip. "So she could control shadows, but wasn't as physically powerful?"

"That's right. An onyx is an odd gem choice for a Champion. Better suited for an assassin than a front-line fighter." Nathan saw Fei's concern growing and added, "But a sapphire is different. Think of it as a way to become a spellblade, without learning sorcery."

Fei nodded, but remained silent. She stared at the three gemstones in Nathan's hand. Her full attention was on them.

"If only I could test out one gem and change later," Fei muttered.

"Unfortunately, there's no known way to do that," Nathan said. And no way was ever discovered in the future. "I'll leave the three gems here. Maybe you'll feel something from them."

"I haven't over the past few days," Fei said.

"Well, maybe today is different."

Not that Nathan believed in that. He had always suspected that the idea of Champions "feeling" their future through a gemstone was because their Bastion rigged the gem to react to their touch and trick them. None of his Champions had ever responded to them.

After placing the gems on a nearby table, Nathan took a short walk with Vera.

"Have you activated your gateway yet?" he asked.

"Leopold said he'd send me the catalysts, but they haven't arrived yet," Vera said. "Not that I know where I'll connect it to. You're rather close to my tower, and I don't know if Bastion Leopold's fortresses will be able to send reinforcements."

"Better to be connected to something rather than nothing," Nathan said. Vera nodded.

"Are you sure you should leave her to decide by herself?" Vera asked, changing the subject.

"It's her future, and she knows her abilities as well as anyone," Nathan said.

"Maybe." She sounded doubtful. "But you're her Bastion. She looks to you for guidance. Even the slightest nudge toward the amethyst and she'll take it. Don't pretend you don't want her to take it."

Honestly, Nathan wanted her to choose the amethyst and to change her enhancement back to the speed one. But he couldn't explain why.

He knew that Fei made for an amazing Champion with amethysts. But she had clearly performed better with her current enhancement. Shouldn't that prove that he needs to push her down an alternative path? Was he blinded by his knowledge of the future?

Nathan held no knowledge about the path not taken by Fei. Would she turn out stronger with a new gem? Or would this be a horrible mistake?

If he hadn't seen Sen's personality shift in this new timeline, he wouldn't hesitate to push the amethyst on Fei. But Sen's changes showed that whatever was happening was for the better. She exuded a level of confidence that Nathan found delightful, and her sorcery improved at a rapid pace.

Maybe Fei could choose a different path as well, and things would be fine. Sen was doing well. Maybe Fei would as well.

"I don't know," Nathan admitted. "Based purely on what I know about her past, I wanted the amethyst. But Champions change as they gain experience. I wouldn't push her into picking her gem this fast if a demonic invasion weren't on the horizon."

"She'll grow into it, won't she?"

"Sure, but what other futures am I closing off?" Nathan shook his head. "I'm beginning to realize that the world is far more complex than I've given credit for. There's no singular path in life. No predestined future set out by the goddess."

Vera's eyebrows shot up. "Those are bold words for a Bastion."

"Borderline heresy, I know." Nathan chuckled darkly. "But if the goddess didn't want us to protect the world ourselves and find our own path, would she have left us alone here?"

Vera remained silent. She walked with Nathan for a time.

"Maybe," she said. "But what if you know what your future should be? Or what somebody else's future should be? Is it right to deny it, because of your feelings about what is the right thing, or allowing choice? What if everybody ends up on the wrong path because of that?"

Nathan's mind whirred. He considered her words.

"Are there wrong paths?" Nathan answered. He shook his head. He knew of at least one. "I don't know. I have a future that I'm working toward. I don't need everybody to be part of that, and they're free to do whatever they want. Right and wrong don't enter into it."

"Hmm. So you'd trample over somebody else's future in order to preserve your own?" Vera asked.

"I'm a Bastion. That's my entire duty in life," Nathan said wryly. "The Federation wants to take land from the Empire, and I'm here to stop them. The demons want... something. I'm stopping them. I kill bandits and enemy Champions. My job is not a nice one."

"You sound more confused than I am," Vera muttered.

Nathan laughed. Long and hard.

How long had it been since he laughed like this, he wondered.

Vera looked at him oddly, as did several of the nearby guards.

"Sorry, but you're right. Can you blame me? My life has changed a lot recently," he said, wiping tears from his eyes.

"I suppose." She sighed. "You lost everything before you came here, didn't you? Effectively a count, denied your inheritance by your father despite being the rightful heir, and now a Bastion. I can see where you're coming from."

The two of them returned to the small garden where Fei stood with a single gem in her hand.

It glittered bright blue in the sun. A sapphire.

"You've decided?" Nathan asked, just to be sure.

"I have."

"May I ask how?"

Fei nodded. "I don't just want to be strong, or fast, or tough. I want to be an amazing warrior who can defeat her enemies no matter what they're like. You've been so amazing in battle with your sorcery, Nathan. How could I not want to have even a sliver of that? And when I get three gems, I'll be able to show you things beyond your wildest dreams." She grinned broadly, showing her fangs.

Holding in a grimace, Nathan nodded. He didn't know how to feel.

"I'll read your mind during the ritual to determine the ability you gain from the gem," he explained. "For later gems, you'll be able to choose, but we don't know how your body will react. So concentrate on the sort of ability you want, and that can help guide me and the binding stone's power."

Her tail swished violently behind her, and Fei nodded several times. Nathan ruffled her hair and heard her giggle when he brushed the inside of her ears.

When she calmed down, he placed the sapphire against her collarbone. It didn't sink in. Fei gasped as the stone touched her skin. A small slit had been cut into her uniform and armor to make way for the gem.

Nathan reached into his mind and channeled the binding

stone. He began the ritual. The sapphire exploded in brilliant, bright blue light, nearly blinding Nathan. Slowly, it sank into Fei's chest. She let out rasping gasps, but remained still.

The process was very painful. Other Champions compared it to being stabbed very slowly.

Eventually, the blue stone sat flush with Fei's collarbone and skin. Her eyes were wide, and almost entirely white. She stared into nothing, and he braced her with his free arm. She looked up at him and nodded.

Diving into her mind, he found it as welcoming as usual. If a little panicked. He took it slow, allowing her to calm down. Eventually he found her core. A satellite of power hung around it, and Nathan felt the tether from it to the binding stone. She was connected to the binding stone, and from it to him.

She was his. The Champion to Bastion connection was now permanent, until death parted them. At any moment, he could feel her life and mind. Understand her state of being. He'd never learned how, but supposedly some Bastions could read the minds and emotions of their Champions. The proof of this was in what he was about to do.

For now, he had a job to do. He reached out for the satellite of power that the gem had installed into her mind. The moment he touched it, Fei's emotions and desires poured into him. His mind instinctively filtered out those not related to the gem.

Although he noted some from earlier that were distinctly related to him and the things she wanted to do to him.

He now knew that she was very, very interested in him. Damn.

Ignoring that, he tuned the sapphire. What felt like hours passed. Fei's desire nudged at him, as did the reaction of her mind when he changed it in certain ways.

The first gemming ceremony was always the hardest. The binding stone was implanting its power into the Champion. It needed to take root, and if the wrong gem was selected or the wrong ability tuned to the Champion, then the ceremony would fail.

Nathan knew how to abort a failed ceremony, but the results could be catastrophic. Champions died from failed ceremonies, their minds turning to mush. Even successful ceremonies had dire consequences due to poor tuning. Nathan had met his fair share of Champions who obeyed their Bastions like slaves, and who were incapable of ever becoming duogem Champions or even using their single gem properly.

Most nations stripped Bastions of their position for a failed ceremony, or for "successful" ceremonies that damaged the Champion's mind. Those rules had changed after the war had begun, but the Empire currently stuck to them. Not that Nathan had any intention of ever doing this to any Champion.

Finally, he pulled away from Fei's mind. Her thoughts poured over him, and she seemed fine.

Nathan looked down at her in reality. She looked exhausted. Only minutes had passed. The sapphire shined from its place in her chest. She smiled at him.

"So what can I do?" she asked.

"Let's go over that another day," Nathan said. He ruffled her hair. "For now, you need some rest."

"Can you groom me again?" she asked dreamily. Her head leaned against his chest.

Those desires from earlier washed over him. He cleared his throat, looked away, and then said, "Of course."

He carried her back to her room, and she dozed. Vera accompanied them, looking thoughtful.

"I told you there wasn't much to see," Nathan told Vera.

"Maybe. But it still satisfied my curiosity," she said.

He shrugged and let her wander off. Vera was due to return to her tower within the next few days. Letting her see a gemming ceremony wasn't a big deal, given how little there was to see. Everything took place in the mental world.

Fei still seemed clean, so Nathan stripped her down and groomed her. She giggled at his touch, and the room filled with her scent as usual.

"Fei," he said. His hand slipped along her taut ass.

She let out a sigh and looked up at him. Her face exuded ecstasy.

His hand drifted lower. Her tongue slipped out of her mouth, and she moaned.

Then her hand gripped his.

"No, not yet," she mumbled.

"We both know you want this," he said.

"I do," she said. "But there's something I want to do first."

"Which is?" he asked.

She smiled. Her body shifted until she sat up in his lap, her mouth next to his ear. He could feel her body pressing against his.

She whispered, "In this next battle, I'll prove that I'm worthy of being your mate."

CHAPTER 22

The sky in the portal turned black the night of the invasion. Scouts reported back within minutes, their shouting echoing throughout the walls of the keep.

Nathan stirred. The noises from outside of his room boded poorly. His head lifted from the pillow, and he stared into the darkness of his room while he waited for his eyes to adjust. Sen moaned below him. She turned in her sleep and rubbed against his naked chest.

The door nearly blew open when Fei knocked on it. Nathan saw its hinges visibly move.

"Nathan!" Fei shouted. "Wake up, something's wrong with the portal."

She pushed the door open and Nathan received a reminder of why locking his door was pointless. Fei's inhuman strength didn't give a damn about how good the steel was or how complex a lock the door had. She pushed the door and it opened. A shame about the frame.

"Nathan!" she shouted again. Then she pouted when she saw him in bed with Sen.

"I'm awake," Nathan said.

"So am I," Sen said. "Goddess, Fei, are you trying to wake the dead?"

Fei didn't say anything, instead choosing to glare at Sen. The beastkin took several seconds to regain her composure and flick on the lights. By which point, both Sen and Nathan were up and getting changed.

"The sky in the portal went dark," Fei explained.

Nathan clicked his tongue. "That means the demons are about to invade through the portal. Gather all the soldiers and officers, Fei. And tell Kuda to send a message to Vera. Maybe she's set up her gateway and can bring reinforcements from Leopold."

Fei obediently ducked off. Sen returned to her room to finish getting ready once she slipped some clothes on. Unwilling to waste time freshening up, Nathan threw on his uniform and rushed to the portal.

The doors were wide open. A dozen soldiers guarded them on this side. They saluted Nathan when he approached and allowed him in. Returning the salute, he entered the portal.

Nathan had been busy preparing for the invasion since Leopold's visit. The portal was no longer a barren wasteland.

Immediately on the other side, a half-dozen automaton hoplites reacted to Nathan's entry. They recognized their creator and deactivated again, lowering their spears. A palisade wall surrounded this side of the gate. Bulky machines sat atop the wall, pointing outward. Small ballista bolts—each about the length of Nathan's leg—bristled from the machines. Dozens more bolts hid within the machines.

These were repeater ballistae powered by the binding stone, each capable of firing a bolt every few seconds. They operated automatically. Even their ammunition was replenished by the binding stone.

The interior gate opened, and Nathan walked through. Over a hundred soldiers milled about here. Another palisade lay farther down the valley and blocked off further descent toward the portal itself. More automaton hoplites stood guard near the wall, and more ballistae defended the wall. Soldiers attended to a few catapults, each of which had automatically refilling ammunition stockpiles.

Looking up, Nathan confirmed that the sky was now pitch black. Below him, the light creeping out from the cracks in the ground had turned a bright white.

Portals didn't always show physical changes such as this before an invasion, but they were a clear sign of overflowing demonic energy. This world was being changed by the energy building up within it. Once they suppressed the invasion, the sky would become red again and the light from the cracks would return to normal.

Nathan considered himself lucky that his first invasion came with such obvious warning signs. While he could read the level of demonic energy flowing from the portal, at best he could only guesstimate when the invasion would happen. The monitoring devices that made accurate observation possible were yet to be invented and Nathan didn't understand them well enough to recreate them. He was a Bastion, not a magical scientist or inventor.

Nobody stood atop the outer palisade. Nathan looked down the valley from the central gatehouse, which was the highest point of the wall. Behind him were his soldiers and summons. Ditches, low-standing wooden barricades, and barbed stakes lined the descent to the bottom of the clearing.

Down there was the beginning of the demonic invasion. Dozens of demons crowded around the craggy rocks near the portal. Every minute or so, another would slowly fade into existence. At first each demon appeared colorless and fuzzy, but they regained their form over the course of ten seconds or so. They would look at their bestial hands and arms, feel their face and body. Then they would pull a weapon of some form out of thin air and join their brethren.

"Shouldn't we be clearing them out?" Sen asked. She wandered up next to him.

"Ordinarily, yes. But I don't know when the portal will tear itself open. If one of us is down there when it happens, we'd be overwhelmed in seconds." Nathan shook his head. "A hundred demons or so is nothing compared to what will come."

"You're really boosting my morale," Sen remarked.

She had adjusted her uniform since joining him. In place of the cloak and rough bandit armor was a black and silver Champion's uniform and a red coat that fell to her thighs. Her breastplate gleamed and stuck out noticeably less than Fei's. A thin strip of tanned skin peeked out at him between her leather skirt and armored greaves.

When he didn't respond to her, Sen made another remark, "I expected there to be bigger walls here. And more summons. Kind of surprised how lightly you're taking this."

"I'm not taking it lightly." Nathan pointed to the sky. "In case you haven't noticed, this isn't our world. Building anything in here requires a lot more power from the binding stone. Given I don't know how big the invasion will be, I need to keep a stock of power in reserve for my sorcery." He shrugged. "Besides, unless I build the walls large enough, the demons will jump right over them."

"Oh. So how do we fight them?"

"To make it clear, we fight them." Nathan gestured to the two of them and grimaced at the soldiers massing below them.

"… they'll die if they fight the demons, won't they?" Sen asked, staring out at Anna's soldiers.

"In droves. They don't have the training or equipment. With enough time I'll turn them into knights capable of going toe-to-toe with demons, but for the most part it's smarter to use summons," Nathan explained.

Sen watched the soldiers prepare the catapults and ballistae for the coming invasion, while Nathan remained silent. Those soldiers who weren't manning siege weapons carried halberds. Not a single bow was in sight.

"What if they break through?" Sen asked.

"The soldiers pull back, and we fight the demons where they are," Nathan said. Sen gave him a look of disbelief. "That's why I have power in reserve. I can create more summons if necessary."

They watched for several long minutes. Demons continued to mass below them. Preparations continued.

Fei joined them. Kuda was trying to contact Vera, but having little success. The sapphire in Fei's collarbone glimmered in the soft light of the world around them.

Nathan tapped into the leylines and confirmed that they were not disrupted anymore.

"That doesn't bode well," he muttered.

"Do we need to do anything?" Fei asked.

Nathan called up a soldier and gave them an order, "Tell Kuda that the leylines aren't disrupted. He'll know what to do."

"Sir," the soldier snapped out, then ducked out of the portal.

"You have a plan for this?" Sen asked.

"Precautions, mostly. Kuda's fairly sharp."

"Sharp doesn't begin to cut it," Sen muttered. "The man doesn't need a knife to cut steak. He can use his mind."

By the time two hundred demons had gathered in the clearing, something began to happen. The air above the mound of rocks seemed to distort. Nathan saw black cracks form in mid-air, and strange gases appeared.

"Don't look directly at it," Nathan muttered.

"You've told us a thousand times," Fei said.

The world roared, and a ten-meter-high hole in the world snapped open. Nathan shifted his gaze slightly to the right. Despite this, a sharp pain built up behind his eyes and he was forced to look away completely.

He grabbed Fei and physically turned her head away. She

whined, but he had seen her ears flatten and knew she had ignored him.

The portal had opened. A tear in space that slowly oscillated between black and white, shaped like a tear drop. Bestial yelling resounded across the valley, bouncing off the cliffs. The demonic horde poured in.

"I didn't think it would hurt this much," Sen said, covering her eyes.

"It shouldn't normally." Nathan bit his lip and glanced back, covering one eye.

The horde wasn't that large. Maybe five or six hundred at most. More would arrive in time, but this was in line with expectations.

But a portal that caused this harsh of a migraine usually came with a larger horde.

In fact, they usually came with a Messenger. Nathan grimaced. Surely one wouldn't arrive this early. Kadria had dismissed his concerns, stating that no Messenger would waste their time on such a small feast.

He didn't point out the fact she seemed pretty focused on feasting on a particular part of him.

Nathan raised an arm. A hush fell over the soldiers behind him. They could see the portal and hear the demons, but not see them.

They waited for Nathan's order.

"All forces, fire at will!"

CHAPTER 23

B oulders tumbled overhead, barely visible against the darkness of the sky. They slammed into the approaching horde. The demons kept charging uphill, even as dozens of them were crushed beneath the tumbling rocks. Their war cries grew in intensity.

More demons collapsed on the front lines, ballista bolts sticking out from their chests and heads. Their brethren trampled them. The automaton ballistae let out an endless series of thunks and plinks as they fired their stream of bolts. Their mechanisms whirred noisily as they reloaded. Larger ballista bolts soared over the wall and into the enemy, spearing several demons at once.

"More of them," Sen gasped.

Another mass of demons spilled out of the portal. The tear in reality fluctuated wildly but emitted no light onto the volcanic rock surrounding it. The new demons wasted no time in summoning their weapons and joining the reckless charge toward the keep.

"Don't worry about their reinforcements. Just cast," Nathan said. "Fei, pick a group of demons and stall them. But don't let them surround you."

"Eh? I can charge into that?" Fei pointed between herself and the hundreds of demons still unharmed by the onslaught of catapults and ballistae.

"They're only regular demons. You're a monogem Champion now. Take your sapphire out for a whirl." Nathan ruffled her hair.

She stared at him for several moments. Then her tail tocked once. She nodded and leaped down from the wall. Her reckless charge toward the demons kicked up a trail of dust.

Next to Nathan, Sen ignored Fei and instead focused on her spellcasting. A pair of triangles hovered in front of her palms. Two massive orbs of fire appeared in front of each hand, each as wide as Nathan was tall.

No, not fire. Lava. The surfaces of the orbs swam with molten rock, and their interiors were more liquid than fiery.

Sen pumped her arms back and forth in a single motion and let out a "Hah!" The orbs of lava flew across the battlefield. Flames burst out from where they landed, and demons exploded into fiery glory. The lava orbs bounced. A trail of lava dripped from them, igniting demons below the orbs.

With each bounce, more demons melted and collapsed to ground as a pile of burning ash. The beasts fled from the lava oozing along the ground, fearing it. Their charge split along the path of each orb and faltered briefly. Boulders crashed into them. More demons went down. For a few brief moments, the demonic assault stumbled.

Then a roar went up from the rear lines. It rippled along the horde. Soon all the demons waved their weapons in the air, their mouths wide open and bellowing their strange language. They charged forward.

Sen held a fist in the air. A pair of squares glowed around it. She cast her fist down.

A meteor turned half of the demons into a smoking crater. Bodies flew. Many of them crashed into the cliffs and some were speared on jagged rocks. Some demons tried to crawl from the crater, their bodies still working despite missing limbs or entire chunks of flesh.

Hundreds more demons spilled forth from the portal, replacing the losses almost instantly.

"Is this normal?" Sen asked. She held her hands together, a single square appearing in front of her.

"Look at how many you're blowing apart," Nathan said. "If this wasn't normal, do you think we'd need trigem or duogem Champions?"

Sen grimaced. "Goddess. How long will this go on for?"

"This wave? Maybe fifteen minutes. The whole invasion? Hopefully just two waves. Maybe three," Nathan replied. He didn't mention that this portal felt wrong to him. The actual demonic assault had yet to surprise him, but he disliked the intensity of the portal itself.

Sen's spell activated and a jet of flame gushed forth. Every demon it touched melted, their bodies blackening instantly.

"I can't believe how little magic resistance they have," Sen mumbled.

"I told you that lower rank spells would be your bread and butter. Stick to them. You'll need to do this for a while."

On the left flank, Fei made contact with her prey. She grinned and drew her scimitar. The demons screeched at her.

A moment later, their screeches transformed into screams of panic and pain. Blue flames ate at their flesh, armor, and weapons. Fei darted into the mob of beasts, cutting a path through the hulking monsters. Those same blue flames wreathed her scimitar and coated her entire body.

When her sword touched a demon, it melted its flesh as if it were butter. Molten droplets of red and black goo pooled on the ground behind Fei. The demons collapsed into pieces. The flames around her body melted weapons before they struck her. Fists and entire arms liquefied like candle wax.

Fei spun through the demons at top speed, whirling around

with her sword. Her eyes glimmered, and she suppressed an obvious desire to laugh.

Nathan watched as the demons recoiled in fear. They tried to give her wide berth, but she danced up to them in the blink of an eye. The entire left flank became her playground. The panicking demons barely noticed the boulders and ballista bolts raining down on them.

Hopefully, she didn't get in over her head. She was using her flames at full intensity. Every swing of her scimitar sent embers flying across the battlefield that could turn a demon into a candle. She was effectively invincible against demons this weak. But the moment she ran out of power in her gem, she'd be crushed by the horde within moments.

Nathan surveyed the battlefield.

The demons slowly pushed forward despite his efforts. Countless more monsters pressed the hesitant front ranks forward, like lemmings pushing their brethren over a cliff and to their deaths.

Except these lemmings might have enough numbers to fill in the chasm beneath the cliff with corpses, thereby making the cliff safe. The demonic horde appeared to be limitless in number.

Leaping over the wall, Nathan drew his sword. A green square shimmered over his hand.

He slashed the air. A hundred meters away, the front rank of demons was sliced in two. Those behind shoved the dismembered bodies out of the way. They charged forward, their bestial faces twisted in fury.

Nathan darted forward. His sword and free hand glowed. The demons stood only meters in front of him. He flung his hands out and unleashed two blasts of wind. Armor shattered, horns crumbled, faces fell in on themselves, and a mass of demons crashed into one another.

Despite the show of power, Nathan quickly found himself surrounded. The demons kept their distance but shuffled around him in a circle. Explosions and bursts of flame disintegrated masses of demons nearby, and blue fire licked up in the distance.

Holding his fist up, Nathan cast a supercharged fourth rank spell. The demons stared at his upraised hand for a moment. Then they bellowed and charged.

Did they even understand what he was doing? Nathan didn't know or care.

Before they reached him, he unleashed his spell by opening his fist into a palm. Countless blades of wind turned every demon close to him into a gory mess.

Nathan lowered his hand and scanned the battlefield. Nothing had changed, he realized. More and more demons poured forward.

He needed a better way to hold them off. Fei would run out of power soon, and Sen was burning too much power too quickly. If the demons broke through in two places at once, or they overwhelmed someone, this invasion would become a disaster quickly.

Given Nathan worried about a nasty surprise coming later, he wanted to hold off on using the binding stone's power for as long as possible.

With a flick of his wrist, he propelled himself toward Fei with a gust of wind. His landing was rough, and he tumbled across the rough, broken ground. A jet of blue fire crashed over him.

Fei screamed, "Nathan!"

He waved off her concern. The fire clung to him and felt tingly, but didn't harm him.

"Gem abilities like yours can't hurt their own Bastion. Calm down," he said.

Fei stared at Nathan in shock, the flames dying down around her body. Behind her, the demons saw an opening and charged forward.

Clicking his tongue, Nathan darted forward. His sword shined and blew apart several demons with a gale thrust. Fei turned and melted several others, then pulled Nathan behind her.

"It's dangerous," she said. Her flames pushed the demons away. "Why are you out here?"

Nathan gave her a look, but held his tongue. He was her Bastion, not a random soldier. Did she think he was going to collapse because a mere demon got a single hit in?

Instead, he said, "I want to pull back and try something else." He cast a supercharged fourth rank spell, but held onto it.

"But I'm doing fine," Fei protested.

Demonic screeching cut off whatever else Fei was going to say. She threw an annoyed look at the intruders, before panic emerged on her face. The approaching horde was larger than before and had spread out while the pair had been distracted.

Nathan swung his sword at the ground between himself and the charging demons. Thunder rang out, and the ground shuddered. A chasm burst into existence. White light blinded Nathan as the chasm reached down to whatever lay beneath this world. The demons tried to halt their charge, but their momentum was too great.

Dozens of demons fell into the chasm. The light prevented Nathan from seeing what happened to them. From experience, he knew that he wouldn't see them again.

"Let's go," Nathan said, grabbing Fei's hand. She stared at him in shock and followed behind him for a few steps.

The ground shook again, and the chasm began to close. Demons screamed as they were crushed between the walls of earth.

Nathan and Fei didn't watch. By the time they leaped on top of the wall and rejoined Sen, the demons had already forgotten what had happened.

Not forgotten, Nathan reminded himself. The demons who saw the chasm were probably dead. Almost every one of the hundreds of beasts charging the wall was a newly spawned demon. The portal had spat them all forth in the time it took for the chasm to swallow the hundreds of their brethren.

"Fei, stay still for a second," Nathan said. He placed a finger against her sapphire and pushed power into it from the binding stone.

Fei's entire body twitched in shock. She stared at Nathan with wide eyes as he topped her up. When he withdrew his finger, her tongue lolled out of her mouth and her eyes had glazed over. She moaned softly.

"Couldn't you at least wait until after the battle to stick it in her and fill her up?" Sen said with a smirk.

"She was almost empty," Nathan said, ignoring the innuendo.

"I'm sure she was. After all, you were busy filling me up earlier." Sen rubbed her belly.

"Do you have to be so lewd?" Nathan said.

Fei blinked and came to her senses. She placed a finger against her sapphire. A satisfied sigh escaped her lips.

"Does the real thing feel that good?" she asked Sen.

Sen glared at Fei. "Why are you asking me?"

Fei tilted her head to one side. Then grinned. "Oh, right. You don't have a gem. Heh."

That had to be on purpose, Nathan thought. He decided to intervene before they began to fight each other, instead of the demonic horde that was closing in on the palisade.

"Focus," he said. "I want the two of you to follow some specific orders. If we pull this off, hopefully the demons will pull back for this wave."

Nathan hid a frown. Given how long it had been since the start of the invasion, he suspected that the second wave of demons had already attacked. The amount of demons they had killed was far too high for a single wave, but there hadn't been a noticeable gap in the assault.

"I'm going to deal with the left flank. Sen, I want you to hit anything in the center with rapid-fire spells. Force them to charge up one side of the valley," he ordered. "Fei, tell the officers to bombard the left flank as well."

"Won't that mean they'll overwhelm the wall on the right side?" Sen asked.

"That's what I want," Nathan said. "Fei, once you give out the orders, gather all the hoplites you can and stand behind the wall on the right-hand side. Once the demons break through, crush them."

Fei grinned. "Oooh. I think I get it."

"Well, I don't," Sen complained.

Nathan ruffled her hair and had his hand batted away for his efforts. "Let's go," he said.

By the time he made it to the left side of the wall, the catapult fire fell exclusively on this side. The demonic advance looked noticeably lopsided. Sen's constant flow of fireballs and flames split the enemy down the center. Fei stood in position behind the wall.

Everything looked good so far.

A pentagon appeared over Nathan's wrists, like a pair of shackles. He held his hands together in front of him, palms crossed. The pentagon glowed blue and slowly spun in a circle.

This was the most powerful spell Nathan knew how to cast without relying on the binding stone. He still wanted to save as much of the binding stone's power for later as possible. But right now, he needed more raw power than he could get with third and fourth rank spells. Even supercharged spells weren't enough. This fifth rank spell did something special.

The demons either didn't see Nathan's spell or didn't care. Boulders and bolts rained down on them. They nearly made it to the wall. Nathan heard Sen shouting at him over the din of the battle.

The pentagon flared in his hands. Nathan pressed it against the wall.

The palisade glowed. This entire half of the wall emitted an eerie blue light. A trickling sound crept into Nathan's ears. Water fell from between the gaps in the logs that comprised the wall, at first slowly, then in a tremendous rush.

Within seconds, the demons found themselves fighting waist high water rushing forward from the wall. They bellowed in surprise and waded through it.

But the water continued to rise. And it began to glow, like the wall behind it.

Soon the demons at the front were picked up by the waves and pushed back, over the heads of those behind them. Waves and the bodies of other demons crashed into the back ranks. The entire charge halted. Weapons lowered.

The demons stared at the tidal wave of water and bodies crashing down the valley. Foam frothed atop the waves, carrying countless corpses in it.

The foam was blood red. The waves shimmered with a magical blue glow.

Demons screamed as the water touched them. The waves ate at their flesh and warped their armor. They tried to flee.

But cliffs stood on one side, and a wall of fire raged on the other. There was no way out.

The tidal wave swept down the valley.

Nathan didn't know how many demons he had killed. A lot. He felt drained. Finally, he let go of the spell and the wall stopped glowing. The water lost its eerie appearance a moment later and instead turned blood red from all the demons it had killed.

A boom rose from his right. Nathan looked over to see that his plan had played out as expected. The demons crashed into the palisade and knocked down a large section of it. Dust blocked most of his view, but he saw demons vanishing into the cloud.

Not that he needed to see the action. The bestial screams and shouts told the story.

Slowly, the demons stopped charging into the cloud. They stood in place, looking lost and confused.

Sen moved her wall of fire closer to them. The demons began to move forward again.

Then Fei burst through the palisade. Her blue flames flickered forward, and dozens of demons melted. The hoplites bounded past her, their spears punching through heads and chests. Their shields shattered horns and broke arms.

Within a minute, the demonic charge became a full-blown retreat. Fei cut down many of them, but didn't pursue too far.

Hundreds upon hundreds of demons awaited her in the clearing around the portal. They stood out of range of the catapults and Sen's magic. Their weapons were raised, and they hungered for her to come too close, so they could surround her.

Fei pulled back. She waved to Nathan from beside Sen. Nathan gave her a tired wave back, still stumbling back along the wall.

"You look like you need a nap," Sen said.

Fei's ears pricked up.

"I'll be fine," Nathan said. "I used too much power. If I have to, I'll top up from the binding stone."

"Why not do it now?" Fei asked, tilting her head to one side.

The answer came in the form of a scout, who ran up to the gatehouse from behind. He saluted and came to a stop.

"Bastion!" the scout yelled. "I'm back from the other side of Gharrick Pass."

"The other side?" Fei asked, confused.

"Yes, Champion," the scout answered. "Kuda sent two of us out to Lady Nair's tower when we couldn't contact her."

"Report, soldier," Nathan ordered. He had a bad feeling about this.

"Yes, sir." The scout paused. "Lady Nair's tower is under attack by the Amica Federation. They have an entire army there. She's surrounded, sir. The pass is cut off."

CHAPTER 24

F ei and Sen stared at the scout in shock. For his part, the scout held his salute. Nathan felt that the man's gaze looked rather distant, however.

Seeing an invading army in your nation was far from comforting.

"Are any of the enemy heading our way?" Nathan asked.

"No, sir," the scout answered. He hesitated. "They seemed focused on the tower. But they had definitely lain siege to it. Both of us saw fire and other sorcery flung from the top of the tower, and a dome barrier was active over the exterior wall."

"Keep an eye on the pass," Nathan ordered. "Alternate with other scouts on a regular basis. Let me know the moment you see Federation soldiers marching toward us."

"Sir!" the scout barked. He dropped his salute and ran back into the keep.

Nathan sighed. The two women looked at him.

"You expected this?" Sen asked.

"I expected something," Nathan said. "A demonic invasion is detectable through the leylines, as is the buildup of energy. We're fighting an enemy Bastion, and he would likely move the moment he felt the portal was close to activating. That's why I wanted Vera to establish a gateway with Leopold. The old man will move against an invading army if he has a clear path, and if he doesn't need to send his Champions riding the long way across the countryside."

"Shouldn't he be moving against them regardless?" Sen said, expression darkening.

"That's what we're here for. Plus, he's holding Forselle Valley. I can't complain too much. It's not as though the Federation can oust him in the north." Nathan shrugged. "Although they may be stupid enough to try."

Speaking of stupid, Nathan turned back to the demonic horde gathered below.

The clearing swelled with the demonic mass, and the portal showed no signs of weakening. Nathan frowned and tapped into the binding stone. A quick search found what he was looking for.

"This must be the last of them," Nathan said. "The demonic energy is running low."

"So they're going to charge us en masse?" Sen asked.

Nathan nodded. "They're only weaker demons, but with their numbers they might be able to overwhelm us. At least, that's what they think."

"So we crush them here and go help Vera?" Sen looked at Nathan in disbelief. "I don't have the stamina to do that, Nathan. There's as many demons down there as we've already killed. And you look like you're about to collapse. Plus, you don't have the energy left in the binding stone to support us away from the keep."

All excellent points.

If Nathan intended to do this the normal way, that is.

Nathan nodded. "You're right. That's why we're not going to do that."

Sen stared at him. "We're leaving Vera?"

"No."

"Then what are we doing?" Sen asked, exasperated.

"Trust me, Sen." Nathan ran a hand through his hair as he thought through his next steps. "Fei and I will take the summons down the valley. I need you to follow us and hit the clearing with your sixth rank spell."

Sen's eyes widened. "Are you crazy? Ifrit hasn't taught me how to control it properly. If I cast that now—"

"You'll use up all of your remaining power. I know." Nathan looked at her. "Do it anyway."

After a lengthy pause, Sen nodded. "Okay. What next?"

"Fei covers me while I do my thing," Nathan said.

Neither woman seemed convinced.

Behind them, the soldiers readied their siege weapons for a second wave. Many of them took the opportunity to drink from canteens or sneak a quick snack. Sweat poured down most of their faces.

The valley wasn't hot, but Nathan wouldn't describe it as cool either. He considered that a positive of battling in here. Once outside, he'd be contending with the summer heat.

Nathan topped up Fei's sapphire again. Sen pointedly ignored the soft moan that slipped out of Fei, and instead meditated. No doubt she spoke with Ifrit about how to cast her sixth rank spell as quickly as possible.

Once Fei recovered from her pleasure-induced stupor, Nathan gave out orders to the officers to hold fire until given other directions. He didn't want to get hit by a boulder while trying to pull off his trick.

Then he, Fei, and Sen leaped down from the wall. The hoplites followed them, streaming out from the gate.

The valley floor appeared unmarred from the earlier battle. Whatever power sustained this place had repaired the char marks, cleaned up the piles of gore, and filled in the many craters. If Nathan hadn't seen the earlier devastation, he might think that nothing had happened here.

Sen screeched to a halt well short of the demons. She held her greatsword in front of her and a red hexagon appeared over it. The surge of power pouring into her spell flooded Nathan's senses, even though he wasn't actively using magical detection. He smelled ash and knew that Ifrit's power was about to show itself.

The hoplites fanned out. Nathan directed Fei to one side of the valley, and she vanished in a blink.

The demons jeered. The horde deafened Nathan with their cries. At least two thousand demons clustered in the clearing, brandishing weapons above their heads and screaming in their bestial language. Within moments, the monsters would begin charging uphill. They had the numbers. Something caused them to hold back, but demons weren't the cautious type.

Once Nathan crossed an invisible line, the demons charged. They spilled forth like an angry red wave.

Nathan drew his sword and slashed across their formation twice. His hand flared with magic both times. The front ranks of the demons collapsed into pieces. But the wave kept charging forward over the corpses.

Blue fire consumed the right flank of the demons. But their numbers proved enough to push through the blaze, and many of them survived long enough to reach Fei. Their bodies blistered and bubbled as they swung at her, but they fought until the end. Fei's scimitar ended their lives with swift, decisive cuts through their torsos or heads.

One demon clipped her head, and she stumbled. Three more demons were on her in an instant, their swords raised. Nathan's sword flickered.

The hoplites were there first. They slammed the demons aside with their bodies and shields. Their spears impaled the beasts and shoved them aside, and a hoplite pulled Fei up. The beastkin shook off the earlier blow, her tail shuddering from base to tip. Then she nodded to herself and gestured for the hoplites to withdraw.

Fei had a connection to Nathan's summons through the binding stone. He let her order them around and turned his attention back to the demons closest to him.

Hundreds of angry, bestial faces closed in on him.

He tapped into his binding stone and let its power flood him. The world slowed down as he entered the mental world of the binding stone. Nathan used this opportunity to check his memory for the most efficient spell he knew.

He needed every drop of power available for what came after this. The binding stone was nearly empty of power. If only Kadria had given him another month. Or three.

With the right spell in hand, Nathan slipped away from the mental world of the binding stone. Time flowed normally again. The demons roared and continued their blistering pace toward him.

Nathan pushed his sword into the ground in front of him with a small flash of power, then cast a third rank spell. A thin wall of rocks burst from the ground. He cast another third rank spell, and veins of magma began to run through the wall.

The demons were only meters away now. Part of the rock wall collapsed. Lava flooded out and onto the demons who broke through.

With one final spell, Nathan blew the wall apart. Lava, razor-sharp rocks, and blades of wind cut into the oncoming horde. The front ranks went down. Then the ranks behind them went down as they ran onto the lava and rocks. The charge faltered. The demons at the rear kept pushing forward.

A crush formed, and the demons pushed many of their kin to their deaths in the lava. The corpses mounted up, and they made a bridge.

Nathan obliterated the corpses with another surge of lava and wind. He continued to stick with third rank spells, with the occasional supercharged one. The hoplites began to throw their spears into the demons.

Eventually, the demons looked for a way around. They pushed toward Fei and found blue death in the form of being melted. The hoplites formed a shield wall and held the demons back.

A few minutes passed. War cries rose up again. The demons charged, convinced this push would work, unlike all the other ones.

It didn't. But the demons never stopped trying.

Nathan glanced back and saw Sen's hexagon glowing blindingly bright. Her crimson coat swirled around her with the force of the power she had summoned.

With a great boom, Sen cast her spell. Then all sound vanished.

The demons froze. They tried to shout, but couldn't hear themselves. They looked around in confusion.

Then one pointed behind them. Then another. Soon, all the demons turned and stared at the portal.

Or what had been the portal.

Where there had once been a gaping hole in the world, there was now a hundred-meter-tall whirling inferno of flames and fury. Orange embers flickered off the tornado. When they hit the ground, each burst into a conflagration large enough to consume a dozen demons. The tornado itself burned blazing white on the inside, and red flames licked the air around it.

The entire world seemed to shimmer with the heat from the tornado. Nathan felt himself sweat even this far away. Standing where he was, the inferno tornado made him feel as though he was standing in front of a blazing furnace. Huge plumes of smoke choked the air. His sense of smell told him that the world was turning to ash.

Huge licks of fire shot out from the base of the tornado. Every demon in the clearing turned to ash within seconds. They didn't even have time to understand what was happening before they died.

Sen flung her arm out, and the tornado moved. Every demon

screamed. For the first time since Sen had cast her tornado spell, sound returned.

Then an enormous arm of flame sprung forth from the tornado and consumed that sound. The screaming of countless demons was snuffed out in an instant.

Those that survived ran. Their eyes were filled with a primal terror. They didn't care about the lava on the ground, or the sharp rocks, or the corpses of their brethren.

The demons knew that death lay behind them. They had to fight and win, or they would all die.

Nathan's sword shimmered, and he cut down a row of demons. More charged him, frothing at the mouth. They moved faster than he thought weak demons could. The hoplites tried to hold them back, but some got through. Several blows rained down on Nathan, and he knew he'd be feeling the bruises for days.

He flexed his fist and turned every demon within fifty meters into meaty chunks. The hoplites bounded away before he finished his spell.

A waste of magic, but he needed to end this.

On the other side, Fei chased dozens of crazed demons who had made it past her. The demons ran like they were possessed. Their speed was nothing compared to Fei, and she cut them down before they reached the palisade.

The tornado continued to blaze. Sen collapsed to her knees, her breath coming out in choking sobs. The spell had a minimum casting time, and she needed to keep it running with Ifrit's obscene power draw. Her hand shook as she held it up, trying to keep the tornado from going out of control.

Demons slipped out of the portal again as Sen's control wavered. The tornado weakened and hovered high in the air.

Nathan approached the portal, ignoring the pests near it. The level of demonic energy powering the portal was low. Low enough to safely pull off what he wanted to do.

"Fei!" he shouted. He gestured for her to deal with the demons.

The beastkin charged across the battlefield, pulling the hoplites with her. She made quick work of the enemy.

Turning inward, Nathan drew on the binding stone. He drew on every ounce of energy it had available.

Then he felt his way along the leylines. He snaked his way out from keep and through Gharrick Pass. After a little while, he found the cairn beneath Vera's tower.

All leylines were connected to one another, which meant that Vera's tower was connected to his binding stone.

Nathan imprinted the route to Vera's tower in his mind. Then he gathered all of his power and began to cast a spell.

No geometric shapes appeared around his body. This was binding stone magic—a form of magic unique to Bastions. Binding stone magic didn't use the rank system of sorcery. The way that Nathan controlled the binding stone, created summons, and built his fortress used this method of magic. Bastions used the innate power of the binding stone to accomplish feats otherwise considered impossible.

Magical scientists deemed this to be manipulating reality. The ability to use a binding stone was the true hallmark of a Bastion's power.

Nathan finished his preparations and focused himself. The inferno had vanished, the last of its embers burning up in the darkness above him. Demons began pouring out of the portal again. Fei shouted something.

Ignoring all of this, Nathan cast his spell.

He connected Vera's cairn with his binding stone.

With a crack like thunder, the shimmering white and black tear in reality vanished. A blast of wind knocked everyone down in the clearing.

Nathan collapsed, and all went black.

CHAPTER 25

"Nathan!"

Nathan stirred. He thought he heard Fei shouting.

"Nathan, get up," Fei said. "Something's wrong with the portal."

A sense of deja vu struck Nathan. Part of his mind panicked. Had he sent himself back in time?

He opened his eyes and remembered where and when he was. Something was wrong with the portal because he had cast a spell on it. Fei was simply panicking.

"I feel like I got hit by a catapult," he groaned, pushing himself to his feet.

Fei yanked him up and let him lean on her. He appreciated both the help and the soft cushions pressing against him.

"Would that even hurt you?" Fei asked, eyes wide.

"Yes. Believe or not, getting hit by a gigantic flying boulder would hurt me," Nathan drawled. "You're a lot sturdier than I am, now that you have your first gem."

"Oh."

Nathan looked around.

No demons remained. The last of their remains seeped into the cracks in the ground and broke down into...

Nathan realized he didn't know what happened to the bodies of the demons in the portal. Outside, their bodies rotted and collapsed like normal. But in this strange place, something swept them away like so much garbage.

But the invasion was over. No more demons spilled from the portal. Fei and the hoplites had cleaned up the few that had remained after he cast his spell.

Where the tear in reality had stood was a much smaller hole in space, roughly the size of a large double door gate. It shined bright white and didn't shift in tone or color. Nothing walked through it.

Nathan frowned. He had hoped that somebody on the other side would notice this and save him the trouble of going to the other side.

"We have to go through," he said. He pushed himself off Fei's shoulders and stood under his own power.

His body ached. The binding stone rung in his mind, empty almost to the last drop.

How long had it been since he had pushed himself this far? When he had fought Kadria, she had destroyed the fortress and directly attacked his network of leylines and binding stones before he even had a chance to use his full power.

If anything reminded him that he had fallen in status as a Bastion, it was this feeling of impotence. He had a single binding stone, with only just enough power to repel a mildly dangerous demonic horde and pull off a nifty trick. He hadn't even fought a Messenger. Or even multiple invasions at once.

It would be a while before he reached the level of power he once held.

"Nathan? Are you alright?" Fei asked softly.

"I just pushed myself too far," he muttered. "Forgot my own limits."

"Shouldn't we pull back then? The portal is—" Fei began to say.

"No," he said. "We need to go through. We have only a few minutes before it collapses. I'll have the hoplites carry Sen back."

Sen kneeled on the ground behind them, where she had cast her tornado. She hadn't moved an inch, and her breathing was clearly labored.

But Nathan needed to push on. He strode up to this new gateway, ignoring Fei's whines about his health. Then he stepped through. Fei followed a moment later.

The white of the portal blinded him, filling his entire vision. It faded quickly. The pair had been transported to an entirely different location. Fei gripped his arm and looked around uncertainly.

"Isn't this…" Fei trailed off. Her tail rubbed against Nathan's leg.

"Vera's tower. I connected the portal to her gateway," Nathan explained.

They were on the third-highest floor of her tower, immediately below her planning room. The gateway glowed behind them, bright white. Nobody else was up here. The tower was eerily empty. Each level was doughnut shaped, with stairwells leading up and down on opposite ends and the empty center leading all the way to the bottom.

Clangs and shouts echoed from below. Nathan walked to the edge of the platform and glanced down. Fei stood behind him, her grip on his arm tightening as he got closer to the edge. She mumbled something about being careful.

Vera's armored summons clustered on the bottom floor, right at the entrance. The door had been destroyed. Spearmen wearing tan and gray uniforms pushed their way inside, but the summons held them back. Corpses piled up, and a pool of blood coated the floor.

Two levels above the fray, Vera hurled balls of fire and light at the attackers. The corpses disintegrated from her onslaught and allowed her summons to push the enemy back to the door.

"Are they trying to wear her down?" Fei asked.

"Wave tactics are pretty normal to deal with sorcerers," Nathan said. "Vera has her cairn, so she can't run out of raw power, but her stamina will run dry eventually. She'll overtax her body from casting too many spells. Then she'll either make a mistake, allowing a Champion to capture or kill her. Or she'll collapse and the fight is over."

"That's horrible," Fei said.

"Given they're using humans for the wave, yes it is." Nathan grimaced. "Usually summons are used." At least, before the war. Perhaps he had been naive in thinking that if he stopped the Empire from falling, then everything would be better.

Nathan looked for a quick way down. He only saw the staircases.

"How come I'm not tired?" Fei asked.

"I did tell you that the enhancement changes you. The binding stone makes you superhuman. That's why sorcerers often become Champions or Bastions. It's one of the few reliable ways to cast spells above sixth rank."

Nathan cursed when he didn't see a faster way down.

Suddenly, a familiar voice shouted, "You're wasting your effort, Nair."

"Sunstorm," Nathan said. "We're running out of time. Let's go."

He leaped down. Fei squawked and followed him, still holding onto his arm. Her quick reaction time allowed her to stick with him.

Despite landing in a roll, Nathan still felt the pain from dropping several stories at once. He felt the fractures and forced himself to ignore the pain blossoming along his limbs.

Fei spotted his discomfort and pulled him over her shoulder. He grimaced but used her superior strength and speed to cross to the other side of the floor.

Vera spun as they approached, her staff glowing with triangles. She stared at them in disbelief, ready to cast her spells at any moment.

"You look like you don't want to see me," Nathan said. "I have a way out. We need to go now."

"How—" Vera tried to say. She shook her head. "Forget it. I'm learning not to question how you do what you do. Lead the way."

Nathan had expected more resistance. This was her tower, after all. Her inheritance.

As they ran for the stairwell up, he glanced down and saw the enemy push through her summons. A seemingly endless wave of Federation soldiers hell-bent on breaking in and killing Vera. Their ferocity was unusual. Somebody drove them to this level of fervor.

Or maybe they thought their commander was more likely to kill them than Vera.

Either way, Nathan found the Federation soldiers unnerving. How did Vera feel after watching them die in droves just to capture her tower?

There was only one floor below the gateway when the Federation completely overwhelmed the summons. The soldiers began shouting and pointing at them. Vera flung spells in response. She looked at Nathan while biting her lip.

"Don't look at me," he said. "I burned all my energy to get here."

"I can tell," she replied.

Nathan felt something nearby. A strong power. He dropped, letting go of Fei.

A wicked short sword cut through the space where his head had been. A boot slammed into his stomach and nearly knocked him off the edge. Fei grabbed him before that happened.

Sparks flew as Sunstorm traded blows with Fei. Blue flames burst into existence.

Sunstorm vanished in a puff of shadow. Fei hoisted Nathan up.

"Keep moving," he growled, stumbling toward the gateway.

Vera looked around wildly, staff glowing with a readied spell.

A pair of shadows appeared, one racing right toward Vera. Her beam of light burst uselessly on Sunstorm's body. Vera's eyes widened, and she raised her staff.

Fei's flames disintegrated Sunstorm's shadow instantly, as if it wasn't there to begin with. Turning, the beastkin intercepted Sunstorm before she reached Nathan.

The two Champions traded blows. Fei's flames ate at Sunstorm's armor and clung to the assassin's skin.

Nathan ignored them and climbed the stairs.

"What about Fei?" Vera shouted.

"She can handle herself," he said.

Grunts and clashes of steel sounded behind them as they ran for the gateway. Nathan paused before the portal and waited.

Fei could handle herself, couldn't she?

Vera stared at the glowing white gateway. "How?"

"Don't ask. Go. I don't know how long we have," Nathan said.

Vera ran through the gateway.

Something appeared nearby. Nathan felt her.

He ducked. Blocked with his sword.

Sunstorm's sword crashed into his and bowled him over. She growled at him. Her armor and clothes had been burned away, leaving her almost naked. She was left wearing only the onyx gem in her collarbone and her black panties. Otherwise, her olive skin was on full display.

Oh, and the burn marks. Blue flames still clung to her, burning at patches of her skin and blackening them. Sunstorm was going to look like she had flown a little too close to the sun after this fight.

Fei crashed into Sunstorm before the assassin readied another attack.

Rising to his feet, Nathan yelled, "Fei, we are leaving."

Sunstorm's head snapped toward Nathan. Before she could do

anything, Fei tripped her. The beastkin darted toward Nathan. A short sword flew at Fei's back, but she spun and batted it aside.

In a puff of shadow, Sunstorm vanished and reappeared right above the gateway. She wasn't giving up, Nathan realized.

Fei hurled a jet of blue flames at the other Champion, while holding Nathan back. Sunstorm's eyes widened. She saw her defeat, no doubt.

If she blocked their way, she'd take the blast of flames head-on and would then have to fight Fei right afterward.

If she ran, then both Nathan and Fei would escape through the portal.

Sunstorm glared at Fei. The assassin ran a finger across her throat the moment before the flames reached her. Then she vanished into her shadows.

The next moment, Fei and Nathan ran through the gateway.

The hoplites and Vera stood guard on the other end. Some soldiers had wandered down as well.

Seconds passed. The gateway remained open. Nathan collapsed on the ground and allowed Fei to stroke his hair. Her tail brushed against his back. He was spent.

Nobody came through. Eventually, the gateway collapsed.

The demonic portal didn't reappear. Over the course of the next several minutes, the black sky regained its color and the light from below turned purple again. The monochrome world they had fought the demons in turned back into a hellscape. Everybody cheered.

Nathan rose to his feet and stumbled back up to the palisade. The soldiers who had come down to see what had happened followed him back. When he stood atop the wall, the remaining defenders watched him in eager anticipation.

He held up his sword and cheered. The soldiers joined in, saluting and throwing their hands into the air.

They had won their first victory.

Nathan left out that they needed to win another. The Federation was coming. But for now, they deserved to celebrate.

CHAPTER 26

"Have you gone insane?" Kadria screeched.

"Given I'm standing in a void talking to a demonic Messenger? Maybe," Nathan said. He crossed his arms.

Kadria paced back and forth in her strange void world. He had visited her immediately after the invasion. The fact that his binding stone was empty concerned him, and there was an incoming enemy army. He doubted she'd help, but maybe he'd get lucky.

Instead, she shouted his ear off the moment he walked in. Nathan looked around.

This place seemed larger somehow. More palatial. Nathan didn't keep track of the furnishings, but he swore there were a few more.

And the room was definitely larger, and not in the mind-bending way. The outline of a rug shifted as Kadria padded back and forth, her bare feet tugging at fibers Nathan couldn't see.

Was she leeching off the binding stone to feather her own nest? Nathan shook the thought away. He didn't have the time right now to concern himself with Kadria. And a slightly larger bedroom for the Messenger was the least of his worries.

"Funny. You'll find yourself enslaved in somebody else's void if you keep pulling stunts like that," Kadria growled. Her eyes flashed.

Nathan noticed that her pupils had enlarged, giving her the appearance of having almost solid red eyes. Her horns had blackened as well. Gone was the Messenger who lusted after his crotch. In her place was a genuine demonic general.

Kadria terrified him right now. He hid the shudders she sent down his spine, but he knew he'd be having nightmares about this.

If she had shown up with this appearance when they first met, he'd never have accepted her deal.

"What's that supposed to mean?" he asked quietly.

"What do you think it means?"

He paused and thought about it. "You said I didn't need to worry about Messengers yet. That the portal was too small to concern them."

Kadria rolled her eyes. "Are you stupid? There must be a Messenger behind every portal. Who do you think creates the things? Do you think those armies of hulking musclebrains are traversing transdimensional space by themselves?"

"What?" Nathan blurted out. "Hold on, but you said—"

"I said that a Messenger wouldn't come through the portal." Kadria ran her hand over her face and glared at Nathan. "Look. Why do you think the portals get worse the more you suppress them? Shouldn't it be the opposite? Use your brain. I turned up when I did because I was looking for competence. I found it, at the end of everything, in a world that had defeated so many other Messengers."

Nathan felt like the world had been ripped out from underneath him. "Other Messengers are doing the same thing you are?"

"Not exactly," Kadria hedged, her tone uneasy. "I can't be too specific. Not yet."

"Why not? We seem to be in this together. Or aren't we?"

Kadria rolled her eyes. "We are. And we'll both be very, very dead if I say the wrong thing at the wrong time. You probably won't understand this, but let's just say that the walls have ears."

Nathan pointedly looked at the closest wall. It didn't appear to have an ear, or the outline of anything at all on it. Kadria kicked him.

"God, you people are stupid," she muttered.

"You mean goddess," Nathan corrected automatically, hiding a grin. He had successfully taunted her.

"Sure." Kadria waved a hand. "In any case, each Messenger has its own goal. They're looking for things. But you know what I know every Messenger wants? Servants. Useful servants. Servants who can manipulate portals using binding stones, which is a power I thought unique to Messengers. Where did you even learn to do that?" Kadria snapped, growing irritable.

A lull fell over the room. Nathan rubbed the bridge of his nose while Kadria huffed and puffed at him.

Then Kadria coughed and straightened herself up. Not that there was much for her to straighten up, given her lack of attire.

"Sorry," she mumbled. "But you Bastions tend to be so terrible at working with your binding stones. Where did you learn to manipulate a demonic portal?"

Nathan frowned. "It was something that an old comrade of mine worked on in my timeline. His theory only really worked on weaker portals, because the power necessary to close a portal is equal to the demonic energy leftover. Plus, closing a portal early will trigger a cascade."

"But you've used it before?" Kadria asked.

"I've tested it on weaker portals." Nathan shrugged. "And my comrade used it in an evacuation once. That's when we learned the spell caused cascades. For what little it mattered at that point. Trafaumh was already a ruin by the time he closed the portal, so creating a bunch of new demonic portals there was a drop in the bucket."

Kadria clicked her tongue. "Just another oddity of your world, I suppose. So many little things drew me there."

Her mutterings continued for several minutes. Nathan didn't pick up anything of particular value from them and eventually grew bored.

"If you didn't notice what we did in my timeline, why does it matter here?" Nathan asked.

"Because this world isn't a maelstrom of death, destruction, and despair?" she asked rhetorically, looking at him as if he were an idiot. Which had been her default look for most of this visit, to be truthful.

"That makes a difference to Messengers?"

"A big difference," Kadria said. She placed one hand high in the air and moved it up and down like a fish. "In your world, large invasions, cascades, trigem Champions, and entire countries being destroyed were normal. A Messenger knew your world was serious business, which attracted major players such as myself. But the individual events don't stand out."

Kadria lowered her hand, and her motions became slower, but much more deliberate. Like waves, Nathan realized. She was making a wave pattern with her hand.

"In this world, the level of activity is far lower. Fewer large invasions, very few cascades, and only the Kurai Peninsula has been destroyed. So every big event stands out."

Nathan licked his lips. "So by converting the demonic portal into a gateway like that, I made a big wave in a small pond?"

"Exactly. And the Messenger behind this portal definitely noticed." Kadria scowled. "And those twins aren't the sort I wanted you to attract. They're the slow burn type. I figured you'd have a year or two before they took an interest in you, then you could flirt for a while before they took you seriously. By which point I could deal with them."

"You know them?"

"Unfortunately." She poked her horns, which had turned back

to their typical shade of creamy white. "Same breed of Messenger." She prodded his crotch with her foot. "In a few ways. Although they don't have my background, and my objective differs from theirs."

Nathan left the void room shortly afterward, with a mumbling from Kadria about how she'd think of some way to help deal with the other Messengers.

She offered no help for his current predicament and instead gave him a look that suggested he needed to dig his own way out.

As much as he wanted to complain, knowing that he had inadvertently attracted the attention of a pair of Messengers bothered him. He welcomed Kadria's help, even if she would be busy for a while.

It ate at him that he didn't question help from a Messenger. Had he really fallen so far that he accepted Kadria's presence in his life? Part of him even felt unhappy that she hadn't pulled down his pants when he had visited.

Nathan shook off his discomfort and left his office. He stopped by a window. The night was moonless and overcast. He couldn't see anything outside, other than the lamps on the walls and lights carried by patrolling guards.

The civilian inhabitants of the fortress surely knew something was wrong. First the soldiers had all piled into the keep, which was a surefire sign of a demonic invasion. Then the men had all come out and cracked open barrels of ale and wine.

At some point after the commotion had started, the tavern opened. People who couldn't sleep, or spouses worried about their significant other in the guards had gathered to wait there. Then the soldiers joined them. The celebrations were ongoing, and Nathan could hear their raucous cheering.

But some guards patrolled the walls, and more than a few had noticed that the scouts were busy. Keen-eyed officers ushered their troops into the barracks and began closing up the kegs. Only a few had been briefed, but word spread fast. All the officers would learn the full details when their companies were back in the barracks.

Nathan wasn't too concerned about the celebrations. He doubted he would need his soldiers at the crack of dawn, so any hangovers could be dealt with.

Although he had to remind himself that these soldiers were relatively green. He was used to men and women who could win a battle, knock back their booze into the early hours of the morning, have a quick nap, and then fight another battle as soon as they woke up.

Kadria was right: this timeline had yet to turn into a pit of despair and destruction. The soldiers had yet to train themselves into boozy warriors. Maybe they wouldn't need to.

Nathan stepped away from the window and made his way downstairs. Few guards patrolled the keep at this time. Those that did saluted him as he passed them.

Eventually, he spotted who he was looking for. Anna and Vera stood outside of one of the receiving rooms.

"We've known each other for years. Once Leopold is here—" Anna tried to say.

"If Leopold comes here," Vera interrupted. "I appreciate your concern, Anna, but I lost my tower due to my own failings. And given Leopold's general inaction, I doubt he'll be saving me from my own missteps anytime soon."

"Don't say that, Vera. Vera!" Anna shouted after the retreating sorceress. She let out a huff when Vera continued to walk away in the opposite direction that Nathan came from.

"I'm assuming she's taking the loss of her tower hard," Nathan muttered.

Anna turned to face him and curtsied. "Bastion Nathan. My deepest thanks for providing me safe harbor during this time of crisis."

Nathan stared at her.

She rolled her eyes. "Goddess, you're really not one for

formalities, are you? The least I can do is thank you for protecting me. From the sounds of it, the Federation means business."

"They do. They have a Champion whose gem ability allows her to specialize in assassination," Nathan said. He nodded in the direction that Vera had retreated. "So, she's taking it hard?"

"Why don't we take a seat and have some tea?" Anna suggested and walked into the nearby room. "I think talking about Vera is the least we need to cover. I hear you used so much magic that you nearly collapsed?"

Nathan followed her inside. Hopefully, this turned out to be a friendly chat, and not an interrogation.

Anna straightened out her skirt before sitting down. Her clothes were much simpler than normal, consisting of a frilly collared shirt, a black pleated skirt, and stockings. No jewelry and minimal sign of makeup. Not that Anna needed much.

Then again, it was past midnight and Nathan had sent a message to Anna to travel here as quickly as possible. If she had arrived in her nightgown, he wouldn't have batted an eye. Instead, she had put in at least some effort to appear like a countess.

Two empty cups sat on the table in the middle of the room. Like most of the receiving rooms in the fortress, this one consisted of several plush sofa chairs around a single coffee table. This particular coffee table had the universal emblem of the Watcher Omria engraved into the glass. In the corner sat a long table where coffee and snacks could be prepared.

Kuda stepped out from that corner with two fresh cups of coffee, then whisked away the empty ones.

"Thank you, Kuda," Anna said with a smile. She fixed Nathan with a glare. "I'm regretting lending him to you. I haven't had a good coffee since he left."

"You were here not that long ago," Nathan replied.

"Then I haven't had a good coffee in my manor since he left," Anna corrected. "Maybe I should move in."

"Right now, you don't have a choice, so feel free to assess your new lodgings against your manor," Nathan said drily.

Anna shot him a sardonic smile. He didn't grace it with a response and instead sipped his coffee.

After a few moments, Anna raised the topic from earlier, "Yes, Vera is upset over her tower. More than that, she's upset that she defended it alone. No reinforcements from the Empire. Nothing from Leopold. Nothing from me." Anna grimaced. "You had demons to deal with, so you get a pass. But I don't, even though most of my private army is partying outside and calling themselves demon slayers."

Suppressing a sigh, Anna drained her cup and asked for another. Kuda was already there and exchanged the cups. A slice of chocolate cake appeared from somewhere as well. Nathan eyed the beastkin, wondering where he hid the dessert. The table behind Kuda was bare, besides a coffee percolator powered by a built-in fire enchantment and a handful of empty cups and plates.

"I don't blame her for being upset, but I don't see it being productive," Anna said.

"Give her time," Nathan said. "I pulled her out of the fire. She's still processing things."

"I would, if we had time." Anna bit her lip. "And if you didn't need her. I'm supposed to be the countess who supports you, but the distinct impression I get from my officers is that…" she trailed off, her eyes wandering to a corner of the room.

Nathan waited patiently for her to finish her thought, or for her to change the subject.

Anna sighed. "I find it difficult to believe that I am, in any way, your superior. My officers told me how the battle played out. They stood behind a wall, unable to see the enemy, and fired catapult shot after catapult shot into the distance. By contrast, you and your Champions flooded the portal, defended a breach in the wall, created a tornado made of fire, and still found time to save Vera."

"That's normal in demonic invasions. There's a reason trigem Champions become legends," Nathan said. "The gap between ordinary humans and Champions is significant."

"Of course. But where does that leave me?" Anna raised an eyebrow. "I can gain the wealth and power that my father felt our family deserved, but all I'm doing to earn it is asking you nicely. I felt that my agreement with Vera would help you, as she would assist you, but she's been less than cooperative."

"You asked for my help precisely because she wasn't cooperative," Nathan pointed out. "Besides, she did help me out."

"And now you've sacrificed a lot to save her. Probably more than she'll ever give you in return." Anna fixed him with her gaze. "Don't lie to me. The soldiers said that Fei practically had to carry you up to the wall. Vera even admitted you couldn't fight when you helped her. What happens if the Federation arrives here in the morning?"

Nathan finished his cup and placed it on the table. Unlike with Anna's coffee, Kuda didn't instantly whisk his away for a refill.

"Let's lay this on the table then," Nathan said, his tone serious. "First, the Federation probably won't march on this fortress straight away. They have no way of knowing that we've been seriously weakened by the demonic invasion. What they do know is that we showed up in Vera's tower despite that invasion. A normal Bastion would assume that means I crushed the invasion without any real difficulty and play it cautiously."

Anna nodded, her eyes bright and expression focused.

Nathan continued while raising two fingers, "Second, even if they do show up, the fortress is well fortified. The barrier will prevent any siege weapons or Champions from knocking down the walls easily. The ditches, walls, and your soldiers—yes, that means you are helping—can keep any non-magical assailants at bay."

Raising a third finger, he said, "Third, it won't take long to recover my power. I'll have enough to top Fei up in the morning.

Once Vera is feeling better, she can help defend. Most of my summons survived the demonic invasion, so I don't need to waste power recreating them. And although Sen's tired, she should be fine in the morning. Even I'll be able to fight. The binding stone is low on power, but I can use my own sorcery."

Anna took a bite of her cake while the explanation soaked in, her gaze wandering. Kuda placed another cup of coffee in front of Nathan. Noticeably, there was no cake for him.

"Sen's the name of the bandit girl you took in, right?" Anna asked.

"You met her last time you were here," Nathan said.

"Mmm," Anna said. She sipped her coffee. "I have two questions about that. More, really, but two for now."

Nathan had expected this to come at some point.

"If she had the power to use such powerful magic before, why didn't she use it against you? Or against me?" Anna frowned. "You seemed to capture her far too easily, and I don't remember Vera mentioning anything about any tornadoes of flame."

Nathan coughed. "Actually, Sen tried to cast that spell both times we met her."

"What?"

"Yes. Fortunately, a sixth rank spell takes too long to cast in a normal battle to be usable without proper support, so she never succeeded. But she tried," Nathan explained.

Anna stared at him, her cup frozen in front of her lips. "You mean when you fought her in front of Trantia the day after you arrived, she—"

Nathan nodded.

Slowly, Anna placed her cup on the table. It shook as she let it go, and Anna quickly placed her hands together in her lap. Kuda's eyes narrowed, and his tail moved for the first time since Nathan had met him.

"I believe I owe you an additional thank you, Bastion," Anna said, her voice flat.

"I just—"

"Do not blow this off," Anna snapped. She froze, closed her eyes, and schooled her expression. "Thank you for preventing Trantia from being turned into an ashen wasteland. The description of the power of her spell made a strong impression on my officers. They believed that she must have been holding back as a bandit." Anna rubbed her face. "Goddess, how did you even recruit her? And don't say it's due to your skill in bed."

Nathan loudly slurped his coffee. This earned him a glare, and he grinned at Anna.

"Fine, keep your secrets," she muttered. "Although I can't believe both she and Jafeila are both interested in you. They'll tear you apart once they find out."

"You think they don't know?" Nathan laughed.

"This is funny to you?" Anna asked incredulously.

Nathan blinked, realizing she was serious. And even a little angry. He glanced at Kuda, who shook his head.

"You don't know much about beastkin, do you?" Nathan said.

"Don't patronize me."

"I'm not. But I'm used to people at least knowing that beastkin are polyamorous," Nathan explained.

Anna looked at him blankly, then she turned her head to face Kuda and raised a questioning eyebrow.

Kuda coughed. "It means that we willing to share our partners. In both the sexual and romantic senses of the word, mistress."

"Sexual," Anna repeated.

"Yes. Different races of beastkin have different preferences, but it is a common trait across our entire species," Kuda explained. "Hence young Jafeila's willingness to pursue Bastion Nathan, even though he is romantically and sexually involved with Sen."

Anna faced Nathan again, her cheeks flushed. "I don't remember Sen being a beastkin."

"There's a concept for this sort of thing happening with

Bastions," Nathan said, feeling sheepish. "The beastkin don't care about the feelings of the humans. This means the human Champions get caught up in the flow of the beastkin Champions."

This was exactly what happened between Nathan and Vala. Vala had been his first Champion in Falmir, and his bond with her had been strong.

Except the beastkin he picked up in the ruins of the Empire didn't really care. They saw Nathan as a strong mate, their Bastion, and ripe for sharing. Vala could push back, but the beastkin didn't play along.

Or even if they did, something invariably happened that broke everything down. The animalistic traits of the beastkin caused some unique sexual problems at times. Vala eventually gave up and let the beastkin join her, and that opened the floodgates.

"I don't remember reading anything like this," Anna mumbled. "And a lot of legendary Bastions don't sleep with all of their Champions like Leopold does."

"The Empire has the largest proportion of beastkin Champions of any nation. It comes with the territory," Nathan said.

"You could say no?" Anna suggested.

Nathan loudly slurped his coffee and ignored Anna's glare.

"Fine," she said, and stood up. Then she mumbled, "Something to keep in mind for the future, I suppose."

"Did you say something?" Nathan asked.

"Yes, but you don't need to worry about it for now." Anna smiled. "Good night, Nathan. I suppose I'll see you in the morning. Or the afternoon, if nobody invades. I wouldn't mind some additional sleep."

Kuda looked unimpressed at the idea of Anna sleeping in until the afternoon. Nathan got the distinct impression that Anna's dream of staying in bed would not come to fruition.

With this conversation over, Nathan slipped away. He made his way to his bedroom. The hallways were silent. Everybody was asleep, save for a few patrolling guards. The celebration outside had ended. Despite all of this, Nathan felt wide awake.

The knowledge of an impending battle pumped adrenaline through his body. His nerves seared his body like fire, and it took everything he had to move calmly.

Maybe this was also a side-effect of using too much magic. Nathan usually kept his calm better, but he felt on edge. His years of experience didn't help him tonight.

He pushed open the door to his room.

"Oh, you're finally back," Fei chirped from his bed.

CHAPTER 27

Fei lay on top of Nathan's bed, her arms wrapped around his pillow. Her body was pressed into the soft fabric, hiding much of her body. He noticed that her hair was messy, probably because she had been rubbing her face against his pillow.

He also noticed that she was naked save for one of his jackets. Her bushy tail was the only thing hiding the tantalizing curves of her bare ass. Fei held as much attraction to him now as she had in his timeline.

"You realize I have to sleep on that, right?" Nathan said, pointing at his bed.

Fei rubbed her face against his pillow and wiggled her entire body from side to side. "All the more reason for me to do this."

The room smelled more of Fei than Nathan at this point. How long had she been in here, he wondered. Her uniform was strewn across the floor, and his used clothes hamper had been rifled through.

"Bad kitten," Nathan said as he sat on the edge of the bed.

He scratched behind Fei's cat ears. She mewled, arching her back. Her eyes curved as she looked up at him and grinned.

"You seem to like it when I'm bad," Fei purred.

The beastkin shifted her body to the side so that she was

pressing her bare legs against him. Her heat poured into him. She licked her lips and rubbed her tail against his back.

Nathan remembered her words from before the battle and realized that Fei was following through. Her arousal was practically dripping onto the bed. She had proven herself and wanted to claim her prize.

"Aren't you tired after the battle?" Nathan asked gently. He ruffled her hair.

Fei shook her head. "I'm fine. And I know you are too." She grinned.

Rather than fine, Nathan would describe Fei as running on fumes. Her eyes were lidded and flickered shut every few seconds. Her ears twitched constantly. She purred incessantly, but her tail rubbed against his back at inconsistent intervals.

She was tired, but knew what she wanted.

"You like it here?" Nathan asked.

"Mmm," Fei mumbled. "It's so much nicer than my village. I get more food, and it's far better. You're nicer than the meisters ever were and let me decide what I want to do. I never thought I'd actually become a Champion. A lot of the other beastkin taken into the academy were sent back to their villages. I was told that most Champions-in-training never receive an enhancement."

She rubbed her face into his pillow. A few seconds later, she came up for air.

"But you made me your Champion right away. You believed in me," Fei said, her green eyes bright and watery. "My instincts have been screaming at me to do so many things to you, but I've known that I needed to prove myself to you."

Nathan blinked. "Instincts?"

Fei grinned at him, her face lewd. She reached behind herself with a hand. Her fingers came up sticky. "Instincts. I'm a beastkin. I want a mate. I'm of age. If I hadn't been taken to the academy, I'd probably have found somebody in my village by now. But I know they wouldn't be anywhere near as good as you. Sen doesn't get it. You probably don't either."

Nathan rubbed her head again. She purred, and he listened closely. The sound was happy. Genuinely happy.

He did get it. He simply hadn't realized Fei had fallen this hard for him.

The Fei he had known had been more stand-offish. Wary. Her experiences with war, Bastions, and humans in general had led her to take a slower approach with him. Wooing her had taken time, and her declaration that he was her mate been a hesitant one. As if admitting it would cause him to disappear. He had never probed the Jafeila from his timeline about what had happened in the past to make her so careful.

Now he wished he had. Had she fallen head over heels for her first Bastion, only to lose him and become heart-broken?

Fei mewled, and Nathan realized it didn't matter.

The Fei in front of him was the real Fei. Right now, he could only touch, feel, and hear one Jafeila, and she was the beastkin rubbing against him in his bedroom.

Nathan shut away his worries and thoughts relating to the Jafeila from his timeline. He didn't forget her, but he did his best to stop actively comparing this Fei to the version he had known. He wanted to make this Fei happy.

A moan rose within Fei's throat as Nathan ran his hand along her taut ass. Her tail wagged. She felt slick to the touch, and Nathan realized this was sweat, rather than arousal.

"Why don't we clean up first," Nathan whispered in Fei's ear. It twitched, tickling his face.

"Don't we do that after?" Fei said with wide eyes.

"We can do both."

Nathan began to strip off outside the bathroom, as if to lure Fei over to him. She stared with wide eyes as more of his skin showed. When his cock popped out, already half-erect, she nearly panted.

Fei bounced off the bed and flung off the jacket. Her breasts jiggled from the movement. Nathan noticed the slickness of her thighs, and the small wet patch on the bed.

As he led her into the shower, Fei became handsy. Her fingers played with his length and she gasped as he began to grow.

She yelped when the shower's cold water splashed over her. Then glared at him.

"We are cleaning up, you realize," he said.

She rolled her eyes, then kneeled in front of him. He admired her plump, naked body. Her voluptuous curves were on show, and she rubbed her hands over her massive breasts with a grin. His eyes wandered lower. He took in her thick, fleshy thighs and the hint of pink he saw between them.

"I'm your mate. I'll do the cleaning my way," she said, interrupting his thoughts.

"Really? I haven't said that you're my mate," Nathan teased.

Her tongue lapped up the liquid dripping from him. She eyed him. "Maybe. But I'm still your mate. I'm your first Champion, so I get to be your mate."

"What about Sen?"

"What about her?" Fei huffed and pumped his length. "I was here first. She can join in if she wants."

Nathan held back a laugh and ruffled her hair. Fei grinned and continued to harden him up. Her eyes widened.

"You're a little bigger than I expected," she mumbled.

"Keep going," he said.

She licked and suckled at his length, her eyes wide. He held her head gently while warm water beat down on the two of them. Her fingers worked beneath her, and he heard her moans around his length.

Slowly, she built up a rhythm. Her head bobbed back and forth. Her tongue lapped up every drop it could. He felt her throat coiling around him, and the pressure of her mouth pleasured him.

Her eyes stared up at his face, lidded but focused. She

watched for every movement he made and adjusted her movements to match. Everything Fei did was to please Nathan. Her fingers moved faster the happier she thought he was, and she moaned harder and longer in response to his groans.

Nathan gently pushed her toward his groin. She responded by taking him all the way. Her eyes snapped wide open when he flooded her stomach. When he pulled out of her mouth with a pop, she followed, her tongue lapping up the beads of white that dripped out.

"We need to clean up, you know," he chided, trying to pull her upright.

She grumbled but let him pull her up. Then he slid her fingers inside her and she smiled like an idiot, leaning against him. She bucked and heaved as she climaxed from his attention, her juices pouring down her legs.

Once out of the shower, Fei dried the two of them off. She stopped him from grabbing a towel and helping, hissing all the while. Her eyes lingered on his erection, which hadn't wavered.

"Is that normal?" she asked.

"Consider it part of the package," Nathan said. Evidently, Kadria's magic still worked.

He led Fei back to the bed. The exhaustion was setting in and he collapsed on the bed. Fei gave him a kiss, their tongues entwining repeatedly for several minutes. She moaned and pressed her body against his. Her hand rubbed his cock.

"You can't go to sleep yet," she said with a smile.

Fei pulled Nathan up. Then she positioned herself on all fours and thrust her ass into the air. Her fingers ensured she was ready, and Nathan smelled her raw arousal in the air.

He pressed himself against her entrance. Fei moaned. His hands sank into her ass while her tail brushed against his chest.

Then he hilted himself in her. Fei sank her head into the mattress, muffling her sweet moans. Although he waited before moving, Nathan found it unnecessary. Fei bucked her hips against his within moments, begging him to start thrusting.

The two fell into a pleasant rhythm. He knew her weak points and preferred speed. She rewarded him by covering his balls and both of their thighs with her juices. The smacking of his body into her ass filled the room as he pushed them both toward climax.

Fei screamed first. Her insides tightened around Nathan as she climaxed. She quivered and moaned, her tongue lolling out on the bed. Nathan didn't slow, and she mewled in pleasure. Her insides contracted around him. She wanted to extract everything from him.

Moments later, he made her his mate for real. He reached his peak and emptied himself. When he slipped out of her, not a drop escaped. The greedy girl. Her fingers rubbed against her entrance, as if to check that she hadn't lost any of her prize.

"More?" she mewled, her eyes wide and watery.

"In the morning?" Nathan gasped out. He was truly exhausted. He collapsed on the bed.

Fei ignored him. She straddled him and slipped him inside of her. "You're still so big and hard."

It was in this moment that Nathan realized the true purpose of Kadria's magic, and the danger it posed to him. If he never grew soft from exhaustion, then his women would never think he was spent.

The physical stimulation kept him awake for hours as Fei rode herself to sleep. She was a very happy beastkin.

CHAPTER 28

As Nathan predicted, the Federation didn't lay siege the next day. Or even the day after.

Three days after the demonic invasion, the Federation rolled up through Gharrick Pass. Innumerable orange banners fluttered in the sky, each bearing the emblem of the Amica Federation. The army destroyed the abandoned checkpoint and defenses at the end of the pass.

"There's a lot more of them than I thought there'd be," Anna said. She stood on top of the outer wall, along with Nathan, Vera, and the others. All of them watched the Federation army encamp.

Anna shivered and held her arms around her body, rubbing her sides vigorously. The day was overcast, and a chill wind blew from the west.

The weather hadn't improved over the past few days. Nathan wondered if it might rain soon. The idea certainly didn't warm the hearts of the besiegers.

Nathan removed his jacket and placed it over Anna's shoulders. She shot him a smile. The sight of her huddling beneath his jacket warmed him. Which was good, because nothing else was.

"You're going to get a chill," Sen admonished him.

"I'll be fine," he said. "And this isn't that large of an army. I expected more."

"Really? For an attack on Gharrick Pass?" Anna asked.

"The Amica Federation is invading the Anfang Empire. This may be the boonies, but it's still part of one of the greatest nations on Doumahr." Nathan shook his head. "I don't have the slightest clue what they're up to. I know the Federation has more soldiers than this on its western front. Where's their Bastion? I've only spotted two Champions, and maybe a single sorcerer."

"Two?" Anna frowned.

Fei chimed in. "The one with the onyx. Sunstorm, I think?" Sen nodded at Fei, and Fei continued, "Plus there's one with an amethyst. She looked human as well."

"Isn't that bad?" Vera said. "They have two monogem Champions. You have one."

"Hey!" Sen said. "I can give as good as any Champion."

Vera eyed Sen, but said nothing.

Nathan ignored the bickering. For her part, Anna took his lead and gestured for him to continue.

"If this is all the Federation can spare, then even if they win, they can't hold the fortress." Nathan stuck his thumb over his shoulder and pointed at the keep. "Without a Bastion, they can't claim the binding stone. Once reinforcements arrive, the Empire will reclaim the pass and this will have been a colossal waste of time, resources, and Champions. To say nothing of the political goodwill between the Empire and Federation."

Nathan frowned. He wondered whether that was Leopold's plan right now. The Bastion promised to send reinforcements, but they had yet to arrive. A duogem Champion could win this battle almost single-handedly, but Leopold hadn't sent one. Was he busy, or waiting to see if Nathan won the battle for him?

Because the Empire would win this war no matter what. With the demonic portal suppressed, the danger of the Empire's collapse had passed. And Leopold knew that the Federation had committed heresy in their invasion attempt. He held all the cards.

"I want to say you have a good poker face, Nathan, but you make a much scarier face when you're thinking about the bigger picture," Anna said. She poked Nathan's cheek. Fei squawked at the sight.

"Do I?" he asked.

"Your jaw locks, your eyes go distant, your nostrils flare, and you seem to exude a much more serious and mature atmosphere," Anna explained. She smiled lightly. "It's cute. I like it."

"You promised you wouldn't call me cute again," Nathan said. "In any case, this army is still worrisome. But it doesn't contain any nasty surprises, such as a duogem Champion or an enemy Bastion. They must be busy elsewhere."

"Like Forselle Valley?" Vera asked.

"They'd have to be supremely arrogant, and supremely stupid, to attack both Gharrick Pass and Forselle Valley at the same time," Nathan said.

"Maybe it's your lucky day."

Nathan laughed bitterly. "Maybe. I'd prefer my lucky day to be the day when this army attacks, personally."

The Federation erected trebuchets to bombard the walls. The stones they launched shattered on the barrier powered by the binding stone. Nathan had set one up a couple of weeks ago, and it projected a dome across the entire fortress, including the exterior ditches.

Next, a sorcerer wearing bright orange robes led nearly a hundred magic users in battle robes to the front of the encampment. The magic users began glowing. They held their palms in front of them, chanting nonsense. At the front, the sorcerer waved his arms about. Eventually, a pentagon appeared around the sorcerer's body.

"What is that?" Sen asked.

"He's fueling his spell with the power of other magic users,"

Nathan explained. "Most sorcerers struggle to cast anything above fourth rank spells. I basically exhaust myself with fifth rank spells unless I use the binding stone or a leyline. That's why sorcerers typically use a cairn."

"Why doesn't he use the leyline then? That's what Ifrit is teaching me to tap into."

Nathan raised an eyebrow. "Let's say you're in enemy territory. Your enemy has complete control over all the resources and weapons. You're running low on supplies. You decide to steal one of his weapons. What do you think happens when you try to use it against him?"

"I don't follow," Sen said, furrowing her brow.

Nathan sighed. "I control the leyline here, Sen. I'm the Bastion. If he taps into the leyline, I make him go pop."

"Oh. Shit."

"Yep. This close together, the leyline and binding stone are essentially the same thing. Think of the binding stone as a super cairn, and I own it. It grants me power, but it can run out. But at least I can stop others from using it. Sorcerers can't quite do the same with cairns, although they can set up traps," Nathan explained.

"Wait, so I'm tapping into your energy reserve when I use the leyline here?" Sen asked.

"More or less."

"Isn't that bad?"

Nathan laughed. "Don't take this the wrong way, but the amount of energy I use from the binding stone is orders of magnitude higher than anything you and Fei use. Bastions are horribly inefficient. I can top Fei up ten times for the price of a single supercharged fourth rank spell. That's why Bastions use Champions and possession. We kind of suck at this fighting thing."

"You flooded the portal by yourself," Sen pointed out.

"And nearly collapsed from the effort." He physically pointed at her. "Meanwhile, you wiped out basically every demon at once with a single spell. I took out a fraction of what you did, for the same effort. And once you're used to Ifrit's power, you'll be able to dip into my reserves and do it time and time again. But I won't. Not to the same degree."

Sen nodded.

Outside the wall, the Federation sorcerer continued to cast his fifth rank spell. Slowly but surely, he prepared something that would probably destroy the barrier.

"Um, shouldn't we do something?" Sen asked. She put a hand on the greatsword slung over her shoulder.

"Feel free. I thought Fei was going to run in while we talked, but maybe she's napping. Or having her tail fluffed by a guard." Nathan shrugged.

"As if she'll let anybody touch her tail other than you. She nearly bit my hand off this morning when I brushed it in bed." Sen rolled her eyes. "Um, what rank of spell?"

"You know what rank," Nathan drawled. "Don't even think about sixth rank."

"But—"

"If you lose control of it, then you're as likely to take out the fortress as the enemy army. You're still tired from the demonic invasion. Plus, there are two Champions in the enemy army, and an enemy sorcerer. They'll detect your spell and may counter it. Don't waste time on high rank spells until you're more talented." Nathan bonked her on the head. "Or else you'll end up like this sorcerer is going to."

Sen grumbled and cast a supercharged fourth rank spell. A meteor shot down from the sky within seconds.

The sorcerer reacted quickly, dropping his own spell. The magic users behind him weren't as fast. While the Federation sorcerer threw up a glowing barrier, his subordinates stared at him like idiots.

Then most of them died, as the meteor hit the ground and turned their formation into a crater. The sorcerer's barrier held, although he looked winded. He dropped to his knees. A handful of magic users remained. They stared at the remains of their comrades, stupefied.

Sen flung bolts of fire at the sorcerer. He protected himself with a wall of earth. It shattered after a few hits, and superheated chunks of earth exploded everywhere. The few remaining magic users went down screaming from the shrapnel.

"He got away," Sen said, lowering her hands.

A tunnel lay where the sorcerer had been. He had dug his way out during the commotion.

"The magic users were expendable to him," Nathan said. "We'll need to get him in the battle. I doubt he'll expose himself like that again."

Rain fell that night. Nathan kept an eye on the Federation from his office.

He had supplies to last a month. If the Federation took too long, then Leopold would arrive and break the siege. Or maybe the Federation would send reinforcements. He didn't know.

But he did know that he gained more strength with each passing day. The binding stone's power restored itself from the leylines, and Nathan became a fighting force again. The Federation couldn't starve him out, and they likely knew it.

But what he really wanted from this battle was to capture Sunstorm. He didn't know who the amethyst monogem was, and he didn't care. She was a Champion that he would defeat in order to win this battle.

But he would capture Sunstorm.

Two more uneventful days passed. The enemy built ladders in their camp. A large battering ram slowly formed into being, with a huge steel cap waiting nearby. The Federation soldiers had brought it through the pass with them, but were busy harvesting the wood for the frame from the nearby forest.

The ditch prevented rams from getting close to the walls, but the main gate had flat land in front of it for obvious reasons. It remained one of the few weak points in the fortress.

Eventually, the mud cleared after that single night of rain. The sun beamed down. The Federation army lined up outside the fortress. Ladders, trebuchets, and the enormous steel-capped battering ram menaced from a distance.

Nathan stood in a tower on the outer wall. Sen and Fei were next to him. His defenders took up positions across the walls, manning ballistae and mangonels. This was a conventional siege, so their training would be of far more use here.

Many of the ladders would reach the walls. The soldiers would fight them off and protect the civilians.

Anna holed up in the keep. Kuda and a handful of hoplites protected her.

The rest of the hoplites protected the keep. Initially, Nathan had planned to send them out and harass the enemy army as they charged. But he didn't have the numbers, and two enemy Champions would make short work of his summons.

Instead, he wanted a defensive force for the keep. Sunstorm might try to sneak in and assassinate Anna, or try something related to the binding stone or portal.

As a precaution, Nathan had sealed the gate to the portal with an additional spell. The entrance to the lower levels had been sealed as well. Only he, Fei, and Sen could get down there now. Not even the summons had access, as he worried that Sunstorm would just carry one down there by force.

Rocks crashed into the barrier. Nathan's thoughts returned to the battlefield.

The Federation soldiers jeered from a distance. Minutes passed. Rock after useless rock exploded on the barrier.

"Fei, would you join Vera on the walls," Nathan said.

"Eh? Why?" she asked.

"There's two enemy Champions. There's a good chance they'll try to pick us off one by one," he explained. "It's better if we're in pairs. You can hold them back long enough if they both attack Vera, at least until me and Sen arrive."

Fei smiled and gave an enthusiastic nod. "Of course. I'll be off then." She darted in and gave him a kiss on the cheek, then leaped out of the tower.

Sen grumbled at the show of affection. "You let her get away with so much."

"You can do the same, you know." Nathan tugged at his gloves. Nothing much was happening yet, so he kept himself entertained with small talk.

"I'm beginning to realize I have to," Sen said. "She may as well not even have her own bedroom, given she spends every night in yours. Does she even use her own clothes?"

"Her uniform?" Nathan offered.

"Sure, but other than that? She steals your worn clothes to wear when off-duty and to sleep in." Sen grumbled.

"You seem upset."

"Not really." Sen crossed her arms. "Maybe a little. We sparred last night, to see who got to wake you up each morning. I lost every round, and she took pity on me and let me share anyway."

Nathan ran a hand over his face to hide his grin. "That wasn't smart."

"I know that now," Sen grumbled. "She's so damn fast. And those flames of hers consume my magic. They're so unfair! What kind of monogem ability are they?"

"The sort that lasts about five to ten minutes under heavy use?" Nathan explained.

Sen blinked.

"Fei's ability is more of a bodyguard ability," Nathan said. "If she's away from me for too long, she'll become less useful. Most Champions have abilities that are less power hungry, so they can operate away from their Bastion or a binding stone for long periods of time."

"So there's a trade-off to some gem abilities," Sen said.

"There's a trade-off to everything a Champion gets from a gem. Fei has a powerful gem ability, but she's weaker than most monogem Champions when not actively using it. And an amethyst or diamond Champion can fight several battles without needing to refill their gem."

In truth, Nathan had misgivings about Fei's sapphire. But he had told himself not to worry about who she had been in his time-line, so he let things go. He told himself that he could adjust her sapphire if necessary. She was going to become a trigem Champion, so there was plenty of room to tweak her future abilities to make her well-rounded.

Shouts rippled along the walls. Nathan looked down to see the mangonels and ballistae begin firing. The Federation soldiers crossed the field. They pushed large wooden shields in front of them, and the frames were mounted on wheels—these were known as mantlets. Behind them came the ram and companies of soldiers carrying ladders.

Nathan scratched his chin. It all seemed like a lot of work for the Federation to put in.

"Sen, light them up," he ordered.

"Seems a bit mean, doesn't it," she said, but raised her arms anyway.

"Last time I checked, they're invading us. They didn't even pay the toll."

"Rude," Sen chirped. A pair of squares hovered in front of her palms.

This was why Nathan didn't worry too much about the siege weapons. In a battle between Champions and Bastions, a conventional army didn't matter. Sen's spells would light the field ablaze. Some ladders would make it to the walls, probably because of the interference of the Federation sorcerer. But not enough to let the Federation's numerical advantage matter.

Nathan felt something in the corner of the tower. He spun and spotted the ball of shadow.

"Down," he yelled. He tackled Sen.

Sunstorm burst into the room. Her eyes screamed murder at Nathan. She looked around wildly, searching for something.

Or someone.

"She's not here," she muttered. Her gaze fixed on Nathan, who stood back up.

"You'll do," Sunstorm said. She pointed her sword at him. "It won't matter if Lilac gets the catgirl's head, if I can give yours to Master Theus."

CHAPTER 29

"You seem angry. Any particular reason?" Nathan asked the woman trying to decapitate him.

Sunstorm growled at him. Her eyes flickered around the tower as she assessed her surroundings.

"I see you replaced your uniform. A shame. You looked better without it," Nathan said. He shifted his sword across his body.

"Do you think that you can give yourself an advantage with words?" Sunstorm retorted. She twirled her swords.

Sen remained behind Nathan. The ladder to the lower level of the tower was in the center, and they needed to get past Sunstorm to use it.

Not that they would. Climbing down a ladder with a blood-thirsty Champion trying to murder him was a terrible idea. Nathan struggled to imagine dumber ways to die right now.

"You're an assassin, aren't you?" Nathan asked.

Sunstorm blinked. "What makes you think that?"

"Onyx gems aren't used by front-line fighters. Teleportation, shadow doubles, the ability to hide in shadow, to create shadows: your gem ability is flexible, and screams assassin. Especially because none of it helps you hit harder." Nathan kept a close eye on the corners of the tower, but saw no shadows. "You're good with your swords, but that's about it. So what else could you be?"

Sunstorm's hazel eyes bore into him. "You seem to know a lot about my abilities given we've fought twice."

"I'm observant," Nathan quipped.

Hopefully, she wouldn't look too deeply. Or assumed he had some other means to know about her abilities. If she escaped again—which was a real possibility given her gem—then she could spread some damaging rumors about him.

"Evidently." Sunstorm twirled her swords again. She showed no sign of aggression. For whatever reason, she was content to hold the two here.

The reason was obvious.

If Sunstorm hadn't interrupted Nathan and Sen when she had, then Sen would have ended this assault before it started. Her spells would obliterate the Federation siege engines.

Nathan hoped that Vera might be able to do some of the heavy lifting. Unfortunately, he heard an ominous crackling sound in the distance. From experience, he recognized that as the sound of spells countering one another in mid-air. Evidently the Federation sorcerer was talented at counter-spells. No wonder he had survived Sen's onslaught.

Nathan found himself torn. Did he continue to stall and hope that Fei arrived, allowing him to capture Sunstorm easily? Or did he send Sen out to deal with the attackers and try to pin Sunstorm down, hoping that he had enough power in the binding stone to weather her assault?

"You seem a little overconfident in your abilities if you think you can defeat both of us," Nathan said.

"I'd say that you seem a little overconfident in the allegiance of your newfound ally," Sunstorm said. She nodded her head at Sen.

A moment passed.

Then another moment.

Sunstorm frowned. "Are... Are you serious, Sen?"

"Um, did you expect me to do something?" Sen asked.

"You were supposed to stab him in the back!"

"Why?" Sen sounded genuinely confused. She looked between Nathan and Sunstorm.

"We're allies! Friends! I promised that I would find you a place in a sorcery school in the Federation. We…" Sunstorm's face turns red, and she glares at Nathan. Her voice dropped to an inaudible mumble.

"Sorry, didn't catch that," Nathan said.

"I don't want you to hear it," Sunstorm growled.

"Um, I didn't hear it either," Sen said. "But I'm pretty sure she's talking about the time I had sex with her."

"What?" Nathan asked.

"Don't say it out loud," Sunstorm screeched.

Sunstorm froze for several moments, then pointed her sword at Nathan. Her breathing deepened, and she bared her teeth.

"Look, just stab him, light his body on fire, and we can go back to how things were. He's wide open," Sunstorm said. "This will all be over, and I can give you the future that I promised you in the Federation."

Sen's eyebrows shot up. "Yeah, I don't think I'll do that. I'll make a similar offer to you, though. Nathan's a lot more attractive than this Theus guy you talked about."

Sunstorm smirked. "No."

"Ouch. That was a fast rejection," Nathan said. He knew he wasn't exactly a model, but was this Theus guy really that attractive?

Not that it mattered, he supposed.

Nathan glanced over his shoulder. The Federation had breached the walls. The fighting was sporadic, but there was a noticeable number of tan and gray uniforms fighting his soldiers. No sign of Fei yet.

He had to assume that meant that this Lilac had engaged her.

"Err, he's a lot smarter?" Sen tried.

"... I have to give you that one," Sunstorm muttered. "But it's not much of a competition. The Federation is still the superior choice, Sen. Didn't you tell me about how the Empire ignored you and your friends? The Federation would have given Derek and everybody else a chance."

"Derek's dead," Sen said flatly. "And Nathan's different."

"Nathan killed Derek," Sunstorm pointed out.

"And he's offering me a future far greater than anything you can. Anything that your Theus can. You can have the same thing," Sen said.

Sunstorm sighed. She scratched the back of her head with the pommel of one of her swords.

"I can only imagine what sweet words you've told her," Sunstorm said. "Or perhaps you are more than you seem."

"Wow. I expected you to try to stab me," Nathan said.

"Sen isn't the first person I've met who seemed unduly impressed with you. A good assassin needs to judge her targets wisely. I'll be sure to mount your head on an appropriately sized board and make it the centerpiece of the room it's in." Sunstorm twirled her swords again.

Stalling over, Nathan assumed.

Fei still hadn't appeared. He had to assume that the other Federation Champion was keeping her busy.

The Federation's choice of tactics surprised him. Splitting up their Champions was the opposite of what he would do. Then again, Sunstorm had believed that Sen would help her.

A puff of shadow signaled the start of the battle. Nathan spun, triangles shimmering into existence over his hands. He grabbed Sen and pushed her toward the ladder. Above him, Sunstorm appeared, swords arcing toward his head.

Nathan's spells fired off, and blades of wind deflected her swords. Nathan thrust upward. Sunstorm narrowly caught his blade between her chest and arm, but she was still falling.

Stepping back, Nathan let go of his sword. His hand flashed as he pointed it at the location that Sunstorm would hit the ground. His wind blast blew Sunstorm to literal pieces.

Tiny puffs of shadow floated in the air where Sunstorm's shadow decoy had been destroyed. Nathan's sword clanked on the stone floor, bouncing several times. Nathan cursed, and nearly bit his tongue off as Sunstorm kicked him square in the jaw.

The glint of metal caught his eye, and Nathan snapped his arm up to catch her sword before she took his head off. Flames overtook his vision. They cleared a moment later, leaving a charred Sunstorm staring at Sen in disbelief.

"Don't light me on fire!" Sunstorm shouted.

"I feel you misunderstood our conversation," Sen said.

"... You really prefer him over me?" Sunstorm muttered, her eyes widening.

Nathan saw the moment Sunstorm's heart broke. It wasn't a pretty sight.

The assassin's fists tightened around her swords. Nathan worried that the threads of her gloves were going to explode. They looked awfully stretched by how tightly Sunstorm gripped her sword hilts.

"I won't let you kill him. If you won't join him, then I have no choice," Sen said. "This is a war. You chose your side. I chose mine."

Sunstorm grimaced. "I wish I could be angry. I should be angry. I don't know what you've done to her, Bastion—"

"Nathan," he said.

"... I know your name," Sunstorm said. Her eyes bore into his again. "Do you actually care for her? Or is she your puppet, like I suspect she is?"

"Does my answer matter to you? I feel like you've made up your mind." Nathan couldn't deny that Sunstorm's opinion of him hurt. He cared for her, even if she hated him right now.

"Hmph. True," Sunstorm grunted out. "In the end, I suppose we can only determine this with swords and magic. If you're half the Bastion you appear to be, then Sen's fate will be in your hands. If you're the lucky charlatan I think you are, then I'll take her back and give her the life she deserves."

Nathan felt that Sunstorm was being a little fatalistic, but that was natural for her.

Before Sunstorm moved, Sen hit her with another blast of fire. Sunstorm shouted something about it being "unfair," but Nathan didn't care.

He grabbed Sen by the waist and leaped from the tower. They soared through the air. Soldiers scurried about on the wall below them. Not all of them wore Empire uniforms.

Nathan's body glowed as he pumped magic into his muscles. He crash-landed on top of several Federation soldiers. They screamed as his magically empowered legs shattered their bones. Sen's flames obliterated the rest.

A battle raged around them. Thousands of Federation soldiers charged the walls, climbing across ditches and hiding behind the wooden mantlets they brought with them. A familiar crackling sound filled the air. Vera and the Federation sorcerer were still going at it, countering each other's spells, and neither had found an edge.

Stones pummeled the Federation soldiers. Arrows and crossbow bolts pierced them. Ballistae pinned them to the ground. A handful of magic users from Anna's private guard unleashed what little firepower they could, and lit fires along the front of the walls.

Hot oil poured down the ladders, knocking soldiers off and sending them screaming to a painful death below. The oil stuck to the wood, making the climb even more difficult for future climbers as their hands slipped and the oil dripped onto their skin. Immediately after, the defenders threw down hot sand. It burned faces, slipped between armor, and stuck to the oil on the ladders.

But the sheer number of ladders was too much. The Federation climbed the walls. The fighting had thickened, and Nathan had dropped right into it.

Elsewhere, the ram crept up to the gate. Ear-shattering booms resounded throughout the fortress as its enormous steel cap slammed into the reinforced gate.

"Get back here!" Sunstorm screamed from the top of the tower. She vanished into the shadows of the tower. Within moments, she would be down here with them.

An arc of blue fire in the distance caught Nathan's attention.

Fei fought with another woman, only a few years older than she was. Lilac, Nathan assumed from the amethyst.

Lilac had the same olive skin and dark hair that Sunstorm did. Another Champion from the Kurai Peninsula, he realized. The Federation had taken in many people from the Kurai Peninsula after its invasion by demons decades ago.

The duel should have been short, in Nathan's opinion. Lilac moved quickly, and her blows were strong. She knocked Fei's scimitar aside with her curved longsword—Nathan had been told by Narime and Sunstorm that it was called a katana. But Lilac couldn't follow through on her blows for one simple reason.

Fei's flames would turn her into ash.

Pieces of Lilac's lacquered wooden armor bubbled and peeled. Fei hurled flames with every swing and dodged backward rather than press the attack. She knew that Lilac was stronger and faster, but it didn't matter. The difference wasn't enough for Lilac to strike a killing blow. The amethyst Champion grit her teeth and swung her sword countless times, scoring scratches and glancing blows. None of them made a difference as her armor peeled away.

Then it happened. Fei held back an attack. No flames swept out from her sword as her scimitar swept high above Lilac's head. She darted back and raised her guard, but the damage was done.

Lilac glanced behind her and saw the Empire soldiers. They kept their distance from the dueling Champions, but were desperately fighting against Federation soldiers.

With a grin, Lilac darted into the melee taking place on the wall. Fei followed with a shout. Empire soldiers dropped like flies as Lilac's sword cut them to pieces.

Even when Fei caught up, she didn't use her flames. Couldn't use her flames. If she did, she'd burn her comrades to death instantly. Lilac deflected Fei's weakened blows and slashed at her with renewed vigor. Blood streamed from Fei's chest as she took deeper wounds.

Lilac retreated every time the Empire soldiers thinned. She knew that her victory depended on being surrounded by human shields.

And Fei had to follow, or Lilac would slaughter the defenseless soldiers.

Nathan cursed. Lilac had stumbled upon a powerful tactic. Fei didn't yet have the control over her ability or experience to easily defeat Lilac in this situation. Now his defenses crumbled, while Fei bled out.

"Sen," he snapped.

"On it," Sen said, raising her arms and casting a fourth rank spell.

Sunstorm appeared behind them. Nathan stepped between her and Sen.

"You don't need to bother," Sunstorm said. "The more Sen focuses on Lilac, the happier I am. I can cut off your head while she's preoccupied."

"Um," Sen said, eyes wide.

"Help Fei," Nathan snapped.

Sen blasted off a wall of flames on the wall near Lilac. The amethyst Champion froze mid-step, finding herself cut off. A pair of fireballs soon followed, but were deflected by Lilac's katana.

Right as Fei closed, Lilac ducked, spun, and leaped at Fei. Fei's eyes widened. She'd left her guard open, not expecting this move from Lilac.

Lilac's sword slid straight through Fei's chest. The two Champions struggled for a moment, each using their strength enhancements to push against the other on the wall. Sen screamed, raising her arms and about to cast a desperate spell.

Nathan slapped her hands down. "Don't! You'll hurt Fei."

Eyes wide and bloodshot, Fei grabbed Lilac's hands. Lilac grinned in return and refused to let Fei pull the sword out. As an amethyst Champion, Lilac had the strength advantage in spades.

"Idiot," Sunstorm muttered. She shook her head. "That duel is already over."

Fei grinned. Lilac blinked in surprise.

Then Fei's entire body exploded in blue fire. Several seconds of blistering agony for Lilac passed before she realized she needed to pull her sword free from Fei's chest. She tried, but Fei held her in place.

Lilac must have wondered why she couldn't overpower Fei. The truth lay in the blue flames. They consumed magic, and the strength enchantment of her amethyst ran through her body. Her body that was being eaten away by the fire melting her hands.

With a vicious headbutt, Fei knocked Lilac to the ground. Both Champions vanished below the parapets. Lilac's screams echoed across the battlefield.

Every soldier nearby stopped fighting. They stared in horrified fascination. Many witnessed the death of a Champion for the first time in their lives. In their minds, they witnessed history.

Not long after, Fei rose. Alone. The katana slid free from her body. Nathan saw the ashen remains of Lilac's hands blow away into the distance, still holding the sword even in death. Blood oozed down Fei's uniform and armor from over a dozen gashes. One of her cat ears bled. She looked around, then picked up her scimitar.

The Federation soldiers dropped their weapons. Many tried to run and descend the ladders. They shouted to retreat to those still climbing. Within minutes, what had looked like the beginning of a crushing defeat for Nathan turned into a decisive victory.

Hundreds of Federation soldiers fled across the field toward their encampment. More ran into the pass, as if already prepared for the loss and didn't want to risk being caught by vengeful Champions.

"Care to surrender, Sunstorm?" Nathan offered the Federation Champion.

After a long, hard look at Sen, Sunstorm threw down her swords. They clattered noisily on the stone.

Nathan blinked. "Can't say I expected that."

CHAPTER 30

Squeals and hisses emanated from the keep's infirmary. Fei tensed and her tail stood on end. Her eyes watered as she stared at Nathan, who watched from the door with crossed arms.

"The more you move, the more it will hurt," Vera chided.

She applied a glowing hand to the wound in Fei's chest. The hole no longer gaped, but the surrounding flesh had swollen. Blood streaked with the water that Vera applied regularly. A large bruise had appeared around it, discoloring Fei's skin and making her naked chest a little less appealing to look at right now.

"I'm a Champion," Fei whined. She hissed as Vera touched her wound and the flesh seared from the magic. Her tail shot bolt upright. Fei continued, her lip quivering, "Can't I let the magic of the enhancement heal me naturally?"

"That magic is the only reason you're still alive," Nathan said. "You have a punctured lung, a high level of blood loss, and one of your tendons has been slashed."

Fei's jaw dropped. She looked at Vera for confirmation, and the sorceress nodded grimly.

"Normally, I would have given you a very different type of spell and moved on to a patient that I had a chance of saving," Vera said. "I rarely see people complaining when half of their veins have emptied out on the ground and their lung is pulling in more blood than air."

"Oh." Fei's voice was nearly inaudible.

"Let Vera take care of you, then get some rest. When the adrenaline wears off, the exhaustion will hit you like a battering ram. You'll sleep like a log," Nathan said.

"Will you visit me?" Fei asked.

"I'll try to be here when you wake up," Nathan promised.

Fei's ears twitched happily, and her tail swished a few times. Then Vera continued to cauterize the wound, and Fei returned to whining.

As Nathan stepped outside, Vera's voice stopped him.

"Are you sure you can trust her?" she called out.

He looked back in and saw that Vera was busy treating Fei. A rhetorical question, in other words.

Standing outside the room was the subject of Vera's question. Sunstorm stood in silence, a shimmering collar around her neck. Her hands and legs were shackled. The restraints prevented her from using her enhancement and gem ability, as there was no way to outright remove the onyx without killing her.

Sen stood next to Sunstorm and looked annoyed. Evidently, she had failed to strike up a conversation with her apparent lover. Former lover.

Nathan didn't know what to make of the revelation. Sunstorm and Sen had never shown any inclination toward sexual relations toward each other, or even toward other women at all. This was entirely new to him, and it had apparently happened before he had arrived in this world. He was thrown for a loop.

Gesturing for them to follow him, he made his way to his office. The sun shined outside. The assault had been relatively brief, and there was plenty of daylight left to clean up. Nathan even had almost all the power from the binding stone left to repair what little damage the keep had sustained. By tomorrow, much of this would be a memory.

Except the casualties. Unfortunately, the binding stone couldn't be used to heal wounds, other than powering his own healing sorcery. Living things were outside his area of expertise. He hadn't understood how Kadria used it to affect his body.

"I didn't expect you to surrender, Sunstorm," Nathan said, repeating a comment he had made several times, to no response. "With your ability, you could have escaped in a heartbeat."

Several moments passed.

Then Sunstorm said, "I want to see for myself what is so impressive about you. Sen has joined you. You turned that catgirl from a greenhorn into a terrifying warrior within weeks. And you terrify the Federation."

Nathan's eyebrows shot up, and he stopped in the middle of a staircase. He looked down at Sunstorm. Her face was impassive.

"Terrify them?" he asked.

"You should have been swept aside here," Sunstorm said. "Instead, I was sent to confirm their fears. You turned up in Nair's tower when you could not possibly have had the resources or time to do so, given you were being assaulted by demons. Even your intervention in the leylines disturbed them, for reasons I don't understand."

"If you were sent here to confirm that I am incredibly danger-ous, shouldn't you have retreated then?" Nathan said. He began walking again.

"Theus will need a scapegoat for his failures. If he had been wise, he would have accepted the advice to focus his efforts here," Sunstorm said, her voice turning bitter.

"Advice from who?"

Sunstorm didn't answer.

Nathan sighed. "I assume that means he actually did attack Forselle Valley at the same time."

Sen giggled. "Didn't you say something about how only some-body really dumb and arrogant would do that?"

"Sounds like our Theus fits the profile." Nathan looked at Sunstorm.

She smirked and looked away.

"I'll take that as a yes," Nathan said. "And that arrogance prevents him from taking advice from those with more experience in warfare. It's an unfortunate problem with many Bastions. The power can get to our heads, and because we make the decisions, we forget that our Champions often have years or sometimes decades of experience on us."

Nathan's original master called it "big dick syndrome." Male Bastions made up the vast majority of Bastions, and they often had sex with their Champions. As such, it was common that they thought with their crotch, and didn't value the opinions of their women.

The original advice that Nathan had received to avoid this had been to avoid having sex with women he wanted to retain as advisers or strategists. That would have worked if said women had respected that advice. Instead, he chose a different path, which was to remember that the trigem mystic fox sharing his bed had been a duogem Champion before he had even been born.

It occurred to Nathan that Narime was in the Federation right now. The fact that the Federation was making these mistakes despite the presence of her wisdom made him realize that many people didn't particularly care about not repeating the mistakes of the past.

"You don't talk like a new Bastion," Sunstorm noted.

"I have a lot more life experience than your average Bastion," Nathan said. "I also note that you didn't say 'Master Theus' this time."

Sunstorm grimaced. "If he doesn't have a place for me, then he's useless to me. He's not worthy of the title."

"Is that all your loyalty is worth? A trade of your skills for the protection of a superior?" Nathan probed.

"Fuck you," Sunstorm spat. "You don't know me. I trade my

talents as a Champion and assassin because they have a known value. Every head I hand my master is proof that I am of value to him, and therefore I get food and shelter for another day. But you're some pompous Bastion from a noble house. You live off the teat of your beloved Empire. If you make a mistake, then somebody will cover up for you."

"If I make a mistake, I'll be dead," Nathan said flatly. "In case you didn't notice, no reinforcements came to help me. Even though you took your sweet time to arrive and assault the fortress. A duogem Champion could have arrived from a nearby fortress any day and swept you all aside, but that didn't happen."

Sunstorm shifted uncomfortably. "That doesn't change the fact that I have to prove my worth. You were given it."

"Maybe. Or maybe that's because you're letting people like Theus tell you how to behave," Nathan replied.

"Don't pretend like you know me," Sunstorm mumbled.

The three of them stepped into Nathan's office. The black door sat at the back. As always, only he saw it. Sen opened her mouth to say something, then looked at Nathan.

"Um, do you want me to help?" Sen asked Nathan.

"Help with what?" Sunstorm growled.

"You'll understand," Sen said gently. "Trust me." She held out a hand.

Sunstorm eyed Sen warily. Her guard dropped, and she smiled back at Sen. Their hands entwined, and they pressed their foreheads together.

Nathan coughed. The two ignored him, gazing into each other's eyes.

"I'll talk to Sunstorm alone," Nathan said. "It'll be easier this way."

Mostly because he didn't know how Sen would react to seeing Kadria again. She didn't remember anything about her encounter with the Messenger, but he didn't want to risk her freaking out.

"Okay," Sen said. She stepped away from Sunstorm. "Remember: Trust me."

Sunstorm nodded. "Fine. I'll trust you." She glared at Nathan. "But not you."

"I don't think you understand what she's asking you to do," Nathan said wryly.

His words passed through Sunstorm's ears to no effect. She leaned toward Sen and held her arms out, her hands still bound. Sen gave Sunstorm a quick hug, but nothing more. Then Sen ducked out of the room.

The disappointment on Sunstorm's face was tangible. Nathan felt his own mood falling just from looking at her.

"If you behave, then you'll be unbound and with her in a little while," Nathan said.

"You're a little too confident in your ability to persuade me," Sunstorm said.

Nathan led her to the room at the back of the office. He confirmed that it was unlocked. Sometimes he couldn't open it.

One time he had opened it, only for it to slam in his face and nearly break his nose. He hadn't seen what Kadria had been doing in her strange void space, but sometimes his curiosity kept him up at night.

Sunstorm stared at him as he walked through a wall—at least from her perspective. He tugged her, and she followed. Surprisingly, she didn't gasp when she entered the void.

She did stare wide-eyed at the Messenger lounging on the bed, however.

Kadria was reading a book. A tome, really. Nathan wanted to compare the thickness of the book to Kadria's chest, but that would require Kadria to actually have one. Suffice it to say, the book could be dropped from a great height and kill somebody.

The lettering on the front of the book was unfamiliar to Nathan. Strangely cursive, and clearly in the form of visual shapes. They vaguely reminded him of the characters that Narime wrote in, but were very different.

"... I know what that is," Sunstorm said after a lengthy pause, her eyes fixed on Kadria. She looked back at Nathan, who placed a hand on her shoulder.

Nathan expected a scream, a shout, or some form of struggling.

Instead, Sunstorm frowned and looked around.

"Are we inside the binding stone?" she asked.

"This isn't the reaction I expected," Nathan said. "You're certainly full of surprises. And no, we're not in the binding stone." At least, he didn't think so.

"Inside the binding stone?" Kadria repeated. She cackled, kicking her legs into the air. Her face remained buried in her book. "The theories you people come up with about the binding stones and leylines are always amusing."

"Then what is this place, Messenger?" Sunstorm said, her brow furrowing.

"My home away from home," Kadria said. Her book vanished, and she straightened up. Nathan noticed that her clothing was askew. The moment he thought that, Kadria tidied herself up.

"That's not an answer," Sunstorm said.

"It's as good an answer as you're going to get. This is my demesne. My little playpen. Eventually it will be ready for a public viewing, but for now it's only for VIPs and their lovely guests." Kadria smirked. "Give yourself a clap that Nathan cares enough about you that you get to be invited. Clap, clap, clap."

Kadria clapped her hands in time to her voice.

Neither Sunstorm nor Nathan joined in.

Sunstorm looked at Nathan. "You care about me?"

"I do," he said. "I know who you are. I even know your true name, Choe."

Sunstorm leaped away from him. Or tried to. The shackles around her feet caused her to trip. She nearly slammed into the floor, but the room shrunk in an instant and Kadria caught her. A moment later, the room returned to normal. Sunstorm and Kadria shot across the room, the assassin held in Kadria's arms.

"Let go of me," Sunstorm shrieked. Kadria tightened her grip around Sunstorm's arms. "I don't know what foul demonic magic the two of you are using, but you won't fool me like you fooled Sen."

Nathan frowned. "It's not magic. You told me your true name yourself, Choe."

"Stop calling me that! I haven't told a single person my name since I left Kurai. Not since—" Sunstorm choked up and looked away.

"Since demons killed your parents in the evacuation," Nathan finished.

She stared at him. Her body slackened. "How... No. Why?"

"I said I care for you. I mean it."

"I have no reason to believe you," Sunstorm muttered.

Running a hand through his hair, Nathan wished that he had an easy way to make her believe him. In the end, he had no choice but to rely on Kadria to remind them of who and what he was.

Kadria smirked at him when he looked at her. "Care to pay the price and have her remember you?"

"Remember?" Sunstorm mumbled.

"That's right. You once loved him so much that you begged him to do things to you no other man ever will," Kadria said. "Or at least, a version of you did."

"I don't like men," Sunstorm said.

Kadria blinked. She ran a finger along Sunstorm's head. In response, Sunstorm's eyelids fluttered and her pupils dilated.

"Huh. What a fun little variation," Kadria mumbled. "Well, no matter. Once you have the emotions, trust, and other mumbo jumbo of your other self, you'll think of Nathan the same way you think of women. Except, you know, he can give you hot, gooey injections."

"I'd rather be dead than let a man touch me with his thing," Sunstorm growled.

"Let's see if you say that in a minute." Kadria laughed.

Before Sunstorm could respond, Kadria placed a hand on the assassin's jaw. Just as happened to Sen, Sunstorm fell silent and her body fell slack in Kadria's lap.

When Kadria was finished, she pulled her hand away. Sunstorm blinked several times. Her gaze fixed on Nathan and she took a deep breath.

"Nathan," she breathed out.

"Choe. Feeling better?" he asked.

"A little," she said. "Give me a minute to process this."

"That's boring," Kadria said. "Where's the emotional reunion? The crying? The kiss? At least tell me what you think about receiving a fat, gooey injection from Nathan?"

Sunstorm glared at Kadria. She looked back at Nathan. "Can I cut her head off? Please?"

Nathan shrugged. "Does your head grow back, Kadria? You'd make a magnificent prize to impress Leopold with."

"Fuck you," Kadria spat, baring her teeth at him. "Make your threats when you have somebody else who can bring back your lovesick puppies."

She certainly took that joke well, Nathan thought.

Nathan coughed. "It's good to have you back, Choe."

"It's good to be back. Even if I appear to have threatened you more times than I care to remember," Sunstorm said with a wince. She rubbed her head. "There was something I wanted to tell you. I can't remember what it was. Strange. I know I could remember it only minutes ago."

Kadria grinned, her eyes practically shining in the void. Nathan pinned her with his gaze, and she tried to look innocent.

"What did you do?" he asked.

"Made things more interesting," she said.

"You made her forget things?"

"Only one particular thing. When the time is right, it will come back. But I don't want her spoiling the show." Kadria giggled. "Think of this like the spice that producers add to an episode to keep the viewers interested."

Nathan and Sunstorm stared at Kadria in confusion.

The Messenger sighed. "I suppose you wouldn't understand that analogy. How about this, then: I'm bored. After a while, you get boring if you win all the time. Plus, I want to make sure that you're winning because you're competent. You have so many advantages. Knowledge of the future because I brought you here. My help in bringing your former lovers to your side. Stress relief from chatting with me. Regular cleaning out of your pipes, courtesy of yours truly. The least you can do is use your brain from time to time."

"Do you genuinely believe that all of my advantages are due to you?" Nathan asked.

"Who else would they be due to?" Kadria watched him, eager for him to bite at her bait.

He chose not to.

"Fine, be that way," Kadria said with a pout. Then she grinned and threw Sunstorm onto the bed. The assassin shrieked. "Now it's time for my payment!"

Kadria crawled on top of Sunstorm. Fingers ran along thighs, and lips kissed skin. Sunstorm moaned under the attention from Kadria. When the assassin spotted Nathan's focus, her face lit up like a tomato and she futilely fought back against her assailant.

"How cute," Kadria mumbled against Sunstorm's neck.

Something entirely different captured Nathan's thoughts.

Kadria's bronzed, plump ass wiggled in the air. Her bangles clinked against each other as she moved against Sunstorm, and the translucent silk strips of cloth attached to her hips waved about. But what really drew Nathan's attention was the tiny strip of black cloth that barely covered her entrances. It stuck so tightly to Kadria's body that Nathan didn't need to imagine what lay underneath.

Nathan ran a finger along Kadria's rear. She gasped in response, but didn't stop moving.

He peeled away the black cloth that Kadria wore as clothing. There was nothing underneath, confirming that Kadria walked around in her underwear.

Nathan stroked Kadria's lower body. When she looked back at him, her eyes were glazed over in pleasure. He rubbed her again, causing her honey to drip down between Sunstorm's legs. Her tongue lolled out of her mouth.

"You're supposed to do that to her," Kadria muttered, her voice oozing with pleasure.

"Do you want me to stop?" Nathan asked.

Kadria didn't respond. She laid her head against Sunstorm's chest and stared at him. He continued to pleasure her, while ignoring Sunstorm's plaintive looks for attention.

Eventually, Kadria's hips bucked as she reached her climax. Nathan maintained his pace. His hand was slick by the time she collapsed against Sunstorm, and she stared into space.

"You seem new to this," Nathan pointed out.

Kadria glared at him. Then, without warning, she vanished with a pop.

Looking around, Nathan realized this wasn't invisibility. Kadria had teleported away or left through some other means. Clearly she hadn't appreciated being the one on the receiving end, even if it was clear that she enjoyed the new experience.

"Nathan, my turn," Sunstorm begged.

He grinned and slipped his fingers into her.

When he finished, and plenty of white flowed out of Sunstorm onto the bed, Nathan let her cuddle up against him.

He suddenly noticed something moving at the foot of the bed. Or someone. He glanced down to see a shimmering shape between Sunstorm's legs. Kadria.

"Enjoying yourself down there?" Nathan asked.

Kadria melted into existence. Her face was a mess of white.

She looked up at him, face red. She grinned. "I couldn't let this amazing stuff go to waste in this silly girl."

Then she buried herself in Sunstorm's crotch again. Nathan's length remained hard, and he somehow knew that Kadria was keen on some gooey injections of her own, if of the oral kind.

CHAPTER 31

"I feel like we're putting too much faith in someone who tried to kill us yesterday," Vera said.

Sunstorm refused to take the bait and continued pointing to Fort Taubrum on the other side of Gharrick Pass.

Nathan had gathered everybody of importance for a strategy session the day after Sunstorm's "awakening." Vera, Anna, Sen, and Fei joined him and Sunstorm in his office. The map of the region sat on the table in the room. A handful of brass markers sat atop the map.

"She's agreed to serve me as a Champion. I've already taken ownership of her gem through my binding stone," Nathan said.

"You can do that?" Vera said.

"Only with the Champion's permission. A gemmed Champion's mind is effectively impenetrable unless they allow the intruder in. If this Bastion Theus had been here, then he could have stopped me, but he wasn't." Nathan shrugged.

"Why does his presence matter?" Anna asked. She nibbled on some warm cookies that the cooks had provided.

"Champions are protected by the magic of the binding stone. Sunstorm chose to lower her mental protection and allow me to transfer her connection to my binding stone. But Theus could have overridden that, given he controls the binding stone," Nathan explained. "It's the same reason why Champions can't use their gem abilities against their Bastion. Which is the other reason not to worry about Sunstorm. Her gem ability can't harm me."

"What about me?" Vera asked. "What if she does things behind your back?"

"There are ways to stop rogue Champions, if necessary," Nathan said.

"This is one of those times that you hide behind your oath, isn't it," Vera accused.

Fei frowned and looked between Vera and Nathan. Sen and Sunstorm looked resigned. They might not have their memories from Nathan's timeline, but they could remember their emotions of the events in it. And they didn't like the idea of a Bastion stopping a rogue Champion one bit.

Sunstorm spoke up, "I was prepared to die for my failures when fighting for the Federation. Master Nathan has offered me a second chance under him. I will not forsake him. And as an experienced Champion, I know what comes from betrayal."

"An experienced Champion? Experienced in betrayal, you mean," Vera commented.

Sunstorm's face remained impassive, but Sen's did not. Nathan placed his hand on her shoulder before she could speak and opened his mouth.

Anna beat him to it. "Vera! Enough!"

"Anna?" Vera leaned backward and stared at Anna in surprise, blinking rapidly. "Surely you find this suspicious as well—"

"But I am also a devout follower of Omria, and understand the value of an oath to her," Anna snapped. "Nathan isn't hiding behind his oath. He's respecting it. You should be thankful that he's sharing as much as he is about Champions and Bastions. Leopold wouldn't waste his breath on us when it comes to this sort of thing. If Nathan's not telling us, then it's probably for damn good reason."

Vera froze, then looked to one side. She covered her mouth for several seconds.

Eventually, the sorceress faced Nathan and looked him in the eye. "My apologies, Bastion Nathan—"

"Just Nathan, Vera," he corrected.

Anna rolled her eyes.

Vera's lips turned upward ever so slightly. "My apologies, Nathan. I forgot that your oath is a matter of faith, rather than one to the state. Perhaps dealing with Leopold too much blinded me, given his close relationship with the Emperor."

"No need to apologize," Nathan said. "In the end, my oath is between me and the Watcher Omria. She will be the one who judges me on my faithfulness." He paused. "And Leopold, I suppose. He can have me executed at the drop of a hat for heresy."

"Don't joke about that," Anna muttered.

"It's not a joke." Nathan sighed and rubbed the bridge of his nose. "But we're getting distracted."

"Indeed," Sunstorm said. "My original point was that the Federation still had considerable resources at Fort Taubrum. This is the staging post used to assault Gharrick Pass."

Nathan placed a finger below Sunstorm's. "Right here is Vera's tower."

"It's not my tower anymore," Vera said sourly.

Sighing, Nathan continued, "Can we assume that there'll be a significant army defending it?"

Sunstorm nodded.

"And this Seraph? Will she be there?" Nathan asked.

Sunstorm bit her lip. "I don't know. She's the brains behind Theus's Champions. The Federation assigned Lilac and me to him purely to provide extra strength, but Seraph runs the entire province. Theus only thinks that she works for him. In reality, she works for one of the regents of the Federation."

"Regent?" Fei asked.

"Several smaller nations make up the Federation, forming a single larger country, and each of these smaller nations—called provinces—is ruled by a regent," Nathan explained. "They use a wide variety of titles, including 'king' of all things, but they're collectively referred to as the regents of the Amica Federation."

"And Seraph works for one of these regents, but never told me who," Sunstorm said.

Nathan had a fairly good idea who it was. He knew who was responsible for the war with the Empire in the first place. But he remained silent. Openly stating the name would raise suspicion from Anna and Vera for little gain.

"If we're only facing one Champion, then this is done and dusted, right?" Anna suggested.

Nathan let out a bark of laughter. "I wish. Sunstorm says Seraph is a highly experienced duogem Champion. I have two monogem Champions, a spellblade equal to a monogem Champion, and a sorceress who can perhaps match a monogem with the help of her cairn."

"I don't follow," Anna replied, giving him a quizzical look. "You have four Champions. They have one."

"Even if we beat her—which is far from guaranteed—she'll likely kill one or more of us," Nathan said flatly. "Each gem provides an exponential increase in power. That's why trigem Champions are legends. A single one can demolish lesser Bastions and several duogem Champions."

The room fell silent. Sunstorm stepped back from the table with a grimace.

Time for a break, Nathan thought. He shooed everybody into a separate room and had some of the newly hired staff bring up lunch. Small talk was had over spiced sausages, potatoes, and bread. A simple meal, but nice enough.

Nathan spent part of it fighting off Fei's wandering hands. She kept trying to eat his food.

After he stopped her from cleaning his plate, she then tried to clean a certain other part of his body. He stopped her from doing that too, much to her annoyance and the relief of the other women in the room.

"So, do you have a plan?" Anna asked him once the plates were taken away.

"Leopold finally responded over the wireless," Nathan said.

"And?"

"He's coming here." Nathan frowned. "Whatever plan I come up with will depend on his support. I don't know what happened at Forselle Valley, or whether Leopold will order me to hold the pass instead."

Anna huffed. "But what do you want to do?"

Nathan smirked. "What do you think I want to do?"

"Given how you've acted since you got here?" Anna walked her fingers across the table. "Go on the offensive. You talk up Seraph and how dangerous she is, but you've said that about everything. I know you have a plan. What you're looking for is an excuse to put it into action."

"And do you want me to do that?" Nathan asked. "You are my countess."

"Let's say that I'm looking forward to ruling both sides of Gharrick Pass."

CHAPTER 32

S eraph drummed her fingers on her desk. The old men droned on and on, their voices projected over the wireless. Her patience had long since worn thin, but she was nothing if not professional.

Snapping at her employers and her current Bastion did her no favors. So she muted herself, poured a glass of wine, and stared at the wall of her office. Nobody else was here. The lights of her office were off. Only moonlight kept her company.

"Theus, tell us again how many Champions you encountered at Forselle Valley?" one of the old men asked, his voice reedy over the wireless projection. This was Grand Meister Korvell, the regent of a city-state within the Federation.

"At least a dozen," Theus said.

Seraph resisted the urge to burst into laughter.

The old men bickered amongst themselves again. Only one of the three didn't believe Theus.

"Pray tell, Theus, where the Empire could get a dozen Champions given their current situation?" the disbeliever asked. He s King George II, whose family split from the Empire a century

Gharrick Pass had originally been part of George's territory, when his family had seceded from the Empire and created their own kingdom. That had lasted for about a decade, before the Empire reclaimed everything west of the Gharrick Mountains. But George pretended he owned the pass anyway. These days his power had faded so much that he had joined the Federation and was a king in name only.

Why the Federation let him call himself a king was beyond Seraph. Korvell had been the head of a merchant guild that ran a city-state from the shadows. George was a noble who could trace his bloodline to the archdukes that ruled the Anfang Empire in the time that the Watcher Omria walked Doumahr. The two held the same status in this meeting, as both were regents.

The last member of this triumvirate of grumbling old men finally intervened.

"Now, George, we all know that our intelligence on the Empire's military resources has been unreliable at times," the last crafty old bastard said, his arrogance oozing through the wireless. Seraph grimaced at the magical device.

High Lord Torneus. Seraph's long-term sponsor, and the regent of one of the founding states of the Amica Federation. The stories behind how he had become the regent were many and varied. He had been one of five ruling council members in his country. The other four abdicated their positions or mysteriously lost the ability to live, just in time for Torneus to become regent.

Seraph suspected the worst of him at all times.

"Don't patronize me," George snapped. "Nothing my spies have given us has been wrong so far. Theus is a dunce."

"If your spies knew what they were doing, I wouldn't have walked into a trap, your majesty," Theus ground out.

"A trap? Bastion Leopold wasn't even at Forselle Valley!"

"Enough," Torneus shouted, his voice crackling over the wireless.

The silence lasted only a few moments.

"Fine. Have it your way, Torneus. But I'll tell you what I do know," George said, his voice laced with bitterness. "The Empire has invaded the Pearlescent Canyon again and restarted their war with Trafaumh. Theus didn't encounter a dozen Champions because the Empire can't spare a dozen Champions at our border."

George paused for a moment, and Seraph suspected he took a drink of water. "They're battling the most powerful nation on Doumahr over the most important religious location to both nations. Omria herself descended there. Those fanatics in Trafaumh will throw everything they can at the Empire. And the Empire will hit back with everything they have. If we can't win now, what hope do we have?"

With those words, George disconnected from the wireless call. A high whine rose from the device, then quickly went away.

"Is that true?" Seraph asked. "Do we have confirmation that the Empire has finally started their war with Trafaumh?"

"That is not your concern," Torneus said.

The hell it wasn't, Seraph thought. If the Empire had already invaded Trafaumh, then that changed everything. Their entire country would gear up for war. Patriotism would skyrocket. Invading the Empire was insanity now. Any victory would be met by three new Bastions a month later, eager to take back their homeland.

"Do you want my recommendation on what to do next, regents?" she pushed. She wasn't going to let Theus dictate the next steps with his peanut-sized brain.

"I don't think—" Torneus began to say.

"Why—" Theus spoke at the same time.

Their voices overlapped, and the connection became a mess of static.

A new voice cut through. Korvell said, "You have had the most exposure to this new Bastion, Seraph. Go ahead."

Torneus and Theus seethed silently. They couldn't openly contradict Korvell. Unlike George, who was considered a pompous fool, Korvell was wealthy and influential.

In most nations, a smart man never angered a noble. In the Federation, people said the same thing about merchants. Money spoke the loudest here, and noble blood thinned with each passing year. Even Torneus trod lightly around Korvell.

"We can't mount another attack in time," Seraph said.

Theus interrupted, "You mean that you can't mount another attack in time. I am more than capable of it. Don't lump your incompetence on me."

Seraph rolled her eyes and took a big gulp of wine. "Of course, Master Theus. But even if you do attack, why would the results differ from your previous assault? That is my point. I can attack Gharrick Pass tomorrow, but I will lose."

Knowing that Theus was about to interrupt her, Seraph spoke quickly, "This new Bastion, Nathan Straub, is far more capable than King George's spies gave credit for. He has defeated two monogem Champions, converted the bandit spellblade we were grooming to become a Champion, and may have even stopped the cascade from happening."

"I confirmed that the cascade took place," Theus growled.

"And then he showed up in Nair's tower the same day," Seraph said. "Given the first thing he did upon arriving at Gharrick Pass was suppress our leyline disruption, it suggests that he has more advanced knowledge of the binding stones than we do."

"If you had attacked him yourself, then we wouldn't be in this mess," Theus said.

"Or maybe nothing would be different, except that I wouldn't be talking to you right now," Seraph said, losing her temper. "I am a duogem Champion, but even I can't instantly suppress a demonic invasion and appear inside a sorcerer's tower miles away."

"But you—" Theus shouted.

"Theus, enough," Torneus said flatly.

Theus shut up.

"Seraph, give us your recommendation for the next move," Torneus said. "I believe we've heard enough of your reasoning."

His tone suggested that Seraph was treading on thin ice.

He hadn't planned on the Empire winning any battles. Torneus's grand ambitions were unraveling, Seraph realized.

"Ask for peace," Seraph responded.

"Ridiculous," Theus snapped.

"Enough!" Torneus thundered. The connection whined so loudly that Seraph thought he had cut her off. "Seraph, explain yourself."

"I already did. We can't attack the Empire. If we do, we'll lose, like we already have. With every passing day, they'll regain their strength. If they can attack us and win, then they will." Seraph felt that she wasn't getting through to them, so she pushed harder. "They're focused on a different war. Our plans have failed. They'll let us back away without raising any fuss. Bastion Leopold is a political animal. But that also means he'll tear us apart if he gets the chance."

"Tear us apart how? You're overstating their strength," Torneus said dismissively. "It's precisely because the Empire is at war with Trafaumh that we don't need to sue for peace. They can't spare additional Champions here. When the moment comes, we strike."

"If they have a dozen Champions at Forselle Valley, they already have the strength," Seraph quipped.

"Don't press your luck," Torneus warned her.

Seraph's lips tightened into a line. Evidently, he knew that Theus was full of shit. Maybe Korvell had bought his excuse, but not anymore.

"I'm afraid that Torneus is right here," Korvell mumbled. "I agree that we cannot go on the offensive, but peace? Impossible.

Too many guilds and trading companies have already factored in our victory. Their profit projections incorporate a Gharrick Pass that does not charge tolls or tariffs, and they must be able to use the mines, forests, and farmland on the arable side of the mountains."

So that was it. The die had been cast before this meeting had been held. The profits of the Federation came before anything else.

Or more accurately, the profits of the wealthiest members of the Federation, who had captured the regencies of almost every state of the Federation.

"Honestly, Seraph, you're too concerned about this Bastion," Torneus said. "You still have our trump card."

"She turned on us," Seraph responded flatly.

"I disagree." Torneus's tone allowed no dissent. "Based on your report, the Bastion has her under his thumb. If she made her move to support us as initially planned, he would have taken her head in an instant."

Seraph remained silent. That wasn't the way she saw it, but she knew better than to argue right now.

A sigh crackled over the wireless before Torneus said, "We're offering her what she's wanted for so long. The Empire has been denying her for years. Denying her lineage for even longer. Unlike them, we honor our promises. Remind our precious contact in the Empire that our offer remains open. She merely needs to fulfill her end of the bargain and deliver us victory at the right moment."

As always, Torneus refused to identify who this contact was. Seraph followed suit, but wondered why that was the case. She knew her identity. Sunstorm had as well.

Did Torneus distrust Korvell or George? Or maybe he thought that the knowledge would leak from Theus to one of his Champions, and from them to the Empire?

Probably the latter, Seraph thought. Torneus didn't become a regent by blindly trusting every idiot under his command.

"Victory, High Lord?" Seraph repeated, her tone questioning. "Are you suggesting that we attack again?"

"As we should," Theus muttered.

"Theus," Torneus said, shutting the Bastion up. Torneus paused, then answered, "No, you are right that being overly aggressive is the wrong choice. But peace is not an option. We will find an opportunity before winter."

By which he meant that Seraph would find an opportunity. She held her tongue again and remained silent as the meeting wrapped up.

Seraph had been a Champion long enough to see where this story ended. Unfortunately, her hands were tied. And she had already sent far too many of her younger brethren to their deaths.

Poor Sunstorm, she thought as she turned off the wireless communication device. Lilac had no real future as a Champion, but Sunstorm's fate saddened Seraph.

Given a good Bastion who cared, Sunstorm had the potential to be a duogem Champion. But onyx gems were poorly understood on the mainland. The legacy of the Anfang Empire meant that almost every Champion used amethysts, diamonds, and rubies. Sapphires also proved popular due to the influence of non-human races. Those were considered honest, reliable gems on the mainland.

Only on the Kurai Peninsula were rare gems such as onyxes used.

Even when somebody understood what an onyx could do, it didn't help Sunstorm. A Champion skilled in assassination was an asset to people like Torneus, but also terrifying. The idea of someone so stealthy and capable of undetected murder, but with the power of a duogem Champion?

Seraph imagined that Torneus slept better now that Theus had told them that Sunstorm was dead.

With a flash of her gem, Seraph vaporized her wine bottle. She scowled. Her fingers dug into the plush upholstery of her chair. For several seconds she fought the urge to turn it into dust.

But then she'd have to get a new one, and she was in the middle of nowhere. She sighed.

Tomorrow was a new day, she supposed. She didn't know how many new days she had left in the Federation.

CHAPTER 33

"Color me impressed. I didn't expect you to stop both a demonic invasion and the Federation," Leopold said, perhaps a little too bluntly.

He joined Nathan in a watchtower within the portal. The two of them stared out over the volcanic plains. No demons wandered here, and none had arrived since the invasion.

"I'm not sure if I should be proud or appalled," Nathan drawled. "Whatever the case, the portal is a heck of a lot larger."

"Yes, that happens when you show off too much," Leopold said.

Nathan blinked. What did he say?

"Haven't heard that before? It's a pet theory of mine, to explain the growth of portals." Leopold grinned, and the edges of his lips vanished into his sideburns. "Portals open because the demonic energy is trying to escape. The faster we defeat the demons, the faster the energy is emitted. We know this. But what if we think of the energy like a river? What does a river do when it flows downhill?"

"It finds the path of least resistance," Nathan answered.

Leopold nodded. "Exactly. That's what I think the portals are. The binding stones are confluence points of leylines, which is why the demonic energy tries to escape here through a portal. When we suppress a portal, the portal grows. And the faster we suppress, the faster the growth." He rubbed his chin while frowning. "It's not a perfect explanation, and many events don't fit the logic, but it explains why portals grow faster in the presence of Bastions and stronger Champions. And why your portal is growing rapidly compared to most."

Nathan had a separate theory, given what Kadria had told him.

But he had to admit that Leopold's theory also made some sense. Kadria had implied that the Messengers didn't pay much attention to their portals, and that Nathan's primary mistake had been to draw that attention to him. That meant that the portals had some automated means of growth.

Was this whole thing some sort of game to the Messengers? Nathan failed to wrap his head around what the Messengers wanted. Kadria seemed oddly content to help Nathan, and even more content to spend time with him. Whatever her aim was, it seemed different to destroying this world.

But he couldn't forget that she had done exactly that in his timeline. What changed her?

"Deep thoughts, I take it?" Leopold asked.

"Knowing that being better at my duty might make the Empire less safe doesn't make me feel better," Nathan half-lied. He told the truth that he didn't like the idea, but he had been thinking of something he couldn't tell Leopold.

"True. That's why we keep our secrets and take our oath. The things that people may do if they knew how this worked are difficult to fathom," Leopold said. His expression was stony.

Nathan wondered if Leopold had some idea of what those things were. The old man worked with people with the power to do very dangerous things, and who might not take kindly to the truth behind Bastions and binding stones.

"I can provide you with some good news, at least," Leopold

said, clapping Nathan on the back. He descended from the watch-tower as he spoke, "After an invasion of this size, it usually takes a few months before they attack again. And if the portal is growing this much, maybe even a year."

"Months," Nathan said flatly.

"Take what good news you can get," Leopold said. His fake smile drifted back into place, but seemed strained. "To your office?"

Ciana and Fei met them inside the keep. Fei's cheeks were bulging with food, and bread crumbs ran down her chin and uniform. By contrast, Ciana was the model Champion, with not a hair out of place. Not that Ciana was a Champion yet.

Fei blushed at the looks she received from Leopold and Nathan. She hurriedly brushed the crumbs away and swallowed her food. Her mumbled apology, flattened ears, and downturned tail earned her a visit from Nathan that night.

Once Nathan and Leopold arrived at the office, the two girls trooped off to a neighboring room. Nathan made some coffee in the percolator, while Leopold examined the map.

"You're rather transparent, aren't you," Leopold said.

"Am I?"

"You have markers in place along the entire border. Last I checked, you're only responsible for defending Gharrick Pass." Leopold's tone was dry. "And that map on the wall is one I am terribly familiar with." He pointed at the smaller map hung on the wall, which covered the north of the Empire and its contested border with Trafaumh.

"I like to stay up-to-date," Nathan said. "Your coffee."

"Thank you," Leopold said. He stared at the map on the wall while he drank. "Do you know why we're fighting over the Pearlescent Canyon?"

"Do you want the official answer, the academic answer, or my opinion?" Nathan asked. He loudly slurped his coffee when Leopold looked at him sidelong.

"You're much more confident this time," Leopold commented. "I suppose you've earned the right. Last time we met, you had defeated some bandits and fought off a monogem Champion. Now you've accomplished more than most Bastions do in a decade. Arguably their entire careers, given you've prevented a war."

Nathan paused at Leopold's comment.

The war with the Federation had been prevented? That was Leopold's view on the matter?

Had Nathan already accomplished what he had come back in time to do? He had been convinced that he had much more to do. Surely the Federation wouldn't give up after one failed assault, given they had gone to the extent of causing a demonic invasion.

"I want your opinion, assuming it's accurate," Leopold said.

"You'll quickly tell me if it's not," Nathan said.

"No, I'll just think less of you." The older Bastion chuckled at Nathan's look. "I live and breathe politics. If I gave away my hard-earned knowledge for free, then I'd have been replaced long ago."

Nathan nodded. If he were younger, he'd judge the old bastard harshly.

Scratch that, he still judged him harshly, but that didn't make Leopold wrong.

"The Pearlescent Canyon is where the Watcher Omria is believed to have descended to Doumahr millennia ago," Nathan explained. "It's a holy place. That's why the Order of Trafaumh will fight for it. They adore Omria and consider the canyon to be a sacred site."

Leopold gestured for him to continue.

Nathan continued, "But the Empire doesn't care about the religious importance. What matters is that the canyon is a reminder of the power of the Empire. When Omria walked Doumahr in the flesh, she backed the Anfang Empire and the Emperor. Every day that the canyon doesn't belong to the Empire is another day that it is reminded of its weakness."

"So you think we're taking back the canyon purely as a show of strength to the rest of the world?" Leopold asked. His expression hadn't shifted.

"I don't pretend to know why we're starting a war now. But I think we want to control the canyon because it's a symbol of the Empire's power. A legacy of the glory days."

Leopold grimaced. "A fairly grim assessment of your homeland."

"Is it wrong?"

"I did say I wouldn't correct you," Leopold said. He paused. "But I will say that your opinion would fit in well with those making realistic plans to help His Majesty. I can tell that you ran a county once. And also why your father didn't like you. He is a nationalist, through and through."

Leopold drained his coffee cup. It hit the table with a hard thud. Nathan frowned.

"Something wrong?" he asked.

"I gave you good news earlier," Leopold said. "I'm afraid there won't be much more to come."

Nathan waited. He heard Fei's excited noises from next door and realized that his office wasn't sound proofed very well.

"The Empire has begun its assault on Trafaumh," Leopold said.

"That's behind schedule," Nathan commented.

In reality, it was on time. Nathan knew that the Empire started the war around now. The difference was that he had already repelled the Federation. In his timeline, the Federation launched their attack within the next few weeks.

"There was some hope that negotiations may allow us to claim ownership of the canyon, under strict terms with Trafaumh," Leopold said. "In practice, those negotiations bought time for the

Empire to get as many Bastions and Champions in place. I was naive to believe we may escape a war."

"So there are no reinforcements coming," Nathan said slowly.

"No."

"Why are you here then?" Nathan asked.

"Because I am an old man who can do what he wants, and everybody is too scared to tell me what to do." Leopold laughed. "That, and His Majesty understands that we're being invaded by the Federation. It's in my hands to salvage the situation. But he needs a victory in the north, and I am his trusted right-hand man. I'll take out the trash trying to sneak in over the mountains."

"I thought you told me that you didn't have any more good news?" Nathan said.

The pair chuckled. Leopold drummed his fingers on the table and stared at the markers.

The arrival of food put their meeting on hold. Nathan stared at what the servant brought in.

Bread, fried eggs, hunks of local ham, cheese, and onions. Nathan was very familiar with the sandwich, but it was the sort of thing one of his Champions made him. Anybody could make it, especially with the fire enchanted ovens and cooktops in a modern kitchen.

Serving it to one of the most powerful men in the Empire seemed like a faux pas.

Leopold picked up the sandwich and bit in. He let out a grunt of approval and took another bite. Yoke ran down his chin, and he wiped it away with a cloth that had been provided.

"This is a guilty pleasure of mine when traveling," Leopold admitted when they finished lunch. "In the capital or my fortresses, my chefs insist on serving me their fanciest and most impressive creations. But sometimes a man prefers simple."

"And loaded with meat," Nathan noted. "Fei would have been impressed by your sandwich."

"Don't lie. I read the reports. Her appetite is part of the reason she's a Champion," Leopold said. "Beastkin eat a lot, but no village can sustain a girl that practically eats a deer every day."

With lunch out of the way, they returned to the main subject. Leopold shuffled some markers around on the map.

He held up one in particular. "This is a Federation Champion, isn't it?"

"It is. Sunstorm, the one that I first encountered with Sen," Nathan explained. He knew what was coming.

"Why is she now part of the Empire according to these markers?" Leopold asked.

"I came to an agreement with her and transferred ownership of her gem to my binding stone." Nathan held his breath after explaining.

Leopold stared at Nathan. Slowly, he placed the marker down.

"Well, I imagine that will terrify Theus," Leopold said.

"You know him?"

"I've heard of him before. My Champions ran into him at Forselle Valley. A thug carved from marble and a face ripped right from a painting. He's stupid. Very stupid. Normally I'd say that losing a Champion would be enough, but I doubt he'll admit it to anyone." Leopold sighed. He rubbed his eyes.

"He doesn't run the show," Nathan said. "A regent does."

"Your new recruit told you that, I take it?" Leopold grunted. "I'm ninety-nine percent certain that High Lord Torneus is behind this. He's a conniving bastard who stabbed his way to the top and helped build the Federation. I'd blame him for a lot of the problems in the world today, but that excuses the people that work with him."

Nathan scowled inwardly. He had been right. Torneus had been behind Seraph.

In his timeline, Nathan had struggled with Torneus right up until the Federation collapsed under the weight of the man's arrogance. The man was the definition of vindictive. What he couldn't rule, he would see burned to ashes around him. In the end,

Torneus didn't live to see it burn. Narime incinerated him first. But the damage had been done. Torneus brought down every nation west of the Gharrick Mountains in Nathan's timeline.

Arguably, he brought down every nation east of the Gharrick Mountains as well, if he was behind the invasion of the Empire to begin with.

Now Nathan had to deal with the bastard again. If he wasn't careful, the same thing could happen.

There was no way that the war had been avoided. If Nathan let this end here, then Torneus would find a new way to bring about the end of the world.

Leopold saw Nathan's face and let out a dark chuckle. "I'm guessing Sunstorm shares my opinion, if that's your reaction. That bodes well. It makes me trust her that much more."

"You said that I prevented a war with the Federation," Nathan said, choosing his words carefully. "Can we really say that's the case?"

"Yes," Leopold answered without hesitation.

Nathan grimaced.

"Hold your horses," Leopold said. He shook his head. "The fact is that we can walk away if we want. The Federation won't attack. Theus is terrified and they won't have the resources. So we can sit on our hands until after winter if we like, which will keep His Majesty happy and the people unaware of the Federation's aggression. That's a possibility."

"And the other?" Nathan asked.

"The other is on your map." Leopold inclined his head at the mess of markers on the map of the region. "We use their attack as a casus belli—that's a justification for a war, if you don't know the fancy term—and invade the Federation. I don't know how much territory we take. I'd wager a couple of binding stones would be a nice start. Those always look nice. And I have some political tactics up my sleeve to keep their neighbors out of it."

"The leyline disruption," Nathan said bluntly.

"You're sharp," Leopold admitted, his eyebrows shooting up.

"Heresy isn't taken lightly by other Bastions. The dark elves and fairies won't intervene if they think the Federation is up to something."

Leopold smirked and said nothing.

Silence fell over the pair. Nathan felt that the choice lay with him, despite Leopold's earlier comment that the Emperor had tasked the old man to do this.

"I have a plan to retake Vera's tower and to capture Fort Taubrum," Nathan said. "But I need your support."

"You need a Champion?" Leopold asked.

"At least one monogem Champion. Preferably two," Nathan said. "Anything less and I think the risk is too high. I'll lose Champions and won't be able to defend what I capture."

Leopold nodded slowly. "Interesting. You realize that Fort Taubrum's binding stone is warded, don't you? The sorcerers from the capital can undo the wards, but it will be weeks. You'll need to defend what you capture without a binding stone."

"As I said, I have a plan. I only need your support," Nathan repeated.

"Your confidence is fascinating." Leopold grinned. "Very well. I will be your support."

Nathan blinked. "I'm sorry?"

"I may not be a Champion, but you know as well as I do that a Bastion backed by binding stones can keep up with a monogem," Leopold explained, his eyes glittering. "So, I'll fight with you on the front lines. I'm looking forward to seeing you in action, firsthand."

Somehow, Nathan felt that he might have made a mistake.

CHAPTER 34

Sparks flew as Fei and Sunstorm clashed. Neither broke through the other's guard, and they both leaped back. They circled.

A crowd gathered in the training grounds. Soldiers and servants pressed themselves against the fence that separated the sparring ring from the rest of the training grounds. An enterprising young soldier began taking bets, and soon odds were set. Money exchanged hands.

The two Champions ignored the peanut gallery. But Ciana and Sen didn't. The pair sat on a bench inside the sparring ring, where the four women had been taking turns to train and spar all morning. Ciana glanced backward.

Nathan waved at her, but ignored her look of concern. He doubted that it hurt for the women to be aware of their popularity in the fortress.

The life of a Champion meant becoming very well known to strangers. Sometimes too well known. Nathan remembered a lot of occasions where his Champions had clung close to him at parties, due to overbearing nobles.

By contrast, the attention from the soldiers was innocent. They respected and adored the combat prowess of Fei and the other

Champions. If Ciana acclimatized to this attention, then it could only help her in the future.

So Nathan continued to read through the paper he had in front of him. He made some notes in the margin as he went through it.

Out of the corner of his eye, he continued to monitor the duel. Some time passed as Fei and Sunstorm fought to prove who was superior.

Neither Champion used their gem abilities. Strictly speaking, this put them on an even footing.

In practice, it showed the raw gap in experience and skill between them.

Both Fei and Sunstorm had the same enhancement. They were both monogem Champions. Both were physical fighters. Sunstorm had a few years on Fei, however. And her background from Kurai went back into her teenage years, whereas Fei was a fresh Champion.

Fei swung, Sunstorm blocked. Fei feinted, but Sunstorm saw through it.

Even when Fei pushed Sunstorm off-balance or seized the advantage, she failed to follow through. Sunstorm's superior foot-work or her experience in recovering from failure allowed her to stay in the fight.

This current spar was desperate and heating up rapidly. Fei rained down blow after blow, pushing Sunstorm to the edge of the sparring circle. A combatant couldn't defend themselves outside of the circle, so a follow-up blow from Fei meant instant defeat for Sunstorm. Even so, the assassin continued to retreat.

She held her ground right at the very edge. The moment that Fei moved in for the kill, Sunstorm dropped both of her swords. As her arms twisted around Fei's sword arm, Fei let out a yell. The beastkin pulled back with all of her strength and rolled. Both women scrabbled with each other on the ground.

Nathan sighed and went back to the paper, realizing he had let himself be distracted by the finale to the spar.

Seconds later, Sen called out, "Victory to Sunstorm. That's four-to-one, so Sunstorm wins."

The crowd groaned. The proceeds from the bets were doled out. Only a handful of people looked happy. Fei was a popular girl in the fortress. That was only natural, given she was the homegrown Champion.

Unfortunately for them, Fei still needed more experience. Her gem ability and raw talent made her an exceptional fighter. But her judgment tended to be lacking.

Such as choosing to engage Sunstorm in a brawl when she had the advantage prior. Sunstorm was an expert in unarmed combat, and Fei wasn't. Reacting faster and pulling back would have been the best option, but failing that, Fei had daggers in her belt. Sunstorm would have had no choice but to let go the moment that Fei pulled out another weapon with her spare hand.

Instead she surrendered her best advantage, was dragged down into the dirt, and quite literally beaten.

The four women milled about in the sparring ring, no doubt deciding what to do next.

Their decision was made for them when the cooks brought out lunch. Boar was the dish of the day, and the wine and honey glaze dripped onto the serving platters.

"Is this going to be enough?" Sen asked.

Ciana gave her an odd look. "Isn't this almost an entire boar? I thought others were joining us."

Moments later, Ciana's look changed to one of horror as Fei tried to stack her plate high enough to raise concerns about the integrity of the plate.

"Fei, you can get seconds," Nathan chided.

"Fine," Fei mumbled, and returned some of the hunks of meat she had taken.

"You get used to her," Sen said.

"Where does she put away all that meat?" Sunstorm asked.

"Her tits, I imagine," Sen muttered.

Sen, Sunstorm, and Ciana stared at Fei's impressive bust, then at their much less impressive chests. Their eyes immediately focused on Sunstorm, and Sen's eyes narrowed.

"You seem to be doing well enough," Sen said. "I thought they were smaller."

"I strap them up in battle," Sunstorm admitted. "They get in the way otherwise. And I'm quite certain that their size is due to my parentage. My mother and sister were both larger."

"Lucky," Sen muttered. "If they get in the way, how do you deal with them, Fei? I can't even fit them in my hands."

Fei tried to answer, but her words came out as a garbled mess.

"Chew, then swallow," Sen told her.

Fei did as told, then said, "Um, practice? I had to hunt daily for my food in my village. I ate too much, so they stopped giving me my allocated ration when I came of age."

"Practice doesn't make things that size move less. I know," Sunstorm said between bites.

"Beastkin physiques are different," Ciana answered quietly. "Because we move so much and are often nomadic, our bodies are much more adapted to physical movement."

Nathan listened in without saying a word. He found their conversation fascinating. Mostly because he was certain they had forgotten that he was here.

Normally when he was around, one of them tried to get his attention and that caused a fight. Usually Fei. He kept things from devolving too far by enforcing a strict rule about no sex outside the bedroom.

"So, what, Fei grows bones beneath her tits?" Sen asked.

"I haven't," Fei objected.

"No, it's more that we have magic within our body that supports our bodies," Ciana said, shaking her head. "We look like humans—"

"Except for the tails and ears," Sen interrupted.

"And the rutting," Sunstorm added.

Ciana blushed. "Let's not talk about that."

So, she was aware of that aspect of beastkin behavior. Fei showed no reaction, which suggested she was not.

Nathan considered that unsurprising. Fei's upbringing didn't involve a good education, and he appeared to be the first man she had shown a serious interest in. It might be another year before her beastkin physiology reared its head. Although Nathan had ordered medicine to deal with it anyway.

The last thing he needed was for Fei to be distracted in battle. She was Nathan's Champion, not his pet.

Ciana cleared her throat and continued, "We look like humans, and largely act like them, but we have differences. The same that fairies and elves do. My stamina is far higher than a human's. Fei can likely run faster and is more dexterous. Wolves can bend steel with their bare hands. Compared to a Champion enhancement, it's nothing, but it matters against ordinary humans."

"And that makes it easier for Fei to fight with large breasts?" Sen said, her voice echoing her disbelief.

"She won't have the physical discomfort or other issues that a human woman would," Ciana said. Then she paused. "Plus, she's a Champion. I think enhancements take care of that anyway. Given the speed she moves at, her bones would break without magical help. She's cutting through steel and running faster than draft horses."

Sen opened her mouth to argue. Then closed it. She grimaced. "Okay, yeah, fair enough. I don't have an enhancement, so I forget how inhuman they are by default. The whole 'magic runs through their veins and makes them inhuman' thing. Huh. No wonder the nights go on for so long."

Sen's eyes pierced Nathan's body. So they did know he was here. He ignored them and continued to eat his lunch while finishing the paper.

"What's that you've got there, Nathan?" Sen asked, refusing his attempt to ignore her and continue eavesdropping.

"An assessment for Ciana," Nathan said. "Leopold asked me to handle her education while he's busy."

"Busy, huh," Sen said. She looked sidelong at Ciana, who avoided her gaze. "Isn't your Bastion supposed to be helping us when we march through the pass soon?"

Ciana remained silent.

"I guess he must be really busy up north, huh." Sen waggled her eyebrows and leaned in close to Ciana, who glared back at her. "He's visiting a couple of his Champions and didn't want you getting in the way of his all day sex romps?"

Ciana pouted. "Probably."

Sen's face split into a grin and she giggled. "Wow. Despite his age, he really is more like Nathan than I thought."

Ciana tried not to appear interested by the comparison. Her horse ears twitched, and her tail swished rapidly from side to side. She cleared her throat and looked innocently at Nathan. "Leopold said he only had time for the visit because Lady von Clair wasn't ready. Is there anything in particular happening?"

"Anna is making some additional preparations with her troops," Nathan said. "And I need to gather more power in the binding stone. It's still summer. We have time before the weather worsens in the pass and makes travel difficult."

"What happens if this duogem Champion attacks us while he's away?" Sen asked, pointing her fork at Nathan as if to challenge him.

"That would make things easier for us," he replied.

Sen scowled. "What if she attacks with a dozen Champions?"

Sunstorm opened her mouth to counter the idea, but Ciana spoke first.

"That would be improbable," Ciana said.

Sen blinked and stared at the unicorn beastkin. Ciana held Sen's gaze without flinching or ducking her head.

Continuing, Ciana said, "The engagement at Forselle Valley suggests that most of the Federation's Champions are located there. Which is reasonable, given how much military strength the Empire has in the north right now. Furthermore, the Federation has significant commitments to the east. Its eastern border touches the Houkeem Desert and is under constant attack by demons invading from the Kurai Peninsula. They also must—"

"I get it, I get it," Sen said. "The Federation is a small nation, with lots of neighbors, and all of their Bastions and Champions are already tied up. Everybody knows that. But what if they decide that it's worth the risk to take us out?"

"They won't," Sunstorm replied. "If they were willing to take that risk, they wouldn't have sent expendable Champions like Seraph and me."

The table fell silent. Sen looked between Nathan and Sunstorm in search of help. This situation was far from her specialty.

"Done," Nathan said, changing the topic. He handed back the paper to Ciana. "I've made notes in the margins regarding some of what you wrote. But largely, there's not much to correct."

"Are you sure?" Ciana asked, eyes wide. She held the papers against her chest.

"Yes. Your knowledge is well beyond what they teach at the academy. At this point, the only ways you'll learn are books, experience, and other Bastions and Champions," Nathan explained. He dug into a side of boar, after pouring some relish over it.

Fei tilted her head and swallowed. "If it's not taught in the academy, how come you can grade her assessment?"

Sunstorm and Sen suppressed smirks, their eyes focusing on Nathan. Surely, he couldn't worm out of this one.

But Ciana shook her head. "Nathan has already proven that he used his time at the academy very wisely. I've learned a lot of what I know from books and questioning the academy's meisters when Leopold takes me there. There's a lot more for me to learn."

"That's a smart approach to take." Nathan smiled, and Ciana ducked her head. "Although you should start thinking about your path."

"My path?"

"Whether you want to become a Champion or a Bastion," Nathan said. "I can't speak for Leopold with regard to your aptitude, but I can say that you know a lot more than most Champions ever learn."

"Should we be offended?" Sunstorm asked.

Nathan shrugged. "There's no reason that I can't tell you more about the secrets of a Bastion. You've taken a similar oath." He left out that Ciana hadn't, which could be a concern under normal circumstances. "Most Champions don't gain anything from knowing this sort of thing. And a lot don't have the aptitude."

All eyes subtly turned to Fei, then back to Nathan.

"So, I should become a Bastion, given the choice?" Ciana said.

"That's not what I'm saying." Nathan paused and chose his words carefully. "Champions rarely make good Bastions, but almost all Bastions make good Champions. But I don't know if anybody could be both a great Bastion and a great Champion, if they somehow had the ability to become both. I'm sure that one of these paths is right for you. Leopold has offered you a choice that very few get. I recommend that you make the most of it."

With those words, Nathan let the women return to their training. He had paperwork to fill out to prepare for the upcoming assault.

CHAPTER 35

A late night invitation from Anna set Nathan's teeth on edge. Generally, being invited by a pretty noble woman to meet her in a private parlor at close to midnight meant difficult times ahead. Nathan had no desire to be tied down to a noble, no matter their status or impressive looks.

Not that he had ever thought about his future beyond being a Bastion. Staring down the end of the world left little time to worry about retirement and things had only become more complicated since coming to this timeline. His worries for the future limited themselves to the next few months or years at most.

Nathan walked through the halls of the keep to the meeting place. More soldiers patrolled the corridors than usual, and the lamps kept everything well lit. The fortress bustled with activity. Outside, supply trains ran along the highways from Forselle Valley and elsewhere in the county.

A young beastkin girl stood guard outside the parlor. Unlike the other soldiers, her uniform lacked Anna's emblem. She worked only for Nathan and was one of his recent hires.

At the sight of Nathan, the guard snapped off a salute. Her wolf ears twitched, and her tail wagged faster and faster with each step Nathan took toward her. But she stared resolutely forward.

Nathan saluted back as he entered the parlor, and the beastkin froze for a moment. He caught her ears shooting bolt upright out of the corner of his eye before the door closed.

"Enjoying your new personal guard?" Kuda said, catching Nathan's attention.

The lights were on, and Kuda was in the room with Anna. Nathan took those as good signs for this meeting. He accepted the coffee that Kuda offered him and took a seat.

Anna sat opposite him and seemed distracted by her thoughts. She idly sipped at her coffee. A handful of papers lay in front of her.

"I wouldn't say 'enjoying,' but I do like having soldiers of my own," Nathan said.

"And the fact that they're all beastkin?" Kuda probed. His lips turned upward at the edges.

"There are a lot of beastkin villages nearby. Wolves near the mountains, cats down by the sea and along the rivers, horses in the plains. I have a lot of ways to make money as a Bastion and not many ways to use it," Nathan explained. "By contrast, the villages out here don't have much. The county that Fei grew up in has denser forest than Gharrick."

Kuda inclined his head in understanding, and his smile vanished. "True. Very true. A rising tide lifts all boats, but it requires the tide to reach those boats to begin with. The beastkin live a harsh life, even though the Empire has banned slavery. Simple solutions only get us so far."

Nathan frowned. Politics. He was never very good at it. The same went for economics.

Logistics. Warfare. Magical theory. Leadership. Even some elements of nation-building such as the mechanisms of bureaucracy, how merchants made money, and taxes. These were the things that Nathan specialized in.

But applying those to a political or economic framework never sat well with him. He could make the leap, if he wanted to. He knew what Kuda meant. The Empire was wealthy, and the nobles especially so. Nathan was extending a helping hand, but Kuda was indirectly questioning if it was enough. He questioned if the Emperor cared about the beastkin at all, given how little was done to help them.

On the other hand, Nathan didn't run an Empire responsible for protecting, feeding, managing, clothing, and housing countless millions. He didn't have to keep unruly nobles in line, who might have aspirations to do worse.

He also had no way to reconcile such ideas with the existence of the academy, and the fact that the Empire had already done more to help the beastkin than most of Doumahr. Every other country beside Falmir and the Empire allowed slavery or a close equivalent.

In the end, Nathan shrugged off Kuda's attempt to politicize the discussion. "Maybe. Maybe not. I'm a Bastion, not a noble or a ruler."

"I could say the same about Bastion Leopold," Kuda countered.

Nathan frowned. "This isn't really a discussion I specialize in, Kuda. War is black and white. Stopping demons is black and white." Or it was, before Nathan met Kadria, but he ignored her existence for now. "But political change?"

Anna spoke up, "If you didn't care, why are you explicitly helping the beastkin?"

"Because they make excellent soldiers and guards," Nathan said. "Wolf beastkin especially are exceptionally strong. If I want to build a unit of knights capable of stopping demons, instead of firing catapults from behind walls, then my best starting point is beastkin."

"Ah. So it's not pity, after all," Kuda said. "My mistake."

Nathan shrugged and drained his cup. "I do feel that part of my duty as Bastion is to share some of my largesse. The binding stone lets me create trade goods from nothing, so I'm not hurting for money. There's a term from Trafaumh about how nobles need to share some of their birthright, because they didn't earn it."

"Noblesse oblige," Anna supplied. "More specifically, it's about how nobles must act nobly, and part of that means to extend our wealth and power to those who do not have it. Saying that it's a controversial topic among nobles is an understatement. Although I imagine you're about to spark a lot of interest in it."

"I am?" Nathan asked. He blinked.

The door opened and Leopold stepped in. Nathan caught the beastkin guard gawking at the older Bastion and gestured for her to calm down. She blushed and resumed her stoic posture.

No wonder Kuda had commented on her when Nathan walked in. She only hid her reaction when she thought somebody was looking.

"Am I interrupting something?" Leopold asked. He eased into a seat with a wince. "My apologies, I had a long ride here."

Nathan looked at Anna in disbelief. "You invited him to a midnight meeting on the same day he arrived?"

"The two of you are going to be busy tomorrow. How else am I going to butt in?" she muttered. Her hands smoothed out her dress, which Nathan belatedly noted was frillier than usual. "We were discussing the idea of noblesse oblige and how the war will cause renewed debate over it."

"Ah, yes, the ethical debate over hereditary nobility." Leopold sighed. "Well, at least I'm sitting down."

"Really? That relates to this war?" Nathan asked.

"To us, this war is about border tariffs, demons, and a power-hungry regent seeking to gain more influence within the Federation," Leopold explained. "But how do we justify the war to the people of the Empire? I hate to say it, but the reality is that it will be through the difference between our nations. We may be changing slowly, but we live in a country of nobility. The Federation is different."

Anna interjected, "Is the Federation really that different to us? All of the regents are people who held power in their former nations. They're nobles by any other name."

"Perhaps. But that's not how they see it. And when they die, their sons and daughters are not guaranteed to become regents. Whereas your children will inherit Gharrick County," Leopold said.

Anna bit her lip but said nothing more.

More politics, Nathan thought. But this time, he understood it. Because it influenced the way he could fight this war, and the way the countries would react to it.

Nathan licked his lips. "This seems like the sort of thing that could spiral out of control quickly."

"Hah, yes," Leopold said. "Hence why His Majesty has left me in charge. Ideally, I intend to make this war about the countries as little as possible. Hence the heresy charge. The more we can pin this on individuals at the top of the Federation, the less this becomes about entire systems of governance. Nobody wants a total war between nations. The instability would threaten the entire world."

Yes. Yes, it would, Nathan thought.

He leaned back in his chair in relief. He didn't want to deal with this political mess. Maybe one day it would rear its ugly head. But today, he fought a simpler war. One about stopping a Federation that had attempted to use demons to attack the Empire and had committed heresy against Omria while doing so.

"Well, it's late. I assume you called us together for a reason, Anna," Leopold asked. He thanked Kuda for the cup of dark coffee, then held it high in the air. As he had been practiced many times, Kuda poured a shot of brandy into the coffee.

Nathan and Anna pretended not to notice. On the one hand,

the elder Bastion's late night drinking habits were his own business, even if they might raise an eyebrow given his age.

On the other hand, worries over poisoning attempts meant that nobody was going to try to pour something into Leopold's drink out of his sight. Nathan didn't need much of an imagination to picture how most of his new beastkin guards would react if they saw Kuda or any other servant slipping something extra into Leopold's drink. Blood would flow, and a promising new recruit would end their career in a traumatizing way.

"You're marching on Vera's tower soon. I want in on the planning," Anna said. She uncrossed her legs and leaned forward, eyes flashing with excitement.

Leopold and Nathan exchanged glances. Neither had expected this.

"Don't look at each other like that. I'm the countess. It's my armies that will support you," Anna said, her voice imperious. Her lip quivered.

Leopold held a hand up and sipped his coffee using his other. Silence fell, and Anna took the chance to regain her composure.

A subtle lean of Leopold's head indicated to Nathan that he needed to take the lead here. He caught the cue, then cleared his throat. Anna turned to him, her lips halfway toward a pout.

"I'm still the Bastion assigned to your county, Anna," Nathan said, trying to mollify her. "If you want to be involved, you can be involved."

"That's not what I mean," Anna muttered. "I said it before, didn't I? I want to be the countess that supports you. My family has protected these lands for generations. I won't be the one who fails to achieve greatness when it's within grasp."

"Quite greedy aren't you," Leopold said, his voice laced with amusement. Anna shot him a cutting look and he winked back at her. "I finally gave you the Bastion you've been asking for, after all of these years, and now you also want to claim his glory?"

"That's not—" Anna stopped talking and scowled at Leopold.

Nathan blinked and looked between the pair in confusion. "Years?"

"Yes, years." Anna rolled her eyes. "I told you when we first met that I wanted somebody to help remind the Empire that this county exists, didn't I? To the south is land held directly by the archduke, and it is mostly occupied by beastkin. North is better, but it's strategically important. Other than the old man here, I don't get my day in court."

"You have a vote in the Diet," Leopold pointed out.

"A vote." Anna crossed her arms. "None of the councils, committees, or even working groups that my father sat on bothered to extend an invitation to me when he passed."

Nathan coughed, and both Anna and Leopold turned to him.

"I'm sorry," Nathan said, not feeling sorry at all. "But, Anna, you told me that you asked for a Bastion only a year ago."

Anna stared at Nathan. Then she glared at Leopold. "You didn't tell him?"

Leopold drained his cup and placed it on the table. He placed his hand over it to indicate to Kuda not to refill it. His eyes focused on Nathan, and he refused to look at Anna.

"I didn't feel it pertinent," Leopold said. "I was unaware you only told him when you asked for an Imperial Bastion, rather than when you requested that the academy accept a specific person to become a Bastion."

"I'm not sure I follow," Nathan said slowly. The room felt colder somehow. Leopold still refused to look at Anna, despite her angry and confused expression.

"You're... Nevermind," Anna muttered and stopped glaring at Leopold. "Fine. I'll explain it." Anna shook her head and faced Nathan. "Before I formally requested a Bastion from the Imperial Army, I spent years helping somebody else to enter the academy. She had been interested almost her entire life, but only when my father fell ill did I gain the ability to sponsor her."

"Because you gained the power of your household," Nathan

said. "You weren't the countess yet, but as the heir, you may as well have been."

Anna nodded. "Exactly. Unfortunately, she was never success-ful. Despite multiple sponsors." Anna glanced at Leopold, who refused to look back at her. "By the time my father passed away, and I took over full control of the household and county, it was something of a lost cause."

"Until you eventually needed military support because your brother left?" Nathan asked, trying to keep the skepticism out of his voice.

"I prompted her earlier than that," Leopold said, his poker face smile back in place.

"You did, yes," Anna said after a long pause. She didn't elabo-rate on why.

Nathan sighed. "That someone. Who was it?"

He had a strong feeling he already knew. There was only one person he had met with a strong enough interest in Bastions and Champions—to say nothing of her bitterness toward Leopold—to have applied multiple times to enter the academy.

"Vera," Anna answered.

CHAPTER 36

"Seraph's not here," Sunstorm reported. "Not yet, anyway."

Nathan nodded and let her take up a position behind him.

Below him, Anna's army formed ranks and prepared for battle. They had marched through the pass today, and Vera's tower wasn't far. Federation banners fluttered around the base of the tower.

Nathan watched from atop the bluffs above the pass. Leopold, Anna, Vera, and his Champions accompanied him.

Ciana remained behind. Leopold refused to risk her in a battle that might involve a duogem Champion. She had attempted to convince Nathan and appeal to him in various ways. He had politely declined. Several times.

One time, Fei had declined on his behalf and thrown a half-naked unicorn beastkin out of Nathan's bedroom. She had not appreciated Ciana horning in on her territory.

On the other hand, Ciana's straightforward seduction attempt made it very clear that she was interested in Nathan. A small part of his mind had worried that she might be more interested in her mentor, but that idea could happily be put to bed.

Curiously, Kuda accompanied Anna. Given neither had any

intentions of participating in the battle itself, Nathan doubted he planned to fight. But he carried a sword and wore light armor nonetheless.

Anna's army was larger than Nathan expected. He had kept a decent defensive force at the keep and left his new recruits behind. Despite this, Anna mustered a significant army, if a smaller one than the Federation defended the tower with.

She had levied soldiers from all across her county. With Leopold's authority—and more importantly, his money—she had even levied soldiers from the beastkin villages to the south. Very little of the army was professional, and most of it had never fought before, but numbers helped. The beastkin's raw power and skill in hunting lent a quality all its own.

Nathan had stepped in and helped organize the army, however. Anna and her officers lacked any experience in command, and had never managed a mixed army like this. Even things as basic as which beastkin played well together were new to them.

A smart man did not put wolf beastkin in the same company as any other beastkin. For one thing, the wolves were unlikely to talk to anybody other than their own kin. Second, most other beastkin became really jittery around large numbers of wolves. Even Fei acted a bit funny when the wolves in the keep gathered in groups of more than three or four.

Given the Federation forces outnumbered his, Nathan organized his offensive to handle it. Ideally, he could rely on his Champions to limit casualties.

Fei and Sen possessed extremely powerful abilities that fell into the category of "anti-army." The downside was that both were so fantastically powerful that Nathan hesitated to use them too much. Fei's flames melted flesh and metal, and guaranteed a painful death for anybody she targeted with them. Sen's spells were less terrifying to witness, but only if she restricted herself to third rank spells.

Even with fourth rank spells, Sen reduced entire columns of men and women to ash.

Ultimately, the Federation soldiers were merely men and women who fought for their nation. They had families. Most probably didn't even know why they were fighting the Empire. Turning countless hundreds of comparatively innocent people into ash didn't sit well with Nathan.

He had done that far too many times in his timeline. Entire battlefields filled with corpses lined his memories as far back as he cared to remember.

If he could avoid doing that here, and instead force the Federation to flee, then Nathan would take the chance. The cost was the lives of the soldiers under him.

That didn't sit well with him either.

War was shit, Nathan thought. It reminded him of why he wanted to prevent this timeline from getting any worse.

"She may not be here now, but I believe it is wise to assume she will be here soon," Leopold said, talking about Seraph. He stroked his bare chin and stared out over the armies. "I'm assuming that's why you're keeping your Champions back?"

"It is," Nathan half-lied. Leopold knew about Nathan's battle plan. This question was purely for the benefit of those around them.

Seraph's presence was the other complicating factor to any plan that relied too heavily on Champions. Even if Nathan didn't care about slaughtering a couple thousand Federation soldiers, sending his Champions to the front line risked the battle in a different way.

The only counter to an enemy Champion was a Champion of his own. And if the enemy Champion was stronger than his, he needed several Champions. Everybody knew this, and armies drew morale from the power of the heroes that led them.

The Federation army held its defensive line around Vera's

tower, not because it was convinced that it could win, but because it knew that it had a duogem Champion backing it.

Nathan imagined a scenario where he sent his Champions against the Federation, recklessly trying to secure the victory as fast as possible, while losing as few soldiers as he could.

Fei burned out companies of soldiers, leaving behind molten piles of flesh and steel. Sen left craters where the enemy had stood in formation. Sunstorm cut down their officers and elites.

Then Seraph showed up and blew one of his girls away. By the time the other two reacted, Seraph could engage another. Nathan and Leopold moved too slowly.

The battle ended before it started. The Federation army lay in ruin. Nathan and his Champions died so early in their careers that they didn't even make the history books.

Not that such a scenario could ever happen. Leopold would have refused to participate in such a foolhardy plan. Despite his age and power, he was far from his binding stones. He had no way to teleport to safety.

Although Nathan suspected that Leopold had some additional defense, an escape plan, or at least a Champion hiding nearby. He hadn't spotted any other Champions, however. And Sunstorm hadn't either.

Everybody watched the soldiers form up into ranks. Many of the beastkin companies grew rowdy, but their officers kept them in check. Most of the officers were older men and women, and their equipment showed wear from previous battles.

"A lot more beastkin responded to the levy than I expected," Anna said. "Some of them even brought their own equipment."

"The Empire dislikes paying to equip a soldier twice," Leopold said. "Many of them will have been asked to fight before and have kept their equipment from the first time. I understand we used to ask every recruit to bring their own weapons, centuries ago, but most people dislike spending their own money in order to fight for others."

"I can require it of them, if they prefer," Anna said.

"Yes, and then you become the countess who forced poor, unarmed peasants to go into battle." Leopold gave Anna a condescending look. "There's your rights as a noble, and then there's what you can actually get away with."

"Noblesse oblige, yes," Anna muttered. "Why did so many beastkin come, then?"

"Because you're paying them a fortune," Nathan said.

Anna blinked and stared at him. Then she looked at Kuda, who nodded in agreement with Nathan.

"I am?" Anna said.

"Actually, I am," Leopold said. "On behalf of His Majesty."

"But I recruited them. They're even wearing my emblem," Anna protested. "I pay my guards well and have offered more for this campaign. But I don't think it's enough to attract hundreds of beastkin from other counties."

Nathan raised an eyebrow. "The lowest paid beastkin here is being paid as much per day as your guards normally earn in a week. The veterans—the officers that keep them in line and who brought their own equipment—are getting paid roughly double that."

Anna's eyes nearly popped out of her head. "That's ridiculous."

"They are at the highest risk of death," Leopold said. "More to the point, that's what the Imperial Army pays levied soldiers. You recruited them under my authority, which means they must be paid according to the standard set by His Majesty."

"By the time they go home, each beastkin will have more money than his entire village makes in a year," Anna said.

"Now you know why so many came out to fight," Nathan said.

"It seems a little unfair to my guards," Anna mumbled.

"Your guards have secure employment. The other soldiers you levied are being paid extra and are protecting their home. They already have livelihoods here, and many will make connections. Some will even remain as soldiers or guards once we take Fort Taubrum, giving them a well-paying job." Nathan pointed to various companies as he spoke, and Anna's gaze followed his hand. "But the beastkin will go back to their villages, in different counties, and it may be years before they have another chance to do more than live off the land. Their homes aren't under threat— at least not yet. They'll still have farmland to harvest and forests to hunt in. They need a damn good reason to risk their lives."

"Goddess, you're good at this," Anna said, staring at Nathan in wonder. "Why did your father disavow you again?"

"I imagine because he actually likes beastkin," Leopold said drily. "Understanding war beyond the idea of stabbing the enemy probably hurt his chances as well."

Nathan hid his surprise. His father in this timeline had issues with beastkin? Nathan spent as little time dwelling on his implanted memories as possible, so he was unaware of this fact.

He really should spend some time meditating on his past in this timeline, in order to avoid any nasty surprises in the future.

Furthermore, Leopold really disliked Nathan's father. Hints had been given earlier, but Leopold no longer bothered to hide his disdain for the other Bastion.

"That explains a bit, yes," Anna said. "Fine, I get it. The beastkin, that is. And also why you've had no difficulties wrangling them into a proper army, Nathan. My captain, Lord Fleitz, fell into despair after his first attempt to bring the beastkin into line."

Nathan had met Fleitz earlier. A straight-laced man roughly the same age as Nathan. He ruled a barony to the north, which included another town in Gharrick County, and owed fealty to the von Clair household. Given Fleitz's defining trait was his love of ale, and the fact he was in the process of expanding the family brewery, Nathan felt no surprise that the man struggled with beastkin.

"I'd take credit for being an amazing general, but the truth is that it's mostly because I'm a Bastion," Nathan admitted. He scratched the back of his head.

Behind him, he heard Fei let out a small whine. He ignored her.

"I imagine the dozens of beastkin currently working for you helped as well," Kuda added. "The veterans fell into line when they saw that you already worked with beastkin."

Fei muttered something that Nathan didn't hear. Glancing behind him, he saw Sen whispering into Fei's ear. The beastkin's ears sat flat against her head, and her tail hung low.

"Is something wrong, Fei?" Nathan asked.

She glowered at him.

Nathan looked at the others, who shrugged. Presumably they hadn't paid any attention to Fei's mood. Given she was his lover, he was more sensitive to her feelings.

Finally, Fei said, "It's not because you're a Bastion."

"Fei?" Nathan asked, surprised.

"They trust you because you proved that you deserve to be trusted," Fei blurted out. Her ears shot up, and her eyes bore into Nathan's. "I spoke to the old warriors, and they all said the same thing: 'Bastion Nathan knows how to lead.' You gave them orders they thought were right. You've done that in all of our battles. It's your experience that makes you trusted, not what you are."

All eyes turned from Fei to Nathan.

Well, wasn't this awkward? Fei talked up his experience, but Nathan shouldn't have it.

Nathan knew he had been coming close to the line in regard to using his wealth of knowledge from his timeline. This outburst proved that he had probably pushed things too far.

But he didn't know if he could stop. What was the point of coming back in time if he failed? Was hiding his knowledge and ability to avoid being found out worth the risk of letting Doumahr fall into ruin again?

No. Not in Nathan's eyes. But he needed to lessen the suspicion building up regarding him. People like Fei adored him and were safe. But what about his enemies?

A declaration of heresy could end everything in an instant.

Leopold spoke up first, "Well, I suppose I was right to take the risk and appoint you as Bastion here. My suspicion that your dismissal by your father made you a good fit has proven correct."

That poker face smile of Leopold's sat firmly on his face. How much did he suspect?

Nathan chose not to think too much about it. He let the topic slide.

Everybody moved onto the subject of battle tactics. The armies were in position. Due to their inferior numbers and the open terrain, laying siege was out of the question. A direct offensive was the only option.

"So we're relying on the soldiers?" Vera asked. "If the Champions are going to hang back as a contingency to deal with Seraph."

"We'll provide limited ranged support for the soldiers," Nathan said.

"Except I'm pretty sure some of us have our own mission." Vera pointed at her tower, which sat inert in the center of the Federation encampment. "We're taking the tower, aren't we?"

"That's the objective of the battle," Nathan asked. "Are you suggesting something else?"

"I have a cairn in my tower. It's tied to my magic. Rather than limited ranged support from back here, I can provide a lot more if I connect to my cairn directly. The Federation will retreat, surrender, or be destroyed once I'm back in control of the tower," Vera explained.

"You brought the idea up earlier," Nathan said.

"And?"

To say that it had been a topic of debate was an understatement.

Anna shot a glare at Leopold, who pointedly ignored her.

The old Bastion favored caution. Use the superior power of the beastkin to win the conventional battle, pepper the Federation with sorcery from afar, and engage Seraph en masse with Champions and Bastions should she appear.

A sound plan. If a little too safe, and likely to cause significant casualties among the beastkin.

By contrast, Anna liked Vera's plan. As Vera lacked any way to boost her sorcery, her spells would be useless against Seraph. The power of Ifrit allowed Sen to harm Seraph, despite her innate protections of two gems. Anna's argument was that Vera contributed more if she took control of her tower.

The fact that Anna argued so strongly in favor of the plan made Nathan question who came up with the idea to begin with. Vera hadn't pushed to be involved with any of the planning. She hadn't floated the idea that she wouldn't join the attack, given her tower was being taken back. But Nathan got the sense she wanted to avoid this battle at all costs.

Something was awry.

"I'm assuming you still can't connect to your cairn from here?" Nathan asked.

"The tower is undamaged, so its wards prevent anybody from tapping into the cairn from outside," Vera said.

"You prevented yourself from accessing your own cairn from outside the tower?" Nathan asked.

"Only if my link was broken. Which it was when you pulled me through the gateway." Vera raised an eyebrow at him, as if to dare Nathan to challenge her on that.

Her words made sense. While Nathan was intrinsically connected to his binding stone, a cairn was merely a local font of magic. There were many ways to disrupt a sorcerer's connection to his cairn. Capturing a sorcerer's tower often employed strategies reliant on breaking that connection, then killing or capturing the sorcerer before he reconnected to the cairn.

After all, once disconnected, it took anywhere from minutes to

hours for a sorcerer to reconnect to his cairn. Vera needed time
once they got into the tower for this plan to work. Somebody
needed to protect her.

Yet another gap between Bastions and sorcerers, and another
reason why sorcerers wanted to become Bastions. A binding stone
was an effectively infinite source of energy, and one that the
sorcerer couldn't lose their connection to.

Or at least, not normally. As Kadria proved, normal went out
the window when Messengers became involved. She had severed
Nathan's connections to most of his binding stones as easily as
Nathan might cut off a sorcerer from their cairns.

"If we're to get you into the tower, we'll need to make a path
and protect you while you reconnect to the cairn," Nathan
explained. This is where any proposal became unstuck during
earlier debate. "I won't put Fei and the others out of position."

"You won't need to," Vera declared. "I have enough power to
push through a few companies of soldiers with the help of one of
your summoned horses. Once there, I can get inside the tower and
activate my remaining summons."

"That's too risky," Anna said. "If we're sending in Vera like
that, then why not push harder? Once she gets on top of the
tower, she'll more than make up for the extra losses we'll take by
being more aggressive. You can't tell me that dragging the battle
out for longer is better for us?"

It could be, Nathan wanted to say. But so much of this
depended on Seraph.

"You're right, if we pull this off properly," Nathan said.
"Which is why I'll go with Vera."

Everybody stared at him.

"But you're in command," Anna said. She looked at Leopold,
who shrugged in return.

"They're your soldiers. You even have your own nobles and
officers commanding them. Fei and Sunstorm are trained
commanders as well. Everybody knows the order of battle,"

Nathan said. "But if we're modifying the plan at this stage, it makes sense that I go with Vera. My binding stone is closer than Leopold's, so I can react more swiftly to any sudden events. Plus, he has more combat experience and is better suited to fighting Seraph."

"It is risky, but an approach I feel I might take if I were feeling reckless," Leopold said.

Nathan couldn't tell if Leopold was chiding him or agreeing with him. He chose to take the words at face value and assume that the old man was letting him do what he wanted.

"Vera?" Nathan asked.

"I won't say no to a chance to get back into my tower sooner," Vera answered. Her eyes met Nathan's. "I didn't expect you or Leopold to stick your neck out like this, but I'll take it. I'll return the favor with an impressive light show once inside."

CHAPTER 37

The strategy session came to a close, and everybody dispersed.

Anna held her own meeting with her officers. Presumably she told them about the change of plans. Nathan suspected at least Lord Fleitz would approach him afterward, if only to confirm specifics.

Normally, a baron might be less willing to annoy his liege by openly looking to somebody else for authority. But Nathan was the Bastion, and Fleitz seemed comfortable with his title. Anna wasn't going to punish one of her few barons, after all.

In fact, Anna seemed to have a surprisingly small retinue for a countess. Most of those present were knights, baronets, and unlanded nobles. Fleitz was the only baron.

Nathan wondered if the other barons had refused to fight, or if Anna hadn't asked. Most barons owed their true loyalty to the archduke, not the local countess. Anna controlled the military and could require their assistance to quell threats—a baron's land comes with the requirement that he bear arms upon request of the Empire—but the barons didn't owe her fealty.

Nobility annoyed Nathan. He found it overly complex. Who appointed whose great-great-great-great-grandfather as baron a couple of centuries ago mattered more than who governed the land he lived in. To say nothing of the bitter power struggle between those at the very top.

Nathan didn't need to imagine the sort of nonsense that must take place between the three archdukes of the Empire, and with the Emperor himself. His true birthplace, the Kingdom of Falmir, had suffered through a truly devastating transition of power. He often forgot that it was still a kingdom in this timeline, calling it Falmir, instead of the Kingdom, as many others did.

"Nathan, the beastkin companies are ready," Fei said, shaking him out of his thoughts.

He rubbed the bridge of his nose and tried to focus himself. As a Bastion of the Anfang Empire, picking fights about the concept of nobility was unwise at best. Better to not waste time thinking about it.

"They know that they're leading the charge?" Nathan asked.

"Yep," Fei chirped. "They didn't seem that surprised. And I think half of their food supplies are actually alcohol." She furrowed her brow in concern.

Nathan stared at her. "Try not to talk too loudly about that. I'm guessing at least one of the old wolves knew how to handle the quartermaster. So long as they share the booze and don't crack open the barrels until after we win, I'll turn a blind eye."

"Isn't Anna paying for all the food and drink?" Fei's eyes widened as she realized what was happening.

"She can consider it a lesson in managing her supplies and logistics better," Nathan said drily. "If she lets the beastkin get one over her like this, imagine what mercenaries will do to her? Better she learns now, and what better way to learn than by picking up the check."

The sun sat firmly above their heads. Not a cloud marred the sky. Banners waved in the air above each army. The enemy encampment had emptied onto the field in front of the pass.

"Still no sign of Seraph," Nathan muttered.

"Isn't that a good thing?" Vera asked.

"I'd prefer to know where she is," he said. "But we can't afford to waste any more time."

Nathan signaled for his army to advance. Slowly, his soldiers marched toward the enemy.

Inexperienced soldiers often said that the waiting was the hardest part. Veterans thought—but rarely said—that watching their friends die while they lived on was the hardest part. Dead soldiers didn't think, but they would probably say that the hardest part was the actual battle, or maybe the part where they lay dying.

For Nathan, the hardest part were these very moments. Watching the armies converge on each other at an agonizingly slow pace. Every second reminded him of past battles. Of battle-fields covered in corpses.

No order could stop the battle now, Nathan knew. That was what made this part of the battle unbearable for him.

He felt forced to watch as the battle inched closer and closer to reality. Eventually, arrows would be fired, or a spell cast, or a melee would break out. Then the battle would be on, and Nathan's mind busy with tactics, contingencies, and ensuring that he played his role correctly.

For now, he waited.

The armies clashed, and Nathan let out a breath he knew he was holding.

"Were you this tense during the siege?" Vera asked, a look of concern on her face.

"No. I didn't give the order to start the siege," Nathan replied.

"Oh."

Everybody else had spread out prior to the start of the battle. Sen hurled fireballs over the heads of the Imperial soldiers. Her figure was easily visible due to the constant arc of flames flying from her, and the glowing triangles around her greatsword. Magical barriers blocked some of her spells, but she shattered most of them. The Federation magic users lacked the power to match Sen.

Fei sat astride an automaton horse next to Sen. Occasionally, the beastkin Champion issued an order, but she mostly watched. Her role was to command the assault and protect Sen if necessary.

Elsewhere, Leopold kept Anna company. Although both Bastions considered it unlikely, Seraph might attempt to assassinate Anna when she attacked. Leopold had the strength to counter her and withstand Seraph's superior power for long enough.

Although not visible, Sunstorm lurked in the distance. She kept watch for Seraph. Her ability to teleport and hide made her invaluable as an early warning system.

The battle dragged on. The beastkin pushed forward. Howls rose up from the front ranks, and the wolves shattered a company of heavily armored knights. Imperial soldiers—beastkin and human alike—swarmed into the opening and tore a hole in the Federation line. Reserves poured forth from the rear of the Federation army, but they had to fight past fleeing soldiers from the front line. Panic ensued.

As the Federation struggled to prevent a full-blown rout, Nathan kicked his horse forward. Vera followed him, and both of them galloped toward the front line.

Fei spotted him and snapped out new orders. The entire battle shifted in a moment. Companies of soldiers that had stayed out of the battle surged forward. The hole in the Federation line was pushed open farther. The Imperial soldiers applied more pressure to the Federation, who fought back fiercely.

A gap opened up in the Imperial lines. Several beastkin ushered Nathan and Vera through the gap. Nathan noticed that all of them were horse beastkin, their long, fine tails swaying energetically behind them.

"Carve a hole," Nathan shouted as he and Vera approached the thick of the battle. He drew his sword.

He blasted a hole in the Federation defenders with a fourth rank spell. Many of those he knocked down got back up, but most didn't. Fire poured down on the rest. Vera's staff blazed with an endless stream of flames. Nathan allowed her to take the lead and blew away any soldiers that got too close.

Spears bounced off the steel frames of the automaton horses they rode. Nathan winced as one soldier successfully hit him in the calf, before blowing away the offender.

Then the soldiers vanished. The horses leaped over a pile of rubble that had once been the outer wall of the tower. Row after row of tents flew past as Nathan and Vera rode toward the base of the tower without stopping. A handful of soldiers and camp followers stared at them. Some grabbed weapons and gave chase.

The doors to the tower were shut. They glowed faintly. Locked with magic.

Nathan leaped off his horse. Vera followed suit more sedately, demonstrating less experience in jumping off horses mid-battle. She strode up to the door and unlocked it. The stone double doors swung open without a sound.

Looking behind them, Nathan realized that the Federation soldiers hadn't given up. Rather than blow them away, he took the simpler route. He unsummoned the horses and followed Vera inside the tower. In the distance, he thought he heard the battle getting closer, as if soldiers were pushing forward to the tower at a rapid pace.

The moment he stepped inside the tower, the doors slammed shut. Vera's back faced him, and she gestured for him to follow him with her hand. She didn't slow down. Her stride was purposeful as she walked across the bottom level of her tower. The tower remained well lit, presumably as the lights drew power from the cairn.

A few corpses remained here, Nathan noticed. Not all of them were on the ground level, which is where Vera had fought off the intruders. But most were.

According to Vera, the doors to her tower automatically locked upon closing. She compared them to a magical deadbolt. Anybody who wanted to open the doors needed a magical key to match the spell keeping them closed. If the Federation closed the doors, or let them be closed for any reason, then those still inside the tower would have been trapped. Some of the corpses probably belonged to people who starved to death.

Accompanying the corpses were the remains of Vera's summons. Plates of armor and weapons, mostly. Vera had more summons within the tower, supposedly. Nathan couldn't see where they might be hidden.

He caught up to Vera and made it to the stairwell before her. Turning while he waited for her, he noticed that she had stopped.

Vera stood close to the center of the room. She didn't speak or react to Nathan's questioning gaze.

This tower contained a cairn. A pile of rocks imbued with magic that allowed sorcerers to easily channel large volumes of magic from the leylines. Nathan suspected that the cairn was underneath them although he didn't see any way in the tower to go underground.

He met Vera's gaze. She stared back at him impassively. No magic came to life in her hands, but that didn't mean much. Nathan couldn't hear anybody outside, or anybody inside for that matter. This tower contained only the two of them.

"So, are you going to join me at the top of the tower or try to kill me here?" Nathan asked.

CHAPTER 38

"At least, I'm assuming that's what you're deciding on now," Nathan added. "I can't tell. I'm pretty convinced that you've been helping the Federation, but you've done a pretty terrible job of it."

"You don't look surprised," Vera replied after a long pause.

"Like I said, I'm pretty convinced that you haven't really been on my side," Nathan said.

"Define 'your side,' Nathan," Vera said.

An excellent question, in Nathan's mind.

"The side that doesn't want an army of demons pouring into the countryside?" Nathan tried. "That stunt by the Federation could have wiped out the entire county. Or even more. A demonic invasion away from a binding stone is notoriously difficult to stop, and attracts unwanted attention."

Vera frowned at him. "Who considers it notorious? And attention from who? You've mentioned more of your secret 'Bastion knowledge' than Leopold has ever let slip. Most of the books I've been able to get my hands on say nothing about many of the things you've mentioned. I asked an old friend of mine about those Messengers you brought up months ago, and he hadn't heard of them."

Of course he hadn't. The idea of demonic generals capable of crushing Bastions like ants was too terrifying for the public to know about. Nathan doubted even the Emperor knew much about them.

"There's an uninhabited peninsula to the east of the Federation that has been overrun by demons. Don't you find it strange that nobody talks much about it?" Nathan said.

Vera remained silent, but grimaced.

"That's the side I'm on, Vera. The one that doesn't want the world turned into an uninhabitable wasteland," Nathan continued. "Hence why I became worried when you didn't seem to be on the same side."

"I helped you stabilize the leylines," Vera protested. "I even fought the Federation when they attacked. How did you even know to suspect me?"

"Initially, I was uncertain. But I grew suspicious of you because of how unwilling you were to take action to stop the bandits," Nathan explained. "The Federation had funded them in the past, the leylines were being disrupted, and now the bandits were attacking a town. But you didn't lift a finger to help an old friend. Anna described you as embittered toward the Empire."

"Are you sure you weren't merely paranoid?" Vera said drily.

"I prefer to think that I plan for contingencies," Nathan replied. He smiled, but it didn't reach his eyes. "One of those included the possibility that either you or Anna were working with the Federation."

"Anna?" Vera scoffed. "You suspected Anna?"

"Briefly." Nathan shrugged. "She had reason to be upset with the Empire. And there was nothing to suggest that she was incompetent—the opposite, in fact. She cares too much about her family, her pride, and her position in the Empire to betray it, however. To say nothing of what would happen to her brother if she betrayed the Empire. He's still fighting against Trafaumh up north, after all."

"You seem convinced from the start that somebody was working with the Federation," Vera said after a pause.

"Because that's how the Federation operates. It expands by creating new provinces and offering power to people who are bitter that they have been overlooked. Torneus is very, very good at finding people who will do things that they otherwise wouldn't, because they have been refused things that they feel they deserve."

Vera stared at him. "You know Torneus?"

"I know how he operates rather well," Nathan said. Elaborating this much was dangerous, he realized. But not talking about the manipulative old bastard hanging over Vera's head was far more dangerous.

"And you thought Torneus was interested in me?" Vera asked.

"Maybe. I didn't know for sure until very recently. Until then, I only had your suspicious behavior," Nathan admitted.

Her refusal to stop the bandits. Her aggression toward him when he first arrived. Her dismissive attitude toward the idea of the Federation attacking the Empire, even though they had been funding the bandits for years.

"But I helped you," Vera protested.

"I'll admit I'm not sure about your motives for doing that," he said, scratching the back of his neck. "But you outed yourself in the battle at the cairn when you chased after Sunstorm. You should have died when you fought her. There's no way that you could have survived a one-on-one fight with her. I assumed that you passed on a message when you chased her."

"… Shit," Vera muttered. "I knew it would look bad in retrospect, but I didn't think you already suspected me by then."

"Really? I all but accused you of potentially working with them when I pointed out that a Federation Champion was skulking around your tower," he pointed out.

Vera blinked. She opened her mouth to reply, then closed it.

Moments later, she covered her face with her palm and stared up at the very top of her tower. Nathan thought she was going to scream in frustration. He glanced around, checking for any signs of an ambush.

Nothing had changed. No summons had emerged from the shadows, and he neither saw nor felt anybody arrive. He couldn't feel Seraph's power outside, either.

"So you knew it was me from the start," Vera said when she recomposed herself.

"Like I said, I suspected somebody. You confirmed my suspicions through your actions," he said. "You wanted to become a Bastion. The Empire refused you. You became angry. Leopold frustrated you because he stopped helping you and continued to keep his secrets, and eventually Anna gave up on you. Then Torneus offered you the binding stone in exchange for betraying the Empire. All you had to do was undermine the defense of Gharrick Pass and constantly mislead Anna."

Vera grimaced and looked away. She didn't refute his story. Maybe he had missed a few details, but he seemed to have gotten it largely right.

"What I don't understand is why you helped me stop the Federation?" Nathan asked.

"… Because they didn't tell me everything," Vera muttered. "I'm not lying when I say that you've told me more about Bastions than anybody else I've ever met. Everybody—Sunstorm, Torneus, Seraph, Leopold—they all know so much more but kept me in the dark. Then you told me what the Federation's plan really was."

"Demons," Nathan said.

"Yes," Vera said. She looked him in the eyes. "That's why I initially helped you. And what I told Sunstorm. I refused to help the Federation with a plan that relied on a demonic invasion of the county."

Something clicked in Nathan's mind. The gap between the

Vera in front of him, who was so angry and bitter at the Empire, and the heroic Vera from his timeline.

They were the same person. There was no gap.

Instead, the heroic Vera saw the consequences of her betrayal firsthand. She saw demonic portals open in her homeland, demons tear apart Gharrick County and destroy Trantia, and possibly even the death of one of her oldest friends.

History never recorded the fact that she helped the Federation destroy the Empire. The Federation never admitted that they were involved in any way beyond attacking the Empire, as intentionally starting a demonic invasion was heresy of the highest order.

What history recorded was a Vera that saw the chaos she had wrought and chose to die fighting against the people who had caused it, rather than silently take the reward the Federation offered her.

Nathan wondered how much of what he thought he knew from his timeline was wrong, or at least slanted. Leopold was a vastly different man to how he had imagined him to be.

"Once I returned to my tower, that wasn't the end of it," Vera continued, bringing Nathan back to the current timeline. "Seraph wanted me to help with the assault on your castle. She explained that you would be in the middle of dealing with a demonic invasion. I realized that she had planned for the possibility that you would stabilize the leylines."

"And then?" Nathan asked.

"Then Leopold turned up and acted like his secretive, condescending self. He seemed more interesting in testing you than stopping the Federation. I was convinced that I was right to support Seraph." Vera gave Nathan a humorless smile. "Except something about you changed him. You were a step ahead of Seraph. You knew about the 'cascade' as you called it. Despite your bullshit explanation about how you didn't understand what was going on, everybody knew that you had been busy planning for a demonic invasion since the moment you captured Sen."

Vera laughed. "Goddess, you even stalled the invasion for weeks. Sunstorm kept asking me if I had heard anything from you, as she became convinced that you had been invaded and Theus had forgotten to tell Seraph."

"You're beating around the bush," Nathan said.

"True." Vera sighed and run a hand through her gorgeous red locks. "I got cold feet."

"Obviously."

She glared at him, and he raised his hands defensively.

"I got cold feet because I realized you didn't deserve this," Vera explained. "Anna didn't either. She had been screwed by the Empire as badly as I had been, but kept going. At first I hated you. You had become a Bastion where I failed. You had what I wanted. But…"

Nathan waited.

"But you lost everything to become a Bastion," she said. "Your family, your home, your title. All gone. And here you are, a Bastion so excellent that even Leopold is impressed. Maybe there was a reason I failed to get into the academy. Maybe there wasn't. But I at least know it's wrong to hold it against you. I couldn't help but imagine if our roles were switched. You're even a sorcerer, and your thirst for knowledge about Bastions must be as great as mine, given how much you've learned so fast."

Vera raised her arms into the air in a shrug, palms open, and gave him a helpless look. For the first time, Nathan saw her not as a powerful sorceress, but simply as somebody who was struggling to find their path in life.

Paths. Nathan saw a lot of diverging paths for people these days. For a man who disliked contemplating his own future, he found himself guiding or shaping the futures of far too many people.

This time that future might end very quickly depending on his decision.

"And do you have cold feet now?" Nathan asked. His voice echoed within the tower.

"The plan was for me to signal Seraph once I got to the top of the tower. She would attack, which would distract your Champions and Leopold. Anna's army will clump up in the center of the battlefield as they try to capitalize on the 'opening' they've made in the Federation ranks," Vera explained. "Easy prey for my spells, especially empowered with my cairn."

"You're dodging the question," Nathan said. "Besides, how did you plan to deal with me? Or any other Champion that went with you? Until you reconnect with your cairn, you're far weaker than a monogem Champion or Bastion."

Vera smirked and wiggled her fingers in the air. Her many rings glimmered in the light. Nathan's eyes ran across the many other pieces of jewelry and adornments on Vera's outfit. He had written them off as aesthetic choices.

It suddenly occurred to them that might have been a mistake.

"What's one of the most obvious tactics to use when facing a sorcerer in control of a cairn?" Vera said.

"Prevent them from using the cairn in the first place," Nathan answered. He stared at her jewelry. His fingers twitched, but he kept his cool. He left his sword in its sheath and didn't touch its hilt.

"Mm-hmm," Vera hummed. "You had Fei beat Sen black-and-blue in the forest. But in my tower, an enemy is more likely to use some grander spell to cut me off. So I have my own tricks to remain connected to my cairn. I didn't lie to you that I'm not connected to it."

"Your jewelry. It channels magic," Nathan said dully.

"That's right. Each of my rings and chains is tethered to the cairn. Even if my connection is severed, their connections remain. So long as I'm inside my tower, I can always draw on my cairn," Vera said triumphantly.

She had an edge that Nathan hadn't anticipated. With the

backing of her cairn, Vera held the raw power of a monogem Champion. Unlike Sen, who lacked the speed and expertise to cast spells while under attack by Fei, Vera was an accomplished sorceress. The Imperial Sorcerer's Lodge recognized her.

"So you eliminate anybody who accompanied you with the element of surprise," Nathan said. "Or at least, you could have, if you hadn't told me about your trick."

"I haven't exactly lost the power of my cairn," Vera said drily.

"No, but if you wanted to blow me away, you would have done it the moment I turned around earlier." Nathan crossed his arms. "I'm a Bastion. I have a binding stone backing me. Giving me any chance to regain the advantage is enormously risky."

"Goddess, you're so damn condescending," Vera snapped. "For all you know, Seraph is waiting in the shadows and will blow a hole in your head the moment I snap my fingers."

"Maybe. Like I said, I do plan for contingencies. There's a reason I came by myself," Nathan answered.

"Really?" Vera shook her head. "Fine then. Humor me. Let's assume I don't have cold feet. I have my cairn. I'm more powerful than you expect. Dozens of summons swarm out from the walls around you. Seraph steps out from the shadows. The doors are locked and you can't get out."

Vera pointed a finger at Nathan. "You are the most important Bastion in this battle. In this region, even. If you go down, both Sunstorm and Fei lose their power. Leopold will surely retreat the moment he realizes you're dead. The Federation will sweep the battle, and then Gharrick County before the Empire can react. Torneus wins."

Nathan grimaced. On the one hand, she was right.

On the other hand, that was only true if the Federation could win the battle after he went down.

"Not quite," Nathan said. "You're forgetting one thing."

"What?"

"I'm a Bastion," Nathan said.

When Vera scoffed, he pointed at the ground below him. Presumably, the cairn sat down there.

"I control the leylines here, through the binding stone. You may control the cairn, but I can manipulate the magic that leads to it," Nathan said.

Vera stared at him, confused.

He continued, "The moment I realize that I'm in an unwinnable battle and cannot escape, I'll overload the cairn. The tower, everybody in it, and within a few hundred meters, will be killed."

"You're kidding," Vera said.

"It's a fairly normal contingency plan for hopeless situations," Nathan said. Or at least, it became one in his timeline. Cairns were simple to overload. "I may even be able to survive it, given I have a lot of power in my binding stone."

"But if you don't, you die," Vera said, her voice hollow. "Your only plan if you were wrong about me was to take down everybody with you? Are you aware of how insane that sounds? You were so certain that you could stop me, or that Seraph wasn't here, that the only backup plan you came up with was to take us with you!" Her voice echoed off the walls. Nathan suspected the soldiers outside heard her.

"Eventually, there comes a battle that can't be won," Nathan said. His eyes bore into Vera's.

"Goddess, of course there is," Vera spat back. "But there's a difference between recklessly walking into a potential death trap and throwing every possible trick at a situation before shrugging your shoulders and blowing yourself to pieces. Imagine if that was my solution? By the time you opened the gateway to my tower to save me, this place would have been a smoking ruin."

"If you're my enemy, why should you care?" Nathan asked.

"Fuck you," Vera shouted, and tried to strangle him from across the room. "Haven't you realized it by now? I don't care about Seraph's plan. To hell with Torneus and being a Bastion. But you! I think you need to step back for a second and remember that there's a long road ahead of you."

Nathan remained silent. Something about Vera's words clicked with him. He had a strange sense of deja vu, but realized it was for a different reason.

"This isn't a glorious last stand," Vera said. "You only became a Bastion months ago. If you die, you throw away years of dreams of everybody who wanted to become one. What about Fei? Sunstorm? Sen? Even the unicorn girl who stares at your ass when she thinks nobody is looking? What happens to them after you're gone?"

Their faces flashed in his mind. So did their older faces, from Nathan's original timeline.

In that moment, Nathan realized his error.

"You're right," Nathan admitted, closing his eyes.

Vera blinked. "You mean it?"

"I didn't plan ahead enough," Nathan said. He ran a hand through his hair and looked at the door. "I do want there to be a future for everybody. Maybe I was a little too fatalistic."

"A little? You basically said that if you were wrong, then death was inevitable," Vera replied. She sighed. "I'm telling you this because the others won't. Your girls admire you to an almost unhealthy extent. You've earned that admiration, but I see a lot of Leopold in you. Being too competent can be a problem as well, as when you finally slip up, you fail to see a way out. I'm used to failure. But you? I get the feeling your first real setback was when your father came back, decided he didn't like you, and disowned you."

Leaving aside that this related to his implanted memories, Nathan understood the comparison. He knew the sting of failure better than she thought he did, but he had risen to greatness far faster than most.

And he also understood the Leopold comparison.

Leopold Tyrim, the right-hand man of the Emperor, and potentially the most accomplished Bastion in the Anfang Empire. He had died gloriously in defense of the Empire in Nathan's timeline. But most people disliked him.

Now that Nathan knew him personally, he saw dimensions that nobody had ever described to him. Leopold was competent. But Nathan saw in him the mistakes that had led to the downfall of the Empire. A highly competent Bastion mired in politics, uncomfortable with his position, and dedicated to his friends, including the Emperor.

Nathan had made similar missteps. They had cost many lives. Falmir had changed drastically as a result of them. And, in the end, he had only barely escaped the consequences due to a mysterious Messenger who offered him an escape from the end of everything. Assuming that Nathan believed that this new start counted as escape.

He needed to avoid making those mistakes again. What he wanted was a future that he could enjoy with those he cared for and loved. Vera was right that he had been too hasty to risk his life like this.

He had only used his contingency plan against Kadria to detonate the binding stone after she destroyed his fortress and killed everyone. Back then, he had nothing left to lose.

But now? He had everything to lose.

With a deep sigh, Nathan got his thoughts in order. "I'll take that on the chin. And maybe more comments after the battle. But if you have decided to fight with the Empire, and not the Federation, why don't we end this battle?"

"I thought you would never ask," Vera said with a bright smile. She bounced toward the stairs, and the two ascended to the top of the tower.

CHAPTER 39

Seraph never made an appearance during the battle. Even after Vera sent the signal to lure her out, the duogem Champion remained absent. Presumably, she knew that Vera had reneged on the deal.

How Seraph knew was another question. She had been described as a savvy operative and commander. Perhaps she smelled a trap and steered clear. Neither Vera nor Nathan found any trace of a spell that might have allowed Seraph to spy on them.

Without their commander and savior, the Federation army collapsed. Vera's spells devastated them. The soldiers broke and fled. Many surrendered on the spot, rather than be run down by hundreds of heavily armed beastkin. The rest ran as fast as they could in the opposite direction of the battle.

Fei saw an opportunity and seized it. She cut off retreat to the east.

Leopold used the same trick, but with less swiftness. He tore the earth apart in front of those fleeing north. Soldiers tumbled into ditches and crashed into pillars of dirt. Desperately trying to scramble to safety, many soon realized how hopeless their retreat was and gave in to the pursuing Empire warriors.

Nathan watched from the top of the tower as a Federation army of thousands dwindled into mere hundreds. Those in the enemy camp didn't bother to flee. The Empire's reputation for mercy prevented a desperate last stand from taking place, or any foolish moves from the Federation soldiers.

After the battle, the prisoners were segregated from the Empire's army. The officers were split out from the common soldiers, and any would-be nobles identified. Although the nature of the Federation made it more difficult to identify who was important.

In the Federation, a noble might be a merchant who bought the land and title. His wealth makes him valuable, but he probably wasn't important. His family would pay a handsome ransom to see him returned, but the impact he would have on any war or negotiations was effectively none. Nathan cared little about these prisoners, although he knew that the ransoms were a nice bonus for the troops and nobles involved in the battle.

But if the noble was somebody in a genuine position of influence, then they mattered a lot. Federation titles were inconsistent, due to the mishmash of countries they had absorbed. A mere lord could be one of the most important people on the battlefield.

Fortunately, Nathan had Sunstorm to help him. She knew many of the nobles involved in the Federation offensive, and the neighboring regions. Although the nobles were shocked to see her wandering around the prisoner camp and investigating them, she picked out the most important prisoners of war.

These high-ranking prisoners became the men and women that Nathan would send back with Leopold after this campaign. Their testimony would serve as proof of the Federation's intent to invade the Empire and cover Nathan's ass.

As for the rest, Nathan left them to Anna to handle. Her adviser, Kuda, likely knew how to handle ransoms and releasing the prisoners.

Nobody wanted to slaughter the surrendered soldiers simply

because they fought for the wrong side. At the same time, releasing them back to the Federation without any penalty could be described as unwise. The enemy soldiers could simply turn back up at the next major battle.

Ransoms were an effective financial penalty, to both the combatant and the nation. The Federation would be less willing to engage in battles. The soldiers were dissuaded from fighting, knowing they might lose more money than they were being paid. And the nobles were especially dissuaded from fighting a losing battle, as their ransoms were exceedingly high.

Assuming the noble made it back at all. No doubt they noticed several of their number being carted off by Sunstorm to separate tents. When your last memory of a general of a losing battle was them being taken away by the victor, a man thought long and hard about being the general of the next battle.

War was a poor business for everyone involved. The Federation started this one for profit. It didn't hurt to remind them that losing a war was very unprofitable.

Leopold wandered up to Nathan and clapped him on the back. "Not joining the celebrations?" he asked.

"I'll need a clear head tomorrow," Nathan replied.

"You're planning to make a move tomorrow?" Leopold asked. "No time to celebrate?"

Shaking his head, Nathan said, "It's not about making a move tomorrow it's about being ready. I'll let others celebrate for me."

The two of them stared out at the soldiers before them. Tankards of ale were passed between many of the men and women. Happiness was the order of the night. Many of these soldiers had seen death for the first time, and they didn't like it. They drank to forget. They drank to celebrate their first victory. They drank because others were drinking.

Leopold spoke up, "You and Vera were in the tower for a long time."

"Were we?" Nathan responded blandly.

Leopold remained silent for several seconds. Eventually, he clapped Nathan on the back again and smirked. "Fine, keep your secrets," he said. "You've done well. I expected things to go worse, but you've planned and dealt with all the eventualities. Or maybe it's just dumb luck."

"How kind of you," Nathan said drily.

Chuckling, Leopold wandered off into the night. He snatched a tankard that a soldier offered and joined in the celebrations with the rest of the men and women.

True to his word, Nathan didn't join in. Instead, he patrolled the exterior of the camp. Just in case. The night was long, especially for a sober man.

Come morning, Nathan woke up to find himself with a lap full of beastkin. Fei groaned when he woke up and pushed her off him. Her cat ears twitched, and her eyelids flickered as she began to slowly awaken.

"It's too bright," Fei moaned.

Clearly, she had been out late with the other beastkin. Her hair and face were a mess. Nathan took some time out of his morning to clean her up. She enjoyed the grooming session, her purring a sure sign that she wanted more, but Nathan chose to avoid anything adult.

There would be plenty of time for fun after the campaign. Right now, they had another battle to plan.

Most of Nathan's war cabinet was present in the command tent when he arrived. Anna, Leopold, Vera, and Kuda were present. Sunstorm arrived not long after Nathan. Notably, Sen was missing.

Nathan wrote her off, as he had spotted her guzzling down far too much ale the previous night. Fei also noticed her absence, and she ducked her head. No doubt the beastkin felt at least some guilt that her drinking competition with Sen was the cause of her absence.

"Don't worry about Sen," Nathan said to Fei. "She's learning a hard lesson about moderating her drinking while on campaign."

Fei nodded but still looked guilty. Nathan debated pushing the subject further. In the end, he let it drop and started the meeting.

"Sunstorm, before I start, any sign of Federation troops nearby?" Nathan asked.

Sunstorm shook her head. Taking that as a sign she hadn't noticed anything else of note, Nathan chose to get on with the show.

"I trust we've all had an enjoyable evening," Nathan said.

"I have. I don't know about you," Leopold said with a smirk.

"We won. That made things enjoyable enough for me." Nathan shrugged.

Anna rolled her eyes. Her face showed no signs of a long night. She must have retired relatively early, or at least avoided drinking too much with her nobles. Nathan knew that she had enjoyed more than a few glasses of wine with them. No surprise, given this was her first campaign and was a wild success so far.

By contrast, Leopold showed his age. The old man had bags under his eyes and looked as if he hadn't slept for a few days. His voice croaked, and he sounded almost as if he'd swallowed a bag of gravel. Despite that, he seemed lively enough. If he was willing to crack jokes, then that probably meant he was fine to plan the rest of the campaign.

"We're not taking at least one more day?" Anna asked.

"Another day is fine," Nathan said. "But that doesn't change the fact that we need to plan ahead."

"So this meeting is purely about planning our next move?" Anna pressed.

"It's about ensuring that we don't lose our momentum," Nathan clarified. When the others looked at him in confusion, Nathan held back a sigh. Leopold understood, but everybody else was too new to warfare to understand the issue that Nathan was trying to avoid.

Nathan scratched his head and tried not to sigh. "We've won one victory. But our objective is to take Fort Taubrum. Many campaigns end because they let the soldiers spend too much time looting, celebrating, or doing whatever the hell they want. That's why it's important that we know when we're moving on the fort."

Anna frowned. "We just crushed the Federation army. Are we really that worried about time?" She looked around at the others.

Leopold raised an eyebrow at Nathan but said nothing. He left this entirely to Nathan. Normally, Nathan would think this is a little too much. But he wasn't a normal Bastion, so he wasn't worried.

"Our real opponent isn't the Federation army," Nathan said. "While it takes time to rally new troops and rebuild an army, the Federation has plenty of other Champions and Bastions. Now that we're threatening them, we're on the clock. Every day that we waste is a day that another Champion or a Bastion could bail out Theus and Seraph."

Vera interjected, "Seraph should be the only one in Fort Taubrum. You're worried about other Champions arriving in the next few days?"

"Yes."

Murmuring met his pronouncement. Kuda whispered something in Anna's ear. She brushed him off, but Nathan wondered if she had sent something to her nobles regarding the time between this battle and the next. Whatever the case, Nathan didn't have the option to care.

Victory was close. If Seraph was the brains behind Theus, then capturing or killing her at Fort Taubrum would end this campaign. The Federation would surely counterattack, but the opening moves in the war would be a solid victory for the Empire. Other nations would think twice before intervening to help the Federation. And that left room for Leopold and the Emperor to work their political magic.

"Fort Taubrum will have its own garrison defending it,"

Leopold said. "We'll still need to defeat it. Besieging a fortress is not easy, especially when defended by a duogem Champion. If we're in such a rush, how do we have the time to lay siege to a fortress?"

Nathan knew that Leopold's question wasn't overly serious, but sometimes he wondered if the old man knew how to be slightly less infuriating. No wonder Vera disliked him. Asking leading questions like this is the sort of thing that makes people dislike you.

"I'm not worried about taking Fort Taubrum," Nathan replied. "The trick is engaging Seraph sooner rather than later. Once she's tied up with our forces, then I can put my plan into action. But if she has reinforcements, or if Theus does something drastic such as abandoning Forselle Valley, then I'll need to drastically alter my plan."

"That sounds like you have an impressive plan." Leopold frowned.

Nathan hadn't explained to Leopold how he planned to seize Fort Taubrum. No doubt the old Bastion had a few ideas. Nathan doubted that any of those ideas were close to the mark. Then again, maybe Leopold had a more active imagination than Nathan gave him credit for.

"How long will it take Theus to get down to Fort Taubrum?" Anna asked.

"Realistically? A day. Maybe two." Nathan waved a hand in the air as if to dismiss the concern that his words raised. "A better question is: how long will it take Theus to panic after Seraph tells him the bad news about this battle?"

Sunstorm scoffed. "He'll panic immediately, but he won't act straight away. The Regents have ordered him to hold Forselle Valley, so he'll be loath to retreat."

"Would he be likely to attack us if we besieged Fort Taubrum?" Anna asked.

"Unlikely," Sunstorm said. "Given the Federation is losing,

he'll revert to his cowardly self. The regents can't exactly threaten him with death if he thinks he's going to die anyway."

Leopold chuckled and shook his head. "If there's one thing that idiot appears to be good at, it's recognizing when he's lost. He pulled out of the battle against my Champions in Forselle Valley far earlier than most Bastions would."

Sunstorm and Leopold exchanged smirks. Their shared disdain for Theus forged a bond between them.

"So that means we have a few days to reach for Taubrum?" Anna suggested.

"At most," Nathan said. "I'm assuming that you want to use all of those 'few days.'"

"If I can, then yes," Anna replied. "Unless we have anything pressing that requires us to march tomorrow or the day after, then I'd appreciate if we have three days encamped here. Fort Taubrum is only a day or two's march north, isn't it?"

After further discussion, they came to an agreement to give Anna the three days that she wanted. Nathan didn't know why she needed three days specifically. He didn't especially care. In the end, Anna had her reasons—presumably noble reasons—and she was lending him her army.

Sunstorm kept an eye out to the north and patrolled significant distances to look for any errant Federation forces that might be of concern. Other than a few small patrols from the towns and nearby forts, she found nothing of interest.

Smaller forts and watchtowers dotted the region. With the time they had available, Nathan sent out Fei and Sen to chase away any Federation soldiers using these defensive positions. Anna's soldiers then took over some of the more heavily fortified locations. They would serve as supply depots and potentially future defensive positions.

Nathan sincerely hoped that they wouldn't need to be used to defend against the Federation. That would imply a major Federation counteroffensive in the future, or that he had failed to push farther into Federation territory before things turned against them.

The three days passed. Anna kept herself busy with her nobles. Additional wagons carrying supplies arrived toward the tail end of the third day. This wasn't what Anna was waiting for, but she took credit for it anyway.

A report from Sunstorm indicated that additional soldiers were traveling through the pass, bearing Anna's emblem. Anna gave no indication to Nathan that they would join the attack on Fort Taubrum. Presumably, these soldiers were here to hold Gharrick Pass and to capture additional Federation territory. Nathan let her do what she wished.

He had his own job to do. His battle with Seraph grew closer.

CHAPTER 40

S en ducked her head through the flap of Nathan's tent. She raised an eyebrow at the noises coming from within, especially now that she saw the source.

"Standing outside, I expected to see both of you wearing much less clothing," Sen said.

Fei mewled. "It just feels so good." She arched her back and her bushy tail stuck out straight.

"What have I told you about moving while I'm grooming you," Nathan said, patting Fei on the ass. She fell back into his lap and flicked her tail against his chest.

Nathan gestured for Sen to enter the tent. She slipped inside and let the flap fall shut behind her.

Glancing back at the entrance, Sen said, "Wouldn't it be a good idea to place some sort of noise suppression spell on the tent?"

"Easier said than done. The tent isn't made from the sturdiest material, and it doesn't provide a proper seal from the outside air," Nathan explained. "Furthermore, spells need to be powered, and I have better things to use my magic on than preventing others from hearing Fei's moans."

"Hey," Fei whined.

Nathan ran a hand along her tail, and she quietened down. Or at least as quiet as she got while being groomed.

Sen took a seat on a nearby crate and closely watched Fei's reactions. The beastkin moaned, mewled, and let out more than her fair share of obscene noises.

"Yeah, definitely still sounds like sex." Sen shook her head. "Not that I came in here to perv or anything."

"Then what did you come in here for? We're taking the fort tomorrow, so it's a good idea to get some sleep," Nathan said.

"I should say that to you," Sen replied. "It seems like you'll be up all night keeping this little kitty company. She's raring to go, judging by the smell. Are you sure you…"

Fei tried to glare at Sen, but the effect was muted by the way her eyes curved and the moans that escaped her lips every few seconds.

"I don't plan to do anything more after this. As always when I'm campaigning, I intend for this to be an early night," Nathan said.

"It's impossible to get him to have any fun," Fei complained. She pushed herself against Nathan, rubbing her scent into his clothes.

He ignored her and continued to stroke her tail and rub her ears.

"Is that what the glass is for? I thought you didn't drink while campaigning," Sen said. She pointed to a small tumbler full of amber liquid.

"That's not for me," Nathan said drily.

Fei pointedly ignored Sen's stare.

"Is that to calm her nerves?" Sen asked Nathan.

"I'm not nervous." Somehow, Fei's denial made her sound more nervous.

Nathan shook his head in response to Sen's question. "Less nervous, more hyperactive. I have no doubt that she'll be fine in the battle tomorrow. What I'm worried about is that she'll try to keep me up all night. And we both know exactly what she'll do when she gets bored."

"The exact same thing that she's trying to do to you right now?" Sen grinned.

Their banter continued for several minutes, and Fei complained the entire time. Nathan idly wondered what the soldiers outside felt about this. No doubt it sounded like he was having sex with one woman, while joking around with another.

Assuming any soldiers were out there to begin with. He was a Bastion—not exactly high on the list of targets that needed protection. His soldiers were more likely to be killed by anybody powerful enough to harm Nathan. Most people that tried to stab him would find their blades shattered on impact with his body.

"I'm surprised that you're not with Sunstorm right now," Nathan commented, changing the subject.

Sen grimaced. "We've been together most the day, but she tends to get a bit awkward at night."

"I was going to ask about that. Things haven't improved?" Nathan asked.

Sen held a palm up facing flat toward the ground and shook it back and forth. "Kind of? It doesn't help that what we think of you and each other is vastly different. She's very keen to pick up where we left off. I am much more in tune with 'old me' than she is, so I feel that she is falling back on our relationship more."

The look that Fei gave Sen was strange, but that was understandable. Not only was the relationship between Sen and Sunstorm confusing, but there was the memory situation to contend with.

Fei didn't know about the alternate timeline. Sen and Sunstorm did, even if their memories were incomplete. At the same time, Sen and Sunstorm remembered their past from this world, which included a sexual relationship between the two of them.

"If you're not interested in her, you can say no," Nathan said.

"The thing is, part of me is interested. I just have difficulty making sense of that part of me." Sen closed her eyes and leaned backward, careful not to topple over. "My memories are a mess, but Sunstorm supported me through a rough patch. But right now, I'm much stronger. I can't help but think that relationship was a crux and that I shouldn't rely on it. For Sunstorm, I think it meant something more."

Sen continued to hedge around the situation. The more she talked, the more Fei looked at her funny.

Fei knew about the relationship between Sen and Sunstorm. Sometimes, she walked in on the two of them doing things in Nathan's room, while they waited for him. That was to say nothing of the activities they sometimes got up to together with him.

But that likely confused her more, as she probably didn't understand why Sen had difficulty with Sunstorm. Fei's understanding of relationships was simplistic at best, so far as Nathan could tell.

Realizing that the situation had grown awkward, Nathan gave Fei a pat on the back and pushed her off his lap. Fei whined in response. Slowly, she crept off his lap and found a new seat.

Right next to him.

Nathan held in a sigh when Fei leaned against him.

"She knows what she wants, doesn't she?" Sen commented with a smile.

Putting on an innocent face, Fei picked up the glass from the nearby table and swirled around the whisky within it. She began to sip the amber liquid.

"It doesn't hurt anyone, so let her be," Nathan said. "I'm assuming you came here for a reason other than sating your curiosity about Fei's moans?"

"I did." Sen nodded. Her hands fidgeted in her lap. "I want to ask you about what I should be doing in battle."

Nathan blinked. "In battle? Well, you have your orders, don't you? They change from battle to battle, sure, but I think you know how to fight."

"No, no, that's not it." Sen shook her head. "I mean, how should I be fighting in battle? I'm a spellblade, right? And you're a spellblade?"

Nathan nodded in response.

"So why do we almost never fight our opponents with our swords? Why do we spend so much time standing back and pummeling them with spells?" Sen asked, exasperation evident in her voice.

Nathan tried not to laugh. Unfortunately, he wasn't holding anything with which to cover his face, so his smile was visible.

"Don't laugh at me!" Sen demanded.

"I'm not laughing at you." Nathan held his hands up in a gesture of surrender. "But I asked this question myself when I was younger. And I've been asked it many times since."

Sen's eyes widened. She asked, "Really? Then what's the answer?"

"Complicated. A spellblade is simply a sorcerer that also uses a sword. But why do we use a sword?"

Sen dithered before answering, "isn't it so that I can defend myself in case a Champion or someone else attacks me in close range?"

"How would you summarize that?" Nathan responded.

Rolling her eyes, Sen said, "Oh, I see what you're doing. This is one of those 'make me give you the answer because I should already know it' situations, isn't it?"

"Then humor me." Nathan waited and crossed his arms.

Fei watched the two of them with wide, curious eyes, while continuing to drink her whisky. She had a taste for the stuff, Nathan noted. While brandy was the favored drink in the Empire, Nathan had always preferred whisky, given it was much more common in his homeland of Falmir. Perhaps Fei liked it because it was exotic to her.

He didn't recall her liking it in his timeline. She had always been more of an ale person back then.

"Having a sword gives me options," Sen said. "If I'm attacked at close range, I can defend myself with it. At long range, I don't have to use it. But is that really all a spellblade is?"

Nathan shook his head. "If that's all a spellblade was, then it would just be a fancy name for 'sorcerer who uses a sword.' Your sword channels magic. You can use it to direct spells, defend against attacks, and use it as a weapon when you go on the offense. What you're experiencing now is a growing pain. When you were a bandit, you used your sword more often than your spells from afar, correct?"

Sen nodded, a frustrated expression crossing her face. Clearly, she was not at home with the shift in focus that Nathan and Ifrit had forced upon her.

"Ifrit has mostly been teaching you long-range spells, hasn't he?" Nathan asked.

"Yes," Sen blurted out. She blinked. "Wait, how do you know that? Can you talk to him in my head?"

"Of course not. I know because that's the traditional way to train a spellblade," Nathan explained. "Or at least, one with as much talent and power as you."

Sen remained silent, although her eyes wandered to the whisky in Fei's hands.

He got the message. Nathan dug up another glass from his trunk. He poured a couple of measures of whisky into it and handed it to Sen. Now that he had produced the bottle, Fei asked for more. He gave her a finger more, and ignored her complaint that he was being stingy.

"When you are less powerful, the gap between sorcerer and spellblade is readily apparent," Nathan explained as he placed the bottle back in his trunk. "But as a Champion, the gap often appears invisible. The spellblade is—to an untrained eye—a sorcerer that uses a sword. That isn't true. But that impression lives on because most opponents are not strong enough to make a powerful spellblade go all out."

"This has to do with the fact that you're always holding back," Sen said, comprehension dawning on her face.

Nathan winked at Sen but didn't confirm her comment. He continued with his earlier explanation, "Being up close and personal with an enemy puts you at risk. It's usually smarter to bombard them from range. Most of your best spells will be more effective at a distance. Until you can cast high rank spells quickly and efficiently, you cannot use them in close-quarters combat."

"Right. So I can only use low rank spells in melee," Sen said. "Ifrit has explained that. But isn't getting up in their face often more effective?"

"You misunderstand," Nathan said. "The point is to learn how to use high rank spells in melee. That's what is truly effective."

"In other words, I'm focusing on long-distance spells as a means of training?" Sen clarified. "That makes it sound like I'm not ready to be on the battlefield."

"If you aren't ready to be on the battlefield, most of this army isn't either," Nathan drawled. "There's no harm in having room to grow, Sen. The same goes for you, Fei. Nobody expects you to be capable of defeating a duogem or a trigem Champion yet. I'm here to train you and help you grow, until you are able to do that."

Sen's eyes widened. "You really think that we will be able to beat a trigem?"

Nathan didn't hesitate, even though he had no confirmation that Sen ever achieved a level of strength equal to a trigem. "I do. I'm here for you. You have Ifrit, and I trust in you." He smiled at Fei and Sen. "Both of you."

Fei squeaked. Her arms wrapped around him suddenly, and he felt something wet splash against his side. He had a bad feeling that was the whisky in her glass. She rubbed her face against his chest. He scratched behind her ears and held her against him.

Sen didn't join in the celebration, however. Concern marred her face.

"If I'm going to be drawing on enough power from Ifrit to oppose a trigem Champion then what will I look like?" Sen asked quietly.

Nathan stood up, shaking Fei off him. He stepped over to Sen.

Bending down, he gave her a kiss. When he pulled away, she stared back at him. He found her expression cute.

"You'll look like yourself," he said.

Sen rolled her eyes. "Of course you would say something like that." But she smiled anyway.

Nathan quickly learned that he had made a mistake by giving both women whisky that night, especially as they demanded more after his pep talk. Maybe he shouldn't have given more to them, but he was feeling good.

He managed to avoid being kept up all night by the two, mostly by dint of the fact that Fei fell asleep halfway through trying to pull his pants off. Her snoring convinced Sen to give up on the idea.

Nathan got a good night's sleep in the arms of both women. He hoped that tomorrow's battle against Seraph didn't ruin his memories of tonight.

CHAPTER 41

A strong wind kicked up around Fort Taubrum. Nathan's army formed a defensive perimeter to the south, but it was unnecessary. The defenders remained firmly ensconced within their walls. Seraph made no appearance.

The sun shined down harshly on Nathan as he looked at the fortress. He noticed that it had been awhile since the fortress's moat had been topped up. The water level seemed oddly low, likely because of the lack of rain on this side of the mountains. The ground was arid, and vegetation was sparse.

"I've checked the perimeter," Sunstorm said after she ran up to Nathan. "There's no sign of Federation forces nearby."

"Good job. Get some rest, then join Fei with the rest of the troops," Nathan said.

He watched as Sunstorm trotted off into the mass of troops nearby. They were busy building the encampment. Siege engines were erected. Patrols ran around the perimeter of the camp. The army settled in for a long siege. Normally, that would be a good idea.

But Nathan had no intention of letting this drag out. He needed to end this soon. Seraph was a wild card. He knew little about the duogem Champion's powers, beyond the fact that they were powerful. All Sunstorm could tell him was that Seraph had some sort of force blast ability. She could blow away objects and people from a distance, and she seemed sturdier than a Champion normally would be with her level of enhancements.

Given Seraph had two jades, Nathan found her powers rather odd. Jades were gems related to nature. A Champion with these gems usually had powers that relate to the natural elements. Control over wind, fire, water, and earth was common. That said, jades were rather flexible, and Nathan didn't understand them in any real depth. No doubt they held secrets that were only known to those from the Kurai Peninsula.

To Nathan, that meant he should minimize conflict with her. As he had said earlier to the others, a drawn-out siege was risky due to the possibility of intervention by the rest of the Federation. More than that, he worried about losing Champions. He had asked for Leopold's help to prevent exactly that, but the only real way to protect everybody was to neutralize Seraph. That meant Nathan needed to put his plan into motion as soon as possible.

Despite his concerns, Seraph didn't make a move on the first day. Night fell uneventfully.

The next morning, Nathan ordered the soldiers to line up in formation in front of the walls. Without siege weapons, many of the soldiers shifted uneasily. They wanted to know why they were out here already. Charging the fortress was suicide. They lacked their siege engines. How could they scale the walls? How could they bring them down?

A dome of light shimmered over the fortress, reminding everybody of the futility of beginning the assault unprepared. To Nathan, it was a reminder of why he needed to move fast. The protective field of magic was further empowered by the binding stone within the fortress. Although inactive, the binding stone would still be tethered into the force field and make it stronger than found at a typical stronghold. Even Sen's magic would struggle to punch through the fortress's protective barrier.

That meant the siege engines his soldiers were building were useless. New tactics were necessary. Fei, Sen, Sunstorm, and the others met with Nathan in front of the army.

"The fortress may not look like much, but I'm worried that you're underestimating it," Leopold said.

"Really? What makes you think that? The fact that we're going to attack the fortress without a single weapon capable of punching through its walls, maybe?" Anna said sarcastically. She shot a cutting look at Nathan.

Nathan ignored her. He waved a hand toward the highway in the distance. "If we're able to seize Fort Taubrum, we'll have cut off one of the largest highways that the Federation uses to transport goods along the Gharrick Mountains up to Forselle Valley. This fortress is of vital importance to the Federation."

"We know," Anna said. "You even told us why we need to hurry. But you can tell me to 'rush, rush, rush' until my ears bleed without making any difference. The siege engines need more time to be built."

"It's because we lack time that we can't wait for siege engines," Nathan said. "Fortunately, we have the means to get into the fortress without them." He looked meaningfully at Leopold.

Leopold's eyebrows raised. The others looked at him, and he shrugged in return.

"I suppose he's not wrong," Leopold said. "The walls and protective field are too strong to get through without siege engines—and we would definitely need siege engines strengthened with powerful magic—but the gate is another matter. I have enough power available from my binding stones to punch through the front gate, if necessary. For me, however, the question is: is it necessary?" Leopold gave Nathan a piercing look.

"Isn't getting into the fortress our highest priority?" Anna asked, seemingly confused.

"Blowing through a magically reinforced gate uses a lot of power that I'd rather save," Leopold said with a smile.

"Power that I'm guessing that you'd rather save for fighting Seraph. At least, that's what I'm assuming comes next." Vera grimaced at the thought of fighting a Champion that had been hyped up to be far more powerful than anyone she had fought previously.

Nathan nodded. Almost everybody understood the reason why Leopold was wary to use so much power to simply get into the fortress. Anna still seemed somewhat confused, but she seemed to understand that the gap in her knowledge was caused by her inexperience with sorcery and warfare, so she let it slide. Although she forced a promise from Leopold and Nathan to explain the details later. Right now, they didn't care to explain everything.

Plus, Anna was likely to understand much better after the battle with Seraph.

Federation soldiers wandered across the battlements of the fortress as they watched. There weren't as many of them as Nathan expected. He wondered if Seraph had committed far more of her forces to the planned ambush at the tower than she should have. Or perhaps she had sent many of her forces away. After all, she surely knew that what really mattered now was the battle between Champions.

Whatever the case, Nathan's battle plan trundled into motion. Leopold took up his position in front of the main gate. Accompanying him were most of the other Champions and sorcerers. Anna took a position in the back of the army, as expected. Nominally, she commanded this army. That kept her out of harm's way, which is where she needed to be once Seraph started unleashing her full power.

Fei and Sunstorm stuck with Nathan up until the start of the battle. They seemed aware that he was up to something. Minutes before the battle was due to start, Leopold wandered up to

Nathan. His eyes lingered on the two Champions who almost clung to the younger Bastion.

"Are you sure about your plan?" Leopold asked. His poker face smile was firmly in place. His eyes held no judgment, but that meant nothing. For all Nathan knew, Leopold wanted Nathan to back away from his foolhardy plan and join the main assault.

"It will minimize casualties," Nathan said.

"You're taking both of them?" Leopold nodded at both Fei and Sunstorm.

Nathan gave Sunstorm a push forward. She stumbled and looked back at him in surprise. With a nod, Nathan indicated that she should join Leopold's force.

"You want Fei?" Sunstorm asked, an undercurrent of hurt in her voice.

"Normally, I'd take you for this sort of mission," Nathan said, one of his hands ruffling Fei's hair. "But you can last longer in open battle. Your gems are built for endurance, and you know how to handle Seraph. Whereas Fei here need to be topped up every few minutes of battle. I'm a little worried about her should she get into a fight with Seraph."

Fei scowled at Nathan and jumped away. She had been enjoying his attention, but she became unhappy the moment that he mentioned that he was "babysitting" her. Leopold and Nathan chuckled.

A hand appeared in front of Nathan. He looked down, surprised to see that it was Leopold's. Looking back up, he saw the old man looking unusually serious.

"For good luck," Leopold said. His poker face smile was gone. In place of it was a genuine smile.

Nathan took his hand and had an unusually firm handshake. When he pulled his hand back he had to shake the feeling back into it.

"Just be careful when you're in there," Leopold said. "I don't know what you think you know, but what you're about to wrangle with is more dangerous than you think. I'm betting you're about to play with fire, and many people have died doing that half-assed." Having said his piece, Leopold accompanied Sunstorm to the front line.

Nathan stared after the retreating Bastion. Had the old man worked out his plan? It seemed unlikely. Then again, what else could Nathan be up to? Nathan wondered if Leopold had attempted this trick in the past. Or perhaps he knew other Bastions who had tried the same thing.

The difference between Nathan and all those other Bastions was that Nathan had the advantage of knowledge from the future.

"Are you really that worried about me?" Fei asked. Her tone sounded unimpressed, even though her words gave the impression that she wanted affection.

"It's not that I'm worried about you," Nathan said. "Rather, I need a Champion to defend me should I run into Seraph. But I also need every Champion to help Leopold at the front gate. My plan is to spend as little time fighting Seraph as possible and she's more likely to focus on holding the fortress gates. But if I do run into her, I need a highly capable Champion to help me fend off a duogem Champion."

"But you said—" Fei began to say.

"And I meant it," Nathan continued. "Your sapphire gem is powerful, but you can't use it for long in a battle. Whereas Sunstorm, Sen, and the others can fight for much longer periods of time without my help. If you're close to me, then I can top you up whenever necessary."

Fei pouted and looked away. His words hurt her. There was no escaping that fact, but they needed to be said. Her capability as a Champion improved rapidly, and she had come a very long way since the nervous beastkin he had encountered when he first arrived at Gharrick Pass. Coddling her did her no favors. She wanted to be a powerful and famous Champion. Nathan knew she had the potential to be a trigem Champion, but achieving that potential meant that she needed to face reality.

"You're thinking about this the wrong way," Nathan said, trying to think of a way to get his message across but blunt the hurt. "Everybody has weaknesses. That is an inescapable fact. What makes us strong is understanding our weaknesses and how to prevent others from exploiting them against us. Right now, you're extremely powerful in short bursts. That means that so long as you're close to me, then very few Champions can defeat you in one-on-one combat. On the other hand, that means you cannot get into extended fights when you're not close to me. That does not make you weak. Rather, it means that you need to pick your battles."

"But what if I have no choice but to get into a battle when I'm away from you?" Fei asked, looking up at him.

"Then you need to find a way to handle fights in those circumstances. A battle does not start the moment that you cross swords with your opponent. It is about positioning, about framing, about taking control of a battlefield, and about maximizing your strengths while ensuring your opponent's weaknesses are exposed."

Nathan wasn't sure Fei got his point, but she wasn't stupid. Simple sometimes, but she had always been the most reliable Champion in his roster for a reason. She had earned her position as the trigem Champion who most often pulled him out of the fire.

As if to prove him right, Fei nodded at him, a look of understanding on her face. She licked her lips and looked up at the fortress walls.

"That's why you're in such a rush, isn't it?" Fei said. "You're setting up this battle to prevent Seraph from gaining an advantage over you. This plan of yours is a hidden strength of yours that nobody knows about, but you'll lose your opportunity if the Federation intervenes. Right?"

Nathan smiled and reached out the hand to ruffle her hair again. Before he could touch her, Fei ducked to the side and looked at him with a triumphant grin. He relented. Although her rapidly moving tail looked awfully inviting.

The two of them continued to wait. Leopold should have attacked by now, but maybe he was waiting for something. He was an experienced Bastion, so Nathan didn't intervene.

What did worry Nathan was the low number of enemy soldiers on the walls. By this point, Seraph must have known that an attack was imminent. This was no drill or intimidation tactic. Nathan planned to attack. Had she seen through his plan and knew that they intended to attack the gate and nothing else?

If she had, then she wasn't showing it. There was still no sign of Seraph in the flesh.

"Why hasn't Seraph showed herself?" Fei asked.

"I'm not sure. By this point she should have responded to one of our actions." Nathan shrugged.

"Does that mean she's not here?" Fei's eyes widened.

"That's unlikely. And by unlikely, I mean very, very unlikely," Nathan said with a grimace. "She's an experienced Champion, and that means she has her own tricks up her sleeve. I'm assuming that she's up to something."

For Seraph to have abandoned Fort Taubrum would mean that the Federation loses a sizeable chunk of their territory. As Nathan said earlier, this fortress protected the highway that cut north-south along the Gharrick Mountains. A lot of merchant traffic used this highway.

Without the fortress's protection, the Federation merchants would have to take a longer route to get to Forselle Valley. Several nations had borders that touched Forselle Valley, not just the Empire and the Federation. It was a major crossroads. If the merchants had to take the long route to get there, then their costs would rise. Higher costs meant lower profits.

No doubt the regents behind this war were furious over the

Empire's counterattack. Not only did they have an expensive war on their hands, but their existing profits were about to fall. Other regents would be furious once they learned the full extent of their losses. The Federation would have no choice but to negotiate with the Empire if they could not take back this land.

So Nathan considered it impossible for Seraph to have already retreated. Doing so would make her a pariah in her nation. Torneus, her backer, would hunt her down for failing him so badly. In such a situation, she was better off trying to hold off the Empire while hoping that Torneus sends reinforcements soon enough.

Nathan shielded his eyes with his hand and looked toward Leopold's position. He saw the old Bastion raising his sword into the air. A crack sounded across the battlefield. A cry rung out across the Empire ranks.

The assault had begun. Fort Taubrum was about to fall.

CHAPTER 42

Seraph finished the last of her paperwork. Placing the last piece of paper on top of her neatly stacked pile of finished forms, she took a moment to look over her handiwork.

Since she moved here under Theus, Seraph oversaw the entire province. This paperwork had been a constant companion. Now all of it lay completed. No more would arrive in her inbox. No more tax estimations; no more monthly reports for the regent; no more pointless status reports for Theus; no more updates to file from the guard captains of the province.

Seraph was alone, as she had been for some time. Her errand boy was long gone. A skeleton crew of soldiers remained to protect the fort. She had sent the rest home weeks ago.

The stares she had received had been questioning when she had ordered so many of them to neighboring forts and towns. Even she had wondered if she was being rash, but events proved that she was right. This new Bastion from the Empire, Nathan Straub, was not an easy foe to reckon with. As she had suspected —despite Torneus's belief otherwise—Nair had proven unreliable as an ally.

When the signal came during the battle over Nair's tower, Seraph had ignored it. Something had felt wrong about the battle.

For one thing, it didn't seem right that Nair could defeat a Bastion by herself. Sunstorm had failed in her place. How could a sorceress like Nair succeed where a trained assassin like Sunstorm fail?

Minutes later—when Nair's spells tore apart the Federation soldiers—Seraph felt vindicated, if empty.

Being right meant nothing if she didn't gain anything.

Outside, Seraph heard jeers from the Empire's troops. An assault must be beginning, she realized. It was earlier than she expected. Much earlier.

She had checked earlier in the day but saw only siege engines in the early stages of construction. That can only mean one thing: the Bastions were going to deploy their might. A reckless approach, but the only one they had.

The halls of the keep were empty as Seraph walked down them. Fort Taubrum had never been well furnished at the best of times, but she had ordered the few decorations to be taken away by the retreating soldiers. The walls stood bare, the lights off, and not a soul stirred in the place.

The ground shook. Dust fell from the ceiling, and Seraph felt her balance shift. Something struck the outer gate with such ferocity to shake the keep itself. Despite this, Seraph maintained her leisurely pace. She walked slowly and surely down the halls, taking in the sights of the keep that had been her home for over a year.

At the end of every chapter of her life, Seraph wondered what she could do differently in the next chapter. She considered it a chance to ruminate on what mistakes she could avoid next time.

Ironic, she thought, that this time she had made the greatest mistakes but had no chance to correct them. Her reflection on the past was purely for self-indulgent reasons. Her last chance to reflect on her life before she went out to face her end like a warrior.

By the time she made it to a balcony overseeing the outer

fortress, the gate had fallen. Dust billowed upward from the outer courtyard. Yelling, shouting, screaming. A cacophony of voices and battle filled the air. Seraph drank it in.

She spotted the glitter of gems. Enemy Champions.

Ducking back inside, she grabbed her prized weapons from the racks in the nearby armory. These consisted of a pair of polished wooden clubs with handles sticking out of from the sides. In her homeland, they were known as tonfas. She held them by the handles, and they protected her forearms during normal usage.

Now armed, Seraph charged back outside. She leaped down from the balcony. The dry dirt rose up to meet her, and she hit the ground in a roll. The battle surrounded her as she rose to her feet. Federation soldiers charged forward to defend the gate but found themselves pushed back. Dozens of Empire soldiers in dark uniforms surged through the wide-open hole that been torn through the wrought iron doors.

Seraph stepped forward and swung one of her arms across the air in a cutting motion. One of the jades implanted in her collarbone glimmered. The dust cloud rising in the air vanished in an instant.

Her vision restored, Seraph quickly found her targets. Behind the Empire soldiers were the enemy Champions. And more importantly, an enemy Bastion. The scouts had noted the presence of a powerful and important man at the battle of Nair's tower. She hadn't believed them, but now she had visual proof.

Leopold Tyrim himself, in the flesh. If she took his head, even Torneus couldn't touch her. She would have slain the most powerful Bastion in the Anfang Empire.

Around him were other Champions and sorcerers. Some dust clung to the ground, so Seraph couldn't get a good look at them. But she saw at least one Champion through the cloud. The glittering gems in her chest were a dead giveaway.

Seraph leaped over the heads of the soldiers. Her jade glittered again, and she fanned out her tonfas. Two waves of magic blasted into the enemy line. Dust poured off the enemies' bodies, and they stumbled and tripped. They stopped, then looked down at themselves in shock.

Every piece of armor and weaponry on the Empire soldiers had vanished. Reduced to dust. Before they could retreat, the Federation soldiers were upon them. Blood flowed.

Fire washed over the Federation soldiers a moment later, and their resistance was snuffed out instantly. They began to fall back from the gate. Even with Seraph standing right there, the soldiers were unwilling to die in the face of a magical inferno.

Seraph stood alone, facing Leopold and his subordinates. Oddly enough, she saw no sign of the infamous Nathan. She looked around to be certain.

Where was he? She had confirmed his presence outside the fortress earlier. His beastkin Champion was missing as well. Seraph had somehow lost sight of the other Champion that had been here. Was she the beastkin? Had she retreated the moment that Seraph had appeared?

If Nathan wasn't here, then where was he? He must be up to something.

In the end, it didn't matter. If Seraph defeated Leopold and the other fighters here before Nathan pulled off his plan, she won. There was nothing he could do to stop her in that case. A Bastion this far from his binding stone had no chance of defeating a duogem Champion.

In fact, she wondered if even two Bastions had a chance against a duogem Champion, this far from their binding stones.

Leopold interrupted her thoughts by throwing a punch at her from across the clearing. Sensing the power behind that punch, Seraph guarded herself with both of her tonfas. A massive wave of force slammed into her and threatened to knock her off her feet.

The fight was on.

Seraph ducked and weaved to avoid the hail of sorcery and

magical power that poured down on her. Spikes of earth exploded from the ground. Balls of lava and jets of flames scorched the earth. Balls of prismatic light burst against the buildings and nearly blinded her.

Her Champion enhancement focused purely on speed. This allowed her to dodge almost any attack, be it a sword swing, an arrow, or a fireball. A more balanced Champion would have allocated some of her enhancement to strength, particularly given none of Seraph's gems enhanced her physical attributes. A pure speed enhancement for an ability focused Champion was extremely rare.

In fact, Seraph had never encountered a speed-focused Champion that didn't use physical enhancement gems in her entire career as a Champion. She knew she was unique. To some, that was a detriment.

Here, though, Seraph proved the depth of her power and ability. None of her opponents touched her. At least, not substantially enough to cause lasting harm.

Growing frustrated, Leopold charged her and tried to bury his battle axe in her head. She met it head-on with one of her tonfas. Her gems glowed. Leopold's eyes widened.

He tried to pull back, but it was too late. Seraph's wave of energy blasted out and into his battle axe. His raw power resisted her—his strength as a Bastion pushing back at her, but it wasn't enough.

For a moment she thought that she would destroy his weapon. Then he really fought back with his power. They had a brief battle of wills.

Realizing the cost of destroying his axe was too great, Seraph withdrew. Leopold raised his guard and held his position. His eyes followed her, but his body didn't.

Behind her, something moved. Seraph spun and unleashed a blast of energy. She only had a moment to see the shadowy figure burst into nothingness as her magic slammed into it and blew it apart. Her eyes widened.

"Sunstorm!" Seraph shouted.

She looked around wildly. Was she seeing things?

That had to have been one of Sunstorm's shadow decoys. It had only been for a second, but she would never mistake those shadow powers for anybody else.

Again, she sensed something. She raised her guard and let Sunstorm come to her. When a blade slammed into her tonfas, she did her best to hold Sunstorm in place.

Before the onyx Champion could retreat from the failed attack, Seraph said, "So you're actually alive."

Mid-jump, Sunstorm faltered. She stared at Seraph in confusion. "You didn't know?"

"I don't recall you sending any messages to let me know that you're actually alive," Seraph said, her tone caught between amused and annoyed. "In fact, I specifically recall Theus telling me that you died. You're one of the best-looking corpses I've seen, I must admit. Can't say I understand why you're trying to kill me, however."

"I understand my loyalties much better now," Sunstorm said flatly.

Seraph's eyebrows shot up. She eyed her old subordinate. She couldn't detect any lies in Sunstorm's expression or her voice.

Loyalties, Seraph thought. How long had it been since Seraph truly felt loyal to anybody?

Around them, the battle stopped. Leopold and the two sorceresses stopped attacking. They seemed as interested in the conversation as the actual participants.

It seemed that Seraph had underestimated her opponent once again. This Nathan was not only a highly capable commander but also very persuasive. Sunstorm had gone from desiring his head to present as a prize, to bowing her own head to him.

"No wonder Theus was so terrified after the failed attack on Gharrick Pass. He told me that you died," Seraph said, unable to hide her smirk. "In truth, he must have felt you convert to the Empire. Not only had he failed to invade the Empire, but he lost one of the Champions lent to him."

"You don't seem too unhappy about this," Sunstorm said, eyeing Seraph suspiciously.

"That's because I'm not," Seraph said. "More than anything else, I feel all the better knowing you're alive and have found your place in the world. If I'm going to go out in this battle, then at least it's with less guilt."

"Guilt?" Sunstorm's expression made it clear that she didn't understand.

Seraph shrugged. She felt no need to elaborate.

For several long seconds, the two women eyed each other off.

Several weeks ago, they had worked together. Sunstorm considered Seraph a woman she admired. Seraph considered Sunstorm to be her most valued and trustworthy subordinate. Both had considered the other to have a very bright future.

In Seraph's eyes, her future ended here. But at least she knew that Sunstorm's hadn't ended with her orders to attack Gharrick Pass. That was more than Seraph knew coming into this battle.

Sunstorm vanished in a puff of shadow. That was the signal that everyone was waiting for. Flames, light, and blasts of power rained down on Seraph.

With renewed vigor, she dodged every attack.

Still no sign of Nathan. She refused to fall here until she saw him. She would fight the man who had recruited Sunstorm to his side. Seraph intended to die here, but she would not lay down and accept death.

Eventually, the attack slowed. Gaping wounds showed on Seraph's arms, legs, and even her torso. Her figure-hugging dress had been all but shredded. Despite that, Seraph had not slowed in the fight.

Before their very eyes, those wounds disappeared. Her flesh stitched itself back together.

"A regeneration ability," Leopold said, his eyes full of wonder. "I have always wondered whether jades were capable of regeneration abilities. Now I have the answer. Something to take home with me to the Empire."

"Assuming you return to the Empire," Seraph taunted.

"You may be tough, but you have done little to prove that you can hurt us." Leopold rolled his shoulders.

He had a point, Seraph had to admit. Despite his age, the man had plenty of endurance.

He and the Champions with him continued their assault without showing many signs of fatigue. Perhaps their plan was to whittle Seraph's gem reserves down.

A foolish plan. They didn't know how efficient her gems were.

More to the point, they were slowly but surely losing the battle.

Seraph let out blast after blast from her gems at Leopold and the others. Their uniforms, their weapons, and even their clothes disintegrated. Only Leopold proved resistant to her attacks. The others had to fight in tatters.

"What game are you playing?" Sunstorm accused.

The assassin didn't bother trying to cover herself up. The Champion enhancement gave her some measure of protection, but the raw power of a duogem Champion allowed Seraph to overwhelm Sunstorm's protections.

The result was something that Leopold likely enjoyed, but only if he looked at any of the nearby women. His focus was surprisingly intense, Seraph thought.

She had heard that he was a lecherous old man. But it seemed that he kept his focus on his opponent during battle.

Still no sign of Nathan.

Seraph grew frustrated. She wanted to end this, but Leopold prevented her from doing so. So many fatal blows had been stopped short by his power as a Bastion. Walls of earth shot from the ground. Or he leaped out from nowhere to block an otherwise fatal blow directed toward one of the sorceresses.

Surely his binding stone must be running low on power, she thought. Then again, he had quite a few binding stones available to him. The issue in defeating him was overcoming his reserves. He couldn't win through raw power, given how far away he was from his fortresses, but his endurance was second-to-none. Such was the power of an established Bastion.

Seraph prepared herself to end the fight using whatever means she had. Eventually her gems would run dry, despite her efficiency. Whatever Nathan was planning surely must be close to fruition. She needed to end this now.

As if her thoughts summoned the man, Seraph felt a very strange sensation run through her body. So did everyone else. They looked up to the sky.

Then they looked down at the ground beneath them. Something churned deep underneath them. Something magical.

"Is that the leyline?" Seraph thought aloud.

Then it clicked. She spun and stared at the keep. A wave of power washed over her, and she realized her mistake.

She had lost this battle before it started. Leaving the keep had been a critical error.

The entire fortress thrummed with energy.

The binding stone had been activated.

CHAPTER 43

I t was no exaggeration to describe the binding stones as the greatest weapons in a nation's arsenal. The Bastions stood as both the greatest defenders and the greatest warriors of each nation. Each binding stone enabled another Bastion to stand on the front line, and contributed a whole slew of new Champions to fight against the demons and enemies of their nation's enemies.

That meant a country needed to defend its binding stones. Bastions defended their activated binding stones using the power of the binding stone itself. They built a fortress, erected defenses, and amassed wealth to hire and maintain an army.

But inactive binding stones could not be defended in this way.

The simplest answer, one might imagine, was to simply activate every binding stone within a nation's borders. But that came with problems of its own.

Active binding stones drew demons to them. And an incompetent Bastion couldn't hold off a demonic invasion.

That meant active binding stones were also active threats to a nation's security. Furthermore, Bastions typically used more than one binding stone. As the most competent Bastions grew in experience and power, they claimed more and more binding stones.

By leaving inactive binding stones available for existing

Bastions to claim in the future, a nation left room for their best Bastions to grow in power.

Of course, an enemy could steal any unclaimed binding stones. To prevent this, nations placed powerful protective wards over their inactive binding stones. These wards were encoded with magical encryption that only Bastions from that nation knew how to decode.

This prevented Bastions from enemy nations from sweeping in, stealing a binding stone, and quickly conquering vast amounts of territory. With these wards, it became safe to leave inactive binding stones lying around.

Given time, sorcerers had the ability to decode wards. But that was the work of weeks, not hours or even days. Campaigns halted in order to capture binding stones. And in the time it took a nation to claim a new binding stone, a counterattack could be mounted.

This limited the power of Bastions, which was the only thing that prevented them from completely dominating the world.

Bastions were extremely powerful. They blunted offensives. They crushed entire armies when they went on the attack. The only thing that could stop a Bastion and his Champions was another Bastion and his Champions.

But that power had a physical range. A Bastion's power dwindled rapidly not long beyond the borders of his nation, once he moved beyond the reach of binding stones.

Or so the theory had always been.

Nathan wondered if what he was doing would have ramifications beyond this one battle.

He deftly undid the wards that protected the binding stone beneath Fort Taubrum. Although he wasn't as practiced at undoing Federation wards as he was at those from the Empire, he still knew how.

Such was the power of coming from the future.

For a normal Bastion, this was playing with fire. One misstep could destroy him. The wards were constructed in such a way that they would obliterate any intruders.

But Nathan was not an intruder, as far as the wards were concerned. He wasn't unraveling the wards like some common thief. He had the keys, magically speaking. Perhaps he fumbled the lock a few too many times, but he still appeared to be an authorized user.

Just as a lock wouldn't seize up on somebody trying to enter their own home using their keys, Nathan didn't need to worry about the wards exploding in his face.

Fei watched Nathan in awe. Her tail swished behind her slowly, and her eyes glued themselves to his back. None of the lamps here were lit, presumably because no one came down here. The stone cellars were dusty, empty, and practically abandoned. The only thing they had found down here was the binding stone, glowing ominously in the dark.

That suited Nathan fine. Seraph made no appearance, although he heard signs of battle in the distance. The constant rumbling sensation that ran through the keep reminded Nathan that he needed to hurry.

After he deactivated the wards, Nathan reached out to the binding stone itself. He found it easier to tether himself to this one than the last one. Part of him suspected that it was due to his recent experience at Gharrick Pass.

The other part felt that it was because Fei wasn't standing on top of him and rubbing her tail against his legs constantly. Although he was used to beastkin looking over his shoulder and distracting him while he tried to do his work, it was still a distraction. Concentration came easier when he wasn't actively pulling his mind away from the sensation of a woman clinging to him.

He claimed the binding stone. A rush of heat blew through his mind. This binding stone hadn't been used in decades, and it made its presence known. Unlike the one at Gharrick Pass, which had been abandoned for centuries, this one wasn't dangerous. Nathan let the sensations wash over him.

Plenty of power sat at his fingertips. The leylines extended for miles in every direction. The fort sprawled out around him, and he felt the damage that had been wrought to it from the battle against Seraph.

"So that's it?" Fei asked, her voice excited.

"Hardly," Nathan said. "We still have a battle to get to."

Fei rolled her eyes. "I know that. I meant that you claimed the binding stone. Now you can beat Seraph?"

Nathan assumed so. How long had it been since he had tested his power against a duogem Champion? Normally, the amount of power he had to use from his binding stones was too high to waste fighting a Champion.

But he lacked other options to defeat Seraph right now. Decades of unused magical power from the binding stone poured into Nathan, desiring to be unleashed. Given Nathan already had a fort to defend this binding stone, he felt there was little harm in using this excess power to defeat Seraph.

"I guess we'll see," Nathan said with a shrug.

"You wouldn't be doing this if you weren't certain." Fei's lips tugged upward. She pressed herself against Nathan's side while rubbing one of her arms across his back.

Nathan gently pushed her away from him. "We can do this later." He pointed above him. "We have a battle to finish."

The two of them rushed through the empty hallways and up the stairwells. The keep remained empty. Nathan heard footsteps in the distance. Too many of them to be only one or two people. The soldiers were retreating, but not into the keep.

Had Leopold already won?

No, Nathan realized. Seraph's raw power could still turn this around.

He confirmed his suspicion when he got outside. A quick glance showed that none of the Empire soldiers had made their way into the fortress itself. Although the Federation had abandoned the courtyard, the Empire had made no progress in seizing Fort Taubrum.

If Seraph successfully held off Leopold, then the battle was lost. Such was the power of a duogem Champion.

Nathan and Fei reached the courtyard. Then both stopped, barely believing their eyes.

"Am I interrupting something?" Nathan asked, mirth filling his voice.

Both Sunstorm and Sen shot glares at him. Sen did her best to cover herself up. Sunstorm didn't bother, as she was in close-quarters combat with Seraph.

For whatever reason, Sunstorm, Sen, and Vera were all in a state of undress. They didn't even carry weapons, save for Vera's obsidian-tipped staff. Leopold was in better shape, although his armor displayed cracks.

Nathan looked at the other woman in the courtyard. Seraph, he presumed. She held a striking beauty, and her silky black hair drew his eye. Oddly, he noticed that she seemed unharmed from the battle, although her clothes were in a similar state of disrepair as the other women in the battle.

Did Leopold have some sort of lecherous attack that obliterated the clothes of the women around him?

Nathan asked the old man as such. He received a glare in return.

"I'm not sure what to say about the fact that the first thing you ask me is if I am responsible for this nonsense," Leopold grumbled.

"Well, you are the only one wearing clothes," Nathan said.

"My apologies for being the only person with magic resistance," Leopold retorted.

The two jades implanted in Seraph's collarbone glowed for a moment. Nathan raised a hand, and a square flickered into existence.

A shimmering wall of light appeared in front of him. Seraph projected a wave of magic power against him, but it exploded uselessly against the protective barrier he cast.

"So you did activate it," Seraph muttered.

She stared at him in wonder and lowered her tonfas. He recognized the exotic weapons, as several mystic foxes used them in his timeline. An odd weapon to see being used by a human Champion.

"You seem to be in a rush to interrupt me," Nathan said.

"My objective here is to kill all of you," Seraph said. She gave him a beautiful smile, the sort that a normal man would remember for a long time to come.

Nathan shrugged and held a hand out to Leopold, as if to gesture for him to continue.

"I can't say I disagree with her," Leopold said, narrowing his eyes. "I'm as curious as she is about what you did. But given she is trying to kill us, I suppose I should explain things to you."

"I'd appreciate that," Nathan said.

Fei moved in front of Nathan, holding her scimitar up and summoning a blue flame over its length. Seraph gave her a dismissive look, before turning her attention back to Nathan.

Monitoring Seraph, Leopold explained, "She has a regeneration ability. It's an immensely powerful one, capable of healing even serious wounds within seconds. I'm assuming that it also makes her resistant to pain and physical injury. Cut her belly open, and she'll ignore it. The flesh will stitch itself back together within seconds. I don't know about limbs, but I imagine that will only hurt her for a few minutes at best."

"I suppose you're not a renowned Bastion for nothing," Seraph said, not bothering to look at Leopold. "Most people underestimate my regeneration ability."

"I appreciate the compliment." Leopold smiled. He continued, "Her other ability isn't a force blast, unlike what Sunstorm said. Rather, it destroys nonliving material. Weapons, clothes, the ground, buildings, and even spells. She seems to have difficulty against magic more powerful than her own, judging from the fact that she struggles to destroy my weapons and armor."

Well, that made for an intriguing pair of abilities. Most duogem Champions had a lot more raw offensive power backing them. But a powerful regeneration ability coupled with a magical attack that couldn't kill people was a very strange pairing.

"What about her enhancement?" Nathan asked.

"Pure speed," Leopold answered.

That made Seraph even stranger.

Nathan had never heard of Seraph in his timeline. Sunstorm never mentioned her. Narime and none of the other Champions from the Federation had brought her up. Given her role in the Federation and starting this war, he found that rather odd. Had Torneus scrubbed her so thoroughly from history?

Part of him wanted to capture her. But she was dangerous.

More to the point, he couldn't rely on Kadria to reawaken her emotions and trust in him. Seraph was an unknown quantity.

Everybody looked exhausted. Seraph appeared unharmed, other than her clothing. But everybody else was covered in scratches, cuts, and all manner of minor wounds.

Nathan realized that—contrary to expectations—Seraph was an endurance fighter.

She outlasted her opponents and took them down after they exhausted themselves. She destroyed their weapons, their armor, and even their spells. Then, when they showed weakness, she finished them off.

"How did you activate the binding stone?" Seraph asked, focusing on her topic of interest.

"Do you really think I'm going to answer that question?" Nathan smirked at her.

"Given your victory is guaranteed, I don't see why you wouldn't," Seraph said.

"Then what? You run away the moment after I answer your

question?" Nathan shook his head. "I'm not stupid. I have the binding stone. I don't intend to share my secrets with just anyone. Sunstorm already explained your role in the Federation, and your relation to Torneus."

Seraph narrowed her eyes and clicked her tongue. She glanced at Sunstorm, as if to suggest that she was annoyed that her identity had been given away. In response, Sunstorm shrugged.

"He already knew about Torneus," Sunstorm said.

"Is that so?" One half of Seraph's lips turned upward. She fixed her gaze firmly on Nathan. "Well, I suppose the only way I find out more is to defeat you."

Nathan let out a laugh. He drew his sword. With a flicker of willpower, he summoned a pair of glowing triangles around the hilt.

Instantly, Seraph surged forward. Nathan barely followed her movement.

Blue flames filled his vision as Fei tried to protect him. A blast of power blew the fire away. Fei's sword disintegrated with another blast of power. Seraph paused her charge and shifted her stance.

Eyes widening, Fei stepped back and tried to protect herself without a weapon.

Enough time had been bought, and Nathan unleashed his spell. A cage of earth exploded from the ground around Seraph. She covered her chest with her tonfas and blasted waves of magic around her. The hardened dirt crashing toward her disintegrated into clouds of dust. But more and more earth burst from the ground in a never-ending tide.

Within moments, Seraph found herself buried beneath a hardened dome of earth.

Fei leaped back and held her position in front of Nathan. He took the opportunity to quickly summon clothes for the women. Seraph might break free momentarily, but a few moments of respite were all that was necessary for the others to get dressed.

Plus, it helped him stay focused if the women wore something.

He also summoned weapons for them, and imbued magic into them from the binding stone so that Seraph's magic wouldn't destroy them as quickly.

As he predicted, Seraph's waves of magic soon burst through the earthen prison. She broke free seconds later.

A pair of fourth rank spells glowed in Nathan's hands. Seraph's gaze latched onto his hands. She reacted quickly and leaped backward. To no avail.

The buildings nearby reached out to grab her, as if they were extensions of Nathan's will. Seraph lashed out at them with her magic. But the magic imbued in them from the binding stone weakened her power, and she was unable to destroy them. She was beaten down to the ground.

Rolling as she hit the dirt, Seraph changed tactics. She charged Nathan again. This time, she pulverized the ground with her waves of power. Dust blew up into the air in dense clouds and prevented him from seeing where she was. But he still felt her presence.

He raised his hands. Triangles appeared at the end of each fingertip, each spell filled with the power of the binding stone.

The triangles burst into brilliant light, and each lanced forward into the cloud of dust. Seraph screamed as several of the projectiles of light punched through her, and she tumbled out of the dust. The moment Fei saw Seraph appear, she charged.

Tonfa met scimitar in a brilliant flash of sparks. Seraph's gem ability slammed into Fei with all the might that she could muster, but could not destroy Fei's sword. Much to Nathan's chagrin, the same could not be said of Fei's clothes.

Seraph's leg swept out, and Fei darted back. Leaping to her feet, Seraph raised her guard. Fei pointed a scimitar at her opponent. Then she blinked when she saw her ungloved hand. She looked down at herself, grimaced, and looked back at Nathan with an upset expression.

There was no time to deal with Fei's concern over her nudity, and Nathan planned to end this.

He had proven his superiority. Seraph lacked the raw power to match his binding stone. With the overflowing power of a binding stone and over a decade of experience using them, he had easily overwhelmed her gems. Seraph didn't stand a chance.

He began to cast a supercharged fourth rank spell. Seraph scowled and fell into a defensive stance.

Before she could charge him, Nathan charged her. Seraph's eyes widened, and her tonfas glowed with magic. His sword slammed into her weapons. Light burst out across the clearing.

Seraph crashed to the ground. Nathan followed through, placing his sword against her neck. Another spell glowed around his sword. The glowing squares hovered menacingly around the hilt of his blade.

"Why didn't you kill me with that earlier spell?" Seraph asked.

"You asked me a question earlier," Nathan said. "The answer is simple: I can activate the binding stone because I know how to unlock the wards. A lock is only as safe as its keys. And I have the keys."

Seraph stared up at him. Then she laughed, and said, "That's it? No grander secret? You had the code to the wards protecting the binding stone? How anticlimactic." She stopped laughing. "Then again, something like this is to be expected of you. You've beaten me every time, not by being supremely powerful or having the largest and greatest army and Champions. But simply by outmaneuvering me at each turn."

Seraph clapped. Or at least, she tried to. She found it hard while holding her tonfas. She looked down at them, and considered dropping them, but decided not to.

Somehow, Nathan found the clapping less irritating than he normally would. He'd had some unpleasant experiences with women clapping around him recently.

"Is this it then? You cut off my head, and the Federation is defeated?" Seraph said.

Nathan paused. Normally, this would be the end. He had slain more than his fair share of Champions. He didn't even know Seraph personally. Kadria had no way to reawaken her lost memories of him.

But for some reason she appealed to him, and not simply physically. Her looks were striking, and her body certainly called out to his. It helped that she was all but naked right now.

Maybe it was the fact that she seemed thoughtful, Nathan thought. Most Champions were pure warriors. Nathan had only considered one of his Champions to be a true strategist. Some of the rest had been commanders, but never advisers in the sense of people he trusted to help guide him in life or manage his fortresses.

Some of them had such talents, but they came from their lives before they were Champions. Whereas it seems that Seraph was different. That intrigued Nathan, because it appeared that the path she walked was wholly different to the path that probably any Champion or Bastion normally walked.

"Was there something else that you wanted?" Nathan asked. He wondered...

"If we're talking about things I want, then it would be for you to have entered my life many, many years ago," Seraph said bitterly. "Given such a thing is impossible, I'm afraid the knowledge that Sunstorm is in safe hands will have to suffice."

Nathan stared at Seraph. Nobody else spoke or moved an inch. Empire soldiers crept through the open gate now that the battle had ceased. But they knew that something was happening and didn't intervene. They made noise but Nathan shut it out.

"I can offer you atonement," Nathan said.

"Isn't that what death is for?" Seraph responded. She closed her eyes.

"Perhaps. But there are many ways to atone. I can make you

my Champion, and your atonement will be toward all the soldiers in the Empire and Federation whose lives you cost, and the civilians whose livelihoods you ruined." Nathan didn't remove his sword from Seraph's neck. He wondered if he was making the right choice.

"And what if I betray you? What if Torneus makes me a better offer in the future, and I can escape my atonement?" Seraph said. Her eyes remained closed.

"Then the Watcher Omria will judge you. She will know you for who you are, and you will suffer for your choices." Nathan tilted his head. "More to the point, I will be your Bastion. If you turn on me, I will destroy you. Atonement through death never stops being an option."

Seraph let out a bark of laughter and opened her eyes. "Well, it seems you're not entirely naive. I'd say you're a fool to recruit an enemy, but Sunstorm seems loyal to you. And the fact that you're aware of your ability as a Bastion to keep your Champions in check makes you a step above Theus."

Theus didn't even know how to keep his Champions in line with the powers of a Bastion? Nathan shouldn't have been surprised, given what he had heard about that idiot.

"So, you accept?" Nathan asked Seraph.

"I do."

With that, Fort Taubrum fell into the hands of the Empire. The soldiers seized the fortress and took the Federation troops prisoner. No Federation reinforcements arrived.

Nathan loved to believe that this was the end of the war. That he had accomplished what he came back in time to achieve. In truth, he wondered if he had instead set this timeline on an entirely different path. One that he didn't understand in the least.

But, for now, he was victorious. The Empire had defeated the Federation, and Seraph was his.

CHAPTER 44

After the battle, life returned to normal. Not that Nathan normally described his life as normal.

Anna's soldiers swept across the region. She sent some home —particularly the beastkin she had recruited using Leopold's authority—but hired many of them permanently.

With her expanded territory, she needed a larger army to maintain it. Most of the guards and soldiers from the Federation couldn't be trusted to protect the region under the Empire, so Anna provided her own soldiers. Additional soldiers increased the financial burden on her, and the war with the Federation meant she lacked the trade income she needed to pay her soldiers. For the time being, Nathan supported her soldiers using his power as Bastion.

Officially, nobody ruled the new territory. But Anna had led the army that captured everything east of Gharrick Pass, so Leopold used that as an excuse to place her in charge of it. Nathan protected the region as Bastion, and Anna ruled it.

Hopefully, this arrangement remained permanent, as Nathan preferred working with Anna over most of the nobles he had dealt with in the past. She had a good head on her shoulders and worked well with his Champions.

Seraph settled in surprisingly easily. She spent most of her time working with Anna and assisting her with the paperwork for the new region. Under Theus, she had run the province. That made her a good fit as an assistant to help Anna quickly establish herself in a new region. Nathan appreciated a Champion that handled his paperwork for him. The farmers and merchants appreciated a steady hand, even if they remained worried about war.

Normally, an invasion came with significant ructions. New merchants moved in, and old merchants were booted out. But Anna was no old money noble with significant connections. She took the land as she saw it and allowed the people already there to maintain what they had. That kept her existing inhabitants happy, preventing any rebellions from rising up. It limited her own financial growth, but Anna couldn't gain much from abusing her power anyway.

Not all the merchants were happy, especially those that relied heavily on trade. Relations between the Federation and Empire remained frosty. Which was a polite way to say that war had not been formally declared, but could be considered to be ongoing regardless.

The Federation never launched a counterattack in response to the Empire's assault. But Theus remained in Forselle Valley with his Champions. Small armies massed on the borders, but never crossed.

Occasionally, Nathan sent Fei or another Champion out to chase away an army that grew too large. No battle ever occurred, as neither side wanted bloodshed. But it served as a reminder that open warfare could break out at any moment.

Torneus had yet to open negotiations with either Leopold or Nathan. Not even Anna heard anything from him. Torneus was clearly bitter over his loss.

As such, Leopold returned to the capital with Ciana. He took with him the political prisoners that Nathan had captured during the battles with the Federation. Those prisoners were the key to making this war favorable for the Empire. Without them, other nations might intervene and make this turn out exactly as it had in Nathan's timeline.

Getting the Emperor himself to intervene was risky. But Nathan and Leopold saw no other choice. They needed to stop Torneus, and they needed to do it without causing the war to grow to involve other countries. Nathan strongly suspected that he had replaced one war—the war that he knew from his timeline —with a different war that he knew nothing about.

So, Nathan whiled away his time, preparing for future battles to come. He fortified Fort Taubrum and Gharrick Pass. He trained his Champions. He learned more about the current timeline. And he enlarged his army, especially his beastkin knights.

Many of the beastkin that fought against the Federation returned to Gharrick Pass in the weeks following the battle of Fort Taubrum. They had been impressed by Nathan. If Nathan took them at face value, he might say that they wished to swear fealty to him and fight for him as knights.

In truth, he suspected that most of them realized that he wouldn't send them to their deaths futilely. That made him a safe option for long-term employment. Being a beastkin was harsh sometimes. Many of them grew up with stories of veterans being sent into the meat grinder. While the battle of Nair's tower had involved many beastkin casualties, very few had been fatal. Comparatively, that made Nathan a highly capable commander.

With so many beastkin joining his side, Nathan finally had the chance to build up an army capable of fighting demons without the aid of Champions. As much as he wished otherwise, Nathan couldn't be everywhere at once. There would be times that demons invaded one of his fortresses while he was absent. His Champions needed soldiers capable of assisting them. That meant knights wielding enchanted weapons and armor, and who were trained to fend off ferocious demons.

The beastkin trained to be the first of those knights. Nathan created enough enchanted weapons and armor for the companies of beastkin that joined him, and they trained under Fei and Sunstorm.

Sen gave the other Champions looks of jealousy, wishing that she had her own subordinates. Nathan hadn't found the opportunity to find many magic users, and knights weren't a great fit for a spellblade. That meant Sen remained a lone wolf for the foreseeable future.

With so much to do, summer quickly passed. The weeks of fall began to pass by rapidly.

One day, Vera opened the door to Nathan's office. She paused when she saw him reading a letter. He waved her in.

"You have a door for your office now, I see," Vera said as she entered.

"I found that although an open door policy works well, I received noise complaints," Nathan joked.

Vera rolled her eyes. "I can't believe you didn't have a door to begin with. Your Champions jump you at every opportunity they get. I'm surprised one isn't on top of you right now."

"Fei's busy patrolling with some of the new beastkin," Nathan said. "She's showing them around the leylines. It helps if they know where they are, in case of an issue like last time."

"Is that likely to happen again?" Vera asked with a grimace.

"Somebody disrupting the leylines in order to cause a demonic invasion?" Nathan considered for a moment whether to give a truthful answer.

In his timeline, the tactic became almost commonplace in wars between nations. By that point, victory was what mattered the most. Allowing a few more demons into the world mattered less than defeating the enemy in the minds of most rulers. Especially when so much of Doumahr was already controlled by demons. How could one or two more portals hurt?

He had thought that things were better in the past. How naive of him.

"There are many reasons to know where the leylines are," Nathan eventually said. "Leyline disruption can be used to shut down the wireless, preventing us from communicating. If for any reason a binding stone is overloading with demonic energy, knowing the location of the leylines is important when demonic portals appear on them. That can happen even without disruption."

Vera scowled. "While that's worrisome to hear, you didn't answer my question."

"And for good reason."

"So the answer is yes." Vera rolled her eyes. "I'm beginning to realize that when you and Leopold are hiding something, it's because that 'something' has a horrible answer."

"That's typically the case with most Bastion secrets." Nathan shrugged. He rolled up the letter he had been reading and placed on the desk.

Vera pointed at the letter. "What's that about? Anything important?"

"Not especially. Ciana asked me some questions about binding stones." Nathan waved in the air as if to signify how meaningless the letter was.

"Ciana? Isn't she in the capital?" Vera grinned. "Oh, I get it. She's being a good little girl and sending you a letter every day, telling you all about her amazing adventures and asking you about her homework."

"Must you?" Nathan groaned.

"The girl adores you. So yes, I'll tease you endlessly. Especially given you already have three women crawling all over you any moment they get. Four, if you count the looks that Seraph gives you out of the corner of her eye," Vera said.

"Seraph doesn't give me any looks like that. Only exasperated ones when I take too long to review her paperwork."

Vera shook her head but dropped the topic.

She wandered over to the window and looked outside. Nothing much was happening within the fortress, as most of the soldiers were out and about.

The fortress had grown to accommodate the many migrants flocking to Gharrick Pass. Merchants flowed through the pass itself, attracting people who wanted to make money from them. Nathan had lost count of how many times he'd expanded the fortress to accommodate them. Ideally, he wouldn't need to bother. He'd let them expand outside the walls.

Right now, allowing that was dangerous. The distance between the frontier of the Empire and this fortress was still too small. Too many people might die if he didn't protect them with fortifications.

"So, have you thought about your next move?" Nathan asked, breaking the silence.

"Well, there was a binding stone nearby. I thought that maybe I might finally become a Bastion, but a certain somebody claimed it himself. What a greedy man." Vera gave Nathan a sidelong look, a cheeky smile on her face.

Nathan didn't rise to her provocation and instead asked, "So you're still intent on becoming a Bastion?"

Vera let out a sigh. "Ideally, yes. But I won't lie that I am rethinking the idea. The Empire won't accept me. Leopold knows what happened here. There's no way I'll ever become a Bastion while he's in the Empire."

"I wouldn't count him out just yet," Nathan said.

"Even if he changes his mind, there are still no binding stones available."

"There are plenty of binding stones available. Just not nearby," Nathan corrected.

"And that's the problem. I'm not sure I want to leave Gharrick County." Vera sighed again and ran a hand through her long red locks. "I grew up here. The next in a long line of sorcerers, all of whom have either used my tower, or practiced sorcery nearby. Inheriting that tower meant everything to me, once."

Nathan waited, suspecting that she was building up to something.

"On the other hand, I'm not so sure I like chaining myself to the past like this," Vera said. "I feel like I need a fresh start. A part of me wonders if that means abandoning my dream of becoming a Bastion, at least for a little while."

"A little while?" Nathan asked. He didn't like the sound of that.

Vera shrugged and avoided his gaze. "You helped me out of a difficult situation. No, let me be frank. I would be dead if it weren't for you. If not at the hands of Sunstorm, then at the hands of Leopold. Becoming a Champion for a short while to repay my debt to you would be a pleasant distraction."

Nathan closed his eyes and withheld a sigh. He had worried that it would be something like this. It seemed that his warning about a Champion being a one-way path hadn't gotten through.

"You said something much earlier, back when we spoke in your tower, about how you like me because I told you more Bastion secrets than others. So, I'm going to tell you a secret that I really shouldn't. One that—should Leopold ever find out that I told you—could have me tried for heresy," Nathan explained.

Vera stared at Nathan. She seemed frozen in place. "You don't have to—"

"Let me." Nathan stared her down. "Remember when I mentioned that becoming a Champion was a one-way path? I meant it. Truly meant it. It's not a metaphor. Accepting any Champion enhancement impairs your ability to become a Bastion. Permanently."

Silence reigned. Nathan waited to see if she would say anything. She didn't, and merely stared at him in shock.

Eventually, she gestured for him to continue.

"While a gem is a permanent change, and can never be

removed, even an enhancement limits your ability to become a Bastion," Nathan explained. "The training enhancements in the academy have a relatively minor effect, which is why Champions can still back away at that point. But once a Champion accepts a full enhancement, their potential as a Bastion is crippled."

"That sounds insane," Vera blurted out.

Nathan kept his face impassive. "There's a reason this is kept secret. There are a lot of implications to go along with it. The main one is that someone can be tricked or forced into accepting a Champion enhancement, and therefore prevented from ever being an effective Bastion. Another is that many people may avoid becoming a Champion, if they knew that meant they could never become a Bastion in the future."

"It's that bad?" Vera's eyes narrowed. "Simply receiving an enhancement has such a powerful impact that they cannot become a Bastion?"

"They can become a Bastion, but they'll never be a good one. Or even a mediocre one. I'm doubtful that a former Champion could even create a duogem Champion," Nathan said. "The effect is that severe. Even if they could, they could never create more than one or two duogems. And never a trigem. Not to mention that their ability to manipulate the binding stone would be far inferior to a true Bastion."

Vera looked up at the ceiling. "Now I better understand why you and Leopold have cautioned Ciana so heavily about rushing into a decision about being a Bastion or a Champion. She wants so dearly to fight for you. I thought that she would sneak off to the battle at my tower. I even kept a lookout for her trying to sneak into any wagons or carts."

Grimacing, Nathan looked away. He had conflicting thoughts about Ciana. He wanted her as his Champion. He adored her. The two of them had been close in his timeline.

But denying her the opportunity to become a fantastic Bastion —if that was what she wanted—was against his nature.

"She told me that tripe that you told her. Or at least, I thought it was tripe." Vera grimaced. "About how someone can only be a great Bastion or a great Champion. I suppose it's right. You can only be one or the other. Because going down one path ruins you for the other."

"That's not what I meant," Nathan snapped. He sighed. "But I suppose it can be interpreted that way. I want her to make the right decision, as it's not something she can rethink later. Even becoming a Bastion then becoming a Champion is hard."

"Why? Does claiming a binding stone impact your ability to become a Champion?" Vera asked.

"Kind of. Binding stone connections are effectively permanent, so you can't become a Champion later. More than that, a lot of the knowledge you learn while becoming a Bastion makes it difficult to be accepted as a Champion." Nathan leaned back in his chair. "Truthfully, a lot of what Leopold and I are teaching Ciana are things that Champions usually never learn."

In the end, Champions were weapons. Nathan did his best to never forget that they were people. People that he was close to and cared for greatly.

But to the nations that funded and trained the Champions, they were powerful weapons.

One didn't teach a sword the mysteries of the world. A sword didn't need to know the ins and outs of politics, or what the implications were if they killed the person in front of them.

A sword's duty was to stab whatever its wielder required it to stab. Champions were the swords of nations, in a way that Bastions could never be. A Bastion wielded Champions in the same way that a soldier wielded a sword.

Seraph was dangerous because she was a sword that knew how to wield other swords, and she appeared to think and act of her own volition. To Nathan, that made her invaluable.

To a nation, that made her terrifying.

No wonder so few nations allowed Champions such as her to

exist. Nathan couldn't help but find it interesting that both Narime and Seraph came from the Federation. Torneus stood as a common link between the two. Did he favor Champions that were more than simple, unthinking weapons?

Nathan wondered what it meant that Leopold was willing to teach Ciana the same things, potentially leading her down the same path as Seraph.

"So, in the end, I cannot make a temporary choice." Vera let out a humorless laugh. "I want to help you and repay my debt, but doing so costs me too much."

"If it helps, I can teach you what little I can about Bastions," Nathan offered. "There are some things that I can't teach you, simply because the academy has refused you, and I don't want Leopold to murder me. But I think I have some leeway with him to teach you a few things. And who knows, maybe there'll be a binding stone available later, when even Leopold can't refuse you."

Vera shot Nathan an appreciative smile. It faded the moment she thought he wasn't looking.

After Vera left, Nathan glanced back down at the letter on the table.

He felt conflicted. Not just over Vera, but also Ciana and Seraph.

For Ciana, the reason was simple. He knew Ciana as a Champion. She might choose to become a Bastion, and he might lose her. If he intervened and pushed her toward becoming a Champion, he could make her his easily.

But with Vera and Seraph, it became more complicated than that.

His uncertainty was because he did not know them. His knowledge of the future did not include Seraph. Vera's recorded history in his timeline was completely wrong.

Nathan reflected on these facts and realized that he had to handle these women the same way that he had handled things when he was younger. Not everything can be known, and not everything can be handled with a surefire plan.

Metaphorically, he stepped into the unknown.

Picking up a pen, he wrote a reply to Ciana. He sent the letter back to the capital, Aleich.

Then he turned around and stared at the black door behind him. He had one last person to speak to. The two of them needed to have a very important conversation.

CHAPTER 45

"So, did this turn out to be everything you dreamed it would be?" Kadria asked.

"I don't recall having the chance to dream before you sent me back in time. So no, it hasn't." Nathan sipped his tea. It didn't taste like anything he had ever drunk in his life. Part of it reminded him of the delicate teas that Narime sometimes served him. Those had been produced in her homeland—before it had been overrun by demons—and were an expensive delicacy.

He sipped the tea again. It tasted sweet. Strangely so, despite having no sugar or honey added to it.

"What have you done to this tea?" Nathan asked.

"Nothing. It's oolong tea. With mangoes. I'm almost certain that you can't get it here, but I figured you might enjoy it. Sweet things are rarer here than I'm used to." Kadria drained her cup, and it automatically refilled itself, the tea appearing from nowhere.

Nathan had no idea what sort of tea she had described. He sincerely hoped he hadn't been poisoned.

Looking around, he noticed that her void room had grown in size. Substantially so.

The bedroom was now more like a suite. Where it had previously been barely large enough to contain a bed, there was now space for a table and chairs. A doorway led off to what Nathan assumed to be a bathroom, although he hadn't investigated it.

He didn't know why Kadria's void room had gotten larger. He suspected he didn't want to know.

More importantly, some color had arrived in this otherwise lifeless void. The table and chairs appeared genuine and colorful against the black backdrop of this strange place. Nathan could see the grain of the wood, the threads that made up the upholstery of the chairs, and the golden straw color of his tea.

Everything else within the room remained an outline. He found the juxtaposition jarring.

For whatever reason, Kadria had chosen a table and chairs as the only colorful things in her room. Presumably so that she and Nathan could sit at them and talk. Whatever food and drink she summoned here also contained color.

"Do you prefer scones or tea cakes?" Kadria asked.

"Are those my only options?"

Kadria shrugged. "I assumed that you might prefer something from your homeland. Your actual homeland."

She smirked, and a plate full of fresh scones appeared on the table. Steam rose from the baked goods. Large dollops of butter, jam, and clotted cream accompanied them in separate bowls.

"I still don't understand how you're doing this," Nathan said, as he held a scone above his face. It smelled real. The tea had tasted genuine as well.

Food never felt, smelled, or tasted anything close to the real thing when created with magic. When a Bastion made food using a binding stone, it was bad enough to drive a man insane over the course of the day. Appearances could be replicated, but nothing else. Magically produced food was all nutrition, no soul.

"If you paid attention to how I do things, maybe you could pick up a thing or two," Kadria commented while smearing hunks of butter, jam, and cream over her scone.

Nathan quickly followed suit and tried not to stuff the thing into his mouth all at once.

It tasted delicious.

"This is the same as your binding stone magic that affects living things, isn't it?" Nathan asked.

"More or less. The difference is that food isn't strictly living, at least normally." Kadria waved her scone around, sending crumbs flying into the void, where they became simple outlines. "The binding stone is part of the world. Magic is just as much a part of the world as anything else, despite the name. People call it magic because they don't understand it."

"That's why we have magical science," Nathan said. "To better understand magic."

Kadria giggled. "Magical science. Such a silly name. You realize the term is an oxymoron, don't you? Science describes how the world works, whereas magic is something that defies the way the world works. Your binding stones defy the natural laws of the world, at least according to normal science. In truth, reality is far more complex than it seems."

"So I've gathered," Nathan said drily.

Kadria wolfed down her scone. "Fine then. You didn't have any dreams, but I know you had something in mind when I brought you to this world. How do you feel now that you've stopped the war? The Empire is safe, no demons are destroying it, and there is no massive wasteland stretching from the Gharrick Mountains to the Kingdom of Falmir. Don't you feel like a hero?"

"Don't patronize me." Nathan glared at her. "I've stopped one war but started another."

"But you did stop the war from your timeline," Kadria said.

"And was that all that you sent me back here to do? I thought you even admitted that you're working with me because you wanted to avoid the end of the world?" Nathan pushed.

"Perhaps." Kadria toyed with a butter knife. "The invasion of Gharrick Pass was the catalyst in your timeline. When the Federation overwhelmed the Empire, it set off a chain of events that inevitably lead to destruction of almost every nation on Doumahr."

"But can't that still happen?" Nathan grimaced and drummed his fingers against the table. The sound echoed around the room. "Like I said, I traded one war for another. By invading the Empire, the Federation opened a hole that allowed the demons a foothold in the middle of Doumahr. But although I've stopped the Federation, now my only choice is to invade them in return. What happens if I tear open that same hole in the Federation? Won't the demons find a way through anyway?"

Finishing the last of the scones, Kadria dismissed the empty plate and the half-empty bowls. She continued to twirl the knife in her hands, as if she wanted something to keep her hands busy.

"That is how cause-and-effect works," Kadria explained, not looking at Nathan. "You change something, and something else happens. How do you think the world would change if you were never born? Do you think it would be exactly the same? That someone else would spring up out of nowhere to do all the things that you did in your world?"

"What if it was the same?" Nathan answered, a trace of bitterness in his voice.

Kadria smirked and finally looked at Nathan. "Ah, I see what you are getting at. We call those predetermined events. They're rare, but some worlds have them. Or perhaps you might call them archetypes of worlds."

Nathan didn't have the slightest idea what Kadria meant. Archetypes of worlds? What was she even talking about? He remained silent.

Continuing, Kadria said, "A predetermined event is something that always happens in some form. Avoiding them is complex. A world may have a war that takes place. Originally, that war is caused by a particularly charismatic leader. But if you remove that leader from the equation, a war takes place because of a different leader, and between different countries. The war is different, the actors change, and even the ideologies and the reasons for the war are different, but the fact that a war happens remains constant."

Kadria spread her hands wide and shook them in the air. "Predetermined events are spooky." She winked at Nathan.

"So, what you're saying is that the war between the Federation and the Empire is a predetermined event?" Nathan asked, trying to follow Kadria.

"Not this war in particular," Kadria replied, looking at a time. "But there will always be a war around this time period. If the Federation and Empire can't start one, then there are plenty of other nations with bones to pick with an old enemy. I may even argue that you're better off with the devil you know, than some unknown maniac that you don't."

"That sounds absurd," Nathan said.

"I did say that reality is far more complex than it seems." Kadria smiled. "Don't worry about it too much. What you should worry about are the wars taking place that you know nothing about."

Nathan grimaced. This was exactly why he had come to meet Kadria.

Beyond the problems he had with Seraph and Vera were the much larger problems plaguing him politically. The Empire waged war with two opponents, and neither war had happened in Nathan's timeline.

The first was the war between Trafaumh and the Empire. Although the Empire had attacked Trafaumh in Nathan's timeline, the surprise attack by the Federation had ended hostilities on the northern front. The Empire had been destroyed practically overnight by the ensuing demonic invasion, rendering the "war" with Trafaumh a historical footnote. As a result, Nathan knew next to nothing about how things might play out.

And of course, there was this new war between the Empire and the Federation. Nathan had a better grasp of the actors here, as he now knew Leopold and had a history with Torneus. But what worried him was that this war was happening at all.

"Trafaumh can take care of itself," Nathan said. "I don't have the time to worry about both wars."

"You're just making excuses," Kadria teased. "What you're really looking for is a reason to go to Falmir, aren't you? Your old homeland."

Nathan shrugged. There was no reason to lie here. "My goals here are twofold: stop the demons from invading Doumahr; and to reunite with my former Champions. If I'm at war with the Federation, then I may as well gather up those nearby. But Vala is in Falmir. I need to find an opportunity to get her back."

"Is that it?" Kadria asked.

She clearly suspected more. Truthfully, he had other reasons to go back. The coup that transformed the Kingdom of Falmir into merely Falmir still stung. He knew that—given the opportunity—the conspirators would bring down the kingdom the first opportunity they had.

Perhaps that was a predetermined event, like this war with the Federation seemed to be. Or maybe Nathan was getting ahead of himself.

Kadria watched him, her eyes searching for something within his.

He waved her off. "For now, I have only one real concern, and that is dealing with the Federation."

"Oh? And here I thought your primary concern would be all the women crawling all over you." Kadria giggled.

Her foot crawled up his leg, her toes pressing into his calf. Higher and higher she crept, until her foot found a familiar location, and pressed into his crotch.

"Don't you appreciate having the opportunity to shape them to your whims? You can make them yours in a way that you never could before," Kadria cooed. She massaged his length, and it slowly hardened under her attention. "I know that you enjoy their constant attention. Aren't they adorable, fighting over you like that?"

He grabbed her leg and pushed it away. Kadria grinned and simply placed her foot back where it had been. He didn't bother trying to stop her this time, choosing to let her have her way.

He had learned that if he pushed back against Kadria too much, she did one of two things: fled, if he got the upper hand; or threw a tantrum and restricted his movement, so that she had free rein over his body.

Right now, he knew that she would do the latter if he annoyed her. He needed to wait until he had a chance to overpower her.

"I am seeing new sides of them that I have never seen before. But they love me for who I am, not because I am manipulating them," Nathan said. "Rather than shaping them, I'm strengthening them. You've proven to me that my Champions need to be far greater than they were when I fought you. The paths they walked down in my timeline may not have been the right ones. As risky as it is, I need to take them down new paths."

Kadria's eyebrows shot up. "Curious. I had thought you would be more resistant to changing them. You seemed so keen to have their memories back. To have them restored to who and what they were in your world—pristine and whole. But it seems that you have come to terms with who and what they are now."

Her eyes seemed to glitter, and Nathan saw in them an emotion he struggled to describe.

He felt that he could describe this emotion were Kadria a normal person. But she was a Messenger, and he wasn't stupid enough to attach human emotions to her.

No more food or drink seemed forthcoming and he had his answers, so Nathan stood up. Kadria whined. He ignored her.

"You are going to return soon, right?" Kadria asked, a plaintive note in her voice.

Nathan glanced at her, raising an eyebrow. "You want me to visit you more often?"

"If you like, I can add color to the bed." Kadria waved a hand at the bed, while refusing to answer his question directly.

Nathan expected something to happen. Maybe for the bed to burst into bright colors, or another bed to melt into existence. Nothing of the sort happened, and Nathan realized that Kadria had simply gestured in its direction.

"Why do you think that matters to me?" Nathan asked.

"You humans tend to like having a better atmosphere for this sort of thing." Kadria placed a hand in front of her mouth and moved it back and forth in an obscene gesture.

Nathan rolled his eyes. So that's what she was interested in.

"If you're thirsty, then I suppose I can make some time for you. Later."

Kadria grinned and clapped. "Fantastic. Oh, before I forget: remember that the twins will visit you sometime soonish."

Nathan paused as he walked toward the door. "The twins?"

Who were the twins? The name suddenly clicked.

"You mean those messengers you warned me about?" he asked, turning to face Kadria again.

Kadria threw herself onto her bed, her hands wandering over her body in a blatant attempt to tempt Nathan into staying. "That's right. They've been asking me about you."

What?

It took every ounce of Nathan's will not to leap over and grab Kadria by the shoulders. "They know about our connection?"

Kadria rolled her eyes. "Of course not. But they know that I'm here. Think of it like when you ask a Bastion about another Messenger. They're asking advice from a colleague. After all, they have an interest in you. Or maybe more like a crush? They want to look their best when they first meet you. First impressions are rather important. They don't want to ruin that first date with you." Kadria giggled.

Nathan ran a hand over his face. He had forgotten about those

Messengers. Another headache for him to deal with while he handled the Federation.

He slipped out of the door and into his office. Nobody was in here. Not that it mattered. For whatever reason, no one seemed to comment on his absence while he was in the void room or where he came from. Kadria's magic somehow prevented others from even noticing her mere existence.

Night had fallen while Nathan had spoken with Kadria. He gazed out at the lamps that lined the battlements. The trees stood bare in the cold, dark night beyond the fortress.

He resolved himself. He didn't know what would come. War was certain, but little else.

What Nathan knew was that he would do anything to get back his former lovers. Narime was the closest that he knew of.

No matter the cost, he planned to get her back. Even if it meant he had to destroy the Federation.

END OF BOOK 1

END OF BOOK II

THANKS FOR READING!

Be sure to leave a review on Amazon here if you enjoyed Heretic Spellblade. I use reviews to determine which series to focus on, so more reviews are always good.

Support me on Patreon

Get early chapters for upcoming books and see early cover art at my Patreon:
     https://www.patreon.com/kdrobertson

Follow me on Amazon

Amazon is often slow to update readers on new releases, so the best way to be notified is to follow my author page on Amazon.

Updates and more

Receive release notice updates on Facebook at:
https://www.facebook.com/authorkdrobertson

You can find updates from me on my website at:
https://www.kdrobertsonbooks.com

BOOKS BY K.D. ROBERTSON

Demon's Throne Series

Demon's Throne

Demon's Throne 2

Heretic Spellblade Series

Heretic Spellblade 1

Heretic Spellblade 2

Heretic Spellblade 3

Heretic Spellblade 4

An Empire Reforged Series

Emperor Forged (Book 1)

Emperor Awakened (Book 2)